SCORING SUTTON

A WAVERLY WILDCATS NOVEL

JENNIFER BONDS

Scoring Sutton: A Waverly Wildcats Novel

Cover Art & Design by Cover Ever After
ISBN (Amazon): 978-1-953794-11-6
ISBN (B&N): 978-1-953794-27-7
ISBN (Ingram): 978-1-953794-31-4
First Edition 2023

www.jenniferbonds.com

For everyone who's ever felt less than; you are enough.

1

SUTTON

"Coming through!" My fingers slip and the box I'm carrying tilts, the contents—and the weight—shifting to one side. I lose my grip and it's all I can do to hold on as I crash into the front door of my new apartment with an unflattering *oof,* the air punching out of my lungs.

Mierda. Using the doorjamb for leverage, I reposition my sweaty fingers and hoist the box in the air, silently praying that, once inside, I can make it to the second floor of the townhouse without getting crushed to death by God knows what.

That would be rampant consumerism and a penchant for hoarding.

Whatever. I'll worry about that in the spring when it's time to move out.

Today, I just need to get my crap inside and up the stairs without killing myself, which really shouldn't be this hard because I'm a freaking D1 gymnast. Strong. Graceful.

Short.

I make it all of two steps into the front hall before I lose my grip on the box again. "Moving days are the goddamn devil."

"There's my little ray of sunshine."

I turn toward the living room and my roommate Madison appears, a big-ass grin on her heart-shaped face. "Blame it on the boxes," I grumble. "They were clearly made for giants with freakishly long arms."

"I told you not to get the extra-large ones."

I don't bother replying. The extra-large boxes were the only ones left because I waited until the last minute to pack—something else Maddie warned me to avoid.

"You're going to hurt yourself," she chides, sounding just like our coach as she darts into the hall and hefts the other side of the box. "And injured athletes—"

"Don't compete." It's Coach Miller's mantra, one she'd happily tattoo on our foreheads if the NCAA would allow it.

Maddie snickers and then we're inching toward the stairs like an awkward turtle, the box suspended between us. I let her ascend first, so I'm bearing the brunt of the weight. It's slow going and by the time we reach the second-floor landing, I'm sweating like a pig and my t-shirt is plastered to my back. We shuffle into my room and drop the box onto the bare mattress.

"One down." Maddie bumps my shoulder, beaming like she's just scored a perfect ten.

Eight to go. I sigh and glance across the hall at Maddie's room. She's already unpacked and decorated. There's a familiar mountain of yellow pillows on her bed and a strand of fairy lights glow softly overhead, giving the room a warm, inviting look that is completely at odds with my own, which, at the moment, is stark white and empty aside from a few cardboard boxes.

Maddie's parents moved her in yesterday. They would've helped me too, but I had to work. Because while Maddie spent her summer lounging by the pool, perfecting her tan and acquiring natural highlights for her golden curls, I was coaching youth gymnastics camps here at Waverly.

I love working with the kids, and the money is good, but it's exhausting. You can't let them out of your sight for a second, which I learned the first week of camp when I caught two of the girls sneaking into the locker room with a bottle of itching powder.

Devious little monsters.

"So your parents really aren't coming?" Maddie asks, pulling me back to the present. "I thought for sure they'd change their minds. I mean, it's our first apartment." She smirks. "No more messy suitemates. No more communal bathrooms. No more cranky RAs watching our every move."

Thank God. Two years of dorm living was pure hell.

"Sorry to disappoint. I told them I could handle it." I shrug, not wanting to admit the truth—even to myself—that they would've bowed out because my sister Gabby, the real star of the Cruz family, had an event this weekend. "It's not like I have that much stuff."

Maddie arches a slender brow.

Which, fair, because I'm a certified packrat. Still, I didn't hear her complaining last semester when she needed a copy of the freshman orientation packet and I was the only one on our floor who could produce one.

She sighs dramatically. "Not gonna lie. I was really hoping for some empanadillas."

"Help me move these boxes and I'll make all the empanadillas your little heart desires."

"If I ate everything my heart desires, I'd split my leotard before the season even starts."

Yeah, right. The girl can eat, but she never seems to gain any weight. I'd kill for her metabolism, but maintaining a strict diet is a small price to pay for the sport I love. After all, nothing beats the thrill of flying through the air and landing the perfect vault.

"Come on." Maddie spins on her heal. "The sooner we get this done, the sooner we get ice cream."

A slow smile curves my lips. "From The Creamery?"

The Waverly U dairy makes the *best* ice cream. It's smooth, decadent, and made with whole milk. Which is why I only eat it on special occasions, because...*gymnast.*

"From The Creamery." She nods decisively. "We deserve a treat to celebrate our first apartment. Plus, we're going to work it off moving all these boxes."

Truth.

Who needs conditioning when you can drag all your crap up and down the stairs in ninety-five-degree weather?

We trek outside for another box—the prospect of Alumni Swirl is a powerful motivator—and are greeted by the thumping bass of hip hop music and a blast of air so hot I swear it scorches my lungs. The sun is blistering and I shield my eyes, squinting against the bright light as Maddie grabs my arm and lets out a high-pitched squeal.

"Do you know who that is?" she demands, gaze locked on a couple of guys playing frisbee next door.

"No clue." They're big and beefy. Probably student athletes. No surprise there. College Park Apartments has a notoriously long waitlist because of its proximity to the athletic facilities. "And unless they're going to move all these boxes, I really don't care."

I turn my attention to the mountain of cardboard filling my ancient Ford Explorer as Maddie ogles frisbee dude.

"If we each take one"—I pull a box to the edge of the trunk —"we can do this in half the time."

Not to mention half the trips.

"No way." Maddie shakes her head, ponytail bouncing. "If

you fall down the stairs and break something, Coach will kill me. Then I'll be dead, you'll be benched, and Coach will get suspended. Even worse, Michigan will kick our asses at the Big Ten Championships in the spring."

I snort-laugh. "You really think Coach would get suspended?"

"Fair point." She sighs and grabs the other side of the box. "Gymnastics is life. They'd probably just slap her with a fine and tell her not to miss a practice."

Laughing, we slide our cargo out of the trunk and shuffle toward the townhouse. This time, I walk backward, relying on Maddie to let me know if I'm going to crash.

We're halfway to the door when she says, "Don't look now, but I think Cooper DeLaurentis is checking us out."

There's a giddy thrill in her voice and I instinctively turn to the frisbee players, all of whom are shirtless and glistening like gods under the midday sun. Sure enough, Waverly's star wide receiver is watching us. Our eyes meet and my stomach drops.

Puñeta. DJ Parker *cannot* be my new neighbor.

I took precautions. I wrote a strongly worded letter. I—

Heart pounding, I scan the guys' faces, searching for the one that haunts my memories.

DeLaurentis. Reid. Smith. Some dude I don't recognize.

Relief washes over me like a Gatorade shower. They're all football players, but I don't know them. Not personally, anyway.

I draw a steadying breath and steel my resolve.

It's fine. I can do this. There are thousands of people in this complex. It's not like I have to socialize with the neighbors. I'll mind my business and they'll—

Maddie groans. "I said don't look!"

"Which basically guaranteed I was going to look." I peek at

my roommate over the top of the box. Her cheeks are flushed, but I can't tell if it's from the heat or embarrassment. Oh, who am I kidding? Maddie hasn't been embarrassed a day in her life. The girl has no shame, which is why I love her. "If you didn't want me to look, you shouldn't have said anything."

"Yeah, but then you would have missed the eye candy." She flashes me a mischievous grin. "You're welcome."

I roll my eyes, but she's back to admiring the view as we inch our way toward the apartment, cardboard digging painfully into the palms of my hands.

"I cannot believe we're going to be living next door to Cooper DeLaurentis."

"Yeah," I deadpan. "It's like we won the hot neighbor lottery."

"Right? Brooke and Soraya are going to be so jealous when we tell them." Her cornflower eyes light up, and I can practically see the cartoon lightbulb glowing over her head. "Maybe he'll invite us to party since we're neighbors. I would give my left ovary to hook up with that man." She wiggles her brows. "Rumor has it football players have amazing stamina."

"*Eww.*" I shoot her a dark look. "There's exactly a zero percent chance I'll be partying with the football team this semester." Or ever. *Been there, done that, have the emotional scars to prove it.* "You shouldn't either. It's like begging for an STD."

Maddie clicks her tongue. "No slut shaming. This is a sex positive environment."

A bead of sweat slides down my temple. She's right, but...

"It's not shaming if it's true." I wipe my cheek on my shoulder. "Besides, I thought you were hooking up with that lifeguard?"

"Do the words *summer fling* mean nothing to you? We're not like, committed or whatever." She laughs and the box shifts between us as I turn to glance over my shoulder. "I don't have time for a relationship."

Real talk. Between classes and gymnastics, free time is nonexistent.

"Fine, but I still think you can do better than some jacked up baller with a tiny dick and a god complex."

"Sounds like the voice of experience," she shoots back, eyes narrowed. "Spill."

"There's nothing to tell."

Because some secrets are so humiliating—so damaging—they can only go to the grave.

"So you're saying that if one of those hard bodied hotties asked you out, you wouldn't be the least bit interested?"

There are plenty of women on this campus who'd be thrilled to score with one of Waverly's gridiron gods, but I'm not one of them.

Not anymore.

"I'd rather eat mat on national TV than hookup with a football player."

2

DJ

"Parker, get your ass over here and put Vaughn out of his misery!" Coop hollers, wiping the back of his hand across his forehead.

"It's too damn hot." I'm not trying to get heatstroke playing Ultimate Frisbee, which is why I'm lounging in the shade while my roommates run themselves ragged. Football training camp is in full swing and Coach Collins will have my balls if I'm not one hundred percent on Monday. "Besides, you and Vaughn make such a great team."

If you enjoy watching them get their asses kicked, which I do.

"He can't even see the frisbee around that giant bush on his face."

Vaughn gives him the finger, but says nothing. He's always been a man of few words. It's a trait I admire since the rest of us are loud as fuck.

"Are we doing this or what?" Reid—our team captain and fourth roommate—asks, spinning the frisbee on his pointer finger. "Because I'm happy to take the win if you want to forfeit DeLaurentis."

Coop bristles, squaring his shoulders. "Fuck, no." He turns to me, a calculating look in his eyes. "Come on, man. I'll owe you one."

And there it is. A favor from Cooper-*I'd-sell-my-soul-for-a-W*-DeLaurentis.

Here's the thing. Athletes are competitive by nature, myself included, but Coop and Reid are on another level. They're the real deal. All-Americans. Heisman contenders. Guaranteed first round NFL draft picks. The prospect of losing at anything —even a meaningless game of Ultimate Frisbee—rankles.

"Well." I peel myself from the lounger. "When you put it like that, how can I resist?"

Vaughn snorts and flops down in my chair as I jog across the lawn.

Enjoy it while it lasts.

Once camp ends and classes start, free time will be a thing of the past. The team is poised for a championship run, but with the loss of our kicker, it's going to take all of us busting our asses to make it happen. Long practices. Brutal conditioning. Late night study halls.

So, yeah. Just the most challenging semester of my entire college career.

No pressure.

My gut tightens, but I breathe through the nerves.

You've got this, asshole.

I'm sure as hell not going to be the guy who drops the ball. Not when most of our starters are graduating in the spring and this is their last shot at a national title. I've still got another year of eligibility, thanks to redshirting as a freshman, but once Coop and Reid graduate, the Wildcats will be in rebuilding mode.

It's just as well. It'll give me a chance to focus on my grades, like I did freshman year. Most guys hate redshirting, but it allowed me to transition from high school to college without being completely overwhelmed. Fact is, if I'd been expected to memorize the playbook *and* pass English Lit, I'd have been screwed.

Goodbye, scholarship. Goodbye, Waverly.

"Get your head in the game." Coop claps me on the shoulder. "If we lose, we'll never hear the end of it."

No kidding. Smith is still bragging about the Madden beatdown he gave Reid last spring.

"What's the play?"

"Go deep." He shoots an appraising look at Smith. "He's fast, but you've got a better vertical jump."

We bump fists and line up, ready to rock the instant Reid pulls the frisbee. Like in football, he has to pass it to the opposition. At which point Coop will catch it, and, if things work out, pass it to me in the end zone.

"Let's do this."

Reid puts the frisbee in motion and I haul ass across the lawn, pivoting around Smith. Reid counts down the possession—six, five, four—and fuck, I need to get open or Coop will have to turn the frisbee over. Smith bumps me from behind, a little friendly contact, and I turn, jogging the last few steps backward as Coop slings the plastic disc my way.

It sails through the air, sun glinting off the shiny white surface. I jump, arm extended, ready to make the grab.

Smith elbows me in the ribs and I get a face full of locs, but it's all good because I've got the disc, fuck you very much.

I come down on one foot, but the momentum of the jump carries me backward and I crash ass-over-elbow into God only knows what.

One second, I'm sailing through the air, disc in hand, the next I'm flat on my back, staring at the summer sky, something sharp as hell stabbing me in the side as I gasp for breath.

"Get. Off. Me."

I'm on my feet in an instant because holy fuck, that stabbing pain is a girl.

Well, a woman. A tiny woman. With cobalt hair.

And she does *not* look happy.

Not that I blame her. I mean, I did just smash her. Well, not like *smash* smash, but...fuck.

"Shit. I'm so sorry." I extend a hand, prepared to help her up. "Are you okay?"

She stares at my outstretched hand like I've got leprosy and I'm not sure how to proceed. On the one hand, I almost knocked her out. On the other, it was an accident, and it's not like I have fucking cooties.

The look on her face would suggest otherwise.

It's not the first time someone's looked at me that way. Doubt it'll be the last.

I plaster a smile on, pretending she's not looking at me like something foul stuck to the bottom of her shoe, and try the apology again. "I'm really sorry. I didn't see you."

Her nostrils flare and I swear to Christ, flames are going to shoot out of her mouth.

Which might be cool if I weren't standing directly in the line of fire.

"You didn't see me?" She huffs out a breath, the silver hoop in her nose catching the light as she gestures to the moving box that's spilled its contents all over the grass. "Then I guess you didn't see my giant box, either."

My teammates cackle like a bunch of fucking hyenas and she mutters something that sounds like "*Asshole ballers*" as I withdraw the hand she clearly has no intention of taking.

Fine. She wants to lie in the grass, that's on her.

"Are you hurt?" A petite blonde springs into action, kneeling beside the blue-haired demon as she sits up. "You didn't break anything, did you?" The blonde inspects her elbow, and she lets out a quiet hiss. "You're bleeding."

Fuck. I didn't mean to plow her over. I just got caught up in the game.

"It's fine. It's just a scrape."

The blonde pops to her feet, ponytail bouncing. "I'm getting the first aid kit."

She bolts before her friend can argue, darting up the sidewalk without a backward glance.

"Well, at least I know where to go if I'm ever in need of First Aid." It's a pathetic attempt to lighten the mood, as evidenced by the howling of my roommates. *Jackasses.* "Ignore them. They're not laughing at you. They're laughing at me getting my ass handed to me by a girl half my size."

"I couldn't care less what you or your obnoxious friends think."

Damn. This girl doesn't pull punches. "I said I was sorry."

She looks up at me, dark eyes brimming with animosity. "Yeah, well, sorry won't fix my broken shit, will it?"

No, no it will not. "I'll pay for any damage."

I've got a little money saved up from my summer job working construction. Assuming the box wasn't full of overpriced designer crap, it'll be okay.

Probably.

"It's fine," she says, words steeped in sarcasm.

Yeah-fucking-right. I may not be the sharpest tool in the shed, but even I can tell it's anything but fine. I should probably walk away now. Clearly this chick isn't into apologies, or even common courtesy, but I'm not a complete prick, so I crouch down to help her put her stuff back in the box.

It's the least I can do after plowing her over.

"Here, let me give you a hand."

I reach for the first thing I see and she springs forward, eyes wide. Our heads knock together—which hurts like a motherfucker—and she lets out a string of curses. At least, I think they're curses. The only word I recognize is pendejo, thanks to two grueling years of high school Spanish.

I hold up the hot pink object she was so desperate to grab. It's silicone and has two rounded prongs like rabbit ears and— *Holy shit, it's a vibrator.*

She snatches it from my hand and heat floods my cheeks.

I'm a hot-blooded twenty-one-year-old and I've had my share of hookups, but I've never handled a woman's vibrator.

Hell, I've never even seen one in real life.

I watch, speechless, as she shoves it in the box.

Could this be more awkward?

Yes, it could. Because my roommates are here to bear witness.

I stare at the girl with the blue hair, forcing myself to meet her icy glare. There's something familiar about her, though I can't put my finger on it. Maybe we had a class together? Or—

Focus, asshole.

Right. This isn't the time for a trip down memory lane.

I need to fix this, assuming that's even possible. "I'm s—"

"I swear to God, if you say you're sorry one more time, I'm going to shove that vibrator down your throat."

I freeze, brain scrambling to switch gears before she makes good on her promise.

"I'm DJ Parker." I flash her a lopsided grin for good measure. We're going to be neighbors for the next nine months, and I sure as hell don't need her glaring daggers at me every time our paths cross. "And you are?"

An emotion I can't identify flickers across her face, but it's gone in an instant. "Not interested."

Irritation blazes up my spine. Is this girl for real?

"I wasn't hitting on you." I throw my palms up in self-defense. "Just trying to be neighborly, but clearly you're not into that sort of thing."

She stands, and because no way am I going to let this woman look down her nose at me, I follow suit.

It's the wrong move. She really is a tiny thing. Maybe five-three or five-four. I've got a solid twelve inches on her and the last thing I want to do is use my size to intimidate her.

"Look, Parker." She plants a hand on her hip, making it clear she's in no danger of being intimidated by my dumb ass. "Some of us are here to get an education, not to play ball, party, and screw our way across campus, okay?"

No. It's not fucking okay.

I've spent my life dealing with other people's assumptions about me and my academic abilities, and I'm not about to stand here and let this girl unload her preconceived, stereotypical notions about football players on me.

Fuck. That.

"You know what? If you feel so strongly about your education, maybe you should talk to the rental office about changing apartments. You know, so all the partying and fucking don't interrupt your studying." I gesture to the trunk of her Explorer, which is still half-filled with boxes. "I'll even help you load your stuff to speed up the process."

She opens her mouth—probably to say something scathing—but no words come out.

My pulse thrums at my temple and we stare at one another in heated silence.

After what feels like an eternity, she turns on her heel and marches up the sidewalk to her apartment, her pert, denim clad ass swaying with each step.

Because of course the devil has a perfect fucking ass.

"And that, my friends, is why Parker will be eternally

single." Coop smirks, looking entirely too pleased with himself. "The man has no skills."

Guilt tugs at my conscience, but I shove it aside. No way am I going to feel bad about trading barbs with the she-devil. Not when she started it.

"Well." Reid rubs the back of his neck. "At least if the townhouse gets egged, we'll know who did it."

Vaughn just shakes his head, like he can't believe I've stooped so low.

That makes two of us.

But with neighbors like that, it's going to be a long semester.

3

———

SUTTON

UN-*FREAKING*-BELIEVABLE. Forty thousand students at Waverly University and I'm living next door to the one person I never want to see again.

I must be rocking some shit karma.

Yeah, and after today, it's going to be next level.

Whatever. Parker got exactly what he deserved.

I push through the door to the rental office, which is blessedly cool, and scan the lobby for someone with a nametag. The place is a madhouse. There are throngs of people milling about with the harried expressions that only seem to appear during moving days and finals.

The line to the rental counter is ten deep, and while I'd like to cut right to the front—because surely this qualifies as an emergency—I queue up behind a guy talking animatedly on his cell.

The sooner I get this straightened out, the better.

Maddie isn't going to like it, but I'll pack and move her stuff, if that's what it takes. Because no way can I spend the next nine months living next door to DJ-*freaking*-Parker.

The man is arrogant. Narcissistic. *Cruel.*

My chest tightens and memories of that night freshman year come flooding back.

The lights. The music. The press of Parker's hard body against mine.

I squeeze my eyes shut and exhale through my nose.

You are not that soft, starry-eyed girl.

Not anymore.

The line inches forward and I silently curse my younger, more naïve self.

Stupid. Stupid. Stupid.

It's almost laughable how innocent and inexperienced I was then.

Blame it on gymnastics. I love the sport, but it doesn't exactly allow for much of a life outside the gym. Especially when you're an elite gymnast.

When it's my turn, I step up to the counter and plaster a smile on my face. The woman behind the desk looks frazzled. Her mousy hair is doing its damndest to escape its braid, and there's a stain on the front of her white polo shirt, proving it's been a day.

Welcome to the club, sister.

"How can I help you?" she asks mechanically, her smile as brittle as my own.

I glance at her nametag, remembering the customer service lessons my parents have drilled into my head over the years.

"Hi, Nancy. I think there's been a mix-up with my apartment."

"I'm so sorry to hear that." And miracle of miracles, she does sound apologetic. "What seems to be the problem?"

Hope floods my chest, and I lean forward, resting my elbows on the counter. "I submitted a note with my rental application requesting an apartment away from the football team, but I've been assigned a unit smack in the middle of them."

She frowns. "You don't want to be housed near the football team?"

"Exactly."

"But you've already moved in?" she asks, brow furrowed.

"My roommate has, but if you could just transfer us to another unit, we'd be happy to pack up."

"I'm sorry. That won't be possible."

My stomach clenches. "Why not? Surely there are other empty apartments. Only student athletes are moving in this early, right?"

Way to sound desperate.

"You've already picked up your keys and signed off on your inspection. Once you take possession of the apartment, there's nothing I can do."

Frustration roars through my veins, but I tamp it down. Acting like an asshole never solved anything, and I'm not interested in becoming a meme.

"It's only been a day. We'll clean everything. I swear." Hell, I'll work my knuckles to the bone scrubbing the townhouse from top to bottom. "It'll be spotless and ready for another renter. One who likes football players." She heaves a weary sigh, but I press on. "If you think about it, it's practically a selling point. I mean, there are tons of women on campus who'd give their left ovary to live next door to Austin Reid and Cooper DeLaurentis."

My roommate included.

Which probably makes me the worst kind of friend, but Maddie doesn't know about freshman year. If she did, she'd move in a heartbeat—and neuter Parker on her way out.

She's loyal like that.

"As much as I appreciate your suggestion, we take our

residents' privacy quite seriously." The rental agent shoots me a patronizing look. "I'm sure you understand."

Oh, I understand all right.

If I don't figure this out, I'm going to spend the next nine months staring at Parker's stupid, smug face.

Should've shoved the vibrator down his throat when you had the chance.

Truth. Then he'd get a restraining order and the complex would have to separate us.

It's not too late.

I file the thought away. Just in case I need a backup plan.

"Look, Nancy. I know this is a highly unusual request, but I did put a note in my application." On an impossible to miss neon orange Post-it. "If you could just pull my file, I'm sure you'll see—"

"Hon, even if you put a note on your application, it's too late to do anything about it. The apartments are assigned based on move-in date, and we are booked solid." She offers me a sympathetic smile, her dark eyes softening. "We've got a twelve-month waiting list. The only option you've got is to sublet, but then you'll have to find somewhere else to live."

I groan. This is total bullshit. I can't ask Maddie to live somewhere else. We chose this complex specifically because of its proximity to the training facilities. Once gymnastics officially starts, we'll be slogging to the gym at the ass crack of dawn. And come winter, we'll be doing it in snow and rain and subzero temperatures.

Coño.

My palms begin to sweat and I wrack my brain for a solution. There has to be something I can do. I can't give up.

Not yet.

"Excuse me." A girl with sleek, asymmetric Fulani braids steps up to the counter, her friendly smile easing my anxiety.

"I couldn't help but overhear your conversation." She gestures to a curvy brunette standing by the door. "My roommate and I haven't moved in yet. We'd be happy to swap apartments with you."

My heart soars. "Really? That would be amazing. Which building are you in?"

She glances down at the paperwork in her hand. "Two."

Maddie and I are in fifteen.

That would put thirteen buildings between Parker and me. The odds of us crossing paths would be slim.

Infinitesimal, even.

"That's perfect. Is it a two bedroom?"

Her face falls. "Four. Our other roommates are moving in tomorrow."

And there you have it. Proof karma is a salty bitch.

"Unless you're willing to swap roommates and apartments, it's a no go." I can't afford to pay for empty bedrooms and I doubt these girls are willing to share just for the privilege of living next door to a couple of hard bodied athletes. "Thanks for the offer, though."

"It was worth a shot." She tilts her head thoughtfully. "What building did you say you were in again?"

I open my mouth to answer and Nancy clears her throat —*loudly*.

Right. Privacy.

I smile at the other girl and step away from the counter just as my phone vibrates in my pocket. When I pull it out, there's a text from Maddie.

Maddie: Where are you? Please tell me you're not at the rental office putting in a transfer request.

The girl knows me too well.

*Me: They won't let us move. We're stuck with the brute squad. *swearing emoji**

Maddie: Sorry, not sorry. It's way too hot to even think about moving again.

She's not wrong, but the knowledge does little to improve my bad mood as I exit the rental office and step back out in the sweltering August heat.

Maddie: What's the big deal? So he saw your vibrator. Half the women on campus have them.

Maddie really doesn't get it.

Because you haven't told her.

Yeah, well, who could blame me for not bragging about the worst night of my life?

I stalk across the parking lot and climb into my Explorer. Hot leather burns the backs of my thighs as I yank the door shut and start the ignition. The SUV rumbles to life and I slump over the steering wheel, silently cursing the universe, karma, and DJ-*freaking*-Parker.

He didn't even recognize you.

Freshman year, the realization would've wrecked me.

Hell, it *did* wreck me.

But I'm not that girl anymore. The one so desperate for acceptance. For something of her own.

After years of living in my sister's shadow—of people lamenting that I'd never move as gracefully as Gabby or tumble as beautifully—I'd been ready to spread my wings and fly at Waverly. Which is why I said yes when the hot guy in my American History class invited me to a party on Greek Row.

Stupid. Stupid. Stupid.

I'd been crushing on Parker for weeks. Imagining what it would be like to run my fingers through his tousled brown hair. Daydreaming about those full, pouty lips locked on mine. Wondering what it would be like to lose myself in those brooding hazel eyes.

It didn't matter that I hardly knew him.

Or that the only time we'd spoken was when he asked to borrow my notes.

I went to that party full of hope and anticipation, butterflies swarming in my stomach.

Parker was already buzzed when I arrived, and he seemed surprised to see me.

That probably should've been my first clue the night wasn't going to end well, but I was determined to roll with it, so I joined him at the beer pong table. By the end of the night, we were both tipsy and when he invited me back to his dorm, I was all in.

It was a short walk, but the night was cool and the crunch of leaves echoed with each footfall. Parker was the perfect gentleman, wrapping me in his sweater and folding me into his warm embrace, one arm slung over my shoulders as we made our way across campus. He smelled like citrus and sandalwood and by the time we got back to his place, I was swooning like a virgin.

My stomach twists at the memory.

Better a fool than a tool.

Maybe. Maybe not.

Parker and I had sex, but there was nothing swoonworthy about it.

The act itself probably only lasted two minutes, and to say it was the most disappointing two minutes of my life would be a gross understatement. It was awkward and uncomfortable and there was no grand finale.

Not for me anyway.

To add insult to injury, he called me the wrong fucking name.

Summer.

I'd never felt smaller or more inconsequential in my life.

Which is saying something given I was raised in a household with a girl who has more gold medals than I have shoes.

My nails dig into my palms, the desire to punch something —anything—rising like the tide.

The following week in class, he looked right through me. No hello. No dip of the chin. *Nothing.*

It was like our hookup never even happened.

Not only had he forgotten my name, he'd forgotten *me.*

I vowed then and there to never be invisible again. To never blend in. To stand out.

By spring semester, I'd dyed my hair blue, pierced my nose, and purged my wardrobe, replacing my boring, vanilla clothing with funky pieces that demand attention.

And despite it all, nothing's actually changed because that asshole just crashed into me like I wasn't even there.

4

DJ

"You should've seen the look on Parker's face when he picked up the vibrator." Coop cackles like a teenage girl. "I swear to God I thought he was going to faint."

My cheeks heat, but I know better than to protest. It'll only fan the flames. And with my luck, inspire the guys to fill my locker with dildos or some shit when I'm not around.

Fuck. That.

If I keep my head down and ignore them, they'll forget all about it by next week when some other asshole makes a fool of himself.

I gesture to the TV with my controller. "Are we doing this or what?"

It's Saturday night and the guys and I are hosting a Madden tourney. Just a small gathering of our teammates, a few cases of beer, and a whole lot of chill after a long week of training camp.

Coop snorts and throws his controller to Vaughn, who's sitting next to me on the couch. "I need another drink. Anyone else?"

Reid and a couple of other guys make noises of affirmation

and someone turns up the music, drowning them out as Vaughn and I face off on-screen.

I lose myself in the game, banishing vibrators and grumpy neighbors to a black hole.

No way am I going to let that shit bring me down tonight.

By the second quarter, I'm destroying Vaughn—no surprise there—and when my running back swaggers into the end zone and spikes the ball, driving up the score, a raucous cheer goes up from our teammates.

"Was that really necessary?" Vaughn mutters, giving me the side-eye.

"Hell yes." I smirk and turn to look at him. "Can't do it on game day. Might as well get it out of my system now."

Coach Collins would lose his shit if I pulled a stunt like that on the field. Which is cool. He's strict, but fair. For a lot of guys on the team, he's the father figure they never had.

So, yeah. No celebrating on the field.

But here? In our living room, surrounded by some of the loudest, most competitive guys I know? You're damn right I'm going to showboat.

Vaughn grunts and I swear to Christ his cheeks turn red. It's hard to tell around the new beard, but I'm pretty sure that's a blush I see. Which is hilarious on a six-foot-six, three-hundred-pound dude.

Imagine if he'd been the one to pick up the vibrator.

He probably would've gone into cardiac arrest.

"Don't worry." Coop jerks his chin in my direction. "There'll be plenty of time to celebrate when we win the national championship."

Reid lifts his beer, as if making a toast. "From your lips to God's ears."

"Man, we don't need divine intervention." Smith grins, lip curling. "We got skills."

He and Coop bump fists, and another round of cheers breaks out as I turn my attention back to the game, sweat beading along my hairline.

The season hasn't even started yet and I'm already stressing.

Fact is, I won't be going pro like Reid or Coop.

I've always known it, but that doesn't lessen the pressure. If anything, it's worse. I have to be unstoppable on the field *and* in the classroom, because unlike my roommates, I won't be drafted in the spring and I sure as shit won't be graduating. While these guys will be playing in the NFL next fall, I'll be a fifth-year senior.

Which means this is also my last chance to land an internship in my major. I've spent the last three summers working at my uncle's construction company—football scholarships don't actually cover all living expenses—and my advisor insists it'll be impossible to break into sports broadcasting without experience.

I don't have connections like Reid or money like DeLaurentis, but I'm a hard worker and I've been busting my ass to maintain a 3.3 GPA. According to my advisor, my best shot for an internship is Sports Stream. The network is based out of Pittsburgh, and though it's not ESPN, they hire one Waverly intern each summer because the programming director is an alumnus.

This year, I need to be that intern.

"Come on, man." Reid throws up his hands as my on-screen receiver fumbles the ball and Vaughn's safety scoops it up and runs it back for a touchdown.

Vaughn snickers and the next thing I know, his safety is doing the griddy.

Someone slaps him on the back and he grins, revealing all of his teeth.

If I didn't know better, I'd be terrified of that look, but Vaughn's marshmallow fluff, so I bust his balls a little.

"Someone's been spending too much time with DeLaurentis. Next, you'll be admiring your reflection and referring to yourself in the third person."

"Screw you." Coop jabs a finger at me. "I don't talk about myself in the third person. I use first person pronouns like the fucking king of campus I am."

"So eloquent," Reid deadpans, shaking his head. "And humble."

Smith snorts. "I'm just impressed my man knows what a pronoun is."

"I'm impressed any of you know what a pronoun is!"

We turn in unison to the party crasher, who stands in the living room entry with her arms crossed. It's the girl from earlier. The one with the blue hair.

For a long moment, no one says anything, myself included. Because what the fuck is happening right now?

"Where'd you come from?" Coop asks, brow furrowed.

Before she can answer, some smartass behind me jumps in. "When a man and a woman love each other very much—"

Coop's middle finger shoots up, but his attention remains locked on the new arrival. "I meant, how did you get in here?"

She lifts her chin, as if preparing for battle. "The door was open."

"Who left the door open?" He scans the room, searching for the culprit.

"I did." Smith ducks his head and gestures to the rest of us. "So we wouldn't have to get up every time one of these fools rolled in late."

"Bruh. That's how stalkers get in." Coop frowns. "And burglars."

It really says something about our lifestyle that stalkers came first.

The she-devil shrugs. "I knocked, but I guess you couldn't hear me over the music."

"What?" Coop shouts, cupping a hand around his ear.

"I said, I knocked but—" She cuts herself off, realizing he's messing with her.

"You should've used the bell," Reid suggests.

She presses her lips together and a beat passes before she answers. "I. Did."

Next to me, Vaughn shifts uneasily and he opens his mouth to reply, but Coop is faster. "It didn't ring."

To her credit, she doesn't make the same mistake twice.

"You should probably put in a maintenance ticket for that." A wicked grin transforms her small mouth. "But in the meantime, maybe you could *quiet the fuck down*?"

Coop's eyes go wide and a ripple of laughter fills the room. Someone shouts "*Dayum*" and some other choice words are thrown around, but it's all in good fun.

"It's Saturday night," Coop says, stretching the words for emphasis. Or maybe he's drunk. It's hard to say because the man loves fucking with people and this girl is making it too easy.

"So? I'm tired and I just want to crash."

He smirks. "What are you, like seventy?"

She arches a brow and scans the crowded room, carefully avoiding my stare. "I know you're all hotshot football players, but surely you have some common decency?"

She's one to talk. What kind of person barges into a stranger's house uninvited?

When no one responds—which is probably for the best—she stalks across the room and turns the speaker off, killing the music.

It's so quiet I can actually hear my heart thundering in my chest.

Which is ridiculous.

The woman is hardly a threat. I've faced guys twice her size on the field. Ones determined to rip my head off.

Forget your head, that one will go straight for your balls.

It might be hot if she weren't glaring daggers at me.

"Are we seriously taking orders from Sailor Moon?" an underclassman asks, breaking the silence.

The blue-haired demon looks down, as if she's completely forgotten what she's wearing, and when she looks up again, her cheeks are scarlet.

My gaze dips to her pajamas. She's wearing a white tank top with a blue and white ruffle around the neckline and a tiny pink bow between her breasts. The matching shorts have blue and white pinstripes and sheer blue ruffles around the leg openings. They're short as hell and reveal miles of toned bronze skin. The girl might be tiny, but she's fit as hell.

My cock stirs with interest because apparently, I'm a masochist now.

"How the hell do you know Sailor Moon?" Reid asks, turning to address the numbnuts who asked the question.

"Pornhub."

The she-devil's blush intensifies, spreading down her neck and over her chest, drawing my attention to the thin cotton covering her small breasts.

Fuuuck.

No way. My cock might be into pain, but I am not. I get enough of it on the field to fulfill whatever dark desires might lurk in my psyche.

I toss my controller onto the coffee table and stand, meeting the she-devil's haughty glare. "On that note, why don't I walk you out?"

Despite her low opinion of football players, I can be a gentleman.

She rolls her eyes. "I think I can find the way."

"Probably, but I'd like to make sure we don't have any more surprise guests tonight."

One is more than enough.

I gesture toward the hall and follow when she marches past, her perfect ass swaying with each step.

"Quit looking at my ass."

"Who says I'm looking at your ass?"

She tosses her hair and it cascades over her shoulder like a crashing wave. "I'm a woman. We always know when men are objectifying our bodies."

Ouch. "Maybe I was just admiring your PJs."

"Right." She turns on her heel as she reaches the front door. "I'm sure you're a huge Sailor Moon fan."

Fuck no. But my cousin is into anime, so I know just enough to be dangerous. And, with any luck, enough to find some common ground so we can smooth things over between us.

Preferably before she breaks in and smothers me in my sleep.

"I can name all the characters."

She snorts. "Which only proves you're active on Pornhub."

I cross my arms because I'm pretty sure strangling a neighbor—even one who identifies as the she-devil—is frowned upon. "Sweetheart, I don't need Pornhub to get off."

"Oh, I know." She sneers, looking me over from head to toe. "I'm sure there's no shortage of broken-hearted fangirls trailing in your wake."

Bullshit. I'm a straight shooter when it comes to sex. My hookups are always the no-strings, one and done variety by mutual agreement. Between football and school, I don't have time for anything else. But if she's so determined to think the worst of me, so be it.

"Jealous?" I brace a hand on the door and lean down until our faces are just inches apart. Her breath hitches and her pupils blow wide, nearly swallowing the umber irises, but she stands her ground. "If you've got an itch that needs scratching, just say the word."

"Don't flatter yourself." She squares her shoulders and pulls herself up to her full height, narrowing the gap between our mouths. We're so close I can't help but notice the perfect Cupid's bow of her upper lip or the lingering smell of mint on her breath and fuck me, I want to taste her. The urge to crush my lips to hers strikes hard and fast, need coiling deep in my gut. "I wouldn't have sex with you if you were the last man on Earth."

Her words are breathy, but they land like a physical blow, each one dripping with venom.

"Good." I push off the wall and take a step back. "The feeling's mutual."

So much for being a gentleman.

She recoils, and before she can deliver another strike, I reach behind her and yank the door open, forcing her to sidestep to avoid being hit in the ass by it.

"Dios mío. You really are an asshole."

"Finally, something we agree on." I smirk down at her, embracing the role she's assigned me. "The next time you want to show off your skimpy little pajamas, use the bell like a normal person."

"Keep your music down and there won't be a next time," she seethes, stepping outside and yanking the door shut behind her.

The slam echoes through the silent hall and I rake my fingers through my hair.

Not my finest moment, but damn. That girl knows how to get under my skin. I may not like her—hell, I don't even know her name—but the sexual tension crackling between us is undeniable.

The guys are in rare form when I return to the living room.

"Looks like you made a new friend," Coop says with a shit-eating grin. "I like her. Seems nice."

I flip him an *up yours* gesture and turn toward the kitchen —I deserve another beer after dealing with the she-devil—but then I get a better idea. "Yo, Coop. Can we get the music back? And while you're at it, crank the volume up a little more."

5

SUTTON

I'M DRAGGING ass when Maddie and I arrive at the gym Monday morning for conditioning. Although our season doesn't officially start until January, we have to train year-round. Plus, I want to be in top form when team practices start next month and I didn't train as hard as I should have this summer. Most of the camps I worked were for level four and five gymnasts and the workouts didn't exactly push me to my limits.

You could've trained in the evenings.

True, but I was dead tired from chasing mischievous girls around all day.

Maddie sprints up the stairs to the gymnastics building—a squat brick rectangle with a modest sign over the main entrance—like she's just chugged a Red Bull. I trail behind, scraping the last of my yogurt from the cup as I climb the cement steps. When I reach the landing, I lick the last bit of strawberry goo from my spoon and toss my trash in the blue and white can.

"What's up?" I ask, joining my roommate, who's made no move to open the door.

"The gym is closed."

"What?" I skim the handwritten sign taped to the door.

Temporarily closed for repairs. Gymnasts may use the facilities at the football building until further notice. Contact Coach Miller or Coach James with questions.

My stomach drops. "Is this a freaking joke?"

The universe can't seriously expect me to train with Parker. Not after Saturday night.

It's bad enough I have to live next door to him.

Maddie's phone pings and she pulls it from the side pocket of her leggings. She taps the screen and her eyes move side to side as she reads.

"Definitely not a joke." She flips the phone around, revealing an email from Coach Miller. "For the next two weeks, we use the football facilities or we don't train. Sounds like maintenance couldn't finish scheduled repairs because of all the summer camps."

I groan, but don't bother to check my phone, which is on silent. No doubt I got the same email.

"No way." I shake my head for emphasis. "No way am I sharing facilities with those entitled douchebags."

Maddie shrugs. "How bad can it be?

Pretty freaking bad.

Because even though I loathe DJ Parker, the pull of attraction is as strong as ever. When he leaned in to make his lewd innuendo Saturday night, those penetrating hazel eyes fixed on me, there was a moment when I imagined his lips brushing mine. When I remembered the feel of his tongue sliding along the seam of my mouth, the press of his muscular body—

Nope. Not even going there.

"Besides, it's only two weeks." Maddie hooks her arm through mine and steers me back down the stairs. "It might even make conditioning more fun. Just think of all the eye candy."

"Eye candy is the last thing we need while training. Does the word distraction mean nothing to you?"

I can practically feel her eyes roll as she says, "We aren't going to get injured while doing cardio."

"Don't be so sure about that. I saw a girl fall off a treadmill at camp and twist her ankle—*because a boy walked past her machine.*"

Maddie giggles. "Yeah, but I'm not thirteen and ruled by hormones."

"So you say," I grumble, adjusting my gym bag as we turn right on University Drive.

"What if I promise to only look while working on my abs?"

"What if we skip conditioning today?" I counter.

"No way. Being accountability partners means actually holding each other accountable." She smirks. "Even when it hurts."

Especially when it hurts.

She's right. I can't afford to skip workouts heading into the season. Once you start, it's hard to stop. The excuses pile up and the next thing you know, your tricks are sloppy and your arms are trembling, and then you get your ass kicked in a televised meet.

We hoof it to the football building, a flashy stone and glass monstrosity that's at least three times the size of the gymnastics building.

The instant we enter the lobby, I pull up short.

"Holy shit." I knew the football team had better facilities than the gymnastics team, but damn. The lobby is cool and quiet, but it's the massive atrium and pristine display cases filled with polished trophies and plaques that draw my eye. Everything about this place screams money from the modern blue and white furniture to the custom Waverly rugs that cover the marble floor. And don't even get me started on the fancy ass Wildcat banners that hang on the walls. "We really need to get some mega-donors for the gymnastics program."

"No kidding." Maddie steps into the atrium and spreads her arms wide, spinning in the shaft of sunlight that streams down from overhead. "I may need to switch sports."

"Don't even think about it." I scan the directory—which, unlike the one in the gymnastics building, isn't a holdover from the seventies—and nod toward the hall on the right. "Looks like the weight room is this way."

"Should we leave a trail of breadcrumbs?" Maddie asks, scraping her hair into a ponytail and securing it with a rubber band from her wrist.

"Why bother?" I shrug and start down the hall. "The janitorial crew would sweep them up long before we return."

Maddie trails behind me, footsteps echoing as she gives a running commentary on all the ways the football building is superior to our own training facilities.

When we reach the double doors marked "Weight Room," I hesitate, pulse thrumming.

Might as well get it over with.

Stalling will only make it worse.

I throw the doors wide and we're greeted by a cacophony of familiar sounds: loud music, intense grunts, and clanging metal.

Home sweet hellscape.

"I think I just got pregnant," Maddie whispers. Whether it's from the gym and its state-of-the-art equipment or the sight of the football team with their bulging muscles on full display is anyone's guess.

Soraya waves to us from a large patch of AstroTurf where she and Brooke are warming up, and we make a beeline for our teammates. Brooke straightens as we approach and flicks the end of her ponytail, a brilliant smile pasted on her sun kissed face.

"How great is this?" she asks, her tinny voice carrying over the sounds of the weight room.

"So great," I deadpan, dropping my bag and throwing myself into my stretching routine. The last thing I need right now is to be drawn into another conversation about douchey ballers.

Hard pass.

"I talked to Coach Collins," Soraya says, rolling her shoulders. "He said as long as we don't interfere with the football team's conditioning, early mornings are fine. They'll be hitting the field soon anyway, so we should have the place to ourselves."

I tune out my teammates' chatter, determined to make this the shortest workout in the history of workouts. As I go through the motions, I scan the weight room, getting the lay of the land. Blue power racks take up most of the space. The racks are lined up in three neat rows that stretch from one end of the room to the other. Each one has a blue and white Wildcat mat below and from what I can tell, all the weights— even the free weights—have the Waverly mascot stamped on them. Cardio machines are on the second level, which is open and overlooks the lower level.

"I'll bet their machines aren't constantly breaking down," Maddie says, catching my eye.

"No way I'm taking that bet." I fish my earbuds out of my pocket and shove them in my ears before hitting play on my audiobook. I make my way to one of the empty racks and use the chin-up bar for hanging leg lifts.

When I'm done, Maddie takes my place and I can't help but notice the guys beside us staring as she brings her feet up and taps them against the bar, her abdominal muscles tightening with each repetition. I try to ignore them and focus on my audiobook, but it's impossible because they're loud as fuck.

"What was Coach thinking, agreeing to this?" a big dude with a fauxhawk asks, crossing his arms.

His partner grunts, but says nothing as he does another squat.

"I mean, how are we supposed to concentrate with all these spinners prancing around?" Fauxhawk smirks as Maddie once again folds herself in half, touching her feet to the bar.

I close my eyes and draw a steadying breath as anger blooms deep in my chest.

They're not worth it…

"Then again, imagine all the kinky shit they can do in bed with that kind of flexibility," he continues, gaze roving across the room. "I'd be down for some of that action."

White-hot fury explodes behind my eyelids. "You know we can hear you, right, pendejo?"

The words are out before I can stop myself.

Fauxhawk's smirk evaporates, and a flush bleeds into his nose and cheeks. "What did you just call me?"

Hands trembling, I yank my earbuds out and stuff them in my pocket. "I said, we can hear you, *pendejo*."

This time I emphasize the word, though I don't provide an explanation.

Fauxhawk stalks forward, eyes narrowed, but before he can so much as utter a word, Parker appears.

Because *of course* he does.

The guy is like a bad freaking penny.

One designed to lure you in with a disarming smile, a chiseled jawline, and the promise of toe-curling orgasms.

Talk about false advertising.

He plants a hand on Fauxhawk's chest, meeting the guy's flat stare with one of his own. "Knock it the fuck off, Langley."

Surprise washes over me and a laugh bubbles up from my deep in my belly. Because in what universe could DJ Parker ever be my hero?

6

DJ

"WHAT'S SO FUNNY?" Langley and I ask in unison.

It's probably the first—and last—time the D-man and I will ever be on the same page. We might be teammates, but the guy's a dick. Despite the she-devil's low opinion of me, I wouldn't wish Langley on my worst enemy.

"I can't decide what's worse," she drawls, adjusting her ponytail. "The cliché sexist pig routine or the knight in tarnished armor."

"Be nice." Her friend drops from the rack, landing lightly on her feet before extending her hand to me. "I don't think we've been properly introduced. I'm Maddie." She nods at the blue-haired demon, who's wearing a black tank top and shorts the same color as her hair. Shorts that reveal even more of her toned bronze legs than those damn Sailor Moon pajamas. "And this is Sutton." She flashes me a knowing grin as her roommate huffs out a breath, sending a loose strand of cobalt hair flying. "Ignore the Addams vibes. She's harmless. Totally warm and squishy on the inside."

Just like a barracuda.

"DJ." I shake her hand, because unlike the sh—*Sutton*, I've got manners. "But my friends call me Parker."

"Nice to meet you, Parker."

They pointedly ignore Langley, and I can't say I blame them. I'd do the same if our positions were reversed. Which is why it's time for him to get gone. "You done here?"

The D-man smirks. "I was just offering to help these ladies with the machines. Looked like they could use a little guidance."

Sutton snorts. "Bullshit. The only thing you were offering was ten different kinds of sexual harassment." She glares up at him, chin jutting out. "It's like you've never even heard of Title IX or the #MeToo movement."

Langley's face goes blank and I know what's coming before he even opens his mouth. "What the fuck is Title IX?"

Maddie rolls her eyes and Sutton shoots her a *told you so* look.

Jesus Christ. It's too early for this shit.

I gesture to Langley's abandoned rack. "Why don't you finish up and move along?"

"I don't take orders from you." A muscle in his jaw tics. "In case you've forgotten, I'm a captain on this team."

And insecure enough to title drop every chance he gets.

"Exactly. Coach catches you harassing our guests, we'll all be running laps 'til we puke." I make a show of scanning the room where our teammates are still grinding through their individualized programs. "No one will thank you for it."

Not when College Park is in the middle of a heatwave and it's hot as balls outside.

He grabs his water bottle from the rack and mutters, "Fuck you" as he stalks off.

"That guy's a team captain?" Sutton sighs. "Why am I not surprised?"

"Only for the defense." I comb sweat-damp hair from my forehead. She already thinks we're a bunch of douchebags and now Langley's proven it with his trash leadership and blatant sexual harassment. *Fucking wonderful.* "He's an asshole, but he plays well and he's just smart enough not to let Coach see what a dick he is."

Maddie grimaces. "I'm sure all the guys on the team aren't like him."

Facts. Reid is a great captain and he wouldn't tolerate that shit on the offense. Hell, he's the one who poached our new kicker from the women's soccer team.

"You know what they say." Sutton flashes me a syrupy smile. "One rotten apple spoils the bunch."

"That's a little harsh, don't you think?"

She shrugs. "I call them like I see them."

Maddie's focus pivots from her roommate to me and back again. When she stops, she's grinning like the goddamn Cheshire Cat.

"Sounds like y'all need to clear the air." She flicks a finger back and forth between Sutton and me. "I'm gonna go do press handstands so you can get started on that."

I don't have the first idea what a press handstand is, but she's not wrong about clearing the air. It's like every time I run into this girl—into Sutton—I say or do the wrong thing.

It's frustrating as hell.

Maddie gives me a little finger wave before sauntering off.

I open my mouth to apologize for Langley's behavior, but Sutton cuts me off. "What do you think you're doing?"

"Helping." *Obviously.* "You're welcome, by the way."

"I didn't ask for your help." She plants her hands on her slender hips and why the fuck am I looking at her hips when she's giving me the third degree? "You think I can't handle a guy like that? Dios mío. He wasn't even original with his gross, misogynistic jokes."

I give silent thanks she doesn't elaborate. The urge to throat punch Langley is real, and something tells me the details of their exchange will only strengthen that desire.

"I have no doubt you can handle guys like Langley." God knows she has no problem handing me my ass. "The point is, you shouldn't have to."

Her eyes go wide, but she recovers quickly. "Whatever. Just don't go thinking three seconds of pseudo feminism is going to get you on my good side."

"You have a good side?" She scowls and a quiet chuckle escapes my lips. *This fucking girl.* "Seriously though. Do you hate all football players, or is it just me?"

She bites her lower lip, and the thrill of victory races up my spine, but when she finally speaks, it's a total copout.

"I plead the fifth."

Well, shit. It's just me then. What the hell did I ever do to her?

A bead of sweat slides down my temple and I swipe it away with the hem of my shirt, frustration gnawing at my gut. I'm not Mr. Perfect, but I'm a decent guy.

Friendly. Laid-back. Fun.

People love me.

Most people.

"Look." I pitch my voice low. "If this is about the, uh, vibrator—"

"It's not."

"Then what is it about? Because if we don't work this out—whatever *this* is—it's going to be a long semester...*neighbor.*"

Sutton studies me, and it's like she's pillaging my goddamn thoughts when she turns those rich, coffee-colored eyes on me. Eyes so dark, they're almost black.

Like her soul.

No way. Sutton might be grumpy AF, but there has to be more to her. After all, her roommate is a ray of fucking sunshine.

"How about we just agree to stay out of each other's way?" she finally says. "If you see me around the apartment complex, just walk on by like you don't even know me." Her eyes narrow. "That shouldn't be too hard for you."

Yeah-*fucking*-right.

I haven't been able to stop thinking about her since Saturday night. Haven't been able to stop thinking about how damn close I was to kissing her—how I ached to taste her—despite the fact that she clearly hates my guts.

"That's it? You're not going to tell me what I did to earn your ire so I can, I don't know, do better?"

"That's not my job." She reaches for her phone, which is resting on one of the rack's crossbars. "If you want to be a better human, that's on you."

Fuck. She's right.

"You're right. I'm sorry. I just—"

Christ. This woman is infuriating. And sexy. But mostly confusing.

Ignoring me, she makes a show of tapping the screen on her phone, making it clear she's done with me.

"His tongue glides over my pussy in slow, sure strokes and my back bows off the bed as I come—"

Holy shit.

Sutton's eyes grow wide when she realizes we can all hear whatever the hell she's listening to and she jabs the screen, aggressively trying to silence the phone.

Several heads swivel in our direction and a chorus of "*Dayum, girl,*" and "*Get it,*" rise above the din of the weight room as she stuffs the phone in the pocket of her shorts, cheeks blazing.

Oh, this is too good. A better man would look the other way. Let her suffer in silence. But, it's too ironic for me to let it slide.

"Forgot your earbuds." I tap my right ear, earning a haughty glare. "I can't believe you had the nerve to give me shit about Pornhub when you're listening to that while you work out."

"It's not porn," she says through gritted teeth. "It's a romance novel."

I smirk, mostly because I know it'll get under her skin and she's cute when she's mad. "Sounds pretty pornalicious to me."

"That's not even a word."

"It should be. Anyway, you shouldn't be embarrassed. I'll bet everyone in this room has looked at porn."

Which is definitely not something I want to think about since *everyone* includes Coach.

She straightens, visibly squaring her shoulders. "I'm not embarrassed."

"Yeah? Then why are your cheeks the color of a chili pepper?"

"Because when it comes to sex, there's a double standard for men and women. One that's thriving if your moronic teammates are any indication."

"Trust me." I scan the area, confirming the guys have gone back to their workouts. It's not the first time something like that's happened in the weight room. Hell, it's practically commonplace. "They aren't judging you. Believe it or not, some of us find empowered women sexy as hell."

"Forget it." She shakes her head, as if casting off the entire conversation. "I wouldn't expect *you* to understand."

A familiar burn sparks in my chest. "Why? Because I'm just a dumb football player?"

Stupid. Idiot. Slow.

Each word cuts like a blade, vicious echoes from my childhood that never seem to fade.

"That's not what I said." Sutton shrugs. "But if the cleat fits..."

Fury claws its way up my throat and I clench my fists at my sides, the familiar feeling of being *less than* settling in my gut like a stone.

No. I'm not going there. Not today.

Fuck her assumptions. And fuck the played out, dumb jock narrative.

That's what you get for trying to play peacemaker.

I don't know why Sutton has beef with me, but I'm over it.

"You know what? You were right." I flex my fingers and back away. "I'll stay out of your way as long as you stay the hell out of mine." I turn to go, but catch myself, unable to resist throwing out a parting shot. "The next time you want to listen to your pornalicious books, use your earbuds so it doesn't distract the football team. Some of us have national titles to win."

7

SUTTON

Parker turns on his heel and swaggers across the gym, broad shoulders emphasized by the sleeveless tee he probably wore just to show off his stupid biceps. Biceps that really aren't that impressive. Lots of guys have biceps the size of my thigh.

Nice guys. Guys who treat women with respect. Guys who remember names.

Guys who don't ghost.

He bends to pick up something on the floor, and my stomach flips.

Parker might be a jerk, but you can't deny he's got a nice ass.

No. He *is* an ass. Big difference. Huge. Because no way am I attracted to that jock hole.

Heat floods my core and I silently curse my stupid body. It may be capable of amazing things, but it's also a traitorous little asshole. That's the only explanation for the fact that, after everything he's done, DJ Parker can still ignite a flare of desire deep within me.

Which is bullshit. Because this morning—despite its humiliating start—has taught me a valuable lesson: *don't get mad, get even.*

8
____

DJ

VAUGHN and I roll into the locker room with just enough time to dress and hit the field.

I've always been a night owl, and morning practices are rough, but it's the last week of training camp, so at least that's something. Even better, Sutton and I haven't crossed paths in days. It's a fucking miracle, but I'm not about to look a gift horse in the mouth.

Not when classes start next week.

I've got enough on my plate without worrying about the she-devil.

Tell it to your cock.

Okay, fine. She may have slipped into my thoughts when I was jerking off in the shower Friday night, but it was one time.

One fantastic fucking time.

Whatever. It won't happen again.

I'm focused now. I have to be. The life of a DI athlete is grueling under the best of circumstances and my circumstances? Far from ideal. Especially since reading assignments—of which there's no shortage—take me twice as long as they should.

Vaughn and I head straight for our lockers and begin stripping. I'm down to my skivvies when Coop joins us.

"Monday can kiss my ass," I grumble, tossing my shorts into the bottom of my locker.

The surrounding guys make noises of assent and I realize Vaughn is almost done dressing. The fuck? Either he set a new world record for speed or I'm even more tired than I thought.

Get it the fuck together, Parker.

Dragging ass on the field is a surefire way to find yourself running wind sprints until you drop.

"Where's Reid?" It's almost time to hit the field and our captain is glaringly absent.

"No clue." Coop flexes his biceps, eyes glued to the mirror inside his locker. "It wasn't my turn to babysit him."

Just then, Reid turns the corner, making his way down the aisle. He looks like something the cat dragged in, but no one comments on it as he opens his locker and discards his stuff. The guy carries the weight of this team and some damn crushing expectations on his shoulders. He's bound to look like ass once in a while, and I doubt he'd welcome me pointing it out.

"Never have I ever seen a bigger douche." Vaughn slaps Coop on the back before he slams the door to his locker and tucks his helmet under his arm. "Don't you ever get tired of admiring yourself?"

"Hell no." A slow grin spreads across Coop's face. "Word of advice: you're going to have a hard time getting laid with that ugly-ass beard of yours."

Vaughn looks genuinely puzzled as his gaze shifts from Coop to Reid and back again. "What's wrong with my beard?"

"Aside from the fact that it needs its own zip code?" Reid asks with the hint of a smile.

"Seriously, bro. Just because you're from West Virginia

doesn't mean you have to look like a mountain man." Coop shakes his head. "You think a girl wants all that"—he gestures to Vaughn's overgrown beard—"scratching her *special place* while you're going down on her?" The air quotes he makes when he says special place send the guys around us into peals of laughter.

Vaughn's cheeks turn beet red above the dark scruff. "Fuck off."

"Don't shoot the messenger," Coop shouts as Vaughn retreats down the aisle, giving us the one-finger salute.

Coop's on a mission to loosen Vaughn up, but from what I can tell, it's not working.

Still, it provides endless hours of entertainment and it's all in good fun. After three years of playing together, these guys are like my brothers. I can't think of anything worse than letting them down. Which is why I'm going to savor the shit out of our last season together and work my ass off to help deliver a national title.

"I hear special teams is practicing on the field with us today," Coop says, closing his locker and turning to our team captain.

Reid's face is carefully neutral. "So?"

"So, that means we'll get to see Carter in action." He grins and wiggles his brows. "I hope she's wearing shorts today."

"Don't be an asshole." Reid glares up at him and peels off his shirt, tossing it in the locker. "It's one hundred fucking degrees outside. Of course she'll be wearing shorts. And no one's going to say shit, got it?"

"That's what I thought." Coop smirks. "The lady doth protest too much."

"As usual, I have no idea what you're talking about," Reid says.

"*Riiiiigght.*"

I adjust my jockstrap and step into my pants. Coop's way off base if he thinks Reid is lusting after our new kicker. My man doesn't do entanglements. No time. Then again, Carter's on the same schedule as the rest of us, so maybe teammates with benefits would suit her just fine. Actually, that's not a bad idea. Maybe it's time I get to know the new kicker. It could be just the distraction I need to banish the she-devil from my thoughts once and for all.

"What the fuck?" Coop stares down at his cock, brow furrowed. Then he does a weird little dance and jams his hand down the front of his pants, scratching his balls. "What. The. Actual. Fuck!" he howls, going to town on his johnson.

I shoot Reid a *WTF?* look before turning back to Coop. "I told you to double bag that shit. Bet it burns when you piss too."

"I don't have an STD, asshole." Coop yanks his pants down and inspects his junk as I lace up. "I always wrap it before I tap it." The volume in the locker room begins to climb and there's more yelling and cussing than usual. Coop kicks off his cleats and strips off his pants before lifting his jockstrap for inspection. "Which one of you assholes put itching powder in my jockstrap?" he yells, holding up the flimsy garment. "That shit's not funny!"

Reid and I both snicker. Coop's one of the biggest pranksters on the team. He probably had it coming.

"Payback's a bitch." I extend a fist to Reid and he bumps it, just as my dick begins to itch.

"Oh shit." I glance down at my cock, panic taking root as the itch intensifies.

Motherfucker.

I untie my pants and yank them down as the sensation spreads, marching across my skin like goddamn fire ants.

I have to scratch. For relief.

Scratching will only make it worse.

Fuck that. I can't *not* scratch. My boys are under attack.

Reid inspects the jockstrap in his hand and decides not to risk it, instead tossing it on the bench as I peel mine off.

The locker room erupts in chaos and Coach storms in, square jaw set. "What the hell is going on in here?" he roars, glancing around at his half-dressed team. His gaze lands on our team captain. "Reid, care to tell me why you aren't on the field yet?"

Reid sighs and rubs the back of his neck. "Well, sir. It seems—"

"Spit it out, son." Coach waves his hand impatiently, and suddenly my itching cock doesn't seem so important.

"Someone put itching powder in our jockstraps," Reid explains.

"Fuckin' pranks," Coach mutters, shaking his head. "Who did this?" he demands, face flushing a deep shade of crimson as he scans the locker room, thick brows pulled low.

It's a waste of time. No one has ever confessed to a prank without a case of beer and a damn good buzz. Not that Coach will let a little thing like a confession stop him from punishing us. The man believes in team punishments, so we'll all pay the price.

"Y'all wanna win a national title and you're wasting my time with this kind of romper-room bullshit?" he bellows. "You have ten minutes to take care of business and get your asses on the field. And when I find out who did this..."

The rest of the threat is lost in the pandemonium of the locker room as he stomps back to his office.

"Who do you think did it?" I ask Reid, using a towel to brush off my junk.

"No clue," he says warily, "but I hope it's not one of our guys."

9

——————

SUTTON

I SCARF down the last of my banana and drop the peel in a trashcan outside Coach Miller's office. Her door is closed, so I sit down in one of the uncomfortable metal chairs that line the cinderblock wall, and make myself at home.

She emailed me this morning to request a meeting, and while she didn't say what she wanted to discuss, there's a small part of me that hopes it's the role of team captain. To build bench strength, Coach Miller typically selects one senior and one junior.

With any luck, that junior will be me.

Nervous energy courses through my body and I drum my fingers on my knees to dispel it. I've been like this all day. Twitchy. Excited. *Hopeful.*

Being named team captain is a big deal. An accomplishment even my parents can't minimize. It may not be Olympic gold, but it's something.

Don't get ahead of yourself.

Right. For all I know, Coach wants to talk choreography.

Sighing, I tip my head back, letting it rest against the wall as I scour my brain for a distraction. I mentally review my homework assignments for the day. It's Monday afternoon, and though it's only the first day of classes, I've already got a crap ton of homework. Mostly reading assignments, but they're also the most time consuming.

If only textbooks came in audio.

Then they'd cost twice as much.

Still, I make a mental note to check into it. The last thing I want to do is replace my pleasure reading with schoolwork, but it's already shaping up to be a challenging semester and I can't afford to fall behind. Coach requires a 3.2 GPA or better from all of her athletes.

If I'm even at risk of getting a C, she'll bench my ass in a heartbeat.

And she definitely won't make me a captain.

My phone buzzes with an incoming message and I pull it out of my back pocket and unlock the screen.

*Maddie: Let me know what Coach says as soon as you talk to her! *fingers crossed emoji**

I hastily type a reply and then delete it, unsure what to say. Maddie's the only one who knows I'm meeting with Coach, and I want to keep it that way, so I type a new message, downplaying my nerves.

Me: Will do, but don't get too excited. It might be nothing.

Her reply is swift and full of confidence.

Maddie: It's definitely something. I've got a feeling.

Oh, boy. Maddie's "feelings" are notoriously unpredictable. Which means I could be the new team captain or I could get saddled with a freshman mentee.

Or worse, embarrassing choreography.

The office door opens and Coach Miller peers out at me. Her auburn hair is pulled back in a ponytail, her angular features on full display. "Come on in, Sutton."

She's got her meet face on, but I'm not sure if that's a good thing because the woman is impossible to read.

I lock my phone and slip it into my pocket as I follow her into the office, nerves taut.

Coach gestures for me to take a seat opposite her desk and when she steps aside, I realize we're not alone. One chair is already occupied.

My stomach drops.

Mierda. No good ever came from a surprise meeting.

The word you're looking for is ambush.

I silence the snarky voice in my head. This isn't the time to get tangled up in my thoughts.

I exhale and take the seat beside Coach's guest. He's mid-forties with short salt-and-pepper hair, and, like Coach Miller, he's wearing a Wildcat polo.

Maybe he's a new trainer or something?

"Miss Cruz, I'd like you to meet Vincent Sharpe, the Spirit Squad Head Coach."

"Spirit Squad?" I echo, losing the thread of the conversation before it even gets started.

Coach Sharpe smiles. "Cheerleading."

What the hell does that have to do with me? I've seen those women tumble. They don't need my help.

Coach Miller takes a seat behind her desk and when she meets my questioning stare, her face remains unreadable. "I assume you know why I've called this meeting?"

"No, ma'am." The only thing I know is that she didn't bring me here to discuss the team captaincy.

She sighs and leans back in her chair, disappointment radiating from her pores. "It's my understanding, Miss Cruz, that last week when Coach Collins graciously allowed us to use the football facilities, you returned the favor by putting itching powder in his players' jock straps."

Coño.

How does she know about that? I didn't tell anyone. Not even Maddie.

Heat floods my cheeks and I know I must look guilty as sin.

If the leotard fits...

Okay, fine, but I didn't expect to get caught.

Which, apparently, was my first mistake.

"Don't bother denying it," she continues. "Coach Collins brought me video footage so I could identify the culprit sneaking into the football team locker room. Your face is clear as day on the film."

Me cago en ná. I should've known the football building would have cameras everywhere. Their program has more funding than they know what to do with, while the gymnastics program is limping along.

Hell, we're lucky to have cameras on the exterior of our building.

So not the point.

And the point is?

I need to find a way out of this mess—*fast.*

"I'm sorry, Coach. It was a silly prank and I shouldn't have done it."

"You're right. You shouldn't have done it. What were you thinking?"

That Parker and the rest of the football goons deserved to be knocked down a few pegs.

But I know better than to say *that* aloud.

"I—" I swallow. "I wasn't thinking clearly."

If I had been, I'd have been looking for cameras. Or, you know, worn a hoodie.

"Do you have any idea how serious this is?" She leans forward, folding her hands on the desk. "A stunt like this doesn't just reflect poorly on you, Miss Cruz. It reflects poorly on my program."

Guilt floods my chest, and my shoulders curl in because she's right. I didn't stop to think about how my actions would affect the team or the coaching staff. I didn't stop to think beyond *my* anger, *my* pain.

Stupid. Stupid. Stupid.

Certainly not the behavior of a team captain.

"You're supposed to be a leader on this team." Coach sighs. "I expected more from you."

And there it is, the gut punch.

"You're lucky none of those young men had an allergic reaction." She frowns, worry lines forming in her brow. "A stunt like this could get you expelled."

Expelled?

My chest tightens, and for an instant, it's impossible to breathe past the fear clogging my throat.

If I'm expelled, I'll lose my scholarship.

No gymnastics.

No school.

No degree.

Just loads of disappointment from my parents.

Sweat dampens my palms. "Coach, I—"

She holds up a hand and I fall silent.

"Coach Collins has agreed to bypass a messy, embarrassing disciplinary hearing *if* you agree to school sanctioned community service."

I straighten, pulse thrumming. "What kind of community service?"

She arches a brow. "Does it matter?"

No, no it does not.

"That's where I come in," Coach Sharpe says smoothly.

"My mascot got a last-minute travel abroad opportunity and now I've got to find a new Wildcat before Saturday's game."

No. Freaking. Way.

"You can't be serious." I shake my head in disbelief. I'm literally the worst person for the job. "I hat— pranked the football team and now you want me to cheer them on as punishment? What kind of sense does that even make?"

The words slip out before I can stop them, earning me a severe look from Coach Miller.

"It'll give you a chance to show your school spirit," she says.

"Serving as the Waverly Wildcat is a big responsibility and a prestigious honor." Coach Sharpe levels me with a hard stare. "The Wildcat is the face of this university. When our mascots graduate, we typically hold tryouts to find a replacement. Candidates go through an extensive vetting process and have to write an essay, face a panel of judges, and demonstrate physical aptitude, including fifty one-armed pushups. However, since we're pressed for time, I'm willing to make an exception."

Lucky me.

"With your tumbling and dancing skills, you'll be a natural fit," Coach Miller adds, though it's unclear which one of us she's trying to convince. "Think of it as an opportunity to bond with your peers and gain additional perspective."

I slump in my chair as the reality of my situation hits me. "If I do this, I'll still be eligible for the gymnastics season?"

Coach Miller nods.

"My regular mascot will return to campus at the end of the semester and will resume all Wildcat duties, including, God willing, any bowl or championship games." Coach Sharpe smooths the front of his shirt. "It's my understanding that your season doesn't officially start until January."

"What about team practices? Conditioning?" I ask, trying to fit the pieces together in my head.

"I've agreed to a certain level of flexibility." Coach Miller flashes me a wry smile. "It won't be easy, but you're going to have to make it work. In addition to performing at all home games, the Wildcat travels with the football team, and also has an aggressive appearance schedule."

Because unlike most schools where multiple students fill the role of mascot, at Waverly there's only one.

And if I take this offer, it's going to be me.

Coach Sharpe tilts his head thoughtfully. "Think you can handle the pressure?"

The sport of gymnastics is all about pressure. Pressure to be the best. Pressure to hold up under intense scrutiny. Pressure to deliver a perfect freaking score. To be a sweet, docile, bow-wearing doll. So, yeah, I'm pretty sure I can handle tumbling on the dugout or the sideline or whatever they call it while Parker trots around in those tight little white pants playing keep away.

I square my shoulders and force myself to meet his stare. "It won't be a problem."

"So you'll do it?" he asks.

My gaze slides from Coach Sharpe to Coach Miller. "Do I have any other choice?"

"This is a gift, Miss Cruz." Coach Miller pauses, giving her words time to sink in. "I suggest you take it."

That's what I thought.

I nod slowly, hoping I don't come to regret my decision. "I'll do it."

"Good." Coach Sharpe rises. "I'm sure I don't need to remind you that the Wildcat's identity is a closely guarded secret. You are not to tell anyone you're filling in."

I nod again. This promise, at least, is easy to make. Because no, I definitely don't want anyone knowing it's me inside that fur suit.

Coach Sharpe scoops up the massive blue and white duffel bag at his feet and hands it to me. "The costume and scheduling binder are inside with everything you need to know, but if you have questions, contact me directly."

Scheduling binder?

What the hell have I gotten myself into?

He grins down at me, a wide smile transforming his face. "Don't you want to open it up and take a look?"

I drag the zipper back to reveal the grinning mascot's head, and I'm nearly bowled over by the smell of rank athletic socks.

Karma, you dirty bitch.

10

DJ

"IDAHO HAD a big season last year and they've got a lot of returning starters," Coach says, pacing back and forth across the front of the weight room where the entire team is gathered. "Expect a tough game tomorrow. We can't afford to underestimate them. Not if we want to bring home the W."

He continues to rail about the home opener, but my eyes are locked on the clock above his head. The minutes tick by on what feels like the longest team meeting ever. We always have a brief download after strength training, usually to discuss the afternoon practice schedule, but Coach has been going for a solid twenty minutes and he isn't showing any signs of stopping.

Welcome to DI football, where your days are scheduled to the minute.

I shift my weight from one foot to the other.

If this goes on much longer, I'm going to be late for class.

Hell, I still need to shower and dress.

Reid bumps my shoulder. "You good?"

"Yeah." *Aside from being anxious as fuck.* "I've got a nine o'clock."

He nods. "Same."

On my other side, Coop snorts. "Since when do you worry about being late for class, Parker?"

It's a fair question. I'm usually a pretty laid-back dude, but not today.

"Since now," I mutter, willing Coach to hurry the fuck up.

Maybe I can skip showering to save time. This morning's workout wasn't too brutal. I subtly sniff my right pit and... *Not an option.*

"Maybe I should raise my hand and ask a few questions?" Coop suggests, flashing his trademark grin. "I'm not sure I entirely understand the Idaho strategy. Might need Coach to elaborate."

"Don't you dare." I shoot him a dark look. "We'll never get out of here."

Not in time for class, anyway.

Coop's grin widens. "Sounds like a challenge. What do you think, Reid?"

"I think you should try acting your age instead of your shoe size."

I snort. "Good luck with that."

"Parker!" Coach barks my name, and I'm instantly at attention. His playing days might be long gone, but Coach is still intimidating as hell.

"Yes, sir."

He widens his stance. "Am I boring you?"

"No, sir." It's a damn lie and we both know it, which is probably why he presses the issue.

"Then why are you talking during my team meeting?" It's a rhetorical question and when I don't answer, he continues. "If you're so confident about the Idaho game, perhaps you'd like to come up here and address the team?"

Fuck no, I wouldn't.

"No, sir."

"Then keep your damn mouth shut when I'm talking," he finishes, pointing his clipboard at me.

I swear, if they made a Coach action figure, that clipboard would be his accessory. He waves it around week in and week out on the sideline. It's become a running joke on the team because it's featured in The Collegian as often as Coach is.

When he finally wraps up, I haul ass to the locker room and take the world's fastest shower, ignoring Coop's ribbing, because yes, of course I washed my balls.

It's 8:45 when I exit the football building and I don't have time to wait for a shuttle, so I hoof it across campus. If I hurry, I might still make it to class on time.

Keep telling yourself that, asshole.

Sweat dampens my brow as I jog up the stone steps to the College of Communications, textbooks jabbing me in the kidney every time my backpack shifts.

I quicken my pace as I enter the building, my sneakers silent on the tile floor. The clock in the entry reads 8:59 and the halls are nearly empty. Most people are still in bed sleeping off last night's hangover or have already slipped into their classrooms to grab seats in the back row.

Thanks to Coach, I'm late for my first Advanced Multicamera Production class.

That's one way to make a first impression.

Yeah, a bad one.

The classroom door is closed when I find it—never a good sign—and I pray Mac Jones isn't the kind of prof to give you the boot for showing up late. Normally I wouldn't sweat missing one class, but I only have Comm 383 once a week and if I miss this three-hour lecture, I'm screwed.

I suck in a breath, paste a smile on my face, and open the door.

The classroom is packed and all eyes turn my way as the door clicks shut behind me.

"Welcome to Comm 383, Mr. Parker." The greeting comes from the middle-aged white dude at the front of the room. He's got longish brown hair that falls almost to his shoulders and the top button on his dress shirt is open, giving him a chill vibe most profs can only hope to achieve. "Ready for Idaho?"

He's not going to give me shit for being late? Mac Jones' cool factor just doubled.

"Yes, sir. Coach Collins has been working us hard to prepare." I flash him an apologetic smile. "Sorry for being late. It won't happen again."

"Call me Mac." He turns to the class. "That goes for everyone."

He resumes his introduction as I scan the auditorium for an empty seat.

There's only one. In the third row. Next to Sutton.

No fucking way.

She's a communications major? Gotta be. No other reason to enroll in this class.

Fuck my life.

There are forty thousand students at Waverly, and I can't escape my salty neighbor.

Mac glances in my direction and it's enough to get my feet moving again. I make my way to the third row and slide into the empty desk next to the she-devil.

"Why am I not surprised?" she whispers, flipping her hair and filling the air between us with the scent of jasmine. "Of course you're on a first-name basis with the professor."

"I've never met the guy before today." I open my bag and pull out my laptop. "But I think it's safe to say he's a fan of Wildcat football. Unlike some people."

She's quiet for a long time, those dark, wide-set eyes fixed on me, and I take the opportunity to study her. Straight nose. High cheekbones. Stubborn chin. She's wearing a loose black-and-white checkered tank top that reveals just a hint of cleavage, red shorts, and chunky black boots. Despite the scowl on her face, she looks fine as hell.

When she finally speaks, I've almost forgotten what we were discussing.

"It's not the sport I have a problem with."

"Thanks for the reminder." It's one I could've done without.

Fact is, I still haven't figured out what it is I've done to piss this girl off and it's driving me nuts. When no one copped to the itching powder incident, I half wondered if it was her. The gymnastics team had access to the building and I sure as hell wouldn't put it past the she-devil.

But even worse?

The little demon slipped into my fantasies again this week with those goddamn Sailor Moon pajamas, nipples straining against the soft white cotton and her silky blue hair—

"Yeah, well, just because you two are besties, don't think it means I'm going to let you copy my notes."

So much for the fantasy.

Screw the fantasy. The reality is even better. Sutton's hot when she's dishing all that snark, which definitely has me questioning my sexual kinks.

Never thought I'd be into pain—or is it degradation?—but here we are.

"I can do my own damn work, thank you very much."

I bump her arm as I pull up a fresh document on my laptop and she huffs out a breath.

So I do it again, a big-ass smile on my face.

I can feel her side-eye, but pretend not to notice.

The seats are narrow as hell and I'm a big guy. We're bound to rub elbows every now and again.

Thank Christ the class only meets once a week.

Any more and there would probably be bloodshed.

Mac holds up a sheet of paper and hands it to a guy in the first row. "I'm passing around a seating chart. Please fill in your name when it comes to you. The seat you currently occupy is now your assigned seat for the duration of the semester." *Fuck me.* "As an adjunct professor, I'm only on campus once a week, and this makes it easier for me to get to know you by name. And because I'm only on campus once a week, my office hours are limited. I suggest you get to know your neighbors should you miss a lecture and need notes."

Yeah, right. It'll be a cold day in hell before I ask Sutton for a favor.

Mac walks us through the syllabus and I tune out, but when he mentions the internship at Sports Stream, I'm all ears.

"You'll notice this class is full." He gestures around the small auditorium. "I'm told there's also quite the waitlist."

No surprise there.

"That's because this class won't be offered in the spring." My pulse quickens at the revelation. "Which means Sports Stream's summer internship will be offered to someone in this class."

Hell yeah.

It's all I can do not to pump my fist in the air. By taking the spring semester off, Mac's effectively cut the number of potential interns in half.

"Keep that in mind with every assignment and test this semester because while the interview process will be heavily weighted, your performance in this class will also be a deciding factor."

No pressure.

Beside me, Sutton stiffens and I can practically feel the tension radiating off her body.

Fuck.

Of course she wants the internship. There probably isn't a person in this room who doesn't. After all, it's the whole point of taking Mac's class.

I shift in my seat, surveying the auditorium and doing the math.

Based on the headcount, I've got a one in fifty shot of landing the gig.

Not great odds, but I'll take them.

After all, I only had a one in thirty-six chance at playing D1 football and here I am, at the top of my game, maintaining a 3.3 GPA—despite my personal challenges.

I've got this. I'm not going to let anything stand in my way. Football might have been the key to higher education, but this internship is the key to my future.

11

SUTTON

I HAVE to land that internship. It's the only reason I registered for Advanced Multicamera Production. Hell, it's probably the only reason anyone here registered, because who wants to take a three-hour lecture on a Friday morning?

That would be no one.

Including *DJ-I-take-up-a-shit-ton-of-space-and-smell-like-freaking-sandalwood-Parker.*

He glances over at me, trying to play it cool, and fails.

Because, like everyone else in the room, he's calculating his odds of landing the internship at Sports Stream.

His gaze sweeps the room and I can practically hear the gears turning in his brain.

Just freaking great.

It's like the universe has completely turned against me. The last thing I need is another reason to despise DJ Parker, yet here we are.

Mierda. I could actually lose this internship to him.

Nope. No way. Not an option.

Winners win. They don't plan for failure, and damnit, I will not fall into the trap of thinking someone else is better suited for this opportunity than me. I've wanted to be a sports commentator for as long as I can remember. Well, that and an Olympic gymnast, but that ship sailed when my little sister's skills surpassed my own, and I'm solidly focused on Plan B now.

So, yeah. DJ Parker isn't getting that internship.

I'll do whatever it takes to win, even if it means sucking up to Mac and lugging wires and becoming a freaking logistics expert.

Advanced Multicamera Production is supposed to teach us everything there is to know about producing a live remote broadcast, which means there will also be on-air opportunities for those of us who plan to work in front of the camera—as opposed to behind it—upon graduation.

The world of gymnastics is small and closely knit, and though there aren't many opportunities for gymnastics commentators, I'm willing to pay my dues and put in the work to remain involved in the sport I love after graduation.

Coaching was never an option for me, a decision that was solidified after working my first summer camp. I love working with the kids and seeing the look of pride on their faces when they master a new skill, but it takes a special person to show up day after day with boundless enthusiasm and energy. That much peopling would suck the energy right out of my introverted soul.

Maddie, on the other hand, will be an incredible coach, and I have no doubt she'll put her business degree to good use when she opens a gym of her own one day.

Who knows? Maybe I'll be the one sitting in the booth giving commentary on her gymnasts' flawless performances.

A girl can dream, right?

Parker shifts and his knee brushes against mine, sending a jolt of electricity straight to my core.

I jerk back, but he makes no move to retract his giant tree trunk of a leg.

"Hey, no manspreading."

"I'm not manspreading." He straightens and moves his leg half an inch. "I'm six-three. In case you haven't noticed, there isn't a lot of leg room for a guy my size."

"That doesn't mean you get to creep into my space."

"It's not like you need it." He glances at my very short, very bare legs and interest flares in his eyes.

"Maybe I do." I shift, crossing my legs in his direction. To defend my space. Not because I want to touch him. Our knees brush, and this time I'm ready for the skin-to-skin contact, for the feel of his warm flesh pressed to mine and the crackle of awareness that passes between us. "Three hours is a long time to be crammed into one of these stupid chairs."

"Tell me about it." He lowers his lashes and I'm pretty sure he's checking out my legs again. "By all means, stretch out. I don't mind a little incidental contact."

I roll my eyes—*hard*. "I'm sure you don't."

"What's that supposed to mean?"

"Oh, come on. Don't sit there and pretend like you don't know your own reputation."

"I don't know what you're talking about," he mutters, brow furrowed. "Since you're such an expert on the topic, maybe you can enlighten me."

I tick the nicknames off on my fingers as I go. "Park-her. BJ Parker. Park-and-ride."

And those are just the ones I can remember. The guy's earned so many nicknames over the last two years, it's hard to keep track of them all.

He snort-laughs and covers his mouth with a fist. He's quiet for a long moment, eyes fixed on Mac, and when he's sure the prof isn't going to come down on him for disrupting the class, he whispers, "That sounds like some bullshit Coop made up. There's no way anyone actually calls me those names."

"Trust me, they do." I nudge his knee with mine, pushing it out of my space and back to his side. "It's disgusting."

"No kidding." His eyes go wide and he looks kind of shell-shocked, which is clearly an act. "It's like I'm just a piece of meat to the ladies. And you had the nerve to accuse *me* of objectifying *your* body?"

"Oh, no." No way does he get to turn this around like he's not the womanizing douchebag here. Especially since I have firsthand knowledge of said douchebaggery. "You were checking out my ass and we both know it."

He twists in his chair, full-on looking at me now. "I'm not sure I feel comfortable sitting so close to you in light of this new information. Maybe I should ask Mac to reassign our seats. I'm sure if I explain the situation, he'd be willing to make an exception to his seating policy."

The pendejo actually raises his hand and panic floods my chest.

Without thinking, I grab his arm and tug it back down. "Don't you dare."

A move like that would kill any shot I had at the Sports Stream internship.

I glance at Mac, but he doesn't seem to have noticed Parker's attempt to catch his attention.

"Damn, girl." He pretends to inspect his arm for damage. Which is ridiculous. I barely touched him. "Has anyone ever told you that you need to relax? Maybe try smiling once in a while?"

I smile. During competitions. When I'm hanging with my girls. And pretty much any time I'm not being forced to share space with obnoxious players who treat women like they're disposable and have the emotional maturity of a twelve-year-old.

"You have no idea what you're talk—"

"Something you'd like to share with the class, Miss...?" Mac asks loudly, pinning me with a questioning look.

Dios mío. Heat floods my cheeks as I force myself to answer. "Cruz. And, no, sir."

"Mac," he returns, correcting me in nearly the same manner he corrected Parker earlier.

The only difference? There's less warmth this time.

Just freaking great.

I shoot a glare at Parker, who smirks.

Because *of course* he does.

"If you're gunning for the internship, I think the idea is to make a *positive* first impression," he whispers, bumping my knee as Mac resumes his lecture about proper field conduct.

"Bite me." I smile, forcing the words through my teeth. "That internship is mine."

"Yeah? Mac will have to learn your name first."

Jackass.

I vow to ignore Parker and his stupid knee and turn my attention back to Mac, determined to redeem myself.

With any luck, he'll forget all about my little disruption by next week.

THREE HOURS LATER, my brain is mush and I'm emotionally drained as I flop down at a table in the HUB. The lunch rush is in full swing and Maddie, Brooke, and Soraya are already eating when I arrive. Maddie slides a grilled chicken salad my way and I flash her a grateful smile.

"You are a lifesaver." I remove the lid and grab a plastic

fork from the tray in the center of the table. "I'm tired, and famished, and I'd probably chew my own arm off if I had to stand in line."

"I hear that." Soraya plucks a baby carrot from the dish in front of her and holds it up for inspection. "I was up until two this morning finishing the reading for Psych Research Methods."

Brooke feigns a snore and Soraya abandons her inspection of the carrot, throwing it at her roommate. Brooke dodges and it flies over her shoulder, landing on the floor.

"Not all of us can major in Home Ec," Soraya says, smoothing a strand of dark hair that's escaped her ponytail.

Brooke grins, utterly shameless. "You mean Family and Consumer Sciences."

"Isn't that what I said?"

Maddie and I exchange a glance and devolve into giggles.

Like us, Brooke and Soraya are total opposites, but somehow it works. This is the thing I love about college gymnastics—the camaraderie. Being part of a real team. One where I'm competing with my teammates, not against them.

It's a completely different feel than elite gymnastics and, after years of standing in my sister's shadow and fighting for every tenth of a point just to be seen, it's allowed me to fall in love with the sport all over again.

Now when I'm fighting for tenths, it's for me—and my team.

"This week is kicking my ass too," I admit, stabbing a cherry tomato with my fork. "I've got an insane amount of reading to do this weekend."

Which I need to squeeze in around my Wildcat duties.

Maddie groans. "Me too, but I'm hoping to get most of it done tonight."

"I like the way you think." Brooke nods in approval. "Then

we can party our asses off tomorrow after the game and spend all day Sunday recovering." Her green eyes sparkle at the prospect. "Oh, better yet, we can get mani-pedis on Sunday."

"I'm down." Maddie turns to me, her sandwich all but forgotten. "Are you sure you don't want to go to the game with us tomorrow? I'll bet we can find someone willing to sell a ticket."

Yeah, right.

Tomorrow is the home opener and the Wildcats are playing Illinois. Or maybe it's Iowa? It doesn't matter. They could play a high school team and it would be standing room only.

"You know I don't do football games."

Not entirely a lie. I haven't been to a game since freshman year, and I sure as hell wouldn't be going tomorrow if it wasn't the only guaranteed way to avoid expulsion.

"You bleed blue and white, yet you refuse to support the biggest athletic program in the school," Soraya muses, studying me. "Make it make sense."

I can't. Not without revealing my humiliating half-night stand with Parker.

"What can I say?" I shrug. "Watching a bunch of dudes play grab-ass isn't my thing."

"Girl, it's everyone's thing." Brooke sighs and rests her chin in her hand. "Have you seen those pants? They leave nothing to the imagination."

I shove a bite of salad in my mouth. No way I'm stepping on that minefield.

"Don't be gross," Maddie chides. "You'd be pissed if some guy said that about our leotards."

Brooke huffs out a breath. "They do. All the time."

"Yeah, and you hate it."

"I believe that's called a double standard," Soraya deadpans.

"Whatever." Brooke grabs the bag of popcorn from her tray and tears it open. "I'm just saying, the view alone is worth the price of admission."

"Speak for yourself." Soraya pushes a piece of salmon around the edge of her plate. "I expect to be wowed with impressive displays of athletic prowess."

Athletic prowess?

I inhale and a piece of lettuce goes down the wrong way, leaving me gasping for breath.

Maddie pats my back and when I clear the lettuce blocking my windpipe, I grab for my water bottle, taking a long swig to avoid saying something I'll regret.

"What?" Soraya looks around the table. "I heard they have a decent shot at winning a national title this year."

A dull throb builds behind my eyelids and I try to remember exactly how many weeks there are in the football season. Judging by today's incessant chatter, it's all anyone's going to be talking about until it's over.

"Oh, hey, anyone want to go shopping this afternoon?" Brooke asks, abruptly changing the subject. "Before I hit the books, I need to find something cute to wear tomorrow night."

Soraya gives her the side-eye. "You have more clothes than a Kardashian. There must be something at home you can wear."

"You'd think that, but you'd be wrong." She plucks a piece of popcorn from her bag and tosses it in her mouth. "If I want to grow my online following, I need to keep it fresh. No one wants to see the same old, same old."

Maddie laughs. "You mean sponsors won't pay for the same old, same old."

Brooke is on a mission to land an NIL endorsement before

graduation, and while it's not my jam, I can hardly blame her. Gymnastics might not be top priority when the mega-donors open their checkbooks, but the top earning college athlete for Name Image Likeness sponsorship deals isn't a football player. It's a gymnast.

A smart, savvy woman who's leveraged her social platforms to amass over two million dollars in endorsement deals as a collegiate athlete.

If Brooke plays her cards right, she can earn enough to set herself up comfortably when she retires from the sport and starts her teaching career.

Soraya's phone vibrates and she checks her messages. "Count me out. I've got study group."

"I'll go with," Maddie offers. "I could use something fresh myself. What about you, Sutton?"

"Pass. Too much homework."

Plus, I should probably use the time to crack open the mascot binder and wash my smelly fur suit before tomorrow's game.

Go, Wildcats!

12

DJ

GAME DAYS in College Park are always a rollercoaster of emotions.

First is my personal favorite, waking up in a cold sweat like, *Holy shit, did I oversleep?*

Then, there's the overwhelming enthusiasm of the fans screaming our names and calling out cheers as we make our way to the football building, quickly followed by, *Fucking fuck. I'm in a hurry and don't have time for another pic because Coach will castrate me if I'm late on game day.*

Don't get me wrong. Wildcat Nation is incredible. The town, the fans, the alumni. Win or lose, they support the hell out of us. It's just that I'd like a little less support before I'm dressed and ready to take the field.

After? Bring it.

I duck my head and adjust my WU ball cap as Vaughn and I turn onto University Drive.

"You realize the hat doesn't actually make you invisible, right?" he asks, quickening his pace.

A bead of sweat slides down my temple and I swipe it away. "It's too damn hot for anything else."

"Preach, brother."

"Besides, not all of us can scare off our fans with just a look."

Not like Vaughn. The guy might be a teddy bear on the inside, but his size, combined with the tats and beard, gives off strong *fuck around and find out* vibes, which come in handy as we approach the football building.

College Park is always a madhouse on game day. Traffic is bumper to bumper and there are tailgates and block parties as far as the eye can see. It's pretty damn amazing, except for the fact that it's taken us twice as long as it should to reach our destination.

Fortunately, we know the drill, so we left early.

Coach expects us in the locker room two hours before kick-off and not a moment later.

Or else.

Vaughn clears a path to the door and I follow.

Some guys might feel emasculated trailing in their teammate's wake, but not me. Better Vaughn's shadow than another dozen fan pics. Today's a big day and I need to get dressed and get my head in the game.

We cross the lobby without drawing too much attention to ourselves and Vaughn peels off to hit the nutrition bar while I make a beeline straight for the locker room, head down, avoiding eye contact.

In addition to alumni and the usual media types crowding the halls, some of the guys have family in town. I pass one of our freshman receivers giving a tour and tug my hat lower.

It's rare my parents can make it to a game, but I knew the distance would be an issue when I accepted Coach's offer to play ball at Waverly. It's a ten-hour drive from South Carolina to College Park and dropping mad cash on airline tickets isn't in the budget.

It's all good though.

They call me before every game and I know they're gathered around the tv back home watching with friends and family. Plus, if my mom were to manage regular visits, it would just mean more frequent inquisitions regarding my grades and love life.

Hard pass.

I swing a right at the end of the hall and as I turn the corner, I collide with someone moving in the opposite direction. The air punches out of my lungs and I take a step back.

The other guy—or should I say girl—got the worst of it.

I glance down and my gaze locks on a familiar pair of coffee-colored eyes.

Oh, shit.

Sutton's flat on her ass, a blue and white duffle bag half her size, sitting next to her on the floor. She glares up at me for all she's worth, but makes no move to stand.

"Sorry." I flash her an apologetic smile and extend my hand. "I was in my head and I didn't see you."

"Yeah." She bats my hand aside. "That seems like a recurring theme. Maybe you should get your eyes checked."

"I'm a D1 football player. My eyes are fine. Better than, actually."

I've got 20/15 vision, but she doesn't need to know that.

"I find that hard to believe." She clutches the giant duffle bag to her chest and climbs to her feet. "You know, since you're constantly running into me."

"Or maybe you're always running into me." I step forward so only the bag separates us. She smells like jasmine again today, and the scent reminds me of home. Warmth floods my body, pooling in my chest and slowly trickling down to my abdomen. "In fact, now that I think about it, it's almost like you're following me. Consider me flattered. I've never had a stalker before."

Her breath hitches—the sound music to my ears—and my cock stirs, desire tightening my balls.

Then, like she knows what I'm thinking, her lip curls. "You. Wish."

Yeah, I kind of do.

Sutton and I might not be able to hold a civil conversation, but who needs words when you've got explosive chemistry?

I'm not sure what it says about me that I find this woman absolutely irresistible when she's pissed.

Probably that you need to get laid.

Maybe. I haven't been with a woman since returning to campus, but it's hardly the longest I've gone without sex.

She stares up at me, a silent challenge glinting in her eyes, and fuck me, I have to meet it. After all, I'm not about to leave a gorgeous woman wanting.

"I'm going to let you in on a little secret, Sutton." I lean in close, savoring the sweet scent of her perfume, and pitch my voice low. "When it comes to women, I prefer to be the one doing the chasing."

Her mouth drops open, and she quickly snaps it shut.

Another beat passes as she looks up at me from under her lashes, the tension between us edging toward combustion. Then my fingers are tangled in her hair, sweeping a blue tendril away from her face. I tuck it behind her ear and my palm grazes her cheek. Her skin is smooth.

Silky.

So fucking soft.

"Don't touch me." The order is little more than a whisper, but I withdraw my hand.

"Just trying to help." I roll my shoulders, letting the

rejection slide off my back. "It looked like you could use a hand."

She sniffs. "I don't need your help."

"You sure?" I glance at the massive duffel, which is still clutched to her chest like the Holy Grail. "That thing is almost as big as you are."

Which isn't suspicious at all.

Yeah, right. I've spent enough time around pranking assholes to know when something is off, and right now, my Spidey sense is in overdrive. Sutton has no business being in the football building, not even on game day.

Hell, especially on game day.

I jerk my chin toward the bag. "What's in there, anyway?"

"None of your business."

The fuck it's not.

"I beg to differ. You see, we had a little issue a few weeks ago. Someone put itching powder in the teams' jock straps. Nasty business. Caused quite the scene. Coach was pissed."

"So?"

"So you wouldn't happen to know anything about that, would you?"

"Of course not." A muscle in her neck flutters and she shifts her weight, as if preparing to make a run for it. "What makes you think I had anything to do with it?"

Only every interaction we've ever had.

"For starters, I can't think of anyone who hates football players as much as you do."

"If that's true, you should probably widen your circle," she snarks, lifting her chin as a pair of athletic trainers walk by, talking in hushed tones.

When they're out of earshot, I press her. "C'mon, Sutton. What are you up to?"

"Nothing."

She tries to sidestep me, but I block her path. "Then let me see what's in the bag."

"No." She twists, moving the bag out of my reach like she thinks I'm going to snatch it from her arms. Which I would never do. *Obviously.* "Keep your eyes and your hands off my bag."

"Relax. I don't bite." A slow smile spreads across my face. "Unless, of course, you're into that kind of thing."

She huffs out a breath. "Yeah, well, maybe I bite. Did you ever think about that?"

"As a matter of fact—"

"Eww." She scrunches up her nose and it's fucking adorable. "Don't you need to suit up or something? Surely you have better things to do than annoy me?"

She's right. I need to get dressed. Taped. Game ready.

Kickoff is in two hours. I don't have the time or luxury of following my cock every which way it twitches. Not today, anyway.

I step aside to let her pass. "For the record, I'm definitely into that kind of thing."

"You're a pig."

"Oink, oink baby."

Without another word, she stalks down the hall. I turn to watch her go, admiring the way her ass moves with each annoyed step. When she reaches the end of the corridor, she throws up a hand and extends her middle finger.

An unexpected laugh erupts up from my mouth and I shake my head.

I don't know what it is about Sutton, but the more she resists my charm, the more I want her.

13

SUTTON

HOW IS THIS MY LIFE?

I stare at my reflection in the mirror, turning to study my pointy ears and furry brown tail. Yes, my tail. Because I have one of those now. As predicted, the costume is too big and smells like it's never been washed, despite the fact that I ran it through the sanitary cycle last night.

Fat lot of good that did.

Ten-to-one, every Wildcat ever has been a dude who didn't have a great handle on his laundry. The thought of sweaty mascots donning the suit year after year triggers my gag reflex, and a shudder racks my body.

Dios mío. I can't breathe. It's too hot.

Fresh air. I need fresh air.

My fingers itch to remove the head, but I force myself to remain still, paws at my sides.

I drag in a shallow breath, hold, and release it slowly.

Waiting until the last minute to try on the costume probably wasn't the brightest idea.

Too late to do anything about it now.

It's going to be a long day. My schedule is packed with

appearances and it's supposed to be another scorcher. Before this day is over, I'm all but guaranteed to join the list of sweat soaked bodies who've contributed to the funky aroma of the fur suit.

Lucky me.

I do a few stretches and practice moving around. The suit is enormous, but the paws keep the sleeves from sliding down too far and while the tail is a pain in the ass, practically dusting the ground behind me, there's not much I can do about it.

You could tie it in a bow.

Yeah, then Coach Sharpe would keel over and I'd be in even more trouble.

At least he doesn't have to worry about me leaking the secret of his little mascot swap to the media. My teammates would never let me live it down if they knew I was filling in. My disdain for the football team is well known and well documented.

A check of the overhead clock tells me I'm out of time.

The football team should be lining up right about now to board the busses that will drive them over to the stadium. Apparently there's a pre-game pep rally to celebrate the home opener, and, according to the binder, I'm supposed to ride with the team and hype them up—whatever that means—as they get off the busses to greet their adoring fans.

With a sigh, I give myself one last look in the mirror and head for the door.

As expected, the football team is fully dressed and has already started filling the busses when I arrive. I move toward the bus in the back and one of the coaches blocks my path.

"You know the drill." He gestures toward the first bus. "Mascot rides up front since you're the first one off."

I nod and change course, silently cursing myself.

It's an obvious mistake, but hardly earth-shattering.

I board the first bus and am greeted by Coach Collins' stern face. He gestures to the empty seat across the aisle and I slide into it, noting the team's quarterback, Austin Reid, is seated behind him.

Thankfully, I don't have a seat buddy either.

The ride to the stadium is short and noisy, but no one talks to me, which is just as well.

Mascots are silent and I need to get into character.

My stomach drops as we pull up to the stadium. There's a sea of blue and white surrounding the players' entrance and from what I can see, the cheer squad is hard at work entertaining the fans.

At the sight of the bus, they scramble to form a human chain on either side of the players' entrance, leaving a wide path for the team.

Our bus pulls to a stop, and the driver opens the front door. I'm immediately hit with a blast of hot air and the raucous cheers of Wildcat Nation. For a moment, I just sit there, processing.

If gymnastics had this kind of support, we'd have a much nicer facility.

And security. The kind that appears to be quietly holding the line behind the smiling cheerleaders.

"Well?" Coach barks, gesturing to the door with his clipboard. "What are you waiting for? We've got a game to win."

Mierda.

I'm supposed to lead the team off the bus. Through that unruly crowd. To the stadium.

I leap to my feet and scurry down the stairs.

The moment the crowd catches sight of me, another boisterous cheer goes up and the cheerleaders shake their pom-poms like their lives depend on it. Excitement crackles in the air, moving around me, but not through me.

I hop down from the bus and, uncertain what's expected, wave to the crowd.

Should've read the handbook in your free time. Or watched a few old games.

Yeah, because I have so much free time.

The cheerleaders each extend one hand into the empty aisle, and when I stare blankly at them, a little girl in a blue and white Waverly jersey at the front of the crowd yells, "You're supposed to give them five."

Of course, I am.

I give her a thumbs up and jog down the left side, slapping palms. At the end of the line, I turn and make my way up the other side, giving out more high-fives as the squad returns to shaking their pom-poms and takes up the Waverly chant.

When I make it back to the bus and none of the players or coaches have descended, I scan the audience, searching for another cue. They're clapping in rhythm with the cheerleaders, so I do the same, positioning myself near the door to the bus. The noise reaches a fever pitch and Coach Collins finally descends, followed by Reid.

I throw up my paw and give them both a quick fist bump as they smile and wave to the screaming fans. This continues as other members of the team hop down from the bus, helmets tucked under their arms. When Parker appears, I make a point of turning my back and waving to the crowd.

Yes, it's petty as hell, but I might as well get some pleasure out of this farce.

For the next twenty minutes, I wave and take pictures with the crowd and by the time the cheerleading squad finally enters the stadium, I'm sweating bullets. I've never slapped so many palms or snapped so many pics in my life.

Perspiration dampens my hair and my tank top is stuck to my lower back, confirming that no, I definitely did not drink enough water to prepare for today's game.

Lesson learned.

As we make our way to the field, I relieve the cheer squad of one of their water bottles, duck into a blessedly cool storage room, and guzzle the contents.

When I catch up, the cheerleaders are warming up on the sidelines as the team does the same on the field. The stadium is packed, and according to the announcer, there are one hundred and three thousand fans in attendance today. Which is wild. Gymnastics is a far more challenging sport and we don't have a fraction of the fans these guys do.

The cheerleaders begin stunting and one of them motions for me to join in, so I throw a few simple tricks for the crowd. Nothing fancy, just a few roundoffs and a couple of back handsprings, which are definitely harder to pull off while wearing a mascot head.

By the time kickoff rolls around, I'm hitting my stride.

I do my part to cheer the team on as they run out of the tunnel and when the Wildcats score their first touchdown, I join the deafening applause as a half dozen male cheerleaders hustle me to the end of the field.

The guys form a line and watch as the kicker puts the ball through the upright. The crowd goes wild once again and the cheerleaders circle around a white, rectangular board lying on the ground.

What the hell?

The cheerleaders stare at me, waiting for...something. I shrug, unsure what I'm supposed to do. The moment stretches out interminably and I can practically feel the eyes of the fans —all one hundred and three thousand of them—boring into the back of my skull, waiting for me to do whatever it is I'm supposed to do in this moment.

A bead of sweat drips into my eye, but the sting is nothing compared to the heat scorching my flesh as embarrassment takes hold.

At least no one can see your face.

"For your pushups," one of the cheerleaders finally shouts, his deep baritone barely audible over the crowd noise.

Pushups?

"One for every point," he adds, using a tone that suggests I better not screw this up.

Ay, cabrón.

A memory from freshman year resurfaces as the band begins to play an upbeat, celebratory tune and I step onto the board. The guys lift it into the air and once it's raised, I wave my paw, extending my pointer finger to signify the number one. The crowd goes nuts and I drop into pushup position, supporting myself with only one arm as I fold the other behind my back. I bang out seven one-armed push-ups to match the number on the scoreboard—because that's the tradition—and the cheerleaders lower my platform to the ground.

The game continues on like this, with me muddling through my duties and feeling like a complete fool. When the student section chants "We want the Wildcat," I'm forced to turn to the same guy who tipped me off about the pushups and cock my head in silent question.

His smile falters, but eventually he takes pity on me and shouts, "They want you to crowd-surf."

Oh, for fuck's sake.

This has to be a joke.

Coach Sharpe can't really expect me to put myself in the hands of thousands of strangers. What if they drop me?

One glance in his direction dispels any doubts I have.

He cuts his eyes at the student section and points subtly.

Fifteen years of gymnastics training and I'm reduced to crowd-surfing in a fur suit.

Fan-freaking-tastic.

Resigned to my fate, I climb the steps to the student section and throw myself at their mercy. A couple of guys in the first row with too much body paint and not enough brain cells hoist me into the air and I stare up at the sky as my peers pass me to the top of the stadium and back down again. It's not as bad as I'd expected, but it's definitely a bizarre experience. Especially since I have to hang onto my tail so it doesn't get caught on anything.

When halftime rolls around, the Wildcats are trailing by three and I'm dying of thirst. I follow the cheerleaders off the field, fantasizing about a bottle of water.

Coach Sharpe falls in step with me as we enter the tunnel.

"What the hell was that?" he demands.

I turn to him, at a loss for words. I waved, clapped, and did the pushups. What else does the guy want from me?

"That was the saddest damn mascot performance I've seen in thirty years of cheer." He shakes his head. "Have you ever even attended a Wildcat football game?"

I shake my head and the utter disbelief on his face is almost comical.

"You'd better get your act together before next week, or you can expect to face the disciplinary hearing."

"You can't do that," I say, no longer worried about staying in character. "We had a deal. I fill in for the Wildcat and nobody finds out about the locker room prank."

"Yes, and today's performance hardly meets the terms of our agreement." He stops walking and I do the same as he turns to face me. "So far, your performance is uninspired, sloppy, and shows a total lack of school spirit."

Ouch. Surely it wasn't that bad.

"I'm doing my best."

After all, I'm a gymnast, not a show cat.

He frowns, and I swear there's genuine disappointment in his eyes. "I sincerely hope that's not true, because if that was your best, it wasn't good enough. Wildcat Nation deserves better."

14

DJ

Damn. Coach wasn't playing. Idaho's improved significantly since we last faced them two years ago. They're making us work today and the heat sure as hell isn't helping. Sweat drips from my hair and slides down my temple, but I don't bother wiping it away. There's more where that came from.

We started the second half trailing by three, and though Carter tied up the score with a field goal, it's anyone's game. Our offense is killing it, but the defense has been spotty.

Fucking Langley.

If he spent more time training and less time being an asshole, maybe we wouldn't be in this position, but football is a team sport, so I keep my opinion to myself. Blaming the defense for giving up another TD every time we score won't solve anything and from the looks of it, the Defensive Coordinator is ready to give Langley and his boys a proper ass chewing when they come off the field.

Serves the prick right.

It's guys like him that give the sport, and its athletes, a bad name. He's a fucking misogynist. It was bad enough when he was giving the gymnasts—giving Sutton—shit, but he's been a real douche to our new kicker too, like it's some kind of flex to be a raging dick.

"Is it me, or does the Wildcat look like he's stoned?" Coop asks, yanking me back to the present. He jerks his chin toward the scoreboard where the Waverly mascot is on camera, looking confused as fuck.

Quite a feat, considering its face never actually changes.

"Beats me." I turn toward the cheerleaders and spot the Wildcat prowling up and down the sideline, tail blowing in the breeze. "He definitely looks smaller. Maybe they got someone new this year?"

Vaughn, who's on my other side, grunts. "No way. They do a big reveal when the mascot graduates. No reveal, no new mascot."

"Really?" Our D stuffs the Idaho quarterback—it's about fucking time—and I watch as the Wildcat lifts his arms, encouraging the crowd to get loud. "How do you know?"

Vaughn pulls a face. "The real question is, how do you not know? It's tradition."

"Probably because I'm not interested in filling my head with shit that doesn't affect me."

Vaughn ignores the dig. "Trust me. It's got to be the same dude as last year."

Swear to Christ, sometimes Vaughn just makes it too easy. "Pretty sexist of you to assume it's a dude. It could just as easily be a chick."

This time, it's Coop who answers. "How many chicks do you know that can do fifty one-armed pushups?" Vaughn opens his mouth to answer, but Coop cuts him off. "Besides your mama."

"You say that like it's a bad thing," Vaughn retorts, hooking his fingers in the front of his jersey. "She could kick your skinny ass."

I snort-laugh. "I'll take that bet. Our boy would tap out the moment he broke a nail."

"Fuck you. I don't give a shit about my nails." Coop smirks. "This face, on the other hand..."

"Yeah, yeah. You're the prettiest girl at the party," Reid says, slapping Coop on the back as he joins us. "But since that won't help us win the game, maybe you could focus on getting your ass into the end zone."

Coop shrugs. "I could, but then Langley would just give up another TD and we'd be right back where we started."

Leave it to Coop to say what we're all thinking.

Reid shoots him a look. "Then I guess it's a good thing this will be our last possession. We need to make it count."

"Hell yeah." I pull on my helmet, adrenaline pumping through my veins as the defense jogs off the field and special teams takes their place. "Let's bring it home, boys."

The tension on the sideline is palpable as Idaho's punter takes possession of the ball. Like everyone else, my eyes are glued to the field, but in my peripheral vision, I catch a glimpse of Coach. He's waving that damn clipboard, but it's too loud to hear what he's saying as he gestures to the field.

Idaho punts and it's a hell of a good kick, coming down inside the five-yard line. Our guy catches the ball and runs it back to the thirty-five, dodging and weaving, before he's tackled.

Sixty-five yards to victory.

The Wildcat roar fills the stadium and then Wildcat Nation is on their feet, screaming and stomping as the offensive line takes the field. My heart is pounding and my breaths come hard and fast as I take my place on the line of scrimmage.

There's nothing quite like the feeling of hearing one hundred and three thousand people cheering you to victory.

It's a fucking trip.

The play clock ticks down and silence falls over the stadium as Reid calls the play.

The ball is snapped and I explode, sprinting past the linebacker who's supposed to be covering me. I cut across the field, my cleats digging into the soft grass, and when I'm near the center, I turn, finding Reid.

He fires a bullet right to me and I snatch the ball out of the air without breaking stride. I throw up an arm to block against the incoming safety and manage to grab an extra yard before he takes me down on the forty-seven.

First down, baby.

My name echoes through the stadium as the announcer credits the play.

Smith and I knock fists as we return to the line of scrimmage, winded, and take our positions.

Reid calls the play, and I mentally shift into blocking mode.

One of the things I love about playing tight end is the versatility of the role. I get to block and receive, depending on the play. It's a hybrid position that requires strength, speed, and damn good footwork, all of which Coach has helped me improve over the last few years.

I draw a steadying breath and brace for the snap.

Across from me, the Idaho defender narrows his eyes. Like me, he's got sweat pouring down his cheeks and his uniform is covered in dirt and grass. He looks tired, but determined as he stares me down, and I know that if I miss this block, the play is fucked.

So don't miss the block.

Easier said than done.

The pressure to deliver is intense, and my chest tightens as I consider the ramifications of failure. This isn't a conference game, but it doesn't matter. We need the win, and I'm not about to let my boys down.

The instant the ball is snapped, I drop-step and crossover, cutting around the defensive end and sealing him inside as I plant my hands on his chest and drive him back, creating an outside lane for my running back.

Reid makes the handoff and Davis, a sophomore who's making his first start today, skirts around me and tears up the field like his ass is on fire. He picks up about five yards before he's tackled.

Not a first down, but a gain is a gain.

I wipe blood from my forearm as I line up for the next play. Not sure how it happened, but I cut myself blocking that Idaho fucker. It's part of the game—not personal—but that doesn't stop me from returning his glare as we face off again.

He grunts something that sounds like "Pussy," but I'm not about to let this asshole get in my head. Not when the game is on the line and we're so close to winning.

Reid calls the play, and the ball is snapped. I dart past the defender, leaving him in my dust, and cut toward the outside. I'm open and the safety, remembering the first play of the drive, moves in to provide coverage.

Joke's on him.

I'm just the backup plan.

Coop is wide open in the end zone.

Reid pulls back his arm and throws the ball downfield, hitting Coop right in the hands. It's a thing of fucking beauty —a perfect spiral—and I throw my arms wide and roar as the scoreboard lights up.

First win of the regular season.

One down, eleven to go.

The stadium erupts, nearly drowning out the band and the Wildcat roar, as one hundred and three thousand voices meld together in raucous celebration.

I'm flying high as my teammates and I gather on the field for our own little victory dance, all of us sweat-soaked and exhausted.

"Good game!" Reid yells, handing out fist bumps and high-fives like TicTacs.

"One and oh, baby!" Smith thrusts his helmet in the air. "This is just the beginning."

Fucking right it is.

We need to go undefeated to guarantee our chance at competing for the national title, because unlike in the NFL, the top four teams in college ball are determined by a selection committee. Then those top four teams compete in a semifinal bowl to determine which two will go on to compete for the national title.

It's totally fucked and it makes for a long, brutal season, especially when you compete in a conference like the Big Ten that's always underrated.

One game at a time.

It's the only way to tackle the season—pun intended.

You can't look too far down the road, otherwise you'll lose sight of what's right in front of you and get your ass kicked by the last team you expect.

You've got to prepare for each game like it's the championship game.

"Party at Sig Chi tonight!" Coop shouts, voice hoarse. "I better see every one of you fuckers there. We've got some celebrating to do!"

Damn right.

It's been a long ass week and I could use an opportunity to blow off steam, especially after this morning's run-in with

Sutton. It's like she's everywhere I go lately. I can't escape her, and I'm not entirely sure I want to, but since she's allergic to fun, I doubt she parties on Greek Row. Which is a good thing since I plan to cut loose and purge the she-devil from my system once and for all.

15

SUTTON

It's Saturday night and I'm sitting on my bed Googling ways to remove sweat stains and foul odors from clothing when Maddie bursts in, all but bouncing on the balls of her feet.

She beams at me, eyes alight, and clasps her hands together in front of her chest. "You'll never believe what just happened."

Whatever it is, it can't be more unbelievable than the fact that I spent the afternoon performing—poorly—for Wildcat Nation, got chewed out by the cheer coach, and then had to make four appearances on campus with my tail tucked between my legs. *Literally.*

"Try me."

She flops down on the edge of my bed, sporting a wildcat tattoo on one cheek and the letters WU on the other. *At least someone knows how to show school spirit.* "I got invited to a party on Greek Row. You have to come with."

So not happening.

I toss my phone on the bed and meet her hopeful stare. "Not interested."

The last time I partied on Greek Row, things didn't end so well. It's a mistake I have no interest in repeating.

Maddie's face falls and I quickly add, "But you should go and have fun."

Fun is the last thing I'd have at a frat party. And that would just spoil the night for Maddie. Really, I'm doing her a favor by staying home.

"Invite Brooke and Soraya. I'm sure they'd be down."

"Yeah," she says, nodding slowly. "But I want to hang out with you. Aside from training, we haven't hung out in ages."

She's right. Not since spring semester. Maddie invited me to visit over the summer, but I couldn't swing it with my work schedule.

There's nothing stopping you from hanging out tonight, except excuses.

Acho. Am I a shitty friend?

Guilt gnaws at my conscience, and as if reading my thoughts, Maddie sighs, looking and sounding utterly dejected.

She's playing me. I know it. But it has been a while since we partied and things are only going to get more hectic this semester with gymnastics, classes, and my Wildcat duties.

Duties I need to brush up on sooner rather than later.

I steal a glance at my open closet. The blue and white duffel bag sits on the floor, exactly where I left it. With Maddie out of the apartment, I could wash the costume and binge old games without worrying about getting caught.

Or you could get your ass out of bed and be a decent friend.

"Pleeease," Maddie begs, her high-pitched whining approaching a frequency only dogs can hear. "I need you."

It's just one party. And it would make Maddie happy. Plus, if our roles were reversed, she'd totally be my wing woman, no questions asked.

"Fine. I'm in."

Two hours later, we meet Brooke and Soraya on the sidewalk out front of Sig Chi. The frat house is a three-story brick mansion nestled smack in the middle of Greek Row. It has white trim, a sweeping porch, and a couple of pendejos sitting on the roof, their legs dangling over the edge as they sip from red plastic cups.

"That's an accident waiting to happen," Soraya says, staring with unabashed disapproval.

"Something tells me the Sig Chi founders would die of shame if they could see their legacy," I add, eyeing drunk partygoers who've spilled out onto the expansive lawn.

"Would you two relax already?" Brooke shoots us a look that says she's not here for any Debbie Downer bullshit.

She's dressed to impress in a slinky red top and a pair of sky-high heels that give her the kind of height most gymnasts can only dream of achieving.

How she manages to not break her neck in those shoes is a complete mystery.

"Okay, so how do I look?" Maddie asks for the eleventy-billionth time as she smooths her freshly straightened locks.

"Ah-maz-ing." Brooke gives her a full body scan, gaze catching on the little black dress that accentuates Maddie's curves. "God, I wish I had your boobs."

I laugh and shake my head, because *same*.

"Are we doing this or what?" Soraya asks, arching a brow. She's wearing a fitted, rust-colored dress that looks incredible against her rich brown skin and for half a second, I wonder if I could pull off that shade of orange. *Not likely*. "It's been a week and Mama needs a drink."

We all burst into giggles at the announcement, which is totally out of character. Soraya rarely touches alcohol, and when she does, she has a firm two-drink limit.

Some girls on the team have given her shit about it in the past, but I respect the hell out of her for standing her ground and not caving to pressure.

"Let's get you that drink." I hook my arm through Soraya's and steer her up the sidewalk, noticing for the first time that there are a handful of football players gathered on the porch. My belly clenches, nerves I didn't know I had standing at attention. I don't know the players' names—hell, I don't even recognize their faces—but they're wearing official jerseys and Wildcat Football apparel, marking them as members of the team.

Probably underclassmen hoping to get laid.

"Who did you say invited you to this party?" I ask, twisting around to look at Maddie.

"I didn't."

"Qué cajones." I shoot her a dark look. "It was the neighbors, wasn't it?"

I should've known. That I didn't even ask just goes to show how distracted this Wildcat thing has me.

Maddie grins, looking far too pleased with herself. "Come on. It'll be fun."

"We have vastly different definitions of that word." I huff out a breath. It's too late to argue, and I didn't put on makeup just to sit at home alone. Besides, why should I let Parker—or the fear of running into him—dictate how and where I spend my Saturday night? I have just as much right to party on Greek Row as anyone. "Fine. But I'm only staying for one drink."

Brooke laughs, the sound carrying on the balmy night air. "That's what they all say."

We climb the front steps of the house and get our red plastic cups from the baby-faced guy at the door. He gives us an appreciative once-over before zeroing in on Maddie.

"Save me a dance?" he asks, brushing a mop of black hair back from his forehead.

"I'm meeting someone," she says, craning her neck to peek inside the dark foyer.

The kid turns to Soraya, completely unfazed. "How about you? Wanna dance later?"

Soraya smiles and pats his cheek. "You're cute, but you don't have the right equipment."

"Huh?"

She ignores him and pushes Maddie through the door. Brooke follows, sweeping past him without a second look.

He turns to me. "I don't suppose you'd—"

Nope. Following Brooke's lead, I step inside before he can finish the question.

"What happened to being attracted to the person and not their sexual organs?" Brooke shouts to her roommate, words barely audible over the thumping bass.

The corner of Soraya's mouth twitches. "I was referring to his brain, not his penis, smutbutt."

A laugh bursts from my mouth, easing the tension that's settled between my shoulder blades. Greek Row is so not my scene. The floor vibrates beneath my feet as I trail Brooke down the dimly lit hall, squeezing between sticky bodies to avoid getting separated from my friends.

I step on some guy's foot and I'm halfway through a shouted apology when Brooke grabs my arm and drags me into the living room. It's crowded, but thankfully, there's room to breathe. There's a beer pong table set up in one corner and, in another, an enormous speaker. Most of the furniture has been pushed up against the wall to create a dancefloor and a couple is going at it on the couch, giving quite the show.

Cup in hand, Maddie heads straight for the punchbowl.

The rest of us follow.

"Is that a good idea?" I ask as a beefy guy in a Sig Chi polo sloshes red liquid into her cup. "You don't even know what that is."

"Or what's been added to it," Soraya says, eyeing the frat bro.

"It's all good." He flashes a boy next door grin that's probably charmed the panties off more than a few women. "It's my job to watch the punch bowl tonight. Anyone tries to slip anything in the mix, they answer to me."

"And that's supposed to make us feel better?" For all we know, he'll abandon his duties at the first opportunity to hook up.

"If I fuck this up, the best-case scenario is that I have to answer to the fraternity president. Worst? Let's just say I'd need to transfer out of criminology."

He glances at my cup and I grudgingly hand it over.

Once we've got our drinks, we carve out a little spot for ourselves on the makeshift dancefloor. We dance and talk and laugh and before I know it, the back of my neck is damp with sweat and my cup is empty.

"I can honestly say I didn't expect to have this much fun on Greek Row," Soraya says, extending an arm over her head as she moves her body to the beat of the music.

Brooke bumps her roommate's hip and winks. "I told you there were better ways to spend a Friday night than studying!"

We dance for another couple of songs and I'm debating the merits of a second drink when Maddie grabs my arm. "This party just went next level."

A loud cheer goes up from the other side of the room and someone starts a Wildcat chant, leaving no doubt as to the identity of the new arrivals.

"Is it me, or did Cooper DeLaurentis get even hotter over

the summer?" Brooke asks, watching the football players over the top of her cup.

They make their way across the room amid raucous cheers and high-fives, their gathered fans eager to get in on the post-game celebration.

And why not? The football team got it done today.

Unlike some people.

Coach Sharpe's disappointed face flashes before my eyes and shame heats my cheeks. I may not have a choice about filling in as the Wildcat, but I've never been mediocre in my life, and I'm not about to start now.

By next week, I'll be the best damn mascot Waverly's ever seen.

Or, if not the best, I'll at least be respectable. Good enough to keep my ass out of a disciplinary hearing, anyway.

Plus, it's an away game. Surely the expectations are lower?

"I'd trade my first-born to the devil himself for a piece of that man," Brooke announces. "Dating a guy like that would do unspeakable things to my follower count."

"Sorry, babe. The odds of locking that down are slim to not in this lifetime." Maddie gives a dramatic sigh as a half-dozen women descend on her crush. "But I doubt it'll keep them from trying."

Brooke tips her head back and drains her cup. "You know who doesn't get enough play? Parker."

Maddie and Soraya shift their attention to the hazel-eyed jackass and, okay, fine, I do too. How could I not when his dark hair is adorably tousled, and he's wearing a fitted black tee that hugs his broad chest like a second skin, showcasing perfectly sculpted pecs?

"Mmm," Brooke purrs. "That boy is fine. And I hear he knows how to take care of a woman, if you know what I mean."

It's on the tip of my tongue to correct her, because Parker most certainly does not know how to take care of a woman, but pointing that out would mean revealing I slept with him two years ago, so yeah, I keep that little gem to myself.

"I have to pee." The bathrooms in this house are probably beyond disgusting, but the punch went right through me and really, anything has to be better than standing here listening to my friends obsess about Parker's killer body.

"Want me to come with?" Maddie offers.

I shake my head. "I'll be fine."

As long as I don't run into Parker.

I press into the sea of writhing bodies, slowly making my way across the room. When I reach the hall, it's easy enough to find the bathroom because the line is twelve deep, other members of the small bladder club chatting and texting as they wait.

A girl at the front of the line smacks her palm against the door and yells, "Hurry the hell up already! I've been waiting ten minutes."

The pressure on my bladder increases at this revelation, and I squeeze my thighs together.

Just. Freaking. Great.

I'm going to pee myself before I ever reach the front of the line.

That's what you get for partying on Greek Row.

It's a mistake I haven't made since freshman year, one I swore I wouldn't repeat. But hey, I haven't hooked up with any douchey football players, so that's something, right?

16

DJ

"My man, looking good out there today!"

A Sig Chi rando holds out his fist and I knock it, pride filling my chest. Everyone's riding high from today's win, including me. Not in a million years did I ever think I'd be part of something as big or important as Wildcat Nation. Our fans bleed blue and white and being part of a team that brings so many people together and gives them such joy is a fucking honor.

One I don't take lightly.

Just the thought of letting the fans down—of letting my team down—dampens my mood as I move slowly through the crush of bodies packed wall-to-wall inside the frat house.

Today's game against Idaho should've been a gimme, but they made us work for every yard and stop, which means we'll be grinding at practice this week.

If you want to be the best, you've got to train like the best.

It's one of Coach's favorite sayings.

One he'll no doubt work into Monday's post-game recap.

But tonight is about celebration, which is why I'm going to get another beer and enjoy the hell out of myself.

The party is lit and sweaty bodies press in on me from all angles, so I almost don't notice when a tall brunette cozies up beside me, batting her lashes.

"Looking good, Parker."

"Thanks," I shout, raising my voice to be heard over the music. "Right back at you."

The response is more reflex than genuine compliment, but she doesn't seem to notice as she leans in, her breasts brushing my chest as she blocks the path to the kitchen.

"I hear Waverly could go undefeated this year."

I shrug and hook my thumbs in the pockets of my jeans. "Maybe. I'm just trying to take it one week at a time."

"Smart man." She smiles, lips parting like the Red Sea. "I'm Alyson, by the way."

"Nice to meet you, Alyson." She's a pretty girl and it's clear she works out to stay fit, but I'm not feeling it. There's no spark. No chemistry. *No snarky banter?* Whatever. "I was just heading to the kitchen to grab another lager, so—"

"What a coincidence," she says, cutting me off before I can give her the brushoff. "Me, too."

Yeah-fucking-right.

Guests drink from the punch bowl or the keg, and while I'm technically a guest, Coop's frat brothers are gracious enough to let us drink the good shit they keep in the fridge. It's a privilege I'm careful not to abuse, but when Alyson hooks her arm through mine, it's clear she's not going anywhere, so I lead the way, cutting a path through the crowd.

It's quieter in the kitchen, just a handful of people standing around talking. I detangle myself from Alyson and grab two bottles of lager from the fridge. She watches, dark eyes calculating, as I pop the tops off and hand her one.

I tip mine to my lips, and take a long pull, willing Alyson to lose interest and move on.

"You're a senior, right?" She sets her bottle on the counter and sashays toward me. "Do you plan to enter the draft in the spring?"

I snort and nearly choke on my beer.

Alyson clearly hasn't done her homework. If she had, she'd already know the answer, but the question tells me everything I need to know about her. She isn't looking to bag 'n' brag. She's looking for something more permanent.

You've gotta give the girl credit for cutting right to the chase.

There are plenty of guys who'd be cool with that kind of setup, but I'm not one of them.

And not just because I'm spread too thin for a relationship.

"Nah." I lean against the counter, crossing my ankles in front of me to stop her advance. "I'll be back at Waverly next year to finish my degree."

"I've heard some guys do that to improve their draft position." She pulls her lower lip between her teeth and looks up at me from under her lashes. "Though you hardly look like you need another year to bulk up."

"I appreciate the vote of confidence, but pro ball isn't in my future." Never has been. I'm a big dude, but professional tight ends are huge. I'd need to grow a few inches and add about thirty pounds of solid muscle to even have a shot. "Plenty of guys on the team looking to go pro, though."

"Yeah?" She quirks a brow like I might start namedropping.

I shrug and take another pull on my beer. As I lower the bottle, I catch a flash of blue hair in the hall.

No way.

It can't be. This isn't her scene.

Only one way to be sure.

"Excuse me." I straighten. "I need to go say hi to a friend."

It's a stretch. I doubt Sutton would ever use the words

Parker and *friend* in the same sentence, but what Alyson doesn't know won't hurt her.

The brunette juts out her bottom lip, but I don't stick around to hear if she protests. I push off the counter and stride across the kitchen, which has two entrances. One at the front that leads to the main hall and one at the back that opens to an old servant's passage.

A passage that leads to what is arguably the world's most disgusting bathroom.

It's so bad, anyone with a cock just pisses off the back porch.

As expected, there's a long line of women waiting to use the restroom and I'll be damned, Sutton is among them.

She's halfway down the line and her back is to me, but there's no mistaking that cobalt hair. It's loose tonight, spilling over her shoulders in soft waves. Waves I'd like to wrap around my fist as I fuck the snark right out of her.

My cock stirs at the fantasy and my gaze dips to take in the rest of her.

She's wearing a black midriff, which exposes the smooth bronze skin of her lower back, a short plaid skirt with stud and chain embellishments, and black combat boots.

It's the hottest fucking thing I've ever seen.

Desire grabs me by the balls and though there's a real possibility she'll kick my ass with those boots, I move toward her.

When I'm right behind her, I lean down and whisper in her ear. "Hey, Shorty."

She stiffens and crosses her arms. "Don't call me Shorty."

"Would you prefer Munchkin? Or Shortstack?" She turns to glare at me over her shoulder, her gorgeous pink lips pursed in annoyance. "How about Babydoll? That would really match your sparkling personality, don't you think?"

"If you call me Babydoll one more time, I'm going to make a very loud, very public announcement about your antibiotic-resistant strain of the clap."

She would too.

"Shorty it is."

Sutton groans and her eyes go round as I drape an arm over her shoulders. "You are the literal worst. Your mom must be so proud."

"She is." I smirk down at her, and when she doesn't shrug off my touch, I add, "Just last month, she said I was the light of her life."

My mom didn't actually use those words, but I'm sure she'd agree.

Sutton shifts her weight from one foot to the other and her shoulder muscles tighten.

"How long have you been standing in this line?"

"I don't know." She glances around, like she's searching for the answer. "Ten minutes?"

So, probably twenty.

"This isn't the only bathroom in the house," I whisper-shout, leaning in close to get a hit of that sweet jasmine scent that always seems to surround her. "There's another one upstairs."

"I'm not going upstairs with you."

"Relax, Shorty." I give an exaggerated eye roll and tilt my face toward hers. "If I wanted to hook up, I'd ask someone who doesn't hate my guts."

She laughs and it's a quiet, husky sound that speaks directly to my cock.

"For your information," she says, lifting her chin. "I'm not short. I'm five-four, which is average."

"For a gymnast?"

"For a woman," she retorts, emphasizing the last word.

Now it's my turn to laugh. "I'm six-three. You're short by comparison."

"Everyone is short by comparison because you're a giant man-child."

"I resent that."

She waves a hand dismissively, shrugging off my arm. "Resent away."

I'm out of snappy comebacks, so I return to the real issue at hand. "As much fun as this is, I have no desire to stand in the bathroom line all night. Are you sure you don't want to ditch this shitshow and go upstairs?"

She nods, but there's uncertainty in her dark eyes.

"Suit yourself." I shrug, pretending I couldn't care less. "But pissing yourself on Greek Row is a whole other walk of shame."

Her eyes dart to the front of the line, which hasn't budged an inch, and back to me. "Fine. But I'm only going upstairs to use the bathroom."

I'm not sure which one of us she's trying to convince, but I grab her hand and lead her down the hall to the back stairs. Sutton's hand is small and warm in mine, and despite the size difference, it works.

I climb the stairs slowly, stretching out this peaceful moment between us because I know the instant we reach the top, she's going to slam a wall down between us again.

Sutton drops my hand the moment her boots hit the landing—no surprise there—and she looks up at me expectantly.

I crook a finger and lead her to the door at the end of the hall.

Up here, the house music is reduced to a dull thumping and though it's dark, I have no trouble finding the key by touch. I slide my fingers along the top of the doorjamb until I hit pay dirt.

Noah, the Sig Chi president, always locks his door during parties, but Coop told me where to find the key ages ago—for emergencies.

I glance at Sutton as I slide the key in the lock.

She's all but hopping from one foot to the other, a look of sheer panic on her face.

If this doesn't count as an emergency, I don't know what does.

I unlock the door and push it wide, gesturing for her to enter. Sutton steps inside and freezes. It's pitch black, but it doesn't take her long to find the light switch. She flicks it and a soft white glow fills the room.

It's your basic frat bro starter pack.

Queen bed. Desk. Lots of Greek life paraphernalia and Waverly shit pinned to the walls.

To Noah's credit, it's spotless.

With a sigh of relief, Sutton disappears into the ensuite and closes the door behind her.

The water begins to run immediately and I try not to think about what she's doing in there. Which is completely ineffective because now all I can think about is that short little skirt she's wearing and what's under it.

My cock swells and I curse.

If Sutton returns to find me with a raging hard-on, the ick factor will be high.

It'll totally validate every shitty thing she's ever said about me.

I think about football, and church, and the wrinkly old dude who lives next door to my parents and probably has wrinkly old dude balls that haven't seen a pair of trimmers since before I was born.

My cock deflates in record time.

Mission accomplished.

The bathroom door opens and Sutton steps out, looking far more relaxed. "Thanks."

"It's all good." I flash her a wicked grin. "Despite what you think, I'm not a complete asshole."

She rolls her eyes, but says nothing as she crosses the room, her boots clunking on the hardwood floor.

Before I know what I'm doing, I lean a shoulder into the doorjamb, blocking her escape.

Sutton freezes, shock and annoyance transforming her pretty face.

"Don't you think it's time we put an end to this game, Shorty?"

She steps forward, meeting me toe-to-toe. "I don't know what you're talking about."

"Bullshit. You know exactly what I'm talking about." I lower my face to hers and *fuck me*. The desire to press her up against the wall and kiss her senseless is like a riptide pulling me out to sea. "You've got beef with me, and I want to know what I did to make you hate me so much."

17

SUTTON

UN-FUCKING-BELIEVABLE.

Parker really doesn't have a clue.

Heat floods my cheeks and I'm not sure if it's secondhand embarrassment or good old-fashioned irritation. Which is stupid. I knew he didn't have a clue, but this is just... I can't even with this guy.

He stares at me, eyes searching mine, and it's a painful reminder that what we shared was so unremarkable—that *I* was so goddamn unremarkable—he still can't remember me.

Or doesn't want to.

I shove the thought away. Nothing good will come from it.

My hands shake and it's another reminder that deep down, in the darkest part of my conscious mind, the part I avoid examining too closely, I still believed he might remember. That seeing me again—at the apartment, in class, on Greek Row—would spark some latent memory of the night we shared.

Wishful thinking, sis.

"Well?" he asks, voice gruff. His playful demeanor has vanished, and he appears as frustrated by this situation—by the fact that we can't seem to stay out of each other's way—as I am. A muscle feathers along his jaw, drawing attention to the angular lines of his face and the scruffy five o'clock shadow darkening his fair skin.

This would be so much easier if he were a troll.

As if sensing the shift in my attention, Parker reaches for me. He scrapes a calloused finger down the side of my face and desire crackles across my skin as he cups my chin.

Heat flares low in my belly, followed by deep-seated self-loathing.

How can his touch still ignite these feelings in me?

"Talk to me, Shorty." His thumb brushes across my cheek and a shiver races down my spine. "What's going on in that gorgeous head of yours?"

No sé.

What I do know is that staring into Parker's eyes won't help me figure it out. I square my shoulders and tip my head back, because no way am I going to let him get the best of me.

Not again.

Which means I need to put an end to this line of questioning. To squash whatever misguided curiosity has him intent on dredging up the past. On figuring me out.

"I don't hate you, Parker." I let a wide smile spread over my face and force a quiet laugh, although my heart is slamming against my ribcage and I think I'm going to throw up. "Hate implies I care about you, which I don't."

It's a shitty thing to say, but I can't go there with him. Can't make myself vulnerable by telling him the truth. Because if he blew me off again—or worse, laughed in my face—I'm not sure I could take it.

So there it is. Despite all the changes I've made—the dye job, the piercings, the clothes—despite how hard I've worked to project confidence, I'm still the same insecure girl I was two years ago, seeking external validation.

That's what happens when you grow up standing in someone else's shadow.

It fucking sucks.

I shove past Parker and clamber down the first staircase I see. I need to get out of this house. It was foolish to come here. To think, even for a second, that maybe he'd changed. That he wasn't an arrogant, self-absorbed prick.

Now who's the pendeja?

My footfalls are heavy on the stairs, but no one pays me a lick of attention. Not even the couple who press themselves against the wall as I fly past. When I reach the landing, I shove through the crowd to the living room, searching for Maddie and the others.

After the relative quiet of the second floor, the music is earsplitting, and maybe it's my imagination, but the dancefloor seems even more crowded than when I left, making it impossible to locate my friends.

Just another reason I shouldn't have gone upstairs with Parker.

One of many.

I know what he's about, but there was the briefest moment when we were bantering back and forth and he offered to find me another bathroom, that I thought maybe, just maybe, he wasn't the guy I remembered.

You thought wrong.

I find my friends dancing near the beer pong table, and when I see Maddie's brilliant smile, a pang of guilt pierces my chest.

The last thing I want to do is ruin her night, but I can't stay here.

"Hey. Can we get out of here?" I ask, raising my voice so she can hear me over the thumping bass.

Before Maddie can answer, Brooke claps a hand on my shoulder. "*Giiirl.* Were you just upstairs with DJ Parker?"

"No." The denial is swift and automatic.

Brooke's eyes narrow and her pupils expand. "You wouldn't lie to us, would you?" She turns to Maddie with an inquisitor's hard stare. "Is she lying? You're her roommate. You know her best."

Maddie shrugs and sips her punch, but when her eyes meet mine over the top of her cup, it's clear she knows I'm holding back.

Which only intensifies the guilt cocktail swirling in my belly.

"We saw you. Just now," Brooke says, pointing over my shoulder. "You came down the stairs and he was right behind you."

Was he?

Doesn't matter.

I take a page out of Maddie's book and shrug. "I didn't see him."

Truth. I was so focused on escape, it never occurred to me he might follow.

I prefer to be the one doing the chasing.

Parker's words come back to me and I can almost hear his sexy rasp as flames lick across my skin.

"Did you hook up with him?" Soraya asks. "No judgment if you did. His body is a work of art."

I arch a brow. "Now who's being gross and objectifying the opposite sex?"

A smile tugs at the corner of Soraya's mouth. "Must be the alcohol talking."

Maddie and Brooke burst into giggles. As much as I want to join them, I can't.

"Seriously, Mads. I'm ready to go."

"You can't leave yet." Brooke grabs my hand. "Not until you tell us if you hooked up with Parker. And, to be clear, if you did, I want all the juicy details so I can live vicariously through you, mkay?"

No, it's really not. But they're buzzed and they have no way of knowing their questions are salt on an open wound.

So tell them.

I can't. Not here. Not like this.

Soraya cocks her head thoughtfully. "Maybe she wants to keep him all to herself."

The very suggestion is laughable. Sure, I'm physically attracted to Parker, but I don't even like the guy. And I certainly don't want him all for myself.

Like that's even an option.

It doesn't matter. They're way off base.

"Or maybe," Brooke counters, "all the fighting and bickering they were doing in the weight room a few weeks ago was foreplay." She turns to me with a hopeful expression. "Please tell me it was foreplay."

"It's not like that," I snap, curling my fingers so my nails dig into the soft flesh of my palms. "Parker and I are not a thing, and we never will be. We hooked up freshman year and the sex—if you can even call it that—was lousy. The cherry on the shit-tastic sundae? The jackass called me Summer because he couldn't even remember my freaking name." A fresh wave of humiliation washes over me and tears sting my eyes. "The following week, he looked right through me like I wasn't even there. But please, continue speculating about his talent in the bedroom."

There's a collective gasp and then Maddie's wrapping her arms around me, giving me a tight squeeze. "I'm so sorry."

Now that the words are out, it's like a weight's been lifted from my chest. For the first time in a long time, I can breathe easily. I don't have to evade or hide or omit the truth.

"We all are," Soraya says, resting a hand on my shoulder.

"We didn't know," Brooke adds, looking contrite and suddenly very sober.

"You couldn't have." Maddie releases me and I straighten. "Because I didn't want you to. I didn't want anyone to know. It was too embarrassing."

And it hurt more than it should have, considering I was used to being overlooked and overshadowed. Used to coming second to my sister. At home, it was always about Gabby's schedule and Gabby's training and Gabby's stupid choreography.

Why had I expected things at Waverly to be any different?

I exhale, blinking back the tears. "At least now you know why I don't like football."

"You mean the stupidest, most overrated, over hyped sport at Waverly?" Soraya asks.

Brooke frowns, pensive. "The one with all those obnoxious, narcissistic jockholes?"

"That's the one," Maddie agrees, nodding emphatically.

A new kind of warmth fills my chest at the show of solidarity. Before I came to Waverly, I didn't have close friends. Not real ones, anyway. The knowledge just reinforces my decision to forgo elite gymnastics and compete at the collegiate level.

"Gracias." I look at my teammates, meeting each of their eyes. "I really couldn't ask for better friends."

"We know." Brooke dusts off her shoulder. "We're kickass like that."

I laugh and spread my arms for a group hug and when we finally pull apart, I'm determined to let them finish the night on a high note.

It's the least I can do after laying my troubles at their feet mid-party.

Timing never was your strong suit.

"Enough about Parker." I shake my head to clear my thoughts. *If only it were that easy.* "That pendejo isn't getting another second of my time or headspace."

The girls' eyes go wide as someone taps me on the shoulder, and when I turn to see who it is, my stomach goes into freefall.

Parker.

His full lips are pressed into a grim line, and his hands are stuffed into the pockets of his jeans, giving him a totally broody, totally hot vibe.

Mierda. How much did he hear?

Enough, judging by the look on his face.

My suspicions are confirmed when he grinds out, "We need to talk."

18

———

DJ

SHAME CLOGS my throat as I meet Sutton's flat stare.

It's no fucking wonder she hates me. What kind of douche calls a woman the wrong name in bed?

Only a total piece of shit.

Fucking fuck.

I deserve every bit of crap she's given me and then some. She shared her body with me and...I don't even remember it.

How is that possible?

She's not the kind of woman you can easily forget.

I mentally recount my hookups over the last couple of years. Despite the rumors, I've never been as popular with the ladies as my teammates. The fact is, I was a late bloomer. I'd been too damn shy to talk to women freshman year and then sophomore year, I'd gotten shitfaced and—

Oh, hell.

My pulse throbs at my temple, a physical reminder of my dumbfuckery.

Is it any wonder she hates you?

"We have nothing to talk about," Sutton says, ice coating

each syllable. I stand there, at a loss for words, as she turns back to her friends. "I'm going to head out. Have fun."

Maddie shoots me a scathing look and offers to walk with her, but Sutton waves her off, promising to text when she gets home. Then she turns on her heel and, without acknowledging me, disappears into the crowd.

Fucking fuck.

How am I supposed to fix this?

"You really screwed up." Maddie tosses her blonde hair as she looks down her nose at me. "Sutton is an incredible person. She didn't deserve to be hurt that way."

"I know." I shove my fingers into my hair and it's all I can do not to roar in frustration. "If I could take it all back, believe me, I would."

In a heartbeat.

If only that were an option.

The girl to Maddie's left raises her dark brows expectantly. "Well, what *are* you going to do about it?"

Fuck if I know. I've made my share of mistakes at Waverly, but this doesn't feel like one that can be fixed with "*I'm sorry.*"

"A simple apology isn't going to cut it," the redhead on Maddie's right says. "Not with the way you treated her."

No kidding. Sutton doesn't strike me as the forgiving type, and the woman can hold a grudge, but I can hardly fault her.

"I know." I duck my head, feeling about two feet tall, despite the fact that I tower over these girls. "I'm kind of figuring this out as I go. Until sixty seconds ago, I didn't even know what I'd done to piss her off."

Because you're a jackass.

Before today, I'd have taken offense at the moniker, but now...

"Fuck." The word explodes from my mouth, but the gymnasts take it in stride. One of the many benefits of partying on Greek Row: anything goes. "I'm sorry. I'm out of my depth here. I feel like complete shit and I know I have to make this right, but I don't even know where to start."

Maddie studies me, her expression thoughtful. "You could start by making sure she gets home safely."

Shit. She's right. There are emergency call stations all over campus, but it's late and Sutton shouldn't be walking home alone. There are all kinds of creeps out there. Drunk creeps. Pervy creeps. Creeps who might get it in their head to hassle a woman.

The lager I drank earlier sours in my stomach.

It's not something I've ever had to worry about because no one in their right mind is going to mess with me and it's not like I've ever had a girlfriend to look out for.

"You're right." I nod slowly. "It's the least I can do."

As I turn to go, one of the girls yells, "And for fuck's sake, don't forget to apologize!"

It's solid advice.

Especially with the way I'm feeling. My head is spinning and I don't know which way is up. For once, I can't blame it on alcohol.

I clear a path through the crowd easily, ignoring the shouts of well-wishers as I focus on my objective. The air is hot and humid when I step outside, but it's an improvement from the close quarters of the frat house and the hundreds of sweaty coeds that would surely have the Fire Marshall quoting occupancy limits.

A quick scan of the lawn confirms Sutton is long gone, so I jog to the sidewalk, gaze sweeping left and right.

My pulse quickens. She's nowhere to be seen.

How is that even possible?

It's only been a minute—two, max—since she walked out.

She can't have gotten far. I turn west and jog toward home.

There are only a few routes she's likely to take, and with any luck, I can catch up to her.

At the end of the road, I turn right and catch sight of her as she steps off the sidewalk and into the shadows.

The fuck?

I put on a burst of speed, ignoring the sweat that beads along my hairline.

When I finally catch up to her, she's cutting across a parking lot.

A dark, deserted parking lot.

At the sound of my footfalls, she turns, eyes wide, and raises what looks like a cannister of pepper spray.

"Glad to see you have some sense of self-preservation." I throw up my hands in self-defense. "But I'd prefer it if you didn't spray me with that shit."

"Don't tempt me." She lowers the tiny black bottle and sighs. "What are you doing, Parker?"

"Walking you home."

She arches a brow. "I don't need a babysitter. I can take care of myself."

Here we go again.

The woman has an independent streak a mile wide. Under normal circumstances, it would be a turn-on. In the middle of the night when she insists on taking shortcuts through deserted parking lots?

Not so much.

"Fair enough, but your friends would feel better if you weren't alone and we're going the same way, so..."

She rolls her eyes and, for the second time tonight, walks away from me, a dark shadow in the milky white glow of the moon.

I fall in step beside her, our footfalls quiet on the blacktop.

"Look, I get that you don't want to talk to me, and I respect that, so how about I talk and you listen?"

She says nothing, just wraps her arms around her midsection and keeps walking.

That has to be a good sign, right?

"I don't blame you for hating me," I confess, which seems apropos since the parking lot we're crossing is attached to a church. "I'd hate me too. Hell, I do kind of hate myself."

More than words can say, because I'm really not the kind of guy who hooks up with a woman and calls her the wrong name. Just the thought of hurting anyone like that—especially Sutton—is a kick in the balls.

"I don't know how to say this, so I'm just going to say it." I shove my hands in my pockets and draw a steadying breath. "I'm sorry. The night we hooked up, I was blackout drunk and I don't remember a thing." She turns to me, disbelief etched in the lines of her face. "I'm not making excuses. I wouldn't do that. The way I treated you was unacceptable. Full stop. I take complete responsibility for my actions, but I wanted you to know the truth." I pause, hating my next words. "To know why I didn't remember."

Hell, why I still don't remember. The entire night is a blank spot in my memory, but there was a condom in the trash when I woke up, and I know the embarrassing story she told at Sig Chi is the truth.

"You invited me to that party," she says through clenched teeth, her words vibrating with hurt and anger. "In American History."

I wrack my brain, searching for the memory. Then it hits me.

Christ. I'd thrown the offer out without much thought. I hadn't even known her name, but she'd let me borrow her notes and it seemed like the right thing to do. I never actually thought she'd show up.

That was your first mistake, dumbass.

"Until now, I didn't even know you showed that night. I certainly never connected the sweet, studious girl from American History with the blue-haired spitfire who handed me my ass on move in day."

Sure, the sweet, studious girl who tied her ink-black hair back with a blue and white Wildcat ribbon was pretty, but pretty girls are a dime a dozen on this campus. Make a sharp turn and you're bound to run into one.

Sutton makes a sound of disgust and sweeps her trademark hair over her shoulder. "After I realized just how invisible I'd become, I made a few changes."

Nausea swirls in my gut. I know what it's like to go unseen. To look in the mirror and feel utterly unremarkable.

And despite the casual way she threw out the information, sharing it cost her.

Vulnerability is never easy, but letting your guard down—even under the guise of sarcasm—with someone who hurt you? That takes guts.

I can't go back and change the past, but here, in this dark parking lot, I can meet her halfway.

A secret for a secret.

"At my high school, being a football player wasn't a big deal." If anything, it was an embarrassment. "Our program was...underdeveloped."

"Well, boo hoo for you," she snarks, and though I can't see her face, I can practically hear her eyes roll to the back of her head as she pivots, turning to walk along the exterior wall of the massive stone church.

"We lost more than we won and the only reason people came to our games was to see the award-winning band."

Hell, it's a miracle Coach gave me a chance, all things considered. But he said I filled a need, and he believed I had untapped potential.

"Okay, so the band geeks got all the ass." She shrugs. "I'm supposed to care about this why?"

"I didn't date. Didn't go to a single party. School and football were my life. When I got to Waverly freshman year, it was more of the same, but the transition was hard. The academics and the game were more rigorous than anything I'd experienced in the past." I probably would've flunked out my first semester if it weren't for the academic center and mandatory team study halls. "I was redshirting and didn't see much playing time, which also meant I didn't get a lot of attention from the women on campus."

"Dios mío." She stops and I turn to face her. "Are you seriously trying to make me feel bad for you right now? Because, spoiler alert, that's not going to happen."

I laugh, low and quiet, the sound devoid of mirth. "I'm not looking for your sympathy, Shorty, and if you let me finish, you'll understand why I'm telling you this story."

"Fine." She makes an *out with it* gesture. "Cuéntame."

"Sophomore year I saw more playing time and everything changed. I started partying with the team, and there were always women hanging around. Women who wanted to hook up with hard bodied athletes. At first, I blew them off, but when the older guys started giving me shit, asking if I was saving myself for marriage, the pressure got to me. I was struggling to find my footing and being the only known virgin on the team wasn't exactly helping. I decided to just hook up and enjoy a little no strings fun." I scrub a hand over my face, wishing I could give my younger self the kick in the ass I obviously needed. "Everyone was doing it and it didn't seem like a big deal."

Her nostrils flare and I press on.

"But when the time came to go through with it, I was nervous and I drank too much. I don't even remember my first time, but from what I hear, it was pretty lackluster." I force myself to meet her eyes because I want her to understand. To know how colossally I fucked up. To know she wasn't the problem. "What was the word you used?" I pause as understanding dawns in her eyes. "Oh, right. Lousy."

19

———

SUTTON

Ay, cabrón.

Parker was a virgin when we slept together? No way. The very idea is laughable. He's gorgeous. Confident. Charming—*when he's not being an ass.* Then again, it explains *so* much. Like the fact that he struggled with the condom and lasted all of three seconds before he shot off like a bottle rocket.

Dios mío. I took Parker's virginity. To a pornalicious Ginuwine song.

The realization steals my breath, and it's hard to meet his eyes.

Maybe it's for the best that he can't remember.

God knows my own first time was underwhelming.

I shed my virginity on prom night, determined to avoid arriving at Waverly completely inexperienced. My date was just as clueless and awkward as I was, but my training schedule left little time for dating in high school and I'd felt like I was behind the curve socially.

Plus, I was curious.

Two awkward hookups and zero orgasms later, my

curiosity is DOA. I bought myself a battery-operated boyfriend and haven't looked back since.

Parker clears his throat, probably waiting for a response, but what the hell am I supposed to say?

Mierda. If only I'd known...

Oh, who am I kidding? We were both drinking, and I'd been crushing on him for weeks. Bad decisions were made all around.

"Being wasted doesn't excuse my actions," Parker says, interrupting my shame spiral. "I know my apology won't erase the hurt I caused you."

"No, it won't." Even if I wish it would.

"Fuck." He rakes his fingers through his hair, making it stand up at odd angles. "I hate myself for doing that to you. For making you feel you did something wrong, or that you weren't enough when I was the problem. I was the one who fucked up. I was the one who wasn't enough," he admits, deflating before my eyes. "If I could take it all back, if I could spare you the hurt I caused, I'd do it in a heartbeat."

There's genuine regret in his voice and I can see the devastation in his eyes, at the way tonight's revelation has wrecked him.

It's been an eyeopener for both of us.

I hadn't realized how drunk Parker was that night, and I couldn't have known that, like me, he was battling inner demons.

His apology won't change the past, but it's a soothing balm to my bruised spirit.

My anger melts away as I search for something—anything—to dispel the awkward silence that's settled over us like a weighted blanket.

"You can relax, Parker. I have no plans to tell people you're a sloppy lay." My words lack their usual punch, feeling more like habit than hostility. "But that doesn't mean you're forgiven."

"Good, because I'm going to enjoy working for it." He takes a step forward, his large body invading my space, the intoxicating scent of sandalwood and citrus enveloping me in a warm embrace. "I've learned a thing or two since our last hookup, Shorty."

No kidding. His reputation is proof enough, but I'm not about to stroke his ego.

"That's what all the boys on campus say." I flash him a sultry smile. "Fact is, twenty-something guys are shit lovers. They're excitable, selfish, and think Netflix is foreplay."

"The key word there is *boys*." He smirks, a silent challenge burning in his eyes. "Is that why you got the vibrator?"

"As a matter of fact, yes." I can't believe we're having this conversation, but there's no way I'm going to back down. Not now. "Unlike some people, BOB has never failed to deliver the big O. Plus, he lets me pick the music and doesn't hog the covers."

A quiet chuckle spills from his lips, the sound scraping over my body like shards of glass and raising goosebumps on my flesh.

"I'll give you the last two, but if a silicone toy gives you the best orgasms of your life, you clearly haven't been with the right guy."

My breath hitches and I silently curse my traitorous body as I stammer, "I believe we've already established that fact."

Desire flares in his eyes and he takes another step toward me, swallowing up the space between us. And like a coward, I retreat, stopping only when my back is against the cool stone wall of the church.

"We also established that I've learned a thing or two since sophomore year."

"Keep telling yourself that, stud." I pat his cheek in a way that should be dismissive, but feels intimate as my fingers stroke the soft stubble on his face.

"I'm happy to prove it." He braces his hands on the stone wall behind me, one on each side of my head, caging me in. "Any time. Any place."

The words are half promise, half threat, and heat blooms low in my belly.

"Hell, I'll prove it right now," he growls, lowering his face to mine.

The offer sounds way hotter than it should, considering we're on holy ground, but there's no denying the growing arousal between my legs.

"What do you say, Shorty?" His breath is hot against my cheek, and as I stare up at him, the only thing I can think about is the press of his soft lips on mine. "Are you going to give me a chance to redeem myself?"

Maybe.

No.

"You had your chance, and you blew it." *Literally.* "I'm not going to have sex with you now just to prove a point."

He smirks. "Afraid you'd like it?"

Abso-freaking-lutely.

It's a reality I'd rather not examine too closely.

"I already told you, I'm not going to—"

The arrogant ass presses a finger to my lips, cutting me off mid-sentence. "Just one kiss."

He trails his middle finger down my cheek. For a big guy, his touch is surprisingly gentle.

Which is definitely *not* a thought I should be having.

I recoil and bite the finger pressed to my lips. To my surprise, Parker groans, long and deep.

It's not the reaction I was expecting, and it's so freaking hot the guttural sound short-circuits my brain. Which is the only reason I agree to his suggestion.

"Fine." The word is a breathy whisper, but I'm in too deep to care. "One kiss."

I hear the lie the instant the words leave my mouth. One kiss will never be enough. Not with Parker.

A slow, predatory smile transforms his handsome face and my pulse flutters at the sight.

This is a mistake.

I know it right down to the soles of my Docs, but it's one I'm going to make and damn the consequences.

Parker presses me up against the wall, his hard body flush with mine as he captures my wrists and pins them to the stone above my head. He shifts and then he's holding both my wrists with one hand as he skims the other down the underside of my arm, leaving a trail of fire in his wake.

"So fucking sexy," he murmurs, fingers skating over the swell of my breast and down to my bare hip. "This skirt has been driving me wild all night."

Before I can respond, he nudges my thighs apart and the soft denim encasing his powerful leg brushes against my sensitive flesh. Then he presses his thigh to my pussy, and I all but purr in satisfaction as every nerve in my body sizzles with anticipation.

It's been so long since anyone's touched me, I'd forgotten it could be like this.

Forgotten the way electricity could hum under your skin like a live wire waiting to be unleashed.

Or maybe it's just Parker's touch that has that effect.

"Bésame." It's a desperate plea, and I'll hate myself for it later, but in this moment that doesn't matter because I can't think past the desire to feel Parker's mouth on me.

He cups my cheek with his free hand and tilts my face to

his, and then he's crushing his lips to mine. The kiss is hungry and demanding and when his tongue skates along the seam of my mouth, seeking entry, I yield without hesitation. He deepens the kiss, his tongue mating with my own in a dance that has my hips rolling and my pussy rubbing against his muscular thigh in search of sweet salvation.

Parker groans into my mouth and the sound reverberates through every muscle and tendon in my body as I lose myself in his touch.

When he finally breaks off the kiss, I'm gasping for breath, but God bless his stamina because he keeps going, trailing open-mouthed kisses across my chin and down the column of my throat. I tip my head back and take what he's offering.

"You taste so damn good," he says, lifting my skirt and gripping my ass with those large, capable hands.

And even though I should tell him to stop, I don't.

Because he was right. I am enjoying this.

With his palms planted firmly on my ass, he pulls me closer, sealing our bodies together.

My eyes drift closed and I concentrate on the feel of Parker's long, hard cock resting snug against my belly. On the way my body tightens with need every time he touches me.

"Eyes on me, Shorty." Parker hooks his fingers in the waistband of my underwear and I have no choice but to comply with his command. "I want to taste you." His gaze dips low. "All of you."

My pulse spikes and a hot flush spreads across my cheeks.

I've never given oral sex much thought. I haven't needed to —until now.

Just because you haven't tried it, doesn't mean you won't enjoy it.

True, but it's just so...intimate.

As if sensing my hesitation, Parker's gaze snaps back to mine. "Have you ever had your pussy licked, Sutton?"

The sound of my name on his lips is nearly my undoing, but I harden my jaw and shake my head.

"Let me be the first," he rasps, lowering his forehead to mine. "I promise to make it so good you'll never look at BOB the same way again."

I nod—because I'm aroused and curious and dammit, I can hookup with whoever I want whenever I want.

Parker drops to his knees and when he looks up at me, there's something like reverence shining in his eyes. He pulls my panties down, his calloused fingers scraping over my outer thighs, and I suck in a breath.

I've never been shy or self-conscious about my body. I've competed before thousands of people in form-fitting leotards that leave little to the imagination, and still, my knees lock as he lifts my skirt, revealing my most intimate parts.

"Relax, Shorty." He slips a hand between my legs, gently nudging them apart. "I've got you."

My core throbs with anticipation as he gently massages my thighs, and when his knuckles graze my slick folds, he hisses. "Christ you're wet."

And because I'm awkward AF, I blurt out, "So far, you've got nothing on BOB."

Parker chuckles, his breath warming my skin.

I'm about to make another snarky comment when he leans forward and licks me right up the center.

Stars shimmer behind my eyelids and *holy-mother-of-God*, why didn't I try this sooner?

My body sings as Parker repeats the move and circles my clit with the tip of his tongue.

Coño. I take back everything I said about his ineptitude.

The boy has clearly learned a few new tricks and if he keeps that up, I'm going to come all over his face.

I thread my fingers through his hair, silently begging for more as I angle my hips toward him.

Parker seems to understand, and he licks my pussy with vigor, his tongue doing things that should probably be illegal.

I never want this to end.

I rock against his mouth greedily as he licks and sucks and then he's sliding a finger inside of me, pumping in and out as I spiral toward climax, each thrust driving my pleasure to new heights.

When he slips another thick digit inside of me, I'm not sure I can take it. My body is wrought with tension and the need to come is riding that fine line between pleasure and pain.

Torment and ecstasy.

Heaven and hell.

The sensation is too much and not enough, and if I'm not careful, it'll split me in two.

"That's it, Shorty." Parker curls a finger toward my G-spot and bears down on my clit, relentless as his thumb massages the sensitive little bundle of nerves. "Come for me."

The orgasm strikes hard and fast and I cry out as the first wave of pleasure crashes over me, drowning out any sense of modesty I possess.

"Good girl." Parker's voice is strained, like he's fighting for control, but I can't think about that now because another wave of pleasure slams into me and my muscles contract around his fingers. "Fuck. The next time we do this, it'll be my cock you're squeezing with that tight little pussy."

Aftershocks roll through my body and my legs are shaking so badly it's a wonder I can stand.

When the last dregs of pleasure subside, common sense comes roaring back.

Did I really just let DJ Parker go down on me? In public. Against a church.

I'm going to get arrested for public nudity or indecency or whatever they call it, and then I'm going straight to hell.

I make a mental note to say ten Hail Marys before bed.

Better make it twenty.

Parker slides my underwear back in place and climbs to his feet, a self-satisfied smile on his sexy face.

"I can't believe I just did that," I say, adjusting my skirt. "And I swear to God, if the words '*I told you so*' come out of your mouth right now, I can't be held responsible for my actions."

"Wouldn't dream of it. My skills speak for themselves."

Yeah, they do.

I turn to go and he slips an arm around my waist, attempting to pull me in for another kiss.

"What do you think you're doing? This"—I gesture back and forth between us—"changes nothing."

"Are you serious? This changes everything."

"No, it doesn't. This was fun, but now we're even." Or as even as we can be, all things considered. I force a smile, striving for confidence, though I feel like I might shatter into a million pieces at any second. "An O for and O."

"Shorty, we're nowhere near even." Parker's eyes go dark in the dim light of the moon. "I still owe you a proper fucking."

A nervous laugh bursts from my lips. "I'm good, thanks."

Liar.

"I told you. I like to be the one doing the chasing." He drags a finger across my cheek and over my lower lip, reigniting the flames deep in my belly. "I won't stop until you're on your back screaming my name with this snarky mouth of yours."

A thrill races up my spine. "That's never going to happen."

It can't. We have too much history, and neither of us needs the complication. Not when we're living in the same building and taking the same classes.

"We'll see." Parker pushes his hair back from his forehead, and when he speaks, his voice is steady. "And just so we're clear, the next time I lick that hot little pussy, it'll be because you're begging for it."

Sweet Jesus.

20

DJ

It's Friday morning and the guys and I are in the locker room dressing for class. Conditioning was brutal, as usual, but Coach's *"Let's kick Buffalo's ass on their home turf"* speech was blessedly short. Buffalo isn't in our conference, but that doesn't mean we can slack off tomorrow. We've got a job to do and one way or another, we need to get it done.

After all, it's the only way to guarantee a shot at the championship game.

I slam my locker door and Vaughn shoots me a look.

"Sorry, man."

"It's all good." He drops onto the bench next to me. "Worried about tomorrow?"

"Not even a little." The team looked sharp at practice this week and our defense seems to be finding their rhythm after the shaky start against Idaho. "We've got this in the bag."

"Fuckin' right." Coop snaps his towel and turns to our team captain. "Think Coach'll let us go out for wings after we check into the hotel tonight?"

"Only if you know a wing bar that doesn't serve alcohol," Reid says, tugging on a pair of athletic shorts.

"Dude, we're going to Buffalo. We can't go to Buffalo and not eat wings."

Reid shrugs. "Take it up with Coach. I'm not about to put my ass on the line for your appetite."

"The fuck?" Coop makes a show of feigning indignation. "You're our captain. You're supposed to have our backs. Right Parker?"

"Look at the bright side, princess." I flash him a shitty grin. "At least you don't have to worry about puffy hangover eyes."

Vaughn snorts. "Because that would be a travesty."

No, the real travesty is that I haven't seen Sutton since we hooked up Saturday night. Our paths haven't crossed this week—not even at the apartment complex—and I'm convinced it's because she's avoiding me, though I'm not sure why.

It could be my confession. Or the fact that we hooked up again.

Hell, it could be both.

The uncertainty has me on edge.

She can't hide forever.

Not when we have Advanced Multicamera Production today.

Unless Sutton dropped the class—which is unlikely with the Sports Stream internship on the line—she'll be there. So will I, since the team bus doesn't leave for Buffalo until two.

"Yo, DeLaurentis. I need to call in that favor you owe me."

Coop eyes me suspiciously as he styles his golden locks. "What do you need?"

I explain, and when I'm finished, he laughs and pulls out his phone. "Joke's on you, Parker. I would've done this just for funsies."

Thirty minutes later, I'm standing out front of the College of Communications when a kid with a Sig Chi pin approaches me with a brown paper bag. He offers me the bag without so much as an introduction, as if he's glad to be rid of it.

"Were you able to get everything?"

He glances around, then nods. "Product is fresh, too."

Jesus Christ. The way he's acting, you'd think we were doing something illicit.

The kid can't be a day over eighteen.

Probably a freshman. Maybe a legacy or rush candidate. Aside from the killer parties, I have no interest in frat life and the only thing I know about their rules is that seniors like Coop hold sway. Which explains how he got this kid to do his bidding at eight o'clock on a Friday morning.

"Thanks." I fish a twenty out of my pocket and offer it to him. "Will this cover it?"

He slouches, uncertainty flashing in his eyes. "That won't be necessary."

The fuck it's not.

I always pay my debts and I have zero interest in owing this kid.

Where he sees a leg up with Coop and the guys at Sig Chi, I see an uneven exchange.

I stuff the cash in his hand and thank him again before heading to class.

Sutton's nowhere to be found when I arrive, so I take my seat and open the bag, removing the rectangular white box from inside. Then I fire up my laptop, keeping one eye pinned to the door.

The minutes tick past and students trickle in one by one, but there's no sign of Sutton.

Where the hell is she? It's 8:59 and Mac will be here any minute.

Shit. Did she drop the class?

Guilt hammers my conscience. She wanted that internship

as badly as I do. If she dropped Mac's class, there can only be one reason.

AKA: one more reason for me to feel like a complete douche.

The door opens and adrenaline surges through my veins, but it's just Mac. He smiles at the class and the door swings shut behind him.

Fucking fuck.

She actually dropped the class to avoid me.

Talk about a kick in the balls.

Despite her words—her insistence that what happened between us Saturday night will never happen again—I know she enjoyed herself. The way she cried out when she came? Maybe that shit can be faked, but there was no faking the way her body hugged my fingers as she came apart on my tongue.

It was fucking perfect.

She was fucking perfect.

Now that I've had a taste, it's going to take a hell of a lot more than a dropped class to put me off her scent.

When I said I wanted her on her back screaming my name, I meant it. Hell, I've been fantasizing about it for the last five days. It's fucking distracting.

I glance at the box on my desk and sigh.

So much for Plan B.

The auditorium door swings open again and Sutton strides in, head down, backpack slung over her shoulder.

Relief floods my chest and I grin as she slides into her seat and starts digging in her bag, a curtain of cobalt hair shielding her gorgeous face from view.

"Hey, Shorty."

She stiffens and glances at Mac, who's unpacking his bag at the front of the auditorium. "Shh!"

"I brought you something."

I lift the lid of the box, giving her a peek at the peanut butter brownies inside. The aroma of chocolate fills the air and, fuck, now I'm hungry.

Her eyes go wide and her tongue darts out, making a sweep of her full upper lip before she regains control. "Are those from Daily Grind?"

"Yup." The café is on the other side of campus and always has a ridiculous line. There's no way I'd have been able to get there and get the goods before class, but thanks to Coop, I didn't have to. "Baked fresh this morning."

Let's just hope it pays off.

"Is this some kind of bribe?" she whispers. "To protect your reputation?"

I roll my eyes and tip my head toward her. "I don't give a shit about my reputation, Shorty."

"So, what?" She scrunches up her nose. "It's some kind of weird sorry-I-screwed-you-over gift?"

"If you don't want them," I counter, closing the lid. "Just say the word."

"Of course I want them." She crosses her legs and her calf brushes mine, sending a ripple of awareness straight to my cock. "They're my favorite."

"I know." Just like I know the sexy sounds she makes when she's coming.

Mac starts his lecture, and she gives me a healthy dose of side-eye. "How could you possibly know that?"

"Maddie told me."

She sucks in a sharp breath and mutters, "Traitor."

"That's a bit harsh, don't you think?" I nudge her with my elbow, savoring the brief skin-to-skin contact. "I'm not the asshole you've made me out to be."

"That remains to be seen."

I should let it go at that, but I can't. Not when sparring with

Sutton is the highlight of my day. "That's not what you said Saturday night."

Her cheeks go pink and she glances around to see if anyone is listening. "We are so not talking about that right now."

If she had her way, we'd never talk about it.

"Fine. I can wait until break." I slide the bakery box onto her desk. This class is long as hell and she might need a pick me up. "Don't even think about running, because I will catch you."

"Nice," she deadpans. "That doesn't sound threatening at all."

"Ms. Cruz." Mac levels his gaze at Sutton. "Correct me if I'm wrong, but I believe this is the second time you've interrupted my class."

An awkward silence fills the auditorium as he waits for her reply.

Sutton opens her mouth to say God only knows what, but I cut in. "I'm sorry, sir. It was entirely my fault. I dropped my pen and asked if she could pick it up for me." I flash him a sheepish grin. "Not a lot of room to maneuver up here."

He nods. "Yes, I imagine it's a tight fit for a man of your size." He starts to turn back to the center of the room and pauses. "Try asking more quietly next time, Mr. Parker."

"Yes, sir."

This time, he doesn't remind me to call him Mac.

Beside me, Sutton huffs out a breath.

Probably imagining all the ways she can de-nut you.

The thought brings an honest to God smile to my mouth as I scrawl a note on a sheet of paper and drop it on her desk.

This conversation is far from over.

21

SUTTON

I STARE at the note on my desk, heart slamming against my ribcage.

This conversation is far from over.

What is there to talk about? So we hooked up. *Again*. It means nothing. Changes nothing.

Just focus on the lecture and forget about him.

Easier said than done. I've never known anyone who takes up as much space as Parker. He sucks the air out of the room, replacing it with cool confidence, quick wit, and devilish smiles.

It's...distracting.

I'm hyperaware of him as Mac lectures about the challenges of filming a live broadcast on location. Though I'm scrawling down notes by hand, his words go in one ear and out the other because I can't stop thinking about the hard bodied athlete beside me. It doesn't help that the guy is like a furnace. Although the air conditioner is going full blast, heat rolls off his body in waves. Which probably makes for great cuddling in the winter months, but is hugely disconcerting since I'm trying to concentrate.

And what the hell was that with Mac just now? Not in a million years did I expect Parker to take the blame for disrupting class.

He saved your ass.

Yeah, because he was trying to weasel his way into my good graces.

Or maybe he did it because he's not a trash human being.

Anything is possible. For all I know, it's part of his plan to earn my forgiveness.

Like that's even possible.

Nope. I will not let DJ Parker charm his way into my life. It's a surefire way to get my heart broken, and I don't have time for heartache. Not with my schedule.

Parker's knee brushes mine and the classroom fades away as electricity hums across my skin. I'm back at the church and Parker's head is between my thighs as he devours my pussy, his thick fingers filling every inch of me as I spiral toward ecstasy, the knowledge that we're exposed—that someone might find us at any second—heightening my pleasure.

Arousal floods my core, and I shift in my seat, trying to dampen my growing need.

Unfortunately, the only thing that gets damp is my panties.

Me cago en ná.

This is so not the time for X-rated fantasies.

I close my eyes and inhale slowly, pushing all thoughts of Parker from my mind.

If I want a shot at that internship, I need to ace this class, which won't happen if I'm daydreaming about orgasms when I should be learning about live broadcasts.

The lecture is torture, and despite Parker's promise to talk more at break, I'm counting down the minutes. I need to get out of this auditorium, if only to get a breath of fresh air that doesn't smell like citrus and sandalwood.

"As you know," Mac says, drawing my attention back to the front of the room. "The culmination of this class is a live broadcast, but I also require my students to demonstrate solid communication and teamwork through a partner project. This semester, you'll be writing a term paper focused on one of the key aspects of production."

He holds up his remote and the on-screen visual at the front of the room changes.

"Partners and topics have been assigned based on the seating chart."

I scan the list and when I find my name, my stomach flips.

Sutton Cruz – DJ Parker.

This has to be a freaking joke. Two years of avoiding the guy and this semester he's blocking my path at every turn. To add insult to injury, Mac assigned us distribution issues, which is going to be just as boring as it sounds.

Where did Waverly find this guy? First the seating chart and now he's assigning partners for group work? It's ridiculous.

Not to mention insulting.

"I see a few surprised faces," Mac continues, voice ripe with amusement. "I know you're accustomed to choosing your own partners for group projects, but you won't have that luxury in the real world. Few of us get to choose our co-workers and regardless of our personal differences, we have to make it work."

Beside me, Parker snickers.

"This is total bullshit," I mutter, tapping my pen on the desk.

"I don't know. I'm thinking this just might be my lucky day."

Of course he's enjoying this. It fits perfectly with his plan to redeem himself in the bedroom.

As if Saturday night hasn't already done that.

I sigh. Clearly I need to squeeze more Hail Marys into my life because WTF.

When Mac finally releases us for a break, I trudge into the hall, feeling like a prisoner marching to her death. Parker is right behind me and when I turn to face him, he's all smiles.

"Hey, partner." He leans one broad shoulder against the wall, hazel eyes dancing with amusement. "How lucky is this?"

"So lucky," I deadpan.

Parker chuckles, low and deep. "It really is, since we're neighbors. Just think of all the time we'll get to spend together."

I straighten and plant a hand on my hip. "Did you put Mac up to this? Request me as a partner because I was avoiding you?"

His grin becomes a full-on smirk. "So you admit you were avoiding me."

So much for being obvious.

"Whatever. You'd better be prepared to work because I need an A in this class."

"Same." He rubs the back of his neck. "My schedule is a bitch with football, so the sooner we can get started, the better."

At least we can agree on that much. My schedule is murder, too. I've got nearly a dozen Wildcat appearances this week, plus the game against Buffalo tomorrow, which, after my performance last week, needs to be top-notch to get Sharpe off my back.

Hopefully, since it's an away game, the expectations won't be as high. Waverly nation is huge, and there will be fans in the stands, but I doubt anyone will expect me to crowd surf.

At least, I hope they won't.

"I'm really swamped, too," I admit. "Why don't we each

take a couple of weeks to research and see what we can learn about distribution? Then we can meet up to figure out an angle for the paper."

Parker narrows his eyes, but when he speaks, his tone is playful. "Is this a stall tactic, or are you just afraid to be alone with me?"

Option C: All of the above.

But I'd choke on my pride before admitting it.

"I have no intention of meeting with you alone." Not when the mere thought of him is enough to make my body hum with desire. And certainly not while he's on a mission to finish what we started Saturday night. "We can meet at the library like normal project partners."

If I had the time, I'd offer to just write the paper myself.

But I don't have the time, so teamwork it is.

Parker pulls out his phone and unlocks the screen. "What's your number?"

It's on the tip of my tongue to argue, but he's right. This project will go much more smoothly if we exchange numbers. Plus, with my luck, if I don't give him my number, he'll just show up at my door whenever the hell he feels like it.

Hard pass.

I recite my number and watch as he punches it in and hits the call button. My phone vibrates in my pocket and I pull it out so Parker can confirm it's his number on the screen.

He snickers as he saves my contact information, and when I see that he's saved my number as Shorty, I follow his lead.

I tap out a fitting moniker and hold up the phone so he can see his nickname: 2PumpChump

Parker's jaw drops and he makes a play for the phone, but I'm ready for him and dance out of his reach.

"You can't leave that. It's offensive and insensitive."

I shrug. "Sometimes the truth hurts."

"What if someone sees it?" he asks, brows pulled low. "I'll never live it down."

"Exactly." I smirk up at him and slide the phone back into my pocket. "Guess you'll have to think long and hard about using my number."

He presses his lips together, but the moment of self-reflection is short-lived. Before I know it, the smug grin is back in place. "Nah. I'll just think long and hard about how to change your mind."

"Don't waste your time. It's never going to happen."

Which is a real bitch because for the first time in my life, BOB feels like a poor substitute for the real thing.

22

———

SUTTON

IT's Saturday afternoon and the Wildcats are playing Michigan State. It's a home game, and the team is 4-0, soon to be 5-0, because although the game has been physical, Waverly has a solid lead. As long as they don't blow it, the team's got this one in the bag.

Too bad there isn't a mercy rule in college football.

It's hotter than a pair of sunburned tits in this fur suit and the game clock is moving slow as hell today. As if that's not bad enough, I'm sweating buckets and my eyes are stinging because I forgot my headband. Or, as us non-marketing folks call it, a sweatband.

So much for the cooler temps the weather app promised.

On the bright side, the costume should keep me warm-ish in the colder months.

Waverly converts on third and long—yes, I know what that means now thanks to my mascot duties—and the crowd goes nuts, drawing my attention back to the game.

The cheerleaders are chanting and jumping, so I do a short tumbling pass down the sideline and end with a split.

Take that, Coach Sharpe.

I'll bet his regular mascot can't do a freaking split. Not a lot of guys with that particular skill outside of the men's gymnastics team.

I pop to my feet and jog past the student section, cupping my ear and gesturing for the crowd to bring the noise.

And just like that, they obey my command.

Turns out, being the mascot is a powerful gig. I can get people to dance, sing, stomp, clap, and cheer with a few silent gestures. Last week, I even got Herky the Hawk to face off with me in a pushup contest when the team played Iowa. I had to flap my arms like a chicken to shame him into it, but still. I'm proud to report that just as the Wildcats kicked Hawkeye ass on the field, I kicked Herky's ass on the sideline.

On his home turf.

It's the little things.

It really is. Especially when your performances are mandatory to avoid possible expulsion.

On the next play, Reid passes the ball to number eighty-seven—Parker—who makes the catch and pivots toward the end zone. Before he can take a single step, a defender in green and white closes in, drops his shoulder, and hammers Parker's right side.

The hit is brutal and I gasp as he goes down, the crunch of protective gear echoing across the field.

Dios mío. How can he possibly walk away from a hit like that?

Parker's crumpled form lies prone in the grass, unmoving, the ball tucked protectively under his arm. My chest tightens, and an eternity passes as I wait for him to sit up or move or do something.

Come on, Parker. Get up.

He doesn't so much as wiggle his fingers.

Fear crawls up my spine, and I clasp my paws together, willing him to move.

Get up and walk it off, you smug bastard!

If he thinks a football injury is going to get him out of doing his half of the AMP term paper, he's got another think coming, so he might as well get up and get on with it already.

Right. Freaking. *Now*.

My attention is laser focused on Parker, as is most of the stadium. When he finally rolls over, it's like the steel band circling my chest has been cut away and I can breathe again, full and deep. I fill my lungs with fresh air as one of his teammates offers him a hand and pulls him to his feet. They do some weird bro handshake and then it's like nothing even happened.

They just go right back to playing the game.

No "*I'm good.*" No "*Sorry for scaring the shit out of you.*" Not even a wave to say, "*Thanks for your concern, but I've got this.*"

What. The. Actual. Fuck?

My head is spinning and my emotions have a severe case of whiplash, but I shake it off and clap along with the rest of the players and fans. Why anyone would want to play a game where their brains are at risk of being scrambled is beyond me. And why are Americans so obsessed with football, anyway? It's archaic and hard-hitting and lacks the grace and beauty of a sport like gymnastics.

Then it's probably a good thing no one asked your opinion.

Fair enough.

The clock finally runs out and the whistle sounds, signaling half-time, my favorite part of game day, second only to the final whistle.

I head for the tunnel, fantasizing about a cold shower and a bucket of water, but Sharpe waves me over.

Right on schedule.

The man has a habit of calling for me whenever there's a water break, and I'm half-convinced it's intentional. Just an extra little twist of the knife on this heinous punishment.

Maybe it's paranoia, but if anyone knows how hot and miserable this suit is, surely it's the Spirit Squad Head Coach.

I follow him into the tunnel and he leads me to a rolling cart that's been pushed off to the side. It's filled with cardboard boxes and though the boxes on top of the cart are open, I can't see the contents.

"What's all this?" I ask, resting my paws on my hips.

Sharpe moves to the far side of the cart, lips pressed into a grim line.

Because that's not foreboding or anything.

"We're trying something different today." He hefts a blue and white device that looks a bit like a paintball gun and has a long white tube bearing the Waverly logo where the barrel should be. "The Assistant Athletic Director for Marketing and Promotions came to see me yesterday. He wants us to try something new this weekend." Sharpe pauses, probably to catch his breath after reciting that absurdly long title. "If it goes well and the fans enjoy it, it could become part of the regular program."

"And what exactly is this mysterious test?"

"A t-shirt cannon."

A t-shirt cannon? He can't be serious.

The look on his face would suggest otherwise.

"With all due respect, sir. I don't have the first clue how to fire a t-shirt cannon."

"It's harmless, Cruz." He holds up the portable cannon for inspection. Because that'll really help. "You just point and shoot." He chuckles like he's just made a hilarious freaking joke. "It's not like we're giving you one of those triple barrel Gatling guns Wisconsin uses." He pauses, giving me a once-over. "Shit. That thing would be bigger than you are. I hear it can shoot 114 t-shirts a minute." His eyes glaze over like a kid on Christmas morning and it's all I can do to not roll my eyes. But since I'm not trying to get sent to a disciplinary hearing, I suppress the urge. "Can you imagine?"

No, I really can't.

That's hardly the point.

"I'm a gymnast, not a...whatever you call a person who shoots t-shirt guns."

"Pay attention, Cruz." He flashes me a pointed stare before returning his attention to the cannon. "I'm only going to show you this once because we're running out of time."

All the more reason to delay.

"Maybe I should practice with it this week and unveil it at our next home game. What's the rush?"

Sharpe makes a sound halfway between a hum of agreement and a grunt of disapproval. "If I had my way, that's exactly how this would go down, but it's not up to me. The manufacturer threw in some kind of sweetheart deal that expires this week." He swipes the back of his hand across his shiny forehead. "The deal's already done, so today it is."

Just my luck. The football program has millions of dollars to spend on everything from custom Wildcat rugs to nutrition bars and they're pinching pennies over a freaking t-shirt cannon.

Waverly has a lot of cool traditions—white out games, fan chants, even the Wildcat pushups—but a t-shirt cannon isn't one of them.

"You just stuff a t-shirt down the tube," Sharpe says, pulling a rolled-up t-shirt from one of the cardboard boxes. "Then you point and pull the trigger."

It looks easy enough, but...

"How am I supposed to manage the gun and the cart?"

"A couple members of my squad will push the cart and refill the cannon as you go. All you have to do is fire into the crowd."

Oh, is that all?

"Relax, Cruz." He pats me on the shoulder and smiles for what feels like the first time since this conversation started. "If I didn't think you could handle it, I'd have figured out a workaround."

I appreciate the vote of confidence more than he knows, but it does little to boost my self-confidence as I take the cannon and try positioning it in my arms. It's heavier than it looks, and getting my finger inside the trigger guard is no easy feat with my furry gloves.

If only they were real paws instead of furry hands.

Then I could foist this task on one of the cheerleaders. But they're not real paws and I can't afford to shirk my duties, so it'll be my furry ass shooting t-shirts into the crowd today.

Coach Sharpe gives a quick nod. "You've got this."

Right. I've got this.

How hard can it be to shoot t-shirts into the crowd, anyway?

23

DJ

NOT TO BRAG, but we're destroying Michigan State and for the first time all season, our defense is playing like a unit. It's exactly the caliber of performance that's expected of us. By Coach, our fans, the conference. It's only week five, but we're starting to look like a championship team on both sides of the ball.

The chatter around town is getting hard to block out. Everywhere I turn, all people want to talk about is the odds of Waverly going undefeated, which bowl game we'll land, and whether I think the team's got what it takes to bring home a national title.

It's fucking exhausting.

Between football and classes, I don't have much energy to spare and I'd rather not spend every waking moment obsessing about what-if scenarios and stressing the game.

Imagine how Reid feels.

I glance at our team captain, who's standing a few feet away. Sweat pours from his brow and he watches the defense intently, unwilling to miss a single play.

Football is his legacy—his future—so maybe it feels different for him, but I doubt it.

Reid doesn't talk about the pressure, but it's got to weigh on him. How could it not when his father is an NFL legend, and he's basically been groomed to play ball his entire life?

I love the game, but when it's time to hang up my cleats next year, I'll be ready.

Beside me, Vaughn upends a water bottle over his head, grinning as the cool liquid pours down his face and beard. "With any luck, Coach will give us a break in the fourth quarter," he says, shaking his head like a wet dog and sending water droplets flying.

"Anything is possible." The underclassmen rarely see much playing time this early in the season, but unless the Spartans put together one hell of a rally, this game is already over. "Why is it so damn hot, anyway? It's almost October. Where are the falling leaves and cooling temperatures?"

Vaughn spouts off some shit about global warming, but it's too loud to hear much of what he says over the roar of the crowd.

Our defense makes a stop on the thirty and the fans go nuts as the Wildcat roar echoes through the stadium. I scan the stands, pride filling my chest at the sight of Wildcat Nation on their feet, cheering us to victory.

Okay, maybe I'll miss this a little.

When else in my life will one hundred thousand people cheer me on?

That would be never.

So, yeah. Enjoy it while it lasts and all that.

Vaughn nudges me and jerks his chin toward the cheerleaders. I follow his gaze and see the Wildcat strutting down the sideline with some sort of blue and white contraption, a couple of cheerleaders trailing behind with a rolling cart.

"What do you think they're doing?"

"Beats me." Vaughn shrugs his broad shoulders, but his eyes remain glued to the mascot who's making his way toward us.

Can't say I blame him. Last year, the Wildcat got it in his head to fuck with the gentle giant and harassed him nonstop for the entertainment of the fans. Needless to say, my man wasn't impressed.

Vaughn's the kind of guy who likes to put in the work and stay out of the spotlight.

He's consistent as hell, but he doesn't have a showboating bone in his body, and constantly seeing his face on the big screen made the big man grumpy as hell.

Now that I'm thinking about it, it's a wonder the Wildcat hasn't resumed his antics, given the popularity of last year's shenanigans.

We watch as the mascot holds up the contraption and, upon closer inspection, I know exactly what it is.

Vaughn grunts "T-shirt cannon," at the same time the word enters my mind.

"That's new," I say, unable to look away as the fans raise their arms and clamber for the Wildcat's attention.

The things people will do to get free shit.

The mascot raises the cannon in the air and when he pulls the trigger, there's a loud *thwump* as a white projectile sails into the stands. A tall guy in the lower section catches it, snatching the t-shirt from the air before the little girl next to him has a shot at grabbing it.

"Asshole," I mutter. "Should've let the kid have it."

The mascot must agree because he shakes his head at the

dude celebrating and rubs the back of one furry forefinger over the other in the universal sign for shame.

Vaughn chuckles and we watch as the mascot moves to the next section, firing off three more shirts. When he approaches the section before the bench, the Wildcat lowers the cannon and points to the crowd, arm swinging like the pendulum on a clock as it sweeps back and forth, encouraging the fans to call for the next shot.

And call they do. The sound reaches a fever pitch and then the Wildcat roar explodes from the sound system.

There's a loud *thwump* and the next thing I know, I'm doubled over, the air punched from my lungs as white-hot pain detonates in my balls.

Fucking fuck.

I groan, my hands instinctively dropping to protect the boys, but it's too late.

Tears sting the corners of my eyes, and I clamp my eyelids shut, suppressing them.

I've never cried on the field and I'm not about to start now, even if I have a busted nut.

"Jesus Christ." Vaughn crouches next to me. At least, I think he does. I can't see him because I'm folded like an accordion and my goddamn eyes are sealed shut, but his voice seems to be at ear level as he asks, "Are you okay?"

"I think my soul just left my body," I pant, gasping for breath. "What the fuck just happened?"

He doesn't answer and when I finally open my eyes, he's holding out a rolled blue and white t-shirt.

"You've got to be kidding me."

He shakes his head. "Afraid not."

I scan the sideline for the Wildcat and he makes an *oopsie* gesture, covering his mouth with both hands as the cheerleaders put the cannon back on the cart.

At least no one else will get shot in the nuts today.

A trainer rushes over and the O-line crowds in as he grills me about my pain level—which is a fucking twelve on a ten-point scale—and suggests I hit the bench while he gets some ice.

Right. Like I'm going to apply an ice pack to my dick in front of one hundred thousand people like a complete and total douche.

"Am I hallucinating right now, or did that just happen?" Coop asks, struggling to speak through fits of laughter.

I straighten, despite the painful throbbing in my groin. "Fuck you and your jokes, DeLaurentis."

Smith slaps me on the back as I hobble over to the bench to await my ice pack. "Man, that's the funniest shit I've ever seen."

"That's certainly one way to make history," Reid says, clapping my shoulder as I pass.

I think he's trying to be supportive, but it's a miss for me.

"That shit is going to be on ESPN and every other network by tomorrow morning," Coop crows. "Our boy is about to reach meme status."

Lucky me.

As I drop on the bench, a video appears on the big screen. It's a clip of the Wildcat with the goddamn cannon. I watch in horror as he lowers the cannon and fires. The camera swings to me and though it missed the initial impact, they got a great shot of me bent in half clutching my balls.

Just my fucking luck.

AN HOUR LATER, I'm chilling in the trainer's room with an icepack on my nuts, celebrating the fact that we're the only team in the conference that's 5-0 when my phone vibrates with another incoming text.

Judging by the timestamps, it's been blowing up since the third quarter. More specifically, since I got nailed in the dick with a t-shirt. So far, it's been a mix of sympathy—mostly from family, plus a handful of cleat chasers—and smartass comments from my friends.

Aside from my parents, I haven't responded to the messages, leaving them on read.

I check the new message and a slow grin spreads across my face when I see it's from Sutton.

Shorty: Heard about the unfortunate incident during today's game.

Fuck. She doesn't even like football. How the hell did she hear about it already?

Because all of Wildcat nation was there to bear witness to your humiliation.

By tomorrow morning, the entire world of sports will have seen it on a highlight reel.

Fuck my life. The guys were right. I'm going to be the hottest meme of the week while the asshole in the mascot costume gets to remain anonymous.

Lucky bastard.

My phone vibrates with another incoming message.

Shorty: Don't think this gets you off research duty. I still expect you to pull your weight.

Naturally.

I snicker and tap out a quick reply.

Me: Is this your way of saying you're worried about me?

She's had my number for weeks and this is the first time she's used it.

Any illusion I had about Sutton's concern is dispelled a

second later when an *In your dreams* GIF appears in the message thread.

Fuckin' right.

And with any luck, IRL too.

Me: There's a party at Sig Chi tonight. You going?

Shorty: You're kidding, right?

Damn. I'd been hoping to pick up where we left off a few weeks ago. Outside of class, Sutton's managed to elude me. Any time I suggest meeting to work on our AMP term paper, she gives me some bullshit excuse about a tight schedule or being slammed with more pressing assignments.

Shorty: I'm surprised you're bothering with Greek Row. Your cock probably doesn't even work after today.

Bullshit. A little ice and my cock will be just fine.

I think.

Me: No worries. My tongue works just fine...as you well know.

For a long time, she doesn't respond. I stare at the screen, waiting for a snarky reply as the ice on my balls melts, but still nothing. Eventually, three little dots appear on the screen.

Then disappear.

Fuck.

The suspense is killing me. What is she doing? Writing a tome?

Maybe she's just going to leave you on read.

My fingers fly over the screen, tapping out another message. It's poor form—desperate even—but I can't seem to help myself.

Me: Happy to stop by and give you a quick refresher.

That's a damn lie. The next time we hook up, it won't be quick and there won't be anything refreshing about it. Given the chance, I'll fuck Sutton boneless. And I won't quit until she's in a sated, exhausted state of bliss.

Her reply is swift this time.

Shorty: Keep dreaming, chump.

The nickname is a blatant reminder of our first disastrous hookup. But it's also a reminder of the promise I made behind that church, when I swore to make her scream my name.

*Me: Oh, I will. *hot face emoji**

After all, it's about time I made good on my promise.

24

SUTTON

DAY OF REST, my ass. With my hectic schedule, Sundays are my only day off. Which means I spent the day washing clothes, cleaning the apartment, and catching up on homework.

It's nearly five o'clock and I've finished most of my reading assignments for the week, with one exception. I flop down on my bed with my Media Management text and a bottle of water, ready to dive into the assigned chapter, which covers work-for-hire contracts. I tried to read it last night, but fell asleep, so here's hoping today's attempt will be more successful.

My phone buzzes on the nightstand, but I ignore it.

Parker's been texting all day, asking when I want to meet up to work on the AMP paper. When Mac assigned it, I suggested we take a few weeks to research independently before meeting up.

That was three weeks ago.

Every time Parker's attempted to set a study date, I've deferred, but I'm not sure how much longer I'll be able to stall. I can't avoid the project forever and, more to the point, the guy is persistent as hell. Which sucks because just sitting next to him in Mac's class each week is torture. It's impossible to concentrate with his large, athletic body crowding me for three straight hours, reminding me of all the sinful things he can do with his tongue.

The prospect of being alone with him again is just—*nope*.

We can always go to the library. At least then we won't be alone and I won't be tempted to rip his clothes off. Or, you know, drop my panties.

There's a knock at my bedroom door and Maddie bursts in, phone in hand. "OMG. Check your messages."

Acho. "Did Parker text you?"

I wouldn't put it past him. Not after the brownie incident.

"What?" She cocks her head and her brow wrinkles, but she casts off her confusion quickly. "No. This isn't about Parker. It's about Brooke."

My stomach flips and I sit up on the bed. "Is everything okay?"

"It's better than okay. United G contacted her about endorsing their leotards." She bounces on the balls of her feet, phone clutched between her hands. "Can you believe she's actually going to get an NIL deal? How freaking amazing is that?"

Pretty freaking amazing. "I should text her to say congratulations."

I grab my phone off the nightstand and, ignoring Parker's texts, go to the group chat I have with Maddie, Brooke, and Soraya. There are seven unread messages...because I'm the only pendeja who hasn't responded yet to Brooke's news.

"Maybe they'll send her enough leos to go around and she can share them with us," Maddie says, leaning against the doorjamb as I send Brooke a confetti filled message.

I drop my phone on the bed and shoot her a look.

"What? A girl can dream. United G is expensive as hell and I'm not too proud to turn down free gear."

I snort because if anyone can afford to buy all the leos her little heart desires, it's Maddie.

"Plus, Brooke will get the newest styles before they're available online." She grins. "The other girls on the team are going to be so jealous. Hell, I'm jealous."

We both laugh and our phones buzz simultaneously with Brooke's reply, a reminder that the discussion is in the early stages and nothing is guaranteed.

It's a practical response, and probably for the best, but I can't help thinking of my abuela's favorite proverb.

El que busca encuentra.

If you search, you will find.

Brooke's worked her ass off for this opportunity, pouring her time and effort into her sport and into building her social following. It's not luck that has United G sliding into her DMs, but hard work and dedication.

If anyone deserves this, it's Brooke.

The doorbell rings, and Maddie and I look at each other in surprise.

"Were you expecting someone?" I ask.

"No." She moves to the window and pulls back the curtain, glancing down at the front stoop. "It's Parker."

Panic floods my body. What is he doing here?

Maddie whirls, her excitement nearly palpable. "Did you invite him over?"

"Of course not." And, okay, maybe my response is a little defensive, but she knows our history now, so she can't exactly be surprised.

She sighs. "Damn. I thought maybe you two finally kissed and made up."

"Not hardly." My cheeks heat and guilt niggles at my

conscience, but there's no way I'm going to admit we hooked up in the church parking lot.

It was a mistake.

A stupid one.

"Want me to go see what he wants?" Her brows shoot up. "Ooh, maybe he brought more brownies. I've got my period and I would kill for something chocolate right now."

"It's fine." I climb out of bed. "I'll go see what he wants." We both know he's most likely here to annoy me, and making her deal with my problems isn't exactly stellar BFF behavior. "There are Reese's in the freezer."

"Best. Roommate. Ever."

She darts down the hall in search of peanut butter cups and I follow, though I take my sweet ass time descending the stairs.

Yes, it's another stall tactic, but at least it gives me time to collect my thoughts before facing Parker.

As if that's even possible.

Truth. The man is infuriating, but he's hotter than the hinges of hell.

I steel my resolve as I grab the doorknob and yank the front door open. Parker stands there, dressed in a pair of low-slung joggers—gray, of course—and a fitted athletic tee that hugs every dip and plane of his muscular chest. His hazel eyes are bright in the fading afternoon light and his shaggy hair looks like he's just run a hand through it, but his smile...

Dios mío.

Parker's smile is warm and inviting and the things he can do with that tongue.

My core heats at the memory and I pray my thoughts aren't written all over my face.

"Hey." He holds up a pizza box. "I figured since you're too busy to meet up and discuss our AMP paper, maybe we could do it over dinner." He flashes me a wolfish grin. "Even you have to take a break to eat, right?"

Yes, but preferably when my mouth isn't drier than the Sahara.

As if sensing my reluctance, he opens the lid and the scent of baked dough and melting cheese calls to me like a siren song.

My stomach growls in response.

A slice or two won't hurt.

Especially since I had a salad for lunch.

"Fine. Let's get this over with." I step aside so he can enter, and when I turn around, Maddie's camped out on the couch, a bag of Reese's in one hand and the remote in the other. Which means we'll have to go upstairs to avoid disturbing her, and vice versa, because our kitchen and living room are one big open concept space. "Parker brought pizza. You want any?"

"I'm good." She pops a peanut butter cup into her mouth. "You two kids have fun."

Yeah, right.

I narrow my eyes, searching her face for signs of duplicity. Could she be in on this with Parker? But no, she looks happy as a clam and totally oblivious to the tension roiling between us.

I grab some plates and a bottle of water for Parker, and we head upstairs.

My belly flips as I open my bedroom door and I do a quick scan to make sure there's nothing embarrassing lying around.

The guy's already handled your vibrator.

Right. It's all uphill from there.

Still, having Parker in my room—in my personal space—is unsettling.

I watch as he sits the pizza box on my cluttered desk and scans the room, cataloguing every picture and memento tacked up on the wall. He pauses on the black and white Bleach anime tapestry, and the soft white lights surrounding it, before his eyes settle on the queen-size bed with its rumpled indigo comforter and stack of Sailor Moon pillows.

"Not what you were expecting?" I ask, hating the defensive edge in my voice.

I do not care what he thinks of my style or my bedroom.

It's for me, no one else.

And, real talk, it's not like I've had to worry about guys seeing it in the past.

He turns to face me, eyes raking over the *Bury Me Next To My TBR* tee that's knotted at my hip and continuing on to the turquoise shorts that barely cover my ass cheeks. "Shorty, this is exactly what I expected."

My pulse flutters and I do my best to ignore the unwanted thoughts and feelings that always seem to bubble up in Parker's presence. "I assume you brought your notes for the project?"

"Yeah. They're in my bag." He drops his backpack on the floor, then opens the pizza box and gestures for the plates. I hand them over and he dishes up two slices, which he offers to me. "Figured we could talk it over while we eat."

"Sounds good."

I settle back into my bed, leaving him the desk chair.

Once we're both situated with our food, he passes me his notes. Some are handwritten, but most are printouts. He's taken the time to highlight the important points, leaving no doubt which of us is more prepared for this meeting.

Way to pull your weight, Cruz.

I skim through the highlighted sections as I eat, noting we've identified a few of the same distribution challenges. It's a promising start considering the fact that we can barely get through class without snarking at one another. I'm nearly done reading when I come across an article with the title circled in red.

"What's OTT?" I ask, dropping my crust back on the plate.

"Over-the-top media services." He leans forward, resting his elbows on his knees. "They're media services delivered directly to the end user. Like Netflix."

I hold up the page with the circled text. "You think this has potential?"

"You don't?"

I'm loathe to admit I don't know enough to have an informed opinion. It shouldn't be a big deal because Parker is a year ahead of me in school. Theoretically, he's taken more classes and has probably studied all kinds of stuff I haven't seen yet, but that doesn't make it any easier to swallow.

"I'm not overly familiar with the topic."

"Hang on." He pulls his laptop from his bag and opens it up. "I wrote a paper about OTT last year that will probably explain it better than I can." He taps on the keyboard, searching for the file as he continues. "There's a lot of information on the subject because of the explosive growth in the last couple of years. That alone would make it easy for us to identify and address the distribution challenges. Plus, I'll bet we'd get bonus points with Mac for relevancy."

Parker stands and approaches the bed, laptop in hand. He crosses the cozy space in a few easy strides, looking perfectly at home, and when he hands me the laptop, his fingers brushing mine. A rush of awareness passes over me, bringing every nerve ending in my body to attention.

Parker must not feel it because he sinks down on the edge of the mattress like it's no big deal that his giant, hulking body is in my bed.

Which it's not.

It's just another piece of furniture.

Just because we're sitting on the same bed doesn't mean we're going to get naked.

Even if I've fantasized about that very thing in this very spot.

So not happening.

Not outside my dreams, anyway.

I clear my throat and force myself to meet his eyes. "I'll just read your paper and then we can decide on a topic."

Parker smirks. "Sounds like a plan."

I lower my gaze to the document on the screen and read the introductory sentence, though for the life of me, I couldn't tell you what it said. So I read it again, still not absorbing a damn thing.

Third time's the charm.

I read it one more time and yeah, no dice.

"It's impossible to concentrate with you sitting there staring at me." I make a shooing gesture. "Can't you find something else to entertain yourself while I read?"

"Sure." He picks up my phone off the bed. "Got any of those pornalicious books I can listen to?"

Yes.

"No."

"Liar." He attempts to wake the phone, but it's locked. "Come on. You want me distracted while you read. This is the distraction I choose."

Of course it is.

"It's that or I stretch out next to you in this bed and take a nice, long nap." He chuckles and the quiet rumble speaks directly to my ovaries. "Now that I think about it, I am pretty tired from yesterday's game."

He arches his back and raises his arms over his head, feigning the world's biggest yawn. The movement reveals a sliver of his tanned, sculpted abs and my blood pressure spikes.

"Don't you dare." I grab the phone from his hand, unlock the screen, and bring up my audiobook app before handing the phone back. I might be disciplined in the gym, but I'm not sure I have the strength to resist Parker here in my bed. Not anymore. Not when I know exactly how good it can be between us. Which is why I need to fortify my defenses. "Knock yourself out, chump. Who knows? Maybe you'll even learn something."

He smirks, letting the dig roll right off his back. "Maybe I will."

25

DJ

I DIG my headphones out of my bag and pair them with Sutton's phone as she pretends to read my term paper on OTT. It's obvious she's not actually reading, because every time I glance her way, she hurriedly lowers her eyes.

Maybe I'm twisted, but the fact that she won't just admit she's as hot for me as I am for her is a fucking turn on.

The thrill of the chase.

Not something I have a lot of experience with since there's no shortage of women on campus eager to hook up with athletes, but there's been the occasional woman who's played hard to get and I dig it. The knowledge that Sutton isn't playing—that she truly believes this thing between us isn't going to happen again—just makes her even more desirable.

I sit down at the desk and scroll through her library. It's like her own mobile porn stash and, not gonna lie, my mind is blown by the endless covers featuring ripped dudes with broody eyed stares.

Somebody has a type.

If these books are any indication, I'm it.

Then again, who knows what's happening between the pages?

I've never been much of a reader, never took pleasure in it like others, but curiosity stirs low in my gut, so I scroll back to the top and press play on her current read.

"We're not finished here, Princess."

He lavished kisses on the backs of her knees, gliding up her smooth thighs and spreading them wide so he could look his fill. When he reached the vee between her legs, she was quivering with need, her pussy wet and glistening with arousal.

Christ. The desire to taste her was visceral, a craving that tested his tightly held control.

He palmed her luscious ass cheeks, kneading the tender flesh.

"If you want me to continue," he said, nipping at her inner thigh. "You will not move. You're going to stand here and take what I give you. Understood?"

She nodded.

"Say it, Princess. Tell me you're going to take it like a good girl."

She turned to look over her shoulder, meeting his gaze with a sultry smile. "Oh, I'm going to take it. Every inch. But I can't promise to be good. Not when being naughty feels so much better."

Holy shit.

It's like a fucking instruction manual.

I listen for another couple of minutes and by the time the couple in the book has climaxed, I'm sporting a semi and I can't think of anything except the sexy little spitfire on the bed next to me.

How the hell does she listen to this stuff in public and not get turned on by it?

Who says she's not turned on?

Facts. She could be horny as fuck right now, and I wouldn't know it.

My eyes slide to Sutton, and she hurriedly looks down.

This was a terrible fucking idea. The study date. The bedroom. The sexy audiobook that has completely derailed my focus.

Nice job, asshole.

We can sit here and pretend like we're working, or we can address the giant fucking elephant in the room. Namely, the fact that I want this girl so badly it hurts.

Maybe that's my bruised ego talking, but I don't think so. I've been hot for her from the moment we met. Or, met again. This Sutton, the one with the nose piercing and snarky mouth, who doesn't take shit from anyone, intrigues me in a way no one ever has.

Like the guy in her audio book, I revel in the challenge. In knowing that she can—and will—meet me toe-to-toe.

"Let me guess." I hold up the phone. "You listen for the plot."

She pulls a face, scrunching up her nose in that adorable way she does when she's annoyed. "What are you even listening to?"

I tell her the title and she rolls her eyes.

"That's not even a spicy one."

"Sounded pretty spicy to me." I rise from the desk chair to return the phone.

"It's like a three out of five on the clitometer."

The moment the words are out of her mouth, she turns scarlet.

It's all I can do not to laugh, but I hold it in. I'm mature like that.

"Tell me more about this clitometer." I drop down beside her on the bed, making myself comfortable as I lean back against the stack of Sailor Moon pillows and stretch my legs out next to hers.

Our thighs brush and she immediately scoots away.

"There's not much to tell," she says through gritted teeth. "It's exactly what it sounds like."

"A rating system for how aroused you get while reading the book."

It's a statement, not a question, and though I didn't think it was possible, her face gets even redder.

Which is ridiculous, given that just a few weeks ago I publicly devoured her pussy.

My mouth waters at the memory of Sutton's taste and the way her arousal coated my tongue.

So fucking sweet.

If I'm not careful, I'm going to have a full-blown hard-on soon.

But since I've never known what's good for me, I hit rewind on the audio book, roll onto my side, and press play.

Dirty talk fills the room and Sutton's eyes go wide, but she doesn't tell me to turn it off.

We listen in silence as the male narrator pleasures his partner, licking and sucking and biting until she's begging for release.

Sutton stares straight ahead, but I couldn't tear my eyes from her if I wanted to. I'm like a junkie needing a fix, and I watch in fascination as her breathing accelerates, her breasts rising and falling in a steady rhythm. The dude in the book slaps his partner's ass and Sutton's lips part, her eyelids falling to half-mast as she curls her fingers in her lap. That's when I notice her thighs are clenched together, the laptop balanced precariously atop them.

The sight of her coiled tight with need is so damn hot, I'm sporting a full erection by the time the woman in the book cries out, her sounds of pleasure so much like Sutton's the night behind the church.

I close the laptop and slide it off her lap and onto the bed.

"I haven't been able to think about anything but the taste of you on my lips since I walked into this room," I admit, voice thick. "Hell, since the night of the Sig Chi party."

She shifts onto her side and props her chin up on her hand, turning the full force of those gorgeous brown eyes on me. She says nothing, but that's okay, because I'm not finished.

"For the last four weeks, you've ruled my thoughts, and I'm not too proud to admit I want another taste." I cup her cheek and drag my thumb across her lower lip. "If that's not something you want, you should tell me now."

Sutton leans into my touch, eyes drifting closed.

Thank fuck.

I close the distance between us and brush my lips against hers.

The kiss is soft and gentle, a spark on the verge of combustion.

She melts against me and a quiet, hungry sound shatters the silence. Then she's gripping the front of my shirt, pulling me closer as she deepens the kiss, her tongue prodding at the entrance of my mouth, demanding more.

Eager to meet the challenge, I tangle my fingers in her hair, wrapping the thick blue tendrils around my fist.

My hard-on strains against the soft fabric of my joggers and I slip my free arm under her body, rolling her on top of me. I position her astride my cock, groaning at the instant friction our bodies create. I want her to know exactly what she does to me, how fucking hard she makes me.

"You feel that, Shorty? It's all you."

She rolls her hips in response, sending a bolt of desire straight to my balls.

Christ. I can't remember the last time I was this turned on. My body hums with energy, adrenaline and lust pulsing through my veins.

I cup the firm, round globes of her ass, trying to slow her down, but she rolls her hips again, the taut muscles of her thighs gripping me tight.

Sutton has an incredible body. I've always known that, but seeing it in action...

Fuck me.

I slide a hand under the hem of her t-shirt, skimming my fingers up her spine until I find the clasp on her bra.

She jerks upright, breaking off the kiss with no warning.

"We can't do this." I stare up at her, trapped between her powerful thighs. "It's a bad idea. We don't have time for..." She gestures between us, fingers splayed. "Whatever this is. Plus, there's the paper we're supposed to be writing. And let's not forget about the sole internship Mac's dangling over our heads."

It's a lot to unpack, so I start with the most obvious.

"Exactly. If anyone deserves a little stress relief, it's us." Being a student athlete carries a lot of pressure, which I'm usually good at managing. But this simmering attraction between us? That's something entirely new. "This doesn't have to be serious. We can keep it casual. Just between us. A way to take the edge off when things get to be too much."

She sucks her lower lip between her teeth, considering. "Just sex?"

"Just sex," I agree, stroking her thighs.

"Enemies with benefits." She flashes me a teasing smile. "I like the sound of that."

"You would." I flip her over again, this time pinning her small body beneath me, though I'm careful not to crush her.

"I'll bet you'd also like to be punished. Maybe I should give you a spanking while we're at it."

Interest flares in her eyes and I swear my dick gets even harder.

"Maybe next time. Maddie's home, so we have to keep it down." Her cobalt hair is fanned out around her like a halo, but she looks far from angelic as she arches a brow and asks, "Think you can manage that?"

Fuck, yeah.

"You know I like a challenge."

She grabs her phone from the nightstand and taps the screen a few times before placing the phone in a docking station.

Soft notes drift from the speaker as she looks up at me. "Just in case."

I lower my mouth to hers and whisper, "We're going to have to work on our trust issues."

This time, when I claim her, there's nothing soft or gentle about it. Our lips crash together and we're a tangle of arms and legs, her fingers tugging at my hair, my fingers tangled in hers as I settle between her thighs. She wraps her legs around my back, rolling her hips to get my cock right where she needs it, and I have to suppress the groan that works its way up my throat.

Keep it down, asshole.

If we get busted, this hookup will be over before it even gets started.

"These clothes have to go," she says, tugging on the hem of my shirt.

"I couldn't agree more." I yank it off and toss it on the floor so I can focus on the woman before me.

Sutton swallows, her throat bobbing delicately as she

brushes her fingertips over my abs. Her touch is featherlight, and it feels so fucking good, I hiss out a breath.

But this isn't about me. Tonight is about Sutton and what she needs.

I promised her a proper fucking and I'll be damned if I fail to deliver.

"Not so fast." I capture her wrist, holding it steady as she attempts to hook her fingers in the waistband of my sweatpants. "I want to take my time with you. Admire every inch of this incredible body."

"Then look. There's nothing stopping you."

No, no there is not.

I drop her wrist and slide her t-shirt up over her abdomen. Her skin is silky and smooth and I pepper kisses along her bare stomach, savoring the scent of jasmine that clings to every inch of her.

She slips her t-shirt off over her head, revealing a plain black bra, which she quickly adds to the growing pile of clothing on the floor.

Her breasts are small and firm and, like everything else about her, they're fucking perfect.

So perfect it takes me a moment to notice the tattoo on her ribs: *I am enough*.

The words are a sucker punch, a reminder that I once made her feel small and inadequate and that no matter how many times I apologize, I can't take that hurt away.

I reach out to touch the tattoo, but Sutton stops me.

"It wasn't any one thing," she says quietly. "It was a lot of things."

My blood heats, the knowledge searing my veins. It's bad enough that I hurt her, but knowing there have been others?

Fuck. It makes me want to throttle something—or someone.

Sutton curls a hand around my neck and pulls me close, pressing a deep kiss to my lips. One that says she doesn't want to dwell on the past. Not tonight, anyway.

That much, at least, I can give her.

I break off the kiss and lower my mouth to her left breast, flicking the dusky peak with my tongue before sucking it into my mouth and biting down.

Beneath me, Sutton whimpers.

I release her and she arches her back, silently encouraging me to do it again.

This time, when I take her in my mouth, I circle her nipple with my tongue, gently massaging the tender flesh.

She sighs and rakes her fingers through my hair, nails scraping my scalp as I make my way to her right breast, licking and sucking and memorizing the goddamn taste of her.

It may be fall in Pennsylvania, but she tastes like summer in the south and I can't get enough of it.

I kiss my way down the taut muscles of her abdomen and remove the spandex shorts separating my tongue from her sweet little pussy.

Sutton is laid out on the bed before me like a goddamn present, all hard angles and soft curves, and when she reaches between her legs and rubs her clit, I nearly lose my mind.

"*Fuuuck.*"

Forget the plaid skirt. This is the hottest thing I've ever seen.

I shove my pants down and free my cock, gripping the base with one hand as I use the other to rub pre-cum on my shaft. Sutton's eyes go dark and she licks her lips as I jack myself with long, steady strokes.

Tension coils at the base of my spine, tightening with each pass.

I've never jerked off with a woman before, but the sight of Sutton touching herself is the best kind of foreplay.

"You're killing me, Shorty." The words are a quiet rasp, and the only sign she hears me over the music is a wicked grin that practically dares me to join her on the bed.

"I'm killing you?" She laughs, the sound deep and throaty. "I'm the one who's been waiting two years for you to deliver a proper fucking."

The way she throws my own words back at me is the sweetest kind of torture. Both an invitation and a reminder.

I strip off my pants and tear through my backpack, searching for a condom.

Thank you, Scouts.

I'm shit at tying knots, but I'm always prepared.

"Still waiting," Sutton chides, opening her thighs to give me a better view of her glistening sex. "Should I just finish myself?"

I jerk upright, foil packet in hand. "I'd love to see you try."

She runs her fingers along the seam of her pussy and I watch, hard as fuck, as she dips two fingers inside herself.

Jesus Christ. Lightning races up my spine, every cell in my body screaming for release.

You're the dumbass who challenged her to finish herself.

I close my eyes and breathe deeply. I will not come like the chump she accused me of being. Because like every other interaction we've had, this is a power play.

A test to see who will come out on top.

"Eyes on me," Sutton orders, her words little more than breathless pants as she throws my own command back at me.

I level my gaze at her as I tear the condom open and roll it over my length.

No way am I going to stand by and watch as she brings herself to completion. I climb over the foot of the bed and crawl up the length of her body, propping myself up on one elbow. Then I grab her right hand and bring it to my mouth, silently daring her to watch as I suck her slick fingers one at a time.

The better to savor every drop.

"Sweeter than Paradise."

A slow smile unfurls on her lips and there's a wildness in her eyes I've never seen before. "Do you want another taste?"

Fuck, yeah, I do. There will never be a time I don't want to eat her pussy, but I haven't forgotten my other promise.

"That doesn't sound like begging."

"It was worth a shot." She looks up at me from under her lashes, amusement glinting in her dark eyes. "I guess I'll just have to settle for your cock."

"Trust me, Shorty. You won't be settling."

I position myself at her entrance and lower my mouth to hers, sucking her bottom lip and taking it between my teeth. She hisses out a breath and I sheath myself to the hilt in one swift motion.

Sutton moans and I swallow the sound with another kiss.

It's as much for my benefit as hers. She's hot and wet and ready and it's all I can do not to groan aloud when her tight channel grips my cock.

We move in unison, our hips slamming together as we make the climb. She meets every thrust, her fingers gripping my ass as she urges me faster and deeper. That we need to keep the volume to a minimum only adds to the excitement, and when Sutton bites her lip to keep those sexy little noises from escaping, I know she's close.

So close.

I want to hear her scream, just like she did at the church, but feeling her come apart under me—feeling her pussy clench me tight—is enough for tonight.

Her hands glide over my shoulders, her nails sinking into my flesh as she anchors herself and wraps her legs around my waist, taking me deeper and squeezing my cock with her inner muscles.

It's too much and not enough.

A total sensory overload. The tension at the base of my spine ratchets up and I swear to Christ I'm going to come.

The fuck you are.

There is no way I'm going to come before Sutton.

Not again.

Determined to stall the pleasure, I clench every muscle in my body. Sweat beads between my shoulder blades as I angle my hips, aiming for the spot that will give her the most intense orgasm. She moans, lips parted, and I slip a hand between our bodies, rubbing circles around her clit.

"Qué rico." The words are followed by a quiet whimper and her eyes roll back in her head.

Fuckin' right they do.

"That's it, Shorty. Come all over my cock like a good girl."

Sutton's breath hitches, her sounds of pleasure coming faster now.

More desperate.

I increase the pace, losing myself in her. In the moment. In a need so wild, I've never felt anything like it before today.

Sutton cries out, her pussy squeezing me tight, and I'm pulled right over the edge with her. I come hard, burying myself balls deep as fireworks explode at the base of my spine. Black spots dot my vision and pleasure sizzles along every nerve in my body as I lower my forehead to hers and we ride out the aftershocks together.

26

SUTTON

"You're going out?" Maddie asks from her favorite spot on the couch, dangling the remote control before me. "I thought we could catch up on our favorite fae lords."

"I wish." I drop my backpack on the floor and flop down on the other end of the couch to put on my shoes. "Parker and I are going to the library to work on our term paper for AMP."

Maddie frowns, a small crease forming between her brows. "On a Saturday night?"

"The football team has a bye week." I bend to tie my sneaker, which is helpful because then I don't have to look her in the eye as I fib. "His schedule is insane. This is the only chance we'll have to put in some quality face-to-face time."

It's not exactly a lie. The bye means we both have the weekend off—the only one we'll get before the season ends— and we're way behind on this paper. Which probably has more to do with the fact that we've been screwing like rabbits for the last three weeks than the fact that our schedules are hell.

The football team is 6-1 after a tough road loss to Nebraska. After Homecoming last week and a record number of Wildcat appearances, I'm freaking exhausted. I'd like nothing more than to lie on that couch and watch fae males strut around shirtless, but this paper won't write itself.

"You're never around." Maddie sighs and slouches down on the couch, propping her feet up on the coffee table. "I feel like I'm living alone half the time."

Acho. I really am a shitty roommate.

And because I'm sworn to secrecy about my Wildcat duties, I can't even explain my constant absence. Not without flimsy excuses, anyway.

"I'm sorry, Mads. This paper is kicking my ass." I slip my other sneaker on and sit up to face her. "Once it's done, I'll have more free time."

Wishful thinking, sis.

Between Wildcat appearances and gymnastics practices, I hardly remember the meaning of the words. It's almost a blessing that Mac's term paper is due before Thanksgiving because it'll be one less thing to worry about while studying for finals.

"I'm calling bullshit." Maddie crosses her arms. "This isn't about a term paper. You've been acting weird all semester."

She's right. I can't exactly deny it because I'm not such a pendeja that I'm going to gaslight my best friend.

"You've been ultra-secretive," she continues, clearly ready to unload everything she's been holding back for the last two months. "Constantly sneaking around and not coming home at night."

Qué revolú. How did the other mascot explain travel for away games? I can't exactly claim overnight study dates and it's not like I have a boyfriend, so I can't say I crashed at his place.

Unless....

I blurt the words out before I can think better of it. "Parker and I are hooking up."

Maddie's jaw drops.

Right there with you, chica.

It doesn't actually explain all my nights away, but I'm hoping Mads will be too distracted by the whole Parker thing to apply logic.

"I knew it!" she howls, eyes sparkling. "I freaking knew I heard sex noises the last time he was over. Plus, the tension between you two is..." She makes a show of fanning herself. "I swear, I get second-hand arousal every time you two are in the same room together."

"I'm going to pretend I didn't hear that." Otherwise, forget being in the same room with them ever again.

She smirks. "I never thought you'd actually admit it, though."

That makes two of us.

"So?" She scoots closer to me, despite the fact that she's speaking at like a million decibels. "How's the sex? I'm assuming he's leveled up since freshman year?"

My face heats and I swear to God, I'd rather visit the gynecologist than have this conversation.

"Would you keep your voice down? He's going to hear you through the wall."

Maddie snort-laughs. "You mean like how I heard the two of you going at it last week when you were supposed to be working on your paper?"

"I never should've told you," I grumble, though I'm glad the tension between us has broken. I hate all this secrecy and I can't wait for this Wildcat business to be over. Maybe I should've just told her about my punishment and been done with it, but I gave my word to Sharpe and I don't want to be the first person in 102 years to break the Wildcat's most honored tradition. "Anyway, it's not like we're a thing. We're just hooking up. For stress relief." I shoot her a warning look. "You can't tell anyone. Not even Brooke and Soraya."

Maddie mimes zipping her lips just as the doorbell rings.

"I mean it." I hop to my feet and grab my bag.

"Fine." She flops back on the couch. "But I expect details later."

I make a beeline for the front door, yank it open, and slip outside before Parker can invite himself in. Maddie will keep my secret, but if he goes inside, the temptation to crack jokes will be too strong to resist.

"Hey, Shorty." Parker slips an arm around my waist and grabs my ass, giving it a gentle squeeze. The number of times he's squeezed my ass in the last three weeks is beyond measure, and I still get a little thrill every time he does it. "It's getting chilly. Maybe we should skip the library and study here."

He leans down and buries his face in my hair before planting a hot, wet kiss on my throat.

"This is exactly why we're going to the library." I give him a playful shove. "Now cut it out before someone sees you."

Twenty minutes later, we're settled into a study room at the library, sitting side by side at a long table. We decided to go with Parker's suggestion to focus on the distribution challenges with OTT. We've both been researching the issues, so tonight's goal is to decide which key points we want to highlight in the paper. Once we have the outline, we can divvy up the work and get writing.

Finally.

I ignore the snarky voice in my head. If anyone is at fault for the delays, it's me. I'm the one who dragged my feet getting started. And I'm just as guilty as Parker for getting distracted by sex during our last two meetings.

Thus the library.

As if reading my mind, Parker says, "You know, we could always close the blinds and—"

"Seriously?" I ask, cutting him off. "We're in the library."

"Exactly." He wiggles his brows, a devilish grin transforming his handsome face. "We could get caught at any moment, so it would have to be quick and dirty and so fucking hot."

He's not wrong.

Desire stirs low in my belly, but I shut it down.

"So not happening. I'm not trading my library privileges for orgasms, no matter how good they are."

Parker chuckles, hazel eyes fixed on mine. When he speaks, it's in that sexy rasp that makes me want to ride his face all night long. "You can pretend the prospect of getting caught doesn't make you wet, but I know the truth." He strokes a finger down my arm and goosebumps pebble my skin. "I knew it the instant I licked your pussy. You get off on the risk."

It's true. Knowing we might get caught at any moment takes the sex to another level. It's why I wanted to keep our hookups quiet.

But I'll be damned if I'm going to admit it. Parker already has too much power over me. Just his touch is enough to make me light up like a freaking Christmas tree. If I start dripping through my leggings, I'll never hear the end of it.

"Technically,"—I flash my teeth—"I get off on your tongue. Or your cock. Or whichever body part is convenient at the time."

"Let me close the blinds and they can all be convenient."

Yes, please.

No, we need to focus. Work first, sex later.

I shove my laptop toward him. "Check this out. I found a

really great study on how fragmentation affects distribution. I meant to send it to you last night, but I fell asleep."

He turns the screen and his eyes go round.

The text is dense, so I get it, but it only took me a couple of minutes to read through it and I was practically a zombie.

"Talk about a mood killer." He shoves his fingers through his hair and clasps them behind his neck as he reads.

Ten minutes later, he's still going and I'm getting antsy because I have nothing to keep me occupied. I could listen to an audiobook, but that feels like a dick move since he's actually working.

"About done there?"

Parker's cheeks flush—something I've never seen outside of the bedroom—and he mutters, "Sorry. I'm a slow reader."

"No need to apologize." And then, because I feel like a Grade-A asshole, I add, "I'm shit at math."

He snorts, but keeps his gaze locked on the laptop before him. "I find that hard to believe."

"Why?" We've never shared a math class, so whatever his opinion is based on, it's not facts.

"Your entire sport is built on a point system." He scrolls down, still not meeting my eyes. "I'm just saying you don't have to diminish your capabilities because you feel bad for me. It's not a competition."

His words are clipped and carefully controlled. I'm not sure if it's embarrassment or anger, but I don't like it. We haven't bickered in weeks—a side-effect of all the orgasms—so where the hell is this coming from?

"I never said it was a competition." I cross my arms, turning his words over in my head. Maybe I should let it drop, but the accusation doesn't sit right. "Last time I checked, we're supposed to be a team."

"Exactly."

Dios mío. For a smart guy, he's being awfully dense.

"Teammates are supposed to lift each other up, not drag each other down."

He turns to me, shoulders rigid. "So now I'm dragging you down?"

"That's not—" I huff out a breath and a strand of my hair goes flying. "Don't twist my words. You know what I meant."

He makes a dismissive sound and I grab his biceps before he can dive back into the article.

"I'm not sure what's going on here, but as long as you write your half of the paper and do it well, we're good." I quirk a smile. "Though I could do without the defensive prick routine."

"Fair enough." Parker exhales and rolls his shoulders. "It's possible I overreacted."

I arch a brow.

"Okay, I definitely overreacted." He scrubs a hand over his face, looking anywhere but at me. "It's a sore subject."

"Want to talk about it?"

It's a stupid question. If he wanted to talk about it, he wouldn't have bitten my head off, right?

Wrong.

"I'm...dyslexic." He pauses, as if waiting for a reaction, but I've got nothing because I had no idea. "When I read something technical like this," he says, gesturing to the laptop, "I need to read it slowly, and often more than once, to make sure I've got the meaning right."

And, like a jerk, I'd been rushing him. "If I'd known—"

A muscle in his jaw tics. "Don't."

"Don't what?"

"I'm not looking for an apology. And I sure as shit don't want—or need—your pity." I nod, understanding taking shape. "I'm only telling you because we're working together and there might be occasions when I need a little extra time."

I open my mouth to tell him it's fine, then clamp it shut. He doesn't need my approval any more than he needs my pity. Everyone reads and learns at a different pace. It doesn't require acceptance; it just is.

So Parker's brain processes information differently. It doesn't change who he is. Doesn't change the fact that he's smart and funny and great at football. It's one aspect of him, not his entire identity. Anyone who feels differently can fuck right off.

"That must've been hard on you growing up," I say, choosing my words carefully.

"It was. Not only because I needed extra time with assignments, but because the accommodations made me a target."

My chest tightens at the word *target*. "What do you mean?"

"When I started school, before my parents realized my brain works differently, I got teased for being slow and struggling with things that came easily to my classmates, like reading." There's a hard edge to his voice when he continues. "By first grade I was falling behind and by second I'd been called stupid so many times I actually believed it."

Anger, red-hot and molten, fills my chest. "Kids can be vicious."

He nods in agreement. "It was so damn frustrating not being able to put the letters and sounds together like my classmates. I tried to hide it, but..." He snorts derisively. "Let's just say there was no hiding it when my second-grade teacher, Mr. Jonas, required us to take turns reading aloud."

The words "I'm sorry" are on the tip of my tongue, but I bite them back. The knowledge that Parker was bullied by callous children burns like acid in my gut, but this isn't about me or my outrage.

"That's when I was finally diagnosed and got the help I needed to succeed in school. Once we realized my brain processed information differently, the school put me on an Individualized Education Plan. My parents were great, but they didn't have any experience with dyslexia, so they scoured the web for tips and tricks. My mom tried everything from putting covered overlays in my books, which didn't do shit, to following the counselor's advice and signing me up for a sport to build confidence." Parker wipes his palms on his thighs, and it's clear that for all his blustering and swagger, he's still insecure about his dyslexia. The realization is like a splinter to the heart, a dull ache relentlessly working its way into the muscle. "Football was a natural fit, and I started making friends, but it didn't stop all the teasing." His eyes shutter, and for an instant, he loses himself in memory. "Tyler Fitzpatrick asked if my initials stood for Dumb Jock Parker and it stuck."

Mierda. No wonder he was so quick to assume I'd written him off as a brainless football player back in August. It may have been unintentional, but it's clear my careless words scraped at old wounds. Wounds no child should have to carry.

I frown. "Didn't your school have anti-bullying policies? Counselors? Zero-tolerance?"

"Yeah, but that stuff only helps so much." He scrubs a hand over his face. "The fact is, some people are born assholes and others are raised by assholes. No amount of anti-bullying rhetoric will change that fact."

"I suppose not." Social media is proof enough.

"That prick made my life hell until eighth grade, when I shot up six inches and decided I wasn't going to take his shit anymore."

"Good for you." I'm not usually a violent person, but in this case... "I hope you kicked his ableist ass."

"Nah." The right side of his mouth hitches up in a crooked grin. "Just the threat had him pissing his pants."

"So typical bully then." I roll my eyes. "I'll bet that pendejo peaked in high school."

"Probably." He shrugs. "I won't let people like him—or their opinions—hold me back. I've got the tools to be successful now, and I've worked my ass off to maintain a 3.3 GPA."

Curiosity unfurls in my chest. "What kinds of tools?"

"When I'm alone, or somewhere I can use my earbuds, I use text-to-speech software. It helps to have the words spoken aloud while I read them. It's better for retention and makes it easier to process the information."

"Wait. You use text-to-speech for your schoolwork, but you aren't into audiobooks?"

His crooked smile becomes a full-on smirk. "TTS has come a long way, but listening to textbooks is nothing like listening to your pornalicious smut."

I narrow my eyes at him. "You say smut like it's a bad thing."

He throws his hands up. "No judgment here. I like my women empowered."

Now it's my turn to smirk. "If that's true, then you know they aren't your women," I tease, making air quotes around the last two words. "You can't actually possess another person."

"Keep telling yourself that, Shorty." He levels those gorgeous eyes at me and heat pools between my legs.

Okay, fine. Maybe he can possess parts of me.

But we are at the library and we are not going to talk about

—let alone have—sex, because that's where this conversation will lead if I don't redirect it.

"Seriously, though. Have you ever tried audiobooks?"

"I gave it a shot when I was a kid, but the selection was shit. So when everyone else was reading Percy Jackson and The Hobbit, I was devouring the movies." Parker drums his fingers on the table, a nervous habit I noticed during our last meeting. "For obvious reasons, pleasure reading isn't a hobby."

"The world of audio has transformed in the last five years." I don't want to push, but there's interest in his eyes when he jokes about my romance books, and something tells me it's more than just the explicit content that intrigues him. "You should give it another try. It's not like listening to a textbook. These days you can find fantasy or whatever else revs your motor in audio."

"Including smut."

"Yes, Parker. Including smut." I laugh in spite of myself. *So much for enemies with benefits.* Over the last couple of weeks, I've begun to count Parker as a friend. "Which reminds me, what do your initials actually stand for?"

"Aww. Is this your way of telling me you want to scream my name the next time we're in bed? Because I can make that happen."

"For the love, do you ever think about anything but sex?"

"Not when it comes to you." He reaches under the table and his fingers slide up my thigh.

"I'm not sure if I should be flattered or insulted right now."

"Flattered," he rasps, pulling me in for a kiss. "I can't stop thinking about you."

A thrill races up my spine, images of Parker fucking me in the stacks filling every dark corner of my mind.

Stay strong, chica.

I turn my head, dodging his lips. "And yet I don't even know your first name."

"Devin Jeremiah." He skims his thumb over my cheekbone. "Now can I kiss you?"

"Devin." It rolls right off the tongue. *Just like your screams when he's going down on you.* "Does anyone call you by that name?"

"Only when I'm in trouble."

"I'll keep that in mind." A flash him a sassy smile. "Now let's get back to work, Devin."

27

DJ

"DAMN, SHORTY." My blue balls and I flop back in the chair. "That's stone cold."

"Work first, sex later." Sutton jabs a finger in my direction. "And don't think for a minute that I'm going to let you off the hook for your half of the paper."

Heat prickles along my skin, but it's not embarrassment or desire. It's something like gratitude. Despite learning about my dyslexia, Sutton won't take it easy on me. She's going to hold me to the same high standard I've come to expect, and she won't stop giving me shit out of some misplaced sense of pity.

Thank fuck.

I hated it in high school when teachers would give me unnecessary accommodations or when my partners for group projects would bend over backward to ensure I had the lightest workload. Or worse, offer to do the project entirely because they were afraid I'd tank their grades.

Dumb jock, my left nut.

I exhale and shove the memories down, putting them in a

box where the passive aggressive slights and childhood bullying can't chip away at my confidence.

"Thanks for not making a big deal about it." I slide Sutton's laptop across the table, returning it to her.

"It's not a big deal." She shrugs. "We all have our stuff. No one escapes childhood trauma free."

"Now that's a hot take if I ever heard one."

"Hardly." She pulls a face and tucks a strand of cobalt hair behind her ear. "Whether you realize it or not, everyone you know is dealing with shit. According to Soraya, it's part of the human condition."

"And she's an expert on the subject?"

"She's the smartest person I know. Plus, she's a psych major."

I nod. Not because I agree we're all damaged, but because that's not a path I want to walk. Not today, anyway.

"What about you?" I narrow my eyes, studying her as I consider the words inked on her ribs. *I am enough.* "What's the story behind the tattoo?"

Sutton stiffens. "Kind of a personal question, don't you think?"

"I showed you mine." I smirk, striving for levity, though this conversation is far from light. "It's only fair."

"I didn't realize we were bartering our childhood trauma." She rolls her eyes. "Besides, it's not a big deal. Not compared to..."

The implication raises my hackles, the muscles in my shoulders bunching on instinct. "Like you said, it's not a competition."

That she would dismiss her own struggles in light of mine is a bitter pill to swallow.

"You're right. I'm sorry." She tips her head back, exposing the long line of her neck as she stares at the ceiling, hair falling over her shoulders in soft waves. "I'm just not used to talking about me."

That, at least, I understand.

Introspection is uncomfortable as hell, and it can't be rushed, so I don't push.

When she finally speaks, her voice is soft, almost defeated. The urge to scoop her up in my arms is nearly impossible to resist. "This might come as a shock, but I was an energetic kid. Always climbing and jumping and basically exhausting my mother, who worked full time and also had a toddler, my sister Gabby, to care for."

I chuckle, imagining a smaller Sutton tearing around the living room like a hellion.

Feels right.

"When I started kindergarten, Mamá enrolled me in an after-school gymnastics program, hoping it would wear me out before I came home. From the very first lesson, I knew it was my sport." A sad smile curves her lips as she continues. "I loved being at the gym and by the time I turned six, I'd been invited to join the competition team. By the time I turned seven, we were spending so much time at the gym that Mamá signed Gabby up for lessons, too. Gabby wasn't interested at first. She'd cry every time she had to put on a leotard. But once it became apparent she was a natural, she took to the sport like a fish to water, determined to outshine everyone around her."

Sutton pauses and though I can see the direction we're headed, the final destination remains just out of reach.

"Anyway, eventually, I qualified for elite gymnastics, and in time, Gabby did too, her skill surpassing my own."

That couldn't have been easy. As an only child, I never had to deal with sibling rivalry, but to share something so important and also be competitors? That had to be hard on their relationship.

"Gymnastics is an expensive sport," she says, still staring at the ceiling, as if afraid to meet my eyes, afraid of what I might see in those dark depths. "My parents supported both of us, but it was clear Gabby had a better shot at the Olympics and the endorsement deals and all the financial support that came with it, so that's where my parents funneled their efforts."

Fuck.

Just the thought of not having my parents behind me one hundred percent is...unimaginable.

"Gabby came first. Her training schedule. Her choreography. Her freaking competition leo." Sutton sighs, chest heaving as if to dispel the negativity. "It got to be...a lot. Always feeling like I was standing in her shadow, always competing with her and coming up short, both in the gym and at home."

No doubt. Playing second string in your own family? That shit would definitely leave a mark.

"I'm sorry you had to deal with that." I take her hand in mine. It's small and warm and though I've never thought of Sutton as delicate, her grip feels fragile in this moment. "No one should be made to feel less than, especially in their own family."

It's hard to imagine Sutton letting anyone overshadow her. The woman I know is bold and unapologetic. She takes what she wants, and she gives as good as she gets. The idea of her being cowed by anything is just...not possible.

Yet here she is, freely admitting it.

"It's not Gabby's fault." She turns to me, meeting my eyes for the first time since we started down this road. "Gabby loves the sport as much as I do. I can't exactly blame her for realizing her full potential."

Maybe not, but she sure as shit can hold her parents accountable for playing favorites and, come on, surely Gabby could see the impact their favoritism was having on her sister?

Unloading on her family won't help.

"You're an elite gymnast." I don't know the odds of reaching that level, but I know it's a long shot for anyone. "That's pretty fucking impressive in its own right."

"It is, but like I said, we all have our own stuff to deal with." She squeezes my fingers, the corner of her mouth twitching. "Which is probably why I internalized your blow off freshman year instead of accepting that you were a playboy douche and moving on."

I shake my head. "Such a smartass."

"You like it." She sticks her tongue out and yeah, I really do. "Anyway, college gymnastics is a better fit for me, so maybe things worked out for the best. I love being on a team and working together toward our shared goals instead of feeling like we're constantly being pitted against one another." She tosses her hair over her shoulder. "Plus, after I land Mac's internship, I've got a bright future in sports broadcasting."

"You really can't help yourself, can you?" I drag her chair closer and draw her in for a kiss, finding her mouth hot and ready.

Like maybe she's also thinking about all the orgasms I could give her in this private room.

Sutton angles her head and I deepen the kiss, my tongue gliding along hers in steady, teasing strokes as I lose myself in the now familiar taste of strawberry lip gloss. Still, it's not enough.

Not even close.

I need more. Need to feel the warmth of her body against mine. To feel her soft curves and muscular thighs. I hook my hands under her ass and pull her onto my lap. She melts against me, breasts pressed to my chest as she slides her hands under my t-shirt, nails raking over my abs and sending a shiver of desire straight to my balls.

Much better.

She rolls her hips and my cock stiffens, ready for action.

It doesn't get any better than this.

A phone buzzes on the table and Sutton freezes.

"Ignore it," I say, breathing the words onto her lips.

Whoever it is can wait.

"It might be important."

"As important as the orgasm I'm going to give you on this table?"

She hesitates, then grabs her phone. "It'll just take a second."

The fuck? I'm going to need to step up my game.

"Dios mío." Sutton's eyes go round. "Brooke just got another NIL offer."

"As in, she's got more than one?"

"United G contacted her a few weeks ago about endorsing their leotards, but they're still working out the details. I guess Pinnacle is interested now, too."

Damn. It must be nice to be in such high demand. "Good for her."

"No kidding." She taps out a quick reply on her phone before sliding it back onto the table. "Brooke's worked her ass off to get an NIL deal. Building a massive online following is a lot of work for an athlete who's not in a high-profile sport like football."

"I wouldn't know."

Her brows shoot up. "None of your roommates have deals?"

The look of disbelief on her face is adorable. "Reid's too focused on the game to worry about that shit, and he'll make millions on his first NFL contract. Cooper's dad is a politician, and he hates being in the public eye, so I don't think he'd be too keen on becoming a spokesperson or whatever."

"What about you?"

"I'd take an NIL deal in a heartbeat." I massage her thighs, thumbs working small circles into the tense muscles. "I've spent my last three summers on construction sites. It's hard, strenuous work. If someone offered me an easier option, I'd gladly accept, but I'm not big enough in the sport."

She ducks her head. "Sorry. I didn't—"

"It's fine." I don't envy my roommates their talents or their choices. "Football got me to Waverly and it'll help me break into sports broadcasting, where I've always wanted to go."

Sutton's eyes shutter and I know we're both thinking about the Sports Stream internship—and the fact that only one of us can get it.

Anxiety squeezes my chest like a vise.

You've always known how it would end.

True, but it was easier to ignore the facts when they were a distant reality. When we were more likely to set each other on fire literally instead of figuratively. But somewhere along the way we became friends, and even though I'm not about to walk away from the internship—from my future—the prospect of disappointing her, of taking something she wants as badly as I do, hurts like a motherfucker.

It's only October.

Right. The intern won't be chosen until December. Besides, there's no guarantee either of us will even get it.

So I do what I do best, squashing all thoughts of the future and sealing them in a box with all the other shit I'm not ready to deal with. Then I crush my lips to Sutton's and lose myself in her warm embrace.

28

———

DJ

"Don't be an asshole."

Coop snorts. "You knew what you were getting into when you hit me up for a ride."

"Trust me, if I'd had any other option, I'd have taken it." But Reid's got shit to do before we leave for Indiana in a few hours and I'm in a time crunch, so public transport was out.

Could've gotten an Uber.

If only I'd thought of that before recruiting Coop for this little adventure.

"It's all good." He snickers and swings the Audi into the Extreme Pleasures parking lot. "I don't mind being a last resort. Especially when it means I get to visit a sex shop."

One look at his shit-eating grin, and I know I'm going to regret bringing him along.

He throws the car in park and I climb out, surveying the empty lot. Thankfully, there's only one other vehicle. The last thing I need is to run into someone I know at a sex shop.

Talk about awkward.

Coop climbs out of the car, practically vibrating with excitement.

Maybe having him as my wingman will prove useful after all. Given his reputation, anyone who knows us would probably assume he's the one doing the shopping. God knows I don't have a clue what I'm doing.

A gust of wind whips at my hair, sending dead leaves tumbling across the blacktop. It's the first weekend in November and a cold front has descended on College Park, bringing gray skies and shorter days, but we haven't seen snow yet, so I can hardly complain.

"What are we shopping for, anyway?" Coop asks, giving the store a once-over. Extreme Pleasures is a squat red brick building with large display windows swathed in flowing white fabric and a discreet sign. "Please tell me we're getting you a fleshlight."

I shoot him the side-eye. "What the fuck is a fleshlight?"

"Ah, Padawan. Much to learn, you still have."

"Dude. If the women on campus had any idea you were such a closet geek, the pussy parade would dry up faster than the Mojave."

He smirks. "Then it's a good thing I know how to keep it on the down low."

Ignoring him, I open the door to the shop, setting off a melodic chime.

If the outside of the shop is discreet, then the inside is definitely...not. The ivory walls and glass top tables are overflowing with sexual paraphernalia, from crotchless panties and colorful vibrators to collars and blindfolds.

"Holy shit." Coop makes a show of scanning the store. "There are dildos as far as the eye can see."

"Welcome to Extreme Pleasures." The greeting comes from our left and I turn to find a tall blonde in a barely-there leather skirt. There's a whip in her hand and she runs her fingers lovingly down its length before placing it on a hook jutting out from the wall. "What can I help you find today?"

"Uh..." I don't have a clue what I'm looking for. Hell, aside from the Bunny of Love, I don't even know what's in Sutton's pleasure chest.

As if reading my mind, Coop snorts and the saleswoman turns her attention to him, a coy smile transforming her pouty lips.

"Hey, Cooper."

He straightens, his laughter dissipating. "Hey."

"I'll let you guys have a look around. Just give me a holler if you need anything."

Is it my imagination or is she making sex eyes at my roommate? I shouldn't be surprised. It's impossible to go anywhere in this town without running into one of his conquests.

The saleswoman winks and returns to unpacking the box at her feet.

"Do you know her?" I ask quietly.

Coop shrugs. "Maybe."

"For fuck's sake, have you really slept with so many women you can't remember them all?"

"It could be worse." He slings an arm around my shoulders. "I could have a drinking problem."

I shrug him off and approach a display table with twenty cocks—give or take—displayed on it. There are a variety of shapes and colors, some big, some small, but damn. How are you even supposed to choose?

Coop joins me and picks up a blue dildo that looks like a fucking tentacle with nobs and ridges all over it. "You know what they say." He smirks and waves the dildo in my face because he's a twelve-year-old, trapped in a twenty-one-year-old body. "Variety is the spice of life, baby."

"I'll remember that when your birthday rolls around." I swat the tentacle away. "Would you quick fucking around? You're going to get us kicked out."

He heaves a long-suffering sigh. "Relax, Mom. We aren't going to get kicked out."

"Only because you banged the saleswoman."

"We don't know that for certain." He puts the dildo back on the table with an appreciative grin. "So what are we shopping for?"

"No clue." I don't have the first idea what would make a suitable gift for Sutton, but after listening to a few of her audiobooks—which are proving quite informative—I'm determined to spice things up in the bedroom.

Can't have her getting bored when things are going so well.

Or worse, finding a new hookup while I'm away.

Just the thought of another man touching her has my pulse thrumming.

"At least tell me who the lucky lady is." Coop rubs his palms together like an old school movie villain. "The suspense is killing me."

"Then you'd better start working on your epitaph, because there's no way I'm answering that question." I shoot him a bland look. "No offense, but I don't need my business getting around the locker room."

"Dude." He plants his hands on his hips, feigning indignation. "Give me some credit. I know how to keep a fucking secret."

True, but... Tension gathers between my shoulder blades. There's no way I'm getting out of this store without evading dozens of prying questions.

So handle your business.

I pick up a silver rod labeled urethral sound and quickly

return it to the display. No way am I shoving a metal rod into my dick. I'm not looking for that much adventure.

"If you don't know what you're looking for," Coop asks, eyeing a sex swing, "how the hell do you expect to find it?"

"I'll know it when I see it."

I hope.

We move through the store, checking out the displays, and I do my best to drown out my roommate's running commentary. We've only scoped out half the store, but he's managed to educate me on fleshlights and done his best to convince me I might need a cock ring.

"Check this out." Coop holds up a box of peach gummy panties. "You can eat your friend *and* her underwear."

"That's it." I point to the door. "Out."

"I see how it is. You're just using me for a ride." He places the panties back on the shelf. "Do I at least get to peek in the bag when you're done?"

That's a big fuck no.

"Not a chance."

"This is bullshit," he mutters, wheeling toward the door. "I'm completely in my element and you're wasting my talent."

Once he steps outside, I'm actually able to focus.

Sutton likes her books spicy, but there's no hardcore kink. Just passionate sex and lots of dirty talk, so... So what? I'm still clueless.

Should've done more research, asshole.

Problem is, once I got through a couple of romance novels, I decided to give fantasy a shot. Sutton was right. Audiobooks have come a long way since I was a kid. The voice actors are incredible, and it's like I can see the story unfold in my head as I listen. I never thought I could be a reader, but I'm halfway through The Witcher series. It's a nice change of pace from listening to music or watching videos during downtime. One I wouldn't have explored without Sutton's encouragement.

"How are you making out?" The saleswoman appears at my side with a toothy grin. "Are you sure there's nothing I can help you with?" She gestures around the store and I subtly wipe my palms on my jeans. "It can be a little overwhelming your first time."

My cheeks heat, but she pretends not to notice.

"If you give me an idea of what you're looking for, I can point you in the right direction."

Fuck. This is so awkward. Never in a million years did I think I'd be talking to a stranger—no, a fellow Waverly student—about sex toys, but here we are.

"I, uh, wanted to get something for my friend. A gift."

The words come out in a rush and I'm not even sure they're intelligible, but she nods, her smile growing wider.

"What's your friend into? Toys, role playing, BDSM?"

"She has one of those vibrators with a rabbit on it." I hold up two fingers like a peace sign and wiggle them to emphasize my point, because apparently, I'm also a twelve-year-old in a twenty-one-year-old body. Which probably explains the fact that my entire face is on fire now. "I wanted to get her something else. For while I'm a way."

"I have just the thing." She crooks a finger and gestures for me to follow. "If she likes vibrators, she'll love the Rosebud."

Rosebud?

She stops halfway down the aisle and picks up a small box with a picture of a silicone rose on the front.

"The Rosebud is our most popular clitoral stimulator." She hands me the package. "It has seven sucking modes and seven vibrating modes for her pleasure. Plus, it's small, discreet, and packs a big O."

I say nothing—because I am in no way prepared to discuss

clitoral stimulation with a stranger—and she continues the sales pitch. The way she lists the product features, we could just as easily be talking about running shoes.

No wonder this place had so many five-star reviews.

I've always thought of adult stores as seedy, rundown shops with creepy employees, but Extreme Pleasures is clean and bright and the staff is clearly knowledgeable.

"I'll take it."

Thirty minutes later, I ring Sutton's doorbell, bag in hand.

She answers the door looking flustered, hair pulled back in a messy ponytail. "Aren't you supposed to be on your way to Indiana?"

Yup. And if I'm late catching the bus to the airport, Coach will have my ass.

"Look at you memorizing my schedule." I attempt to pull her in for a kiss, but she twists out of reach. "If I didn't know better, I'd say you were going to miss me while I'm away."

"Just certain parts." A taunting smile transforms her luscious mouth. "BOB is great, but he doesn't do oral."

Thank Christ. I love eating Sutton's pussy. Just the thought of it has my cock stirring.

No time.

"I got you something." I dangle the discreet white bag from my fingertip and her brows shoot up. "To keep you company while I'm away."

Sutton narrows her eyes in suspicion, but takes the bag, immediately glancing inside. She gasps. "You didn't."

"Oh, I did."

The laughter that spills from her lips is high and bright. Music to my fucking ears.

"This thing was in my social feed a few weeks ago. According to the reviews, it gives such powerful orgasms, you'll never need a man again."

"Bullshit." I snort. "No silicone toy will ever make you come as hard as I do."

She leans against the doorjamb, crossing her arms. "Don't be so sure about that, Devin."

A thrill races up my spine. I fucking love the way she says my name, and I'll do whatever it takes to hear it again.

"Tell you what, Shorty." I slip an arm around her waist and pull her close, not giving her a chance to evade me this time. "I'll call you tonight and we can test that theory together."

Her breath hitches and she presses a soft kiss to my lips. "It's a date."

29

SUTTON

I'M NOT sure what it says about my life that I'm holed up in a hotel room, channel surfing and bored out of my mind as I wait for my— My what? Sex buddy? Frenemy with benefits? Whatever. It doesn't matter. Parker and I don't need a label. We're casual.

Keep telling yourself that, sis.

Ignoring the snarky voice in my head, I flip through the channels again. Since the identity of the mascot is top secret, I'm basically sequestered to my room during away games. Normally, I don't mind. But tonight?

It's freaking torture.

Anticipation coils low in my belly and I glance at my phone again, double checking to make sure I don't have any missed calls.

So much for playing it cool.

What I need is a distraction. Unfortunately, cable tv isn't it. I could try Netflix, but my laptop is all the way across the room and I'm too comfortable to get up.

Liar.

Okay, fine. It's after nine and Parker will be calling soon.

My gaze slides to the silicone rose on the nightstand. It's a vibrant shade of red, adorable, and according to the web, all but guaranteed to deliver an out-of-body experience. So yeah, I'm curious.

You could try it out solo.

It's tempting. Just the thought of it has my pussy dancing the cha-cha.

But a promise is a promise, and we agreed to test it out together.

I pick up the toy, holding it in the palm of my hand. When Parker showed up at my door earlier, I'd panicked. I'd been trying to cram the last of my stuff into an overnight bag for the Indiana trip and he was the last person I expected to see before departure, but the fact that he'd bought me a gift was even more surprising.

Is that something friends with benefits do?

Am I supposed to get him something now?

No. That would probably be weird.

Then again, what's a pair of handcuffs between friends?

Goosebumps pebble my skin at the thought of restraining my big, sexy FWB. Of seeing sweat bead along his brow and watching as his taut, sinewy muscles strain for release beneath me. He'd be completely at my mercy, the same way I'm at his when he's—

My phone pings with an incoming text, and I drop the vibrator on the bed, scrambling to see who the message is from.

Please don't be Parker cancelling.

With my luck, his roommate is probably in for the night.

The guys are supposed to rest up before a game, but it's inevitable that some of them find their way down to the bar for a beer. Something I learned during my first away game when I nearly got caught sneaking down to the lobby for a bottle of water in my pajamas.

Mamá: You'll never believe what just happened!

The message is on a group chat with my dad and me. Before I can guess at the big news, another message pops up, which is so on brand I can't help but smile.

Mamá: Gabby's been invited to the National Team training camp in January!

My chest tightens as I re-read the message, pride and disappointment wrapping themselves around my heart like a pair of gymnastics grips. I'm thrilled for my baby sister, but I can't deny there's a tinge of disappointment as well. Disappointment she still has a shot of reaching goals I never will. Of realizing a dream that slipped through my grasp and making our parents proud.

It's a bittersweet feeling.

One that comes with a crap ton of guilt.

Me: That's amazing! She must be freaking out.

That's one explanation for why she didn't tell me herself.

Papá: We're so proud of her. This could be her big break! First the National Team, then the Olympics!

And there it is... Like I need a reminder Gabby is the shining star of the family.

Mamá: Make sure you send your congratulations.

I will—of course I will—but I'm sure she's getting plenty of props at the gym.

Papá: We're proud of both of you, corazón de melón.

Nice save, Dad. Throwing in my childhood nickname—melon heart—is also a nice touch.

Mamá: The camp is the third week of January, so we'll have to miss the Rutgers meet, but I told Gabby you'd understand.

Oh, I understand. Gabby's sport comes first—like always.

Way to be a jealous pendeja, Cruz.

Frustration claws at the back of my throat. I hate feeling this way. Hate feeling this messed up combination of love and jealousy. Just once, it would be nice if my parents put *me* first.

Amor y celos, hermanos gemelos.

How many times have I heard my abuela say love and jealousy are twin siblings? Too many to count. But I can't think about that right now, so I tap out a quick reply.

Me: It's fine. I'm sure someone else can use the tickets.

Tickets I've already purchased because Rutgers was the one and only meet my parents agreed to attend this year.

It's not a big deal.

But it sure as hell feels like one right now.

Me: I hate to cut this short, but I've got a big day tomorrow, and I was just about to crash when you messaged.

It's only a partial fib, and since it's a text, my parents are none the wiser. They respond with the usual kissy face emojis and I flop back on the pillows, phone resting on my stomach as I stare up at the ivory ceiling.

Something's got to give.

Maybe, but now isn't the time. Gabby's going to train with the National Team and I don't want to say or do anything that will diminish the experience for her. She's worked hard, and she deserves this opportunity. Not to mention the excitement that comes with it.

I just wish my parents could muster the same level of enthusiasm for my gymnastics career. The Big Ten Football Championship might not be the Olympics, but it's a big freaking deal to me.

My phone rings and I snatch it up, glancing at the screen before swiping accept.

"I was just about to give up on you."

Parker laughs, the quiet rumble soothing the ache in my

chest. "It took a little convincing to get Vaughn out of the room."

"I figured it was something like that."

"Try not to sound too excited." There's a brief pause. "Did I catch you at a bad time?"

"No." At least, I don't want it to be a bad time, even if my mood is crap. "It's nothing like that."

"Then what is it?"

I bite my lip, hesitating. The last thing I want to do is rehash the discussion, but I need to get this toxic mess out of my head.

"I was talking to my parents. It was..." I sigh. "Honestly? It was so typical I don't even know why I'm upset."

We're both quiet for a long moment and for the first time, I wish I could crawl inside his head and read his thoughts.

Which isn't creepy at all.

"Talk to me, Shorty." There's genuine concern in his voice and it all but melts my resolve. "Whatever it is, you can trust me."

My pulse accelerates as the weight of his words settles in my bones. Two and a half months ago, I wouldn't have trusted Parker with a class assignment, let alone my deepest feelings —feelings I haven't even shared with Maddie—but that can of beans was spilled weeks ago. I scrub a hand over my face and exhale, clearing my mind. Parker already knows about my rocky relationship with my parents. There's no point holding back now.

"My sister was invited to train with the National Team in January." The instant the words are out of my mouth, I want to suck them back in. To put a stop to whatever is happening between Parker and me. We're already in too deep, sharing secrets and exchanging gifts. I'm no expert, but even I can see we're riding the line between friends with benefits and—

Nada.

It's what we agreed to. No catching feelings.

"And?" he prompts gently.

"They texted to share the good news and say how proud they are of her. Which I get, I really do. But then they said training camp conflicts with my home competition schedule and they're bailing on the Rutgers meet." I pick at a loose thread on my t-shirt. "It wouldn't be a big deal except it's the only meet they could attend." There's a sound of disgust on the other end of the line, and my guilt increases tenfold. "Sorry. I didn't mean— I'm probably being sensitive. Getting upset about nothing."

"It's not nothing. You're entitled to your feelings, Sutton." That he doesn't call me Shorty tells me just how passionately he feels about the subject. "Your parents made a promise, and yes, this is a huge accomplishment for your sister, but that doesn't minimize your achievements. At the very least, they could've offered to come see you compete a different week instead of canceling altogether."

"I know, but—"

"No buts." He huffs out a breath. "They're your parents. They should have enough pride and joy to go around. It's literally in their job description."

He's right. I know it down to my toenails, which are currently painted a shade of blue called Midnight Kiss—*Go Wildcats!*—so why am I defending our screwed-up family dynamic?

Because you're too much of a coward to face it head-on.

Coño. I hate it when my subconscious is smarter and more evolved than I am.

"No one deserves to be treated like an afterthought. Especially you."

"Especially me?" More like, even me.

"A smart, strong, talented woman with independence for days."

I laugh in spite of myself. "I seem to recall you weren't such a fan of my independence when we first met."

"Let's just say I've seen the error of my ways."

"Have you now?" I scoop up the rose vibrator from where I dropped it on the bed. "Took you long enough."

That earns me another quiet laugh. "You can't rush perfection."

"Did you just deem yourself perfect?" I arch a brow, though he can't see it. "Someone's getting cocky."

"Speaking of cocks..."

A giant grin splits my face. "Real smooth, Parker."

"I try." He pauses and my core tightens, the tension between us blazing like wildfire. "Tell me what you're wearing, Shorty."

Mierda. We're really doing this.

I glance down at my Wildcat tee and gym shorts. So not sexy.

"I'm wearing a black lace thong and matching bra."

That, at least, is true.

He growls appreciatively and I shimmy out of my shorts.

"Are you in bed?"

"Yes."

"Damn." There's a hungry edge to his voice and when he speaks again, the words are barely a rasp. "I wish I could be there to see you laid out before me like a goddamn offering. All that silky skin just waiting for my mouth."

Arousal pools between my legs. "What would you do with that filthy mouth of yours?"

As if I don't already know.

"You know exactly what I'd do. I'd lick every inch of your gorgeous body, starting with the sliver of skin just behind your ear. It's so fucking sensitive you'd arch beneath me on contact, your breasts pressed to my bare chest, our hot flesh sealed together just the way we like it." *Yes.* My pulse quickens, my breaths coming faster with each delicious scene he paints. "My mouth is watering just thinking about it."

Mine, too. I switch the phone to speaker and lay it on the nightstand.

"Then I'd work my way down to your breasts, licking and sucking those perfect tits until I took your nipple between my teeth, biting down so hard you'd see stars. Christ, I love the feel of your body beneath me. Love parting those powerful thighs to admire your pussy." He exhales, and, from the sound of it, he's fighting for control as I spread my legs and slide my hand down the front of my panties. "Are you wet, Shorty?"

"So wet." I drag a finger up my center and slowly circle my clit, a quiet sigh escaping as I give myself over to the sensation.

"That's right. I want to hear you." The line goes silent except for the slow metallic drag of a zipper. "Don't you dare hold back. I want every moan. Every whimper. Every gasp of pleasure."

"They're all for you, Devin." I couldn't hold back, even if I wanted to.

"Fuckin' right they are." My core clenches at the fierce, possessive tone. "Are you touching yourself? Imagining my tongue working your clit? Thinking about how good it would feel to have my cock buried inside you?"

"Yes."

"That's because no one makes you come like I do. No one knows the rhythm of your body the way I do. Like a goddamn symphony for my ears alone."

There's no point protesting. We both know it's true.

But...

"Are you sure about that?" I circle my clit again, every

muscle in my body going taut as I imagine Parker's thick digits wrapped around his cock. "I've got my new friend Rose here with me."

"Yeah?" The quiet slap of flesh echoes down the line as he jacks himself. "Should we invite her to the party?"

Abso-freaking-lutely.

"The more, the merrier." I switch the Rosebud on, setting it close to the phone so he can hear the quiet hum as I wriggle out of my thong.

"*Fuuuck.* I wish you were here."

Tenderness warms my chest, but it's quickly consumed by a tide of molten desire, the knowledge that Parker is somewhere in this hotel, stroking his cock, heightening my arousal.

"Mmm." I grab the Rosebud and drag it across my stomach, relishing the gentle vibrations. "So good. I'm not sure if I should start with my nipple or—"

"Spread your legs like a good girl." My thighs part instantly. "I want that Rosebud on your pussy," he rasps. "It'll be like I'm right there with you, sucking your clit until you scream."

I press the Rosebud to my clit and *Dios mío.*

A strangled cry escapes my throat. The onslaught of sensation—a combination of sucking and blowing—is almost too much to bear. Devin makes noises of encouragement, but I barely register them. Pleasure radiates through every nerve in my body, the tension between my legs coiling tighter and tighter as I race toward climax at light speed.

"Qué rico."

"That's right." Parker's breath hitches and it's possible he's holding out, waiting for me. I don't know. I can't think past the intensity building between my legs, the promise of an explosive orgasm hovering at my fingertips. "Come for me, Shorty."

With the palm of my hand, I rock the vibrator against my clit, losing myself in the fantasy as I spiral toward oblivion.

"I'm going to—"

White light explodes behind my eyelids and I cry out, pleasure ripping through my body like an avenging angel. It's unlike anything I've ever experienced. Every nerve in my body sings and my back bows off the bed, the sheer intensity of the orgasm threatening to split me in two as a warm liquid dampens my thighs and sheets.

"Fuck, yes," Devin roars, riding out his own climax on the other end of the line. A beat passes before he announces, "We're going to have to do this again."

"Yeah, we are." I scoot up in the bed, examining the wet spot on the sheets. "No pressure, but I think Rose just made me squirt."

He's silent so long, I check to make sure I haven't dropped the call. "Devin?"

"Shit." He chuckles and heat prickles along my exposed skin. "I never thought I'd actually be competing with a toy."

"Don't sell yourself short. The phone sex was A+ work." I grab my cell off the nightstand and switch it back to talk mode, bringing it to my ear as I curl up against the pillows. "Do you do this a lot?"

"Phone sex? No." He snorts. "Is that what you heard on campus?"

"No." I pause, pulling the sheet over my body. "You just seemed...very comfortable with the whole thing."

"That's because I've been listening to your pornalicious audiobooks."

"Really?" I grin, doing my best to suppress a laugh. "Well,

good news then. If you don't make it as a sports commentator, you can always try your hand at narrating audiobooks."

"Let me guess. You volunteer as tribute to help me practice?"

"You know what they say. Practice makes perfect."

30

SUTTON

"Come on, Shorty. I'm dying here." Parker's hands settle on my shoulders and he squeezes gently, his long fingers soothing my tired muscles. It's Sunday night and we're holed up in my room, putting the finishing touches on our AMP paper. "We'll be quick. Then we can get right back to work distraction free."

I grin, but keep my attention fixed on the laptop before me. "Last time I checked, sex was a major distraction."

"Exactly." He leans down and his breath is hot against my ear as he whispers, "Once I lick your pussy, I'll be way more focused."

My core clenches and I press my thighs together beneath the desk. "You're insatiable."

"What can I say?" He nips my ear and I lean into it, the scrape of his teeth doing unholy things to my body. "You have that effect on me."

"The feeling's mutual." But someone has to be the responsible adult here and clearly it's not going to be Parker. Not tonight, anyway. "Work first. Sex later."

It's practically becoming my mantra.

Mamá would be so proud.

Or not.

Parker's a great guy. Smart, considerate—despite my initial perception of him—gorgeous, and an athlete to boot. But he's not long term.

Hell, he's not even short term because we are not a couple.

"Suit yourself." He straightens and shoves his hands in the pockets of his joggers. "It's just that I haven't been able to stop thinking about Friday night."

Same, but... "What about it?"

I shouldn't encourage him—we have work to do—but I'm already turned on, so screw it.

"I've been thinking of all the creative ways I could use the Rosebud on your body." He pauses and I turn to face him, curiosity getting the best of me. "I've finally decided which we're going to try first."

"And?"

A slow smile spreads across his face and it's pure challenge. "I could bend you over the desk right now and show you."

An image of Parker bending me over the desk, legs spread wide as he wraps my hair around his fist and enters me from behind, incinerates every other thought in my brain.

"Think about it, Shorty. You could have my cock filling every inch of you as Rose works your clit." I squirm, trying to relieve the growing ache between my legs. "Just say the word."

Yes.

I clamp my lips shut before the word can escape, but it's futile. Devin's eyes sparkle with laughter, leaving no doubt he can sense my inner turmoil.

Mierda. I'm so in over my head.

Enemies with benefits was one thing, but this? How am I supposed to give this up when Parker gets bored and moves on? Because he will tire of this arrangement, eventually.

That's the whole point, right?

To keep it casual.

To have a little fun and then go our separate ways.

A clean break.

Which is why you should enjoy it while it lasts.

But first, homework.

"In case you've forgotten, this paper is due by midnight. If we're late, Mac will dock our grade, and I for one will not jeopardize my shot at the Sports Stream internship for sex." I shoot him a pointed look. "No matter how good it promises to be."

"Fine." He groans good naturedly and spins on his heel. "Have it your w—"

His words are cut off and his eyes go round as he stumbles and goes down, one foot caught in the strap of the duffle bag I carelessly tossed in the corner. He lands on all fours with a thud that shakes the entire room.

My heart jackhammers in my chest and I leap to my feet, but Devin's faster.

He grabs the bag. "What's in this thing, anyway?"

"Don't!"

Too late. The zipper slides open with a quiet hiss and his curiosity morphs into confusion.

You had one job, Cruz.

"Is this what I think it is?"

"That depends." I wrap my arms around myself and force a smile. "Do you think it's a super cozy Wildcat onesie for cold winter nights?"

He shoots me an incredulous look.

I shrug and flop back into my chair. "It was worth a shot."

"You're—" He shakes his head and a tuft of dark hair falls over his brow. "You're the Wildcat?"

"Surprise!" I throw jazz hands, though I'm far from excited about his discovery.

"How?" His brow furrows as he tries to work it out. "You're on the gymnastics team. How can you possibly do both?"

At least he's asking the right questions.

And as long as he's doing that, he's not thinking about the incident with the cannon.

"Funny story." I tuck a loose strand of hair behind my ear. "Remember when the football team got pranked with itching powder?"

His eyes narrow. "It *was* you. I knew it!"

"Guilty as charged."

He chuckles, taking the news surprisingly well. "That was dirty, you know."

"Yeah." I huff out a breath. "So was how that asshole treated Maddie in the gym."

He mutters something that sounds like, "Fucking Langley."

"Anyway, I got caught and that,"—I gesture to the bag—"is my punishment. The real Wildcat got a last-minute study abroad opportunity, and I was given the choice of facing a disciplinary hearing—and possible expulsion—or filling in for the semester."

"Lucky break."

"So lucky," I deadpan. "Just a few more weeks and I can put this nightmare behind me."

The football team is 8-1 after trouncing Indiana yesterday. There are only three more games in the regular season and then I'm off the hook, assuming the regular mascot returns to campus as planned. The way Waverly's playing, the team is all but guaranteed a bowl appearance. Thankfully, that won't be my problem.

Imagine the performance Sharpe would expect for a bowl game.

I shudder.

"It could be worse." Devin frowns and I see the moment the realization hits him. "You shot me in the nuts with a t-shirt."

"Oopsie." I duck my head. "In my defense, they didn't give me time to practice, and the Wildcat roar scared the crap out of me. I didn't mean to pull the trigger."

"*Riiight.*" He drags the word out, a smile tugging at the corners of his mouth.

"That roar is loud as hell." I can hardly fault him for being skeptical. Not after the itching powder. "If it's any consolation, Coach Sharpe chewed me out big time afterward."

"Rightfully so," he grumbles. "My boys are scarred for life."

I roll my eyes. "Your boys are fine."

A fact I can confirm firsthand.

"True." He zips the bag and tosses it aside before turning his gaze back to me. "But if you want to kiss and make up, they'd be down."

"Duly noted." I swipe my tongue across my lower lip, filing the suggestion away for later.

"Wait a minute." He climbs to his feet and shoves his hands through his hair. "Are you telling me we could've been hooking up at away games all this time and you never said a word?"

"Yes?"

He groans. "We were literally in the same hotel Friday night and you didn't invite me over to try out your new toy?"

"Trust me. I'd have much rather been screwing my brains out. It was boring hanging out in my room alone and keeping a low profile." I arch a brow. "I couldn't even go to the vending machines for fear of getting caught. Frankly, I don't know how the real mascot did it."

You can bet your ass that if I ever meet him, I'm going to ask.

Devin shakes his head, apparently still in disbelief.

Right there with you.

"I knew the Wildcat looked shorter this year. The guys and I were talking about it at the home opener. Coop said you looked stoned." He smirks. "And that there was no way a woman could do fifty one-armed pushups." He rubs his hands together like he's about to dive into an entire carton of ice cream. *Mmm. Double chocolate chip would really hit the spot right now.* "I can't wait to see the look on his face when I tell him you're filling in."

"Wait. What?" I shake off all thoughts of ice cream. "You can't do that."

Devin's face falls. "Do what?"

"You can't tell anyone I'm filling in for the mascot." I stand and press my palms to his chest, determined to make him understand. "The mascot's identity has to remain secret. It's tradition."

He wiggles his brows. "Traditions are meant to be broken."

"You're thinking of rules." I offer him a tight-lipped smile. "If I screw up, Sharpe will have my ass in front of the disciplinary board in a hot minute."

"You're serious." He wraps his arms around my waist and pulls me close. Heat radiates from his body and he smells so freaking good. I inhale the delicious scent of sandalwood and citrus that is so uniquely his, and as I stare up at him, his eyes soften. "Relax, Shorty. Your secret is safe with me."

Relief floods my veins. "Thank you."

It would be tragic to make it this far, only to have everything fall apart now.

"No need to thank me." His hands slide down my backside

and he palms my ass cheeks. "I don't play dirty. Except in the bedroom."

I laugh in spite of myself. Because *of course* he brought the conversation back to sex. "Keep it in your pants. We've got a paper to finish."

—————

31

DJ

"I'M GOING TO GRAB A DRINK." I close my laptop and swing my feet over the side of Sutton's bed before crossing the room to stand behind her. She's sitting at the desk, back straight, perched on the edge of her chair. It looks uncomfortable as hell, and yet, she hasn't moved in two hours. "You want anything?"

"A refill would be great, actually." She hands me her water bottle without looking up from the screen. "I'm just going to do one more read through and then I think we're done."

Praise Jesus. We've been at it for two hours, working in a shared document to strengthen our conclusion and ensure the sections we each wrote blend smoothly to create one cohesive analysis. If I don't get a break soon, my brain is going to melt and leak out of my ears.

I plant a kiss on the top of her head and turn for the door, careful not to trip over her bag this time. I shake my head, still unable to wrap my brain around the fact that Sutton is the Waverly mascot. Not in a million years would I have guessed my sassy little spitfire was inside that suit cheering the team on.

Hell, I'm pretty sure she doesn't even like football.

Which explains so much.

When I reach the bottom of the stairs, I cross into the open concept living room and kitchen to find Maddie sprawled on the couch watching tv.

"Hey, Maddie."

"Parker." She smirks, which is oddly disconcerting on her pixie-like face. "You two are working awfully late tonight."

"Paper's due at midnight."

She makes a noncommittal sound as I stride to the fridge and open the door. It's the complete opposite of the fridge in my apartment, which is always crammed full. There's an assortment of yogurt, a pitcher of filtered water, a takeout salad, and a couple bottles of Powerade I brought over with me. I grab a Powerade and the pitcher of water and push the door shut with my foot. Maddie's still watching as I set my haul on the counter and twist the top off Sutton's water bottle.

"I guess that means you won't be hanging around the apartment anymore." I must look confused because she adds, "You know, now that the paper from hell is finally done."

"I— Guess not."

Unease stirs in my gut as I fill the water bottle. Will Sutton want to end our arrangement when the project is finished? I'd hoped we could keep this thing between us going through the end of the semester. Or, at least until things with the internship heat up.

I'm not ready to let her go—not even close—but we never discussed an expiration date.

That's because you were thinking with your cock.

Facts. I don't even think we agreed to exclusivity. Not that I'd hook up with someone else while we're sleeping together. She wouldn't either. I know that with certainty. It's not her style. Still, the realization that she might not want me as badly as I want her is a kick in the balls.

"I'm sure you're both glad to be done with it," Maddie continues. "You guys have spent an insane amount of time together."

My head snaps up and water splashes over the side of the bottle. "Excuse me?"

"Personally, I've never invested that much time in a group project, but maybe I just haven't found the right partner. I've certainly never been as *enthusiastic* as you two. From the sounds of it, you two have had some pretty *heated* discussions up there." She nods toward the ceiling and twirls a strand of hair around her finger, that smug grin still fixed in place as I grab a towel and mop up the spill. "According to Sutton, it's A+ work, so high five for that."

I stiffen. Is Maddie fucking with me right now? Does she know Sutton and I have been hooking up? More importantly, does Sutton know Maddie knows?

Doesn't matter. I'm not saying shit. I promised to keep our arrangement secret, so that's what I'm going to do.

"Let's just hope Mac agrees." I return the pitcher of water to the fridge. "We're going to need it if we want a shot at that internship."

"Who knows?" Maddie shrugs. "Maybe something even better will come along."

"Doubtful. There is nothing more important to me right now than scoring that internship. It could make or break my future."

"Talk about shortsighted." She sighs and turns back to the tv. "Swear to God you and Sutton are peas in a freaking pod."

Okay, this is just getting weird. I screw the top on the water bottle, grab my Powerade, and say goodnight.

When I return to the bedroom, Sutton's hunched over her

laptop, lost in thought. Her fingers fly across the keyboard and I peek over her shoulder just in time to see her make a correction to my part of the paper.

"What are you doing?" I slide her water bottle onto the desk and twist the cap off my drink before taking a long swig.

"Just making a few corrections."

She backspaces and changes conscience to conscious.

My gut hardens and I replace the cap on my drink as she continues, pausing when she finds a mistake. In my section. Again.

Sweat beads along my hairline and I roll my shoulders to slough off my frustration. When it comes to academics, the only thing worse than having someone else read a paper I've written is having them point out the errors. I usually have the tutors at the academic center look over my work after I do the usual spellcheck and read-aloud stuff, but I didn't have time with the AMP paper.

You should've made time.

Fuck. Instead of visiting a sex shop Friday, I should've tried for a walk-in appointment at the academic center, but I was sure I'd nailed the paper. I read over it several times. Validated all my citations. Triple checked my references.

And you still couldn't see the mistakes.

The ones that are so obvious to Sutton.

Shame blazes through me, scorching the back of my neck.

Stupid. Idiot. Slow.

The words echo in my head like a broken fucking record.

One I wish I could forget. One I've worked so hard to put behind me.

Not hard enough.

The crunch of plastic shatters the silence and I glance down at the dented Powerade bottle in my hand.

Sutton hits save on the file and glances up at me. "You okay?"

No, I'm not fucking okay. I'm standing here like a dumbass while she corrects my work. "I'm good."

She pulls up her email, where she's already drafted a submission note to Mac, and attaches our finished paper. "You don't look okay. Did something happen while you were downstairs?" She turns back to me, eyes wide. "Was it Maddie? I meant to tell you, but she knows we're hooking up. She'll probably give you a hard time. Just for fun."

"It wasn't Maddie." Though that certainly explains her weird commentary.

Sutton frowns, turns back to the laptop, and hits send. Then she stands and turns to face me. "What is it then? You were fine when you went downstairs and now, you're not."

I set my bottle on the desk and step away, putting some distance between us.

"You were fixing my part of the paper."

"I told you I was doing one more read through." Her brows knit together in confusion. "What's the big deal?"

"The big deal is that instead of telling me what needed revised, you took it upon yourself to make the corrections."

"That's the point of editing. To fix what needs fixing."

"I can pull my weight." She reaches for me, but I sidestep her, ignoring the hurt that flashes across her face. "You don't have to coddle me or pick up the slack."

"That's not what I was doing."

I snort and cross my arms. "Bullshit."

"No, bullshit is you getting upset because I fixed a few typos." She huffs out a breath. "Everyone makes mistakes. It's not a big deal."

"True, but if it was anyone else—if you didn't know I had

dyslexia—you'd have called me out for sloppy work instead of fixing it."

Her eyes narrow. "Is that what you think?"

"It's what I know."

"For your information," she says through gritted teeth. "I'm not in the habit of shaming my partners. Especially when their work is top-notch. I'd be a shitty partner if I behaved that way."

"It's not shitty to hold people accountable."

"Agreed. But that's not what we're talking about here. You did the work, and you did it well, which is why I corrected the typos without making a fuss." She's calling them typos, but it was more than that. I wrote the wrong damn word. "It wasn't a power play or some underhanded method of putting you down." She wraps her arms around her midsection. "If I'd known the changes would upset you, I'd have pointed them out so you could correct them."

"Okay." That's all I wanted. To be treated like anyone else. No special treatment.

She nods. "Okay."

A beat passes and we stare at one another, neither of us willing—or able—to break the silence.

Sutton licks her lips, tongue gliding over the tender pink flesh in a way that has my cock stirring.

"Did we just have our first real fight?" A smile tugs at the corner of my mouth.

"I think so." She spins on her heel, sashays over to the nightstand, and yanks the drawer open. When she turns back to me, Rose is resting in her palm. "And now," she says, voice low and husky. "If you're done being a stubborn ass, I believe we have unfinished business."

I quirk a brow in silent challenge.

"You." She takes a step toward me, hips swinging. "Me."

Another step. "Rose." She swaggers past, trailing a finger across my chest. "The desk."

My pulse spikes and my feet are cemented to the floor as she sets the toy on the desk and plants her palms on the surface, that perfect ass on display. She turns to look over her shoulder and when our eyes meet, my cock springs to attention.

Fuuuck.

"Come on, Devin. You can spend the night stewing about that paper or you can make my fantasies come true." She flashes me a devilish smile. "Unless you'd rather watch?"

32

SUTTON

Nothing like a hard-hitting game of football to get the adrenaline pumping.

I'd known Michigan would be a rough game—it's all anyone's talked about on campus this week—but it's turning out to be brutal, both on the field and in the stands. The fans are in rare form, vacillating between pride and frustration, the mood in the stadium shifting with each play.

"Come on, ref! He was clearly holding. Get your head out of your ass!"

Case in point.

The heckler seated in the front row at the forty-yard line hasn't shut up since kickoff.

There should be a rule against assholes getting such good seats.

Look, I've never cared about football, but it's impossible to stand on the sideline each week and not become invested in Waverly's dream of making a championship run. A dream that will end today if they don't turn things around.

We're up by three, but it's late in the fourth quarter and nothing's guaranteed. Not with the way this game has been going. If they lose...

I can't think about it. Can't think about how it'll crush Devin.

On the bright side, my performance has been on point.

I nailed my pushups. Slayed the t-shirt cannon. And my pre-halftime dance was freaking spectacular, if I say so myself.

Which I do.

Obviously.

Even Coach Sharpe complimented my performance today, so, #winning.

The sun disappears behind a cloud and a cold breeze whips through the stadium, cutting straight through my fur suit. *Spoiler alert*: it isn't nearly as warm as I thought it would be.

I need to get moving. It's the only way to stay toasty since I can't exactly wear a winter coat under the mascot costume. Not if I want to tumble, anyway.

I jog down the sideline and position myself at the thirty just as Waverly snaps the ball. Reid drops back, scanning the field for an open receiver. He spots someone downfield and fires off a bullet, but it's intercepted.

"Austin Reid is picked off!" the announcer bellows, words barely audible over the groans of the fans. "I can't believe it!"

The Michigan defender runs it back and my stomach drops.

Nonononononono.

He covers ten yards before Parker tackles him from behind.

More angry shouts go up from the crowd and I cover my eyes with my paws.

When I look again, the Michigan offense is taking the field and Coach Collins is ranting like a madman, gesticulating wildly with his clipboard. Someone snatches it from his hand just as he approaches the ref.

Smart move.

That thing could do some real damage.

On the sideline, Parker claps Reid on the back and they exchange a few words. I'm too far away to hear what's said, but I can read their faces easily enough.

This is it. The moment of truth.

If Michigan scores, it's all over. The game. The championship run. Everything.

The hopes and dreams of Wildcat Nation permeate the air, making it hard to breathe. It's like being trapped inside a pressure cooker, the weight of expectation pressing down.

Imagine how Devin feels.

Mierda. This must be torture for the guys on the team.

Every eye in the stadium is fixed on the defense as they settle in at the line of scrimmage. They can't afford to give up another touchdown. There's not enough time left on the clock. They have to hold the line.

Michigan snaps the ball. It's a running play and they pick up three yards.

Not enough for a first down, but it's a start.

On the second down, they attempt to pass, but the receiver can't pull it down.

"Incomplete!" the announcer declares. "But what a play by Michigan."

Whose side is he on, anyway? It's a freaking home game. He should be rooting for the Wildcats.

"Michigan is third and long. They need to convert here or they'll be forced to go for it on the fourth down, giving Waverly strong field position."

Thanks, Captain Obvious.

I can't bear to watch.

You don't have a choice.

Okay, fine. I have to watch, but there must be something more I can do.

That's the whole point of the mascot, right? To influence the fans.

I turn to survey the crowd. The student section is on their feet, refusing to accept defeat.

And that's when it hits me.

"Let's make some noise," I whisper.

I throw up my hands, gesturing for the crowd to pump it up. They're slow to respond, so I cup my ear in an *I can't hear you* pose. The first few rows start a D-fence chant and I thrust my paw in the air before turning to the next section and giving them the same *make some noise* gesture.

They're faster to respond and then I'm on the jumbotron in full view of the entire stadium, raising Wildcat Nation to their feet in support of the defense. The crowd noise is so loud, I can't hear myself think. There's no way the offense will hear the play call.

Michigan snaps the ball as the crowd reaches a fever pitch and—

Yes! *Yesyesyes.*

One of our defenders sacks the quarterback, laying him flat-out on his back, and I punch both fists into the air in a wild victory dance.

"This is it, folks. Fourth and long," the announcer says, clearly feeling the momentum shift. "If the Wildcats can make the stop, they take possession and have an opportunity to run the clock down."

The teams line up for what might be the most critical play of the game, and I do my best to get the crowd back into the play. I don't know if the noise helped the defense or not, but it sure as hell didn't hurt.

Michigan snaps the ball, and the quarterback tries to

punch through the D-line. He gets tackled at the line of scrimmage and the crowd goes nuts.

As predicted, Coach Collins runs down the clock and the Wildcats win by three.

Pride swells in my chest as the guys celebrate on the field and when Devin removes his helmet, revealing sweat-slick hair and the world's biggest smile, my belly flips.

He deserves this.

For the first time, I find myself truly invested in the Wildcats' success. Not because failure on my part means expulsion, but because Devin and the other guys on the team have worked hard. Stood up to the pressure. Given Wildcat Nation hope.

Sure, some of them are undeserving douche canoes, but they just might be the minority.

When the cheer squad files off the field and through the tunnel, I hang back.

Most of the players have left the field, but not all of them.

I linger in the hall near the team locker room, and my patience is rewarded when Devin rounds the corner, helmet tucked under his arm.

He grins when he spots me, that gorgeous smile transforming his handsome face, softening the hard angles. "Now, this is what I call a pleasant surprise."

I wave awkwardly.

Because of course I didn't think this through.

If I had, I'd have remembered I can't actually talk because...*mascot.*

Then again, who needs words?

I crook a finger and gesture for Parker to follow.

His grin widens, and he trails me around the corner to a tiny nook that serves who knows what purpose. We can't be seen by anyone glancing down the hall. Someone would have to walk right past to spot us, which shouldn't be a problem because this won't take long.

"Was it my imagination or were you cheering extra hard during the fourth quarter?" he asks, backing me up against the cinderblock wall.

I hold up my paws in a *Who knows?* gesture.

Devin's a big guy, but with his pads, he's huge. His broad shoulders nearly span the width of the nook and though he's sweat soaked and dirty, he's never looked sexier.

"Hmm." His gaze slides over me and even though I'm covered from head to toe in fur, he must like what he sees because heat flares in his eyes. "The teeth are a nice touch," he says, voice like gravel. "But they have to go if I'm going to kiss you."

Yes, please.

Arousal pools between my legs and I make no move to stop him as he pushes my Wildcat head up, so it's resting on top of my head.

He moves in close, his body pressed to mine, but he makes no move to kiss me.

"So?"

"So what?" I challenge.

"Were you cheering for me in the fourth quarter?"

Now it's my turn to smirk. "Just exercising my school pride."

"School pride, huh?" He cups my cheek with his free hand, his calloused fingers scraping over my heated flesh as he takes my lower lip between his teeth and tugs gently. My nipples go hard and I gasp as he releases me. "Is that what we're calling it now?"

"Call it whatever you want." The words don't matter. Only the action. "Just kiss me while you're doing it."

He drops his helmet and in one swift move, he lifts me

into the air, pinning my back to the wall. I wrap my legs around his waist and crush my mouth to his. The kiss is hot and wet and when his tongue surges into my mouth, I nearly come undone, a quiet moan slipping from my lips as I rock my hips against him. He smells like grass and dirt and fresh air.

The salty undertone that's uniquely his only serves to heighten my arousal.

I need this man inside me right-freaking-now.

"Fuck." He pants, breaking off the kiss. "You're going to send me to the locker room with the world's biggest hard-on."

I grin and roll my hips in response, tension coiling low in my belly.

"Give me twenty minutes to shower and I can meet you at your place."

"Can't." I shake my head for emphasis because words are hard. "I still have. Two appearances. This afternoon."

He growls in frustration. "Tonight then?"

I nod and roll my hips because I can't *not* rub my clit on this man right now.

"That's it, Shorty. Ride me like a good girl." Eyes locked on mine, he slips a hand between our bodies and presses his thumb—at least, I think it's his thumb—to my clit. "I know just how you like it."

Qué rico.

He really does.

And because there's no shame in my game, I hold his gaze, letting him work me toward climax, each quick rotation of his thumb delivering a burst of pleasure that drives me higher as I spiral toward release.

My core clenches and I whimper.

I need more. More pressure. More contact.

More Devin.

It's only been a few months, but like the well-trained athlete he is, he's learned to play my body like a champ.

He presses down on my clit and I bite my lip as pleasure radiates through my body.

"Shh," he whispers. "We don't want to get caught, do we?"

I shake my head, still biting down on my lip to muffle the sounds of gratification desperate to escape my traitorous mouth.

"Someone could walk by at any moment and catch us. They'd see me rubbing your clit and know this hot little pussy belongs to me."

"Yes." I don't know if I'm agreeing or encouraging him, but when he presses down again, his thumb tracing a rough circle around that sensitive bundle of nerves, I explode.

Pleasure courses through my body like an electrical current and I arch into him, greedily savoring the aftershocks as he claims my mouth, the kiss soft and gentle this time.

When we finally break apart, I'm grinning like a fool.

"Text me later?" he asks.

"Of c—"

"Holy shit! Is Parker doing the mascot?"

Coño.

Devin winces, eyes slamming shut, as a string of expletives burst from his mouth. He lowers me to the ground and I scramble to pull my Wildcat head down. He's a big guy and if I can't see the newcomer, maybe he can't see me either.

Here's hoping.

Devin turns and I peek around him to glimpse Cooper DeLaurentis and Austin Reid. They look about as shocked as I feel right now.

"Don't you have somewhere else to be?" Devin barks. "Like the shower?"

Cooper smirks. "I could ask you the same question."

"We got tagged for interviews," Reid says, raking a hand through his damp hair. "We didn't mean to interrupt." His attention pivots from Devin to me and back again. "What you do off the field is your business."

"Yeah." Cooper throws up his hands, one of which is clutching a helmet. "As you were. We saw nothing."

Reid gives him a shove and they continue down the hall to the locker room.

Devin turns back to me, the ghost of a smile touching his lips when he sees my Wildcat head is back in place. "At least one of us gets to keep our secret."

33

DJ

Thanks to my post-game activities with Sutton, I'm the last one to leave the locker room and by the time I get home, I'm dragging ass. All I want to do right now is scarf down a pizza and catch a nap.

The upside of Sutton's Wildcat duties is that I can rest up for tonight.

The downside? My balls are blue as shit.

I can take it though. Hell, the anticipation will make the payoff that much sweeter.

And with any luck, those Wildcat appearances won't take long.

I fish my keys out of my pocket just as the streetlights come on. The temperature is dropping fast, and the sun set half an hour ago. Short days are one of the things I hate most about winter, second only to the cold. Before enrolling at Waverly, I wore shorts year-round and didn't own a coat, but Pennsylvania is a far cry from South Carolina, so yeah, I had to expand my wardrobe.

I dart a glance at Sutton's apartment as I slide my key in the lock.

The idea of her walking home alone in the dark sets my teeth on edge and I make a mental note to text her. Maybe we can meet up when she's done and I can walk her home. Or better yet, maybe we can grab a bite to eat and *then* I can walk her home.

God knows I'm a bottomless pit on game days and she probably hasn't eaten since she put on the Wildcat costume this morning. The memory of her nearly empty fridge seals the deal. Yeah, I'm definitely taking her out for dinner. My girl needs to keep her strength up. Between gymnastics and mascot performances, she must be burning calories like mad.

What she needs is a big-ass cheeseburger. Some fries. Maybe even a milkshake.

Decision made, I turn the key and open the door.

The instant I enter the apartment, goosebumps prickle the back of my neck.

Something's wrong. It's too quiet.

Especially for a game day. There's always music playing. Or football on tv. Someone cooking or screwing around on the Xbox.

Yet there are zero signs of life.

Which can't be a good thing.

I drop my bag in the hall and head for the living room.

My roommates are lined up on the couch like they're in timeout.

Because that's not weird at all.

"What's going on?" It's the obvious question, though I'm not sure I want the answer. Not when they're all staring at me like...I don't know what.

"Why don't you sit down?" Reid gestures to the empty loveseat and my Spidey-sense goes on high-alert.

"Is there a reason you're treating me like a guest in my own house?" Shit. If that's not a red flag, I don't know what is. "Am I about to be voted off the island?"

"We've already got one drama queen in this house," Vaughn says, nudging Coop. "Let's not add another."

"Dude." Coop huffs out a breath and slowly turns to face him. "We talked about this. Positive, affirming statements only."

"That *was* positive." Vaughn strokes his beard like he's fucking Dumbledore. "It was a warning. Like those fables they tell kids to keep them on the straight and narrow."

"Straight? Narrow? Do you even hear yourself right now?" Coop turns to Reid, who's seated on his other side. "And you think *he's* the sensitive one."

What. The. Actual. Fuck?

It's like my roommates have been replaced by The Three Stooges.

Reid closes his eyes and I'm pretty sure he's counting to ten.

He had a rough game today, and he's dealing with personal shit—something to do with our kicker, Carter—which is enough to trigger my guilt complex. My feet are moving before I consciously decide to follow his suggestion.

"What's up?" I lower myself onto the loveseat. Whatever it is, it must be important. Why else would they all be sitting here in silence, waiting for me?

Reid clears his throat, visibly uncomfortable. "We weren't sure how to bring this up, but after what happened today..." Unease roils in my stomach. "With the Wildcat."

For fuck's sake. He can't be serious. His last hookup was headline news. And every one of us has walked in on a Cooper DeLaurentis hookup at some point. But I get caught one time and it requires an intervention?

"What he means is, we weren't sure if we *should* bring it up," Vaughn interjects.

"Tomayto, tomahto." Coop shrugs. "The point is, we respect your privacy, but we also want you to feel comfortable. After all, we're roommates."

"Friends," Reid amends.

"Practically brothers." Vaughn reaches over to clap me on the shoulder. "We love you and support you. Unconditionally."

"Good. I—" I shift uneasily, searching for the words that came so naturally to Vaughn. "I love you guys, too." Though I'm not in the habit of saying it.

"There's no judgment here." Reid's jaw is set and when his eyes meet mine, they're brimming with sincerity. No surprise there. He's always been a standup guy. "You can be your authentic self and live your truth, whatever that may be. You don't need to hide. Not with us."

Wait. What?

"When you're ready to take the next step," Coop adds. "We'll be right by your side."

"Exactly." Reid nods, like it's a done deal. "We just wanted you to know. After what we saw earlier, we—"

"Hold up." I throw up a hand, struggling to make sense of their words. "What exactly do you think you saw?"

Reid and Coop exchange a look, and it's our team captain who speaks. "You were hooking up with the guy in the Wildcat suit."

Fucking hell.

It all makes sense now. The intervention. The offers of support.

The assumption that the mascot is always a dude.

"It all makes sense now," Coop says, echoing my thoughts. "Why you don't hook up much. Why you've never dated."

"I don't have time for distractions." *Sutton isn't a distraction.* If anything, I've been more focused, determined to carve out time for her. Still, I double down, narrowing my eyes at Coop. "You of all people should understand since, as far as I know, you've never had a girlfriend either."

He waves a hand, brushing my protest aside. "This is why you kicked me out of the sex shop, isn't it? You didn't want me to see what you were buying."

For a smart guy, he's pretty thick sometimes. "I kicked you out because you were acting like a jackass!"

"How is that different from any other day?" Vaughn asks, coaxing a laugh from Reid.

"But... We thought..." Coop frowns, brow furrowed. "Aren't you gay? It took us a minute to pick up on the signs, but today they were hard to miss." I shake my head, but I don't get the chance to reply because he gets a second wind. "Is it a furry kink, then? Do you have a fursona? Because that's okay too. Whatever you're into, we've got you, brother."

It's official. I've entered The Twilight Zone.

Vaughn cocks his head. "What's a furry?"

"We'll talk later." Coop winks at him. "Patience you must have, my young Padawan."

"The point is," Reid says, clasping his hands together. "However you get your rocks off—furries, feet, nylons—we support you."

Jesus Christ. Did he just suggest I might be turned on by nylons? Sutton is turning me into the laughingstock of the team. First the t-shirt cannon, now this?

If I wasn't so crazy about her, I'd be offended. Maybe this thing between us started as redemption—or, as Sutton likes to call it, enemies with benefits—but that was just noise. We're good together, and it's not just the sex, though the sex is fucking spectacular. I love the way she challenges me. Gives as good as she gets. Doesn't back down and stands up for what she believes in. She's smart. Loyal. Driven.

"Parker?" Reid prods, interrupting my thoughts.

"Sorry, I—"

Just tell them Sutton's the Wildcat.

Not an option. I made a promise and I'm not about to go back on my word. Not when it took so long to earn her trust. Not when her gymnastics scholarship is on the line.

So what if they think I'm gay? Or into furry shit?

It doesn't matter.

I care about Sutton too much to hurt her.

Besides, I'm not so fragile I'm defined by my sexuality. My roommates are way off the mark, but their hearts are in the right place. If there was ever any doubt these guys had my back, it's been erased.

"What can I say?" I shrug and flop back on the couch. "I dig the Wildcat suit."

Facts. Today's stadium hookup was hot as fuck. Hell, I might even ask Sutton to wear the costume for a little role play later tonight.

"Damn, Parker." Coop shakes his head and I swear to God there's awe in his voice. "I always figured you for the vanilla type." He leans forward, bracing his elbows on his knees. "Can I ask you a personal question?"

"Like I could stop you." I curl my fingers, gesturing for him to lay it on me. The sooner we get this over with, the sooner I get my pizza.

"This ought to be good," Vaughn mutters.

"There's just one thing I want to know." The asshole looks me square in the eye and grins. "Does the fur tickle your balls when you're hooking up?"

34

SUTTON

"YOU STILL WITH ME?" Devin nudges my arm, but he's grinning, one of those brilliant smiles that reaches all the way to his eyes.

"Sorry." Heat floods my cheeks. "I spaced."

At the worst possible time.

I scan the studio to see if anyone else noticed, but Mac's busy explaining lighting technique to a group of students gathered around the main set. Those of us working in the wings are cast in shadow, so I doubt he can even see me crouched in the dark, sorting cables like my GPA depends on it.

Which it does.

"Relax, Shorty. We've got this." Devin grabs a mess of black cables that all look the same and attempts to untangle them. Mac's assigned us audio production, which means if anything goes wrong with the microphones or sound effects during today's mock broadcast, we're screwed. "I was up half the night memorizing the setup."

That makes one of us.

Me? I dropped like a stone after practice last night.

Between my course load, gymnastics, and my Wildcat duties, I'm spread thin. Like, transparent.

Only one more week to go.

It's the Friday before fall break—not that it's much of a break since the football team has a road game at Rutgers tomorrow and Maryland at home next Saturday—but I'm looking forward to a few days off. I haven't seen my family in months, and it'll be nice to sleep in my own bed.

The reprieve from my hellish schedule is just an added bonus.

Maryland is the football team's last regular season game.

It's also my last Wildcat appearance.

Hallelujah.

"Since you have the cables memorized, I'll leave you to it." I stand and turn my attention to the lavalier mics laid out on a rolling electrical cart.

"Any plans for Thanksgiving break?"

"I'm going to sleep late, veg on the couch, and do absolutely nothing."

"What?" He stares up at me in mock horror. "No great big turkey dinner where you eat until it hurts and slide into a food coma while the rest of the country watches football?"

"Not this year."

My mom texted a few days ago to let me know she won't be cooking a traditional Thanksgiving meal this year.

No pavochon. No mofongo stuffing. No flan de coco.

Worse, I can't even complain without looking like a pendeja.

"Why not?" Devin frees a cable and sets it aside. "What's different this year?"

"My family is skipping the traditional holiday meal to support Gabby." Which apparently means strict diets all around. Even my dad—whose sweet tooth is bigger than mine

—is watching what he eats. "She needs to be in the best physical shape possible, heading to the National Team training camp in January."

I get it. I do. I can't exactly afford to pack on the pounds either, but it's one freaking meal.

One I look forward to all year.

Thanksgiving's always been a special day for my family. It's the start of the holiday season and the magic it brings. It's a tradition my grandparents started long ago in Puerto Rico, and though I've only visited the island once, the knowledge that we share the same traditions makes me feel closer to them, even when we're an ocean apart.

Devin's face falls and I know instinctively that he's reacting to the change in my mood. To something he saw on my face or in my voice. "It's one meal."

"You're preaching to the choir." *Which is why it's best to change the subject.* The last thing I want to do is bring him down. "What about you?"

His entire demeanor changes and his face lights up.

"Thanksgiving is the social gathering of the year in my family. Mom spends the entire week preparing and my extended family comes in from all over the state." He chuckles. "It's cool though. I don't get home much during the school year, so it's nice to see everyone." He glances up at me and there's a mischievous glint in his eye. "The best part is kicking my uncle's ass at flag football. My team has a six-year winning streak." He puffs out his chest. "Soon to be seven."

A laugh bubbles up from my stomach and I shake my head. "Nice."

"It is. In fact, it's one of my favorite traditions." He holds up a hand, as if expecting more snark. "And before you go feeling sorry for him, you should know he used to run the score up on my team when I was a kid."

I arch a brow. "So you're saying the competitive streak runs in your family?"

"Damn, right."

"I'll keep that in mind."

It's something I can't afford to forget. Not even for a second.

"Oh, no." Devin rocks back on his haunches, studying me. "You've got that look."

"What look?" I'm careful to avoid eye contact as I confirm the mic batteries are properly charged.

"The one that says you're sweating our term paper."

"Well, I wasn't until you brought it up." My stomach twists. "But now that you mention it..."

"Relax. We aced it."

"I like your confidence." Still, I won't be satisfied until I see the grade for myself. "I wish Mac would just hand our papers back already. They're in his bag." Which is laying on the anchor desk like a beacon of academia. "If he'd just pass them out, then we'd all be able to concentrate."

Devin chuckles, low and deep, the sound reverberating through my body as he grabs a cable that's snaked around the cart. "We'll have our grade soon enough."

I sigh. He's right. This isn't the time to worry about things beyond our control. We need to finish the audio setup and impress Mac with our flawless execution. He'll be announcing the candidates for the Sports Stream internship soon, and I need to be on that list.

You're not the only one counting on that opportunity.

My palms go damp, and I glance at Devin. He's still working on the cables, a tuft of chestnut hair obscuring his forehead, completely oblivious to my attention. Mac hasn't given us a specific date, but with the semester drawing to a close, it seems likely he'll announce the candidates any day now.

Even if we both make the short list, only one of us can land that internship.

Mierda. I really should've thought this through before we started sleeping together. It didn't seem like a big deal at the time. The fight for the internship was so far away. A distant worry. Now it's here and... My chest tightens. The last thing I want to do is take an opportunity from Devin. He wants it —*no, needs it*—as badly as I do.

I never imagined our enemies with benefits arrangement might develop into something more. We may not be #couplegoals, but I care about Devin and I don't want to hurt him.

Not now, not ever.

He's a good person. Smart. Caring. Motivated. A rockstar in bed. That he actually likes my snarky side is just the icing on the cake. He's nothing like the fuckboy I imagined.

And that's a problem why?

Because even though I told myself it was just sex, somewhere along the way, I developed feelings for Devin.

Feelings I can't—won't—allow to impact my future.

That shouldn't be a problem.

After all, we're just friends with benefits.

"Almost done there?" He climbs to his feet. "Looks like we're next up for inspection."

I lift my gaze just enough to confirm Mac is winding down with the lighting group as I slide a battery into the first lavalier transmitter. It locks into place and I move down the line, ensuring all six mics have a battery pack. We only need three for today's broadcast, but it's always better to be prepared.

Just in case.

If I've learned anything in this class, it's that things on set can get buggy, and I want Mac to see we're ready to troubleshoot if needed.

"All set." I wipe my palms on my thighs.

"What frequency should this be on?" Devin asks, picking up a transmitter.

"I didn't realize there would be a pop quiz." I flash him a playful smile. "If I'd known, I would have studied more."

"Smartass." He flicks my nose. "Lucky for you, I like my women sassy."

"Your women?"

He rolls his eyes. "You know what I mean."

"Yes, and lucky for you, my mouth is one of my best traits."

"Don't I know it." He places the transmitter back on the cart and checks the next one. "These are on the same frequency."

My heart stutters.

That's not possible. I checked them. Didn't I?

I grab the first mic, check the frequency and move to the next.

Ay, cabrón.

He's right. It's such a rookie mistake. Broadcasting 101. I quickly adjust the settings and continue down the line.

"Why the hell would anyone set them to the same frequency?" It makes no sense. Each mic needs to be on a separate frequency to pick up the wearer and avoid interference.

Devin stares over my shoulder, probably keeping an eye on Mac. "For the same reason all the cords are tangled."

"People are assholes." I reset the last transmitter and place it back on the cart. "Thanks. That was a good catch."

One I should have made.

One I would have made if I'd been focused on my job instead of bantering with Devin.

"No worries." He shoves his hands into his pockets. "It could've happened to anyone."

"True." *False.* "But you didn't have to point it out. You could've let me flounder in front of Mac."

Something dark flashes in his eyes. "I wouldn't do that to you. You're my partner."

I purse my lips, choosing my next words carefully. "I'm also your competition for the internship."

"Yeah, and if I get it, which I'm pretty sure I will," he says, grinning, "I want to do it on my own merit. Not because I was a dick and screwed over my partner."

He's baiting me. I know it right down to my toes, but I will not fall for it.

Not today.

I match his smile. "So you're playing the academic integrity card?"

"Exactly." He shrugs. "It's a classic."

True, but if we weren't sleeping together, would he have made the same choice? I'm not sure I want to know the answer and the realization leaves a bitter taste in my mouth.

It shouldn't matter.

But it does.

35

———

DJ

DESPITE THE NEAR miss with the microphones, Sutton and I killed the sound portion of the mock broadcast. Mac only had good things to say about our prep, and to his credit, he even noticed the clusterfuck that was the cables when we arrived in the studio.

Maybe that's because he was the culprit.

My gaze slides to the main stage, where he stands behind the anchor desk, congratulating today's hosts. Could Mac have been the one to screw with the mics and tangle the cords? Maybe it was a test to see if we're prepared for the realities of studio work.

If so, we passed with flying colors.

Sutton and I make a good team. There's no denying it.

Beside me, Sutton shifts her weight.

She's wound tighter than a spring today. Not that I blame her. Every week, every project, brings us one step closer to the Sports Stream internship.

I sling an arm around her shoulders, wrapping her in a tight embrace. She fits perfectly, as if the spot at my side was carved for her alone. "Nice work today, Shorty."

"Thanks. You too."

Her words are clipped and while a bystander might think she's annoyed, I know her well enough now to recognize she's in the zone. Most likely thinking about our term paper. Which is probably the only reason she doesn't shrug me off given we have an audience.

No one's paying attention to us, though.

Like Sutton, most of our classmates are watching Mac or the clock, doing a piss-poor job concealing the restless energy that has them in a stranglehold.

It's nearly eleven, and he still has to hand back the term papers before dismissing us.

On a good day, eleven o'clock means a chaotic mass exodus, everyone eager to get an early start on the weekend.

On the Friday before a Thanksgiving? It's likely to be a stampede.

"Good work today, everyone!" Mac raises a hand, gesturing for silence. "As promised, I've got term papers to hand back before we break for the holiday. If one member of each group could come forward when I call your names, I can get you out of here on time."

Sutton tenses and I lower my mouth to her ear as he begins calling names. "Why don't you grab our paper, Shorty?"

She nods, and when her eyes meet mine, they're brimming with gratitude.

Did she really think I'd make her wait one second longer than necessary to see our grade?

Not a chance.

Mac calls off names in quick succession and our classmates dart forward to collect their papers.

"Cruz and Parker!" Mac calls, lifting our paper in the air.

It's folded to protect our privacy, but it's still a weird

experience, reminiscent of high school. Most profs would've entered the grades directly into WildcatPATH, the system used to record all student information, but Mac isn't like other profs, probably because he's not actually an academic at heart. He's a broadcaster first, a teacher second.

It's one of the things that makes him so effective.

Sutton slips out from under my arm and makes her way to the front of the studio. Her back is to me, blocking my view of Mac, but he must say something to her because she gives a curt nod as she accepts our paper.

She turns on her heel and clutches the paper to her chest, not even glancing down to check our grade.

What the hell did he say to her?

I flex my hands at my sides, each step she takes back to me feeling like a goddamn eternity.

"Mac wants to see us after class," she whispers.

"Why?"

"No clue, but I'm guessing it has to do with our paper."

My gut tightens.

It's probably nothing.

"I can't look." Sutton thrusts the term paper into my hands, eyes squeezed shut. "You do it."

Fuck it. If it's bad news, it's best to just get it over with.

I draw a steadying breath and turn the paper over, forcing myself to read the notes scrawled at the top in red ink. "Excellent work. A+."

"A+?" Her eyes go wide and she grabs the paper. For an instant, she just stands there staring at it, but when she lifts her gaze to mine, she's beaming. "We got an A+!"

"Yeah, we did." She flings herself into my arms, her sweet floral scent filling the air as I pull her close. "I told you we aced it."

"Wait." She pulls back, her excitement fading. "If our

paper was solid, do you think he wants to see us about the internship? Are we finalists?"

I sure as fuck hope so.

"Only one way to find out."

Mac dismisses the class and we join him on the set along with two other students, Preston, our resident know-it-all, and a quiet girl whose name I think is Kali.

"I know you're all anxious to get started on your fall break, so I'll make this quick." Mac grins and surveys the group, pausing just long enough to make eye contact with each of us. "Congratulations. You four are the finalists for the Sports Stream internship."

Sutton inhales sharply, but I don't dare turn to look at her.

Shit's getting real.

"Interviews will be held the first Friday of December at the Sports Stream office in Pittsburgh. I'll be canceling class in order to attend, but don't expect any handholding." He pauses, letting his words sink in. "The interview process is rigorous, as is the intern position. You can expect to complete a panel interview, an aptitude test, and a live broadcast. This is an opportunity to showcase what you've learned at Waverly, and I expect you to do the university proud. Understand?"

There's a round of assent from the group and Preston's "Yes, sir," is the loudest of all.

The arrogant prick probably thinks he's a lock for the internship.

At least he's consistent.

The asshole spent the first half of the semester bragging that his father plays golf with someone in the Sports Stream executive suite, so it's par for the course.

Guys like that always underestimate the competition. He couldn't possibly conceive of someone like me—someone with a blue-collar background and no connections—beating him at anything. I seriously doubt he'd put respect on Sutton or Kali's names either.

Ten to one, he's a misogynist.

"I'll send each of you an email with the interview details, but if you haven't already completed a mock interview at the Career Counseling office, I strongly encourage you to do so. It's great preparation for the real thing."

I glance at Sutton out of the corner of my eye. She nods slowly, soaking up Mac's every word.

Forget Preston. How the hell can I go head-to-head against Sutton?

Because you don't have a choice.

Sweat beads along my brow. I've busted my ass for this opportunity. I can't throw it away for a woman, even one as incredible as Sutton. As much as I care about her, I have to go full-throttle for this internship. It's the best chance I have of landing a position in sports broadcasting after graduation.

Things would be a lot less complicated if you weren't sleeping with the competition.

True, but I wouldn't change a damn thing.

I used to think having a woman in my life would be a distraction, that it would derail my focus and drain my energy, but I was wrong.

Being with Sutton helps me relax and recharge. I can talk to her about things I can't talk about with anyone else. Like being dyslexic. And steamy audiobooks.

Hell, it's practically self-care.

This internship could change everything.

No. I won't let it.

"If you have questions, please email me." Mac claps his hands together. "And, of course, enjoy your fall break."

We thank him and file out of the studio.

Sutton's quiet as we make our way to the front of the building and it's not until we exit that she finally speaks. "So."

"So." My breath comes out in a white puff and I shove my hands into my pockets. Although the sun is shining, it's chilly this morning and there's a breeze rustling the dead leaves that litter the front steps of the communications building.

"We should probably talk." She wrings her hands. "About the internship."

Anxiety rolls off her like a nor'easter, and though I want to soothe her nerves, I don't have the first damn clue what to say.

So much for not letting this opportunity change things.

"Maybe we should take a—"

I don't let her finish that sentence.

"Look, I don't want this to change things between us." I glance around, confirming there's no one in earshot. "We've got a good thing going. The internship doesn't have to change that."

"We're competing for the same position." She scrunches up her nose, the tip of which is turning pink from the cold. "I don't think we can just ignore that fact."

"I'm not suggesting we ignore it."

She cocks her head and the sun glints off her dark irises. "Then what are you suggesting?"

I wish I knew.

"I—" I shrug, adjusting my backpack and stalling for time. "I'm saying the internship has nothing to do with our hookups. There's no reason we can't keep the two things separate."

She sucks her bottom lip between her teeth, considering. "I don't know. It feels messy."

Maybe, but...

"It's only messy if we make it messy. We're adults, Shorty." I smirk, knowing full-well she can't resist a challenge. "I think we can agree not to let our incredible sexcapades interfere with the interview process, don't you?"

"It's not me I'm worried about," she retorts, crossing her arms. "Unlike some people, I'm not ruled by my sexual organs."

My dwindling condom supply would suggest otherwise, but I know better than to point it out.

"Technically, I'm ruled by hormones."

She laughs, low and husky. And despite the fact that it's colder than a witch's tit, my cock stirs.

"Now, if we're agreed"—I wrap an arm around her shoulders and steer her down the stone steps—"I suggest we head back to your place for an orgasm or five before we have to leave for Rutgers."

"Deal." She reaches across her body, offering me her right hand. I shake it. "May the best candidate win."

36

DJ

My PARENTS gawk at the stadium tunnel in awe as we line up for the Senior Day program. It's a cold, crisp day, and despite the threat of snow, the sun is shining. From the looks of it, all of Wildcat Nation has descended on College Park, ready to cheer us to victory. The stadium is vibrating with excitement —literally, the cement tunnel is damn near shaking—as the fans stomp their feet, performing a spirited cheer.

With last week's win over Rutgers, we're heading into our last game of the regular season with a 10-1 record.

Soon to be 11-1.

If things go our way today, we advance to the Big Ten Football Championship game.

But first, we have the Senior Day presentation.

Despite the chill, sweat builds around the collar of my jersey, a byproduct of nerves and adrenaline. I'm game ready in cleats and pads while my parents are wearing their Sunday best. It makes for an odd combination. One that's repeated throughout the players' tunnel as the seniors on the team line up with their loved ones.

It's a big day.

Not only because it's the last time most of these guys will play ball in Wildcat stadium, but because it's an opportunity to recognize the people in our lives who've provided endless love and support over the years. It would be easy to claim each of us got here on our own talent, but it wouldn't be true. Few of us would've made it this far if the people who believed in our potential hadn't sacrificed nights and weekends driving us to practices. If they hadn't cheered us on at every game and tournament. Invested in summer camps and developmental coaching.

For me, those people were my parents.

Pride shines in their eyes and, despite some earlier drama at the football building, spirits are high. Mom and Dad enjoyed meeting the other parents. No surprise there. Mom's always been a social butterfly. And my dad? Well, he may be an introvert, but it's safe to say he was starstruck by Reid's father, a future Hall of Famer.

Hell, I think he's still riding high, a goofy-ass grin on his face as he turns to me.

"When you started playing ball, I never imagined we'd one day be exiting the Wildcat tunnel together." Tears glisten in his eyes as he rests a hand on my shoulder. "I'm so proud of you, son."

"We both are." On my other side, Mom grabs my hand, giving it a gentle squeeze. "You've worked so hard to get here."

She doesn't say it, but I know she's not talking about my dedication on the field, but in the classroom. My academic career may have started off lackluster, but I'll be damned if it ends that way.

I grin. "You're making it sound like I've already peaked."

"Let's hope that's not the case." She hooks her arm through mine, looking up at me with a mischievous glint in her hazel eyes. "Which reminds me, do you think Coach

Collins will let us take part again next year since you're going to be a super senior? It's not every day a couple of small-town yahoos like your father and I get to take the field before such a large crowd."

I snort and shake my head. "I don't think that's how this works."

Then again, who knows?

For all his bluster, Coach is a softy. If he knew my mom wanted to participate in Senior Day again next year, he'd probably make it happen.

"Are you ready for your Sports Stream interview?" Dad asks.

"As ready as I can be."

I have no clue what to expect. Sure, Mac gave us parameters, but who knows what kind of aptitude test they're going to spring on us?

My father breathes into his hands, attempting to warm them. "Have you been preparing? Answering practice questions online? Created a résumé?"

He fires the questions off so quickly, they're impossible to answer.

"There's no such thing as being too prepared," he adds. "Your uncle offered to practice with you over the phone, if you need help. He's interviewed hundreds of people in his line of work. Might be good practice for you."

"I'm good." No disrespect to my uncle, but I've been through his interview process. It's not what I'd call challenging, and the skills he's looking for on his crews are a far cry from what Sports Stream requires. "I'm working with the office of Career Counseling here at the university."

His brows knit together. "What's that?"

"They help with job placement, provide résumé critiques, and assist with interview prep. To ensure students know what to expect during a job search." I shift my weight and switch my helmet to my other hand. As much as I love chatting up my parents, it would be nice if the announcer could hurry the fuck up. I'm ready to hit the field and standing around on concrete isn't exactly comfortable when you're wearing cleats. "I've got a mock interview scheduled this week. After, they'll give me feedback on my answers, body language, what areas could use some work, and stuff like that."

"That's incredible." Dad shakes his head in wonder. "You've got so many opportunities your mother and I never had. I'm glad you're making the most of them."

I spin around, facing both of my parents.

"The only reason I have these opportunities is because you guys worked so hard to make them for me. I couldn't have done any of this without you." Emotion clogs my throat, making it hard to speak. "Your support is everything."

And that's the God's honest truth.

I never could have done this on my own.

My parents exchange a look, one I can't decipher, and my father cups my cheek, something he hasn't done since I was a kid. "You did this on your own, DJ. You worked hard and you should be proud."

I nod, tears stinging the backs of my eyes. "I am. Thank you, sir."

"Now." Mom pulls herself up to her full height. "What about that girl you mentioned? The one you've been working with all semester. Is she up for this internship, too?"

"Yes, ma'am." No need to elaborate.

"Well, don't worry. I'm sure you'll outshine her."

"Not that I don't appreciate the support," I say, stifling a laugh. "But I'm sure her parents told her the same thing."

"Maybe, but I'm right." A self-satisfied smile curves her lips. "Speaking of women... Are you dating anyone?"

Fuuuck.

Not this again.

"I told you. I'm not dating. Between school and football, I don't have time."

She already grilled me over Thanksgiving dinner, in front of friends and family, so I don't know why she's bringing it up again. She can't possibly think the answer's changed. It's only been two days.

Both of which I've spent with her.

Still, she looks hopeful.

Probably because she's not buying what you're selling.

Mom's always been good at spotting a lie, no matter how small, but technically, it's not a lie because Sutton and I aren't dating.

Yet.

Over the last few days, I've started to think it's a situation that needs to be rectified.

"You need to make time." Mom sighs, her breath forming a white cloud as she exhales. "You can't spend your entire life working or you'll wake up one day old and alone and full of regret."

I turn to my father. "She's been watching A Christmas Carol, hasn't she?"

"You know your mom." He chuckles and his shoulders shake. "She made me watch it in the hotel room last night."

She sniffs and shoots him an exasperated look. "Don't let your father fool you. He's the one who picked it."

"It was that or one of those over-the-top Hallmark movies," he says, wrapping an arm around her waist and pulling her in for a kiss. "I picked the lesser of two evils."

She smiles and her cheeks, which are red with cold, turn a deeper shade of crimson. "I love those movies."

"And I love you."

It's the same reason I watch the sappy holiday romcoms with her.

Mom always plays them while we bake Christmas cookies. It's a longstanding tradition, one we've upheld for the last three years, even though it means moving cookie day to the middle of December when I get home from school.

"Here we go!" Coach Collins shouts, sparing me any further talk of my love life.

The announcer kicks off the Senior Day presentation by introducing Reid. As he takes the field, his escort is announced and then his academic achievements and future goals follow before a previously recorded message is played on the big screen. In the message, Reid thanks his father and the fans for their support before he ends with "Go Wildcats!"

The crowd goes wild and pride fills my chest as I watch my teammates take the field one by one. Pride at our shared accomplishments. At how we've all grown and changed since freshman year. We aren't done—not by a long shot—but I can't help but marvel at the difference three years makes, and I can't wait to see what the future holds for each of these guys, though I'll sure as hell miss them when they're gone.

Sutton will still be on campus next year.

With my parents at my side, I step up to the tunnel opening, waiting for my name to be called. I scan the sideline for the Wildcat, and just as my name echoes through the stadium, I spot her waving a blue and white Waverly flag that's almost as tall as she is.

Later. Think about it later.

Right now, we've got a game to win.

⁓

Four hours later, I'm standing on the sideline with my boys, gripping Vaughn's jersey, as the game clock runs down, cementing our 30-0 win over the Terrapins.

The stadium erupts and Reid pumps his fist in the air, far too chill as I leap onto the mountain man's back. "Eleven and one, baby! We fucking did it!"

"Hell yeah, we did," Vaughn shouts, reaching around to slap me on the biceps as our defense jogs off the field, celebrating the first and only shutout of the regular season. "Nothing like finishing on a high note."

No kidding. With our record, we're guaranteed a bowl appearance. The question is, which one? Bowl matchups won't be determined until after the division championship games are played. If Ohio loses today, we advance. If not...

No point sweating it now.

It's out of our hands. All we can do is wait and hope we're in.

It has to be enough.

I drop to the ground and clap Coop on the shoulder, but it's clear he's not in the mood to celebrate. After the shitshow at the football building earlier, I can hardly fault him. Reid whispers something in his ear before turning to celebrate with the rest of the team, ever the dutiful captain.

When we finally make our way back to the locker room, Coach doles out some rare praise before reminding us to stay the fuck out of trouble. By the time he tells us to hit the showers, my brain is on auto-pilot. I wash up and when I get back to my locker, Reid's trying to convince Coop to grab a bite to eat with him and his father.

I run a towel through my hair, drying the shaggy locks. I'm in desperate need of a cut, but I like the way it feels when Sutton runs her fingers through it, something she tends to do while we're lying in bed.

My skin pebbles at the thought of her nails scraping against my scalp, and it's impossible to suppress the shiver that races up my spine.

"Dude, you need thicker skin," Vaughn says, buttoning his jeans. "It's not even cold in here."

"My skin is just fine, fuck you very much." I throw my towel at him, but he deflects it and it lands on the bench in a soggy white lump. "In fact, it's perfect for California where the championship game will be played."

"I know that's right!" Smith chimes in, extending a fist to me. I bump it as Vaughn kisses his fingertips and points to the sky. "Where are we celebrating tonight?"

"I'm keeping it low-key." I grab a pair of boxer briefs from my locker and slip them on. "My parents are taking me out to eat."

He looks at me like I've just announced I'm going to dip my balls in hot wax.

"Yeah, man. But what're you doing after?"

Fucking my girl, if I'm lucky.

"I'll probably just head home and crash."

He makes a dismissive sound and turns his attention to my roommates. "You believe this shit?"

"It's Senior Day." Reid shrugs. "We've all got family in town."

Smith nods, but he's clearly disappointed as he turns to a couple of underclassmen on the other side of his locker.

The last thing I want to do tonight is hang out on Greek Row and get shit-faced. I haven't seen Sutton since I got back to campus yesterday, and with winter break approaching, I want to spend as much time with her as I can.

You could invite her to dinner.

With my family?

No way. Dad would tell embarrassing stories. Mom would pepper her with questions. They'd make assumptions.

The realization isn't as unappealing as it should be.

I grab my phone before I can change my mind.

Me: Hey, Shorty. Want to grab dinner? My treat.

Technically, my parents are treating, but it's whatever. Everyone knows free meals are the kryptonite of every college student ever.

Shorty: Aren't you having dinner with your parents?

Me: Trust me. They won't mind.

In fact, my mom would be thrilled.

There's a long pause and three little dots hover on the screen before disappearing. I stare at the message thread, heart pounding, but nothing happens.

No message. No bubbles. Nothing.

What's taking her so long? I know she's there. She just messaged me.

I have two bars, but maybe I dropped the signal. I raise my phone in the air, searching for another bar.

Finally, a new message appears.

Shorty: I don't want to intrude on your family thing. Hit me up if you want to hook up later.

Disappointment pierces my chest, and it's only when I read her message again that I realize I wanted her to meet my parents. Wanted them to meet her. Wanted this night to be more than it is.

But that's not going to happen, because as much as I care about Sutton, we aren't on the same page.

Hell, I'm not even sure we're reading the same playbook.

37

SUTTON

Hit me up if you want to hook up later? I groan and tip my head back, silently cursing my stupidity as I hover outside Coach Sharpe's office.

Buen trabajo pendeja. A guy invites you to meet the fam and not only do you decline, you suggest a casual hookup instead?

Real smooth.

In my defense, the offer came out of left field.

Or is it right field?

Whatever. It doesn't matter. The point is, I never saw it coming. That's not what Devin and I are about. We're casual. No labels. No expectations. No meeting the family.

Apparently, he didn't get that memo.

Ahogarse en un vaso de agua.

Right. I'm probably making a big deal out of nothing.

It was a casual, last-minute invitation. He was probably celebrating with the guys, feeling great about today's shutout, and made the offer without thinking. For all I know, he invited the whole team.

I draw a steadying breath and check my phone, hoping for a response.

Nothing.

I stare at the screen, willing him to say something. Anything.

Heck, I'd settle for a GIF at this point.

I'd wanted to say yes. To accept the dinner invitation, even though the idea of meeting his parents scares the crap out of me. I missed him over break and though we exchanged a few texts, it wasn't the same.

If he offers again, say yes.

Or I could text and say I changed my mind?

A pair of pristine white sneakers enter my field of vision and there's a quiet *snick* as Coach Sharpe unlocks the door to his office. "Thank you for waiting, Miss Cruz."

Like I had a choice.

I stuff my phone in my back pocket and look up, realizing for the first time that he's not alone. Coach Miller is with him, her face a blank mask.

Mierda.

Why is she here? The last time we all met like this, it didn't end well.

Dread pools low in my belly and a cold sweat beads between my breasts.

I'm supposed to be turning in my Wildcat costume today.

That was the deal.

So why is she here?

Only one way to find out.

I grab my duffle bag from the floor and trail them into the office, déjà vu sweeping over me as I drop into a chair opposite Coach Sharpe's desk.

His office is light and airy, the white walls lined with colorful cheer photos and polished trophies that reflect the late afternoon sun.

The atmosphere does little to put my nerves at ease.

Coach Sharpe sinks into an oversized leather chair before leaning forward and folding his hands on the Wildcat blotter that covers his desk.

He clears his throat and adrenaline spikes through my system. "Miss Cruz."

I nod and wipe my palms on my thighs.

"As discussed previously, being part of Waverly's longstanding mascot tradition is no small undertaking. The Wildcat is our greatest symbol and students who take on the role have big shoes—and expectations—to fill."

I swallow though my mouth is drier than a cotton ball.

"I'd like to start out by congratulating you on rising to the occasion." A smile breaks across his face and relief washes over me, my shoulders going loose. "We got off to a rocky start, but you made the mascot your own this season and you've done a commendable job." He pauses. "Despite the unpleasant circumstances that led you to the role, I knew you could do it, if you put in the work."

"Thank you." A smile tugs at the corner of my mouth. "It was actually kind of fun once I got the hang of performing."

He flashes me a quizzical look. "Would you like to stay on for the rest of the semester?"

Not even a little. "I appreciate the offer, but with gymnastics ramping up, that won't be possible."

Coach Miller grins.

Unlike Coach Sharpe, she knows just how hard it's been for me to get in my twenty hours of conditioning and practice while fulfilling my Wildcat duties and maintaining my GPA.

"Very well." He gives a curt nod. "Our regular mascot will be stateside next week, so I think it's safe to say you can officially hang up your paws."

Thank you, sweet baby Jesus.

Coach Miller shifts in her chair, turning her body toward

mine. "I asked Coach Sharpe if I could be here today because I've been watching you closely this semester, Sutton."

I stiffen, my muscles going taut.

"Over the last three months, you've shown a great deal of determination and fortitude as you worked to juggle your responsibilities and meet your obligations."

"Thank you."

A warm glow sparks in my chest. I wasn't looking for praise, but it's nice to have my efforts acknowledged. This has been the most challenging semester of my college career, but it's also been the most rewarding, which is strange since I haven't actually been competing.

"You may not realize it, but you've grown tremendously this semester, both as a leader and as a person. You embraced the role of the Wildcat and whether you meant to or not, you impressed me." No small feat. The woman is unflappable. "Which is why I'm naming you Junior Captain this year."

I bolt upright, heart hammering against my ribcage. "Really?"

"You've earned it." She gives me a pointed look, one slender brow arched. "Lucky for you, I believe in second chances."

You know, I think I'm starting to believe in them myself.

"Thank you." There are about a hundred more where that came from, but I manage to hold them back. "I won't let you down, Coach."

I'm walking on air as I exit the building. I pull out my phone to text Maddie the news, but I don't get a chance because I've got fifteen unread messages.

*Brooke: The United G deal fell through. They decided to "go in a different direction." *sobbing emoji**

I nearly drop my phone as I reread her text. Brooke's been negotiating the name, image, likeness deal with United G for weeks. They said she was the perfect athlete to endorse their brand.

How could this happen?

I scan the rest of the thread, so lost in the exchange I barely notice my fingers stiffen from the cold as I make my way up University Drive.

Soraya: That's bullshit. They've been stringing you along for months.

Maddie: I'm so sorry.

Brooke: I can't believe this. Just last week, the rep told me they were drawing up the contract, but that I had to be exclusive, so I declined the Pinnacle deal.

No. *Nonono.* I'm no expert, but my father works in sourcing and I've picked up a thing or two about negotiations over the years. Rule number one? A deal isn't done until the contract is signed by both parties.

Maddie: Can you go back to Pinnacle and say you changed your mind?

Brooke: I already tried. They gave my spot to someone else.

Soraya: Did you explain to United G that you declined the other offer in good faith?

Brooke: Yeah. The rep said there's nothing she can do.

Of course. Because to United G, it's just business. Another day, another dollar. I want to be surprised, but... There was a story in the news recently about a female athlete who was pregnant with her first child and her sponsor wanted to cut her pay as a result. Some crap about her not being at peak performance.

Brooke: Some bullshit about the executive team changing creative.

Soraya: That's seriously fucked.

Brooke: Tell me about it. I worked my ass off to keep my content fresh, and this is what I have to show for it?

Maddie: I will NEVER wear another United G leo.

Maddie: In fact, I'm throwing every single one I own in the trash right now.

The message is followed by a hot garbage GIF.

Soraya: Agreed. They're trash, just like their management.

*Brooke: *sad face emoji**

My fingers fly over the screen as I type a reply, anger fueling my movements.

*Me: I'm so sorry, Brooke. Girls' night at our place? We can eat ice cream and burn our leos together. *fire emoji**

No way am I going to continue supporting a company that treats athletes like disposable, interchangeable assets. I'd rather compete naked than be seen wearing one of their leotards after the way they've treated Brooke.

We make plans to meet up and as I walk home, frustration twists my stomach. The way United G treated Brooke is inexcusable. If she'd had someone looking out for her, someone with experience to help navigate the murky waters of NIL, this never would've happened.

But she didn't.

She was on her own because she's twenty years old and hails from a family of scientific researchers. Her parents might be experts in their fields, but Brooke said herself that they know jack about negotiating endorsement deals.

And United G took complete advantage.

After all, it's easy to screw over inexperienced athletes when you've got deep pockets and there's no one to stop you.

It's the way of the world.

No. I refuse to accept that jaded outlook. Brooke—and every other student athlete hustling to excel at their sport and put fans in the seats—deserves better.

If only there was a way to make it happen.

38

SUTTON

"WHAT WOULD you say is your biggest weakness?"

Parker rolls his eyes, but flashes me a confident smile, full lips parted to reveal a row of pearly white, camera-ready teeth. "I'm a perfectionist. I like things done right and I'm not one to cut corners, even when it saves time."

"Dios mío." I nudge him in the ribs. "You got that answer from one of those *How to make a great first impression and ace interviews* sites, didn't you?"

His face goes slack. "I can neither confirm nor deny."

I snort-laugh. "Yeah, well, that advice was probably written by a guy with Cheetos fingers who still lives in his parents' basement and spends all his time on Reddit because he can't hold down a job."

"Woah." He throws up his hands, feigning surprise. "Tell me how you really feel, Shorty."

It's Friday night and we're lounging on my bed, practicing for the Sports Stream interview tomorrow. We've both done mock interviews at the Career Counseling office as Mac suggested, but there's no such thing as being too prepared, right?

Neither of us has ever been on a professional interview before and though the counseling office told us what to expect, my stomach is twisted in knots.

Or maybe that has something to do with the big sexy tight end in my bed.

The one who's driving me to Pittsburgh tomorrow in his roommate's Jeep so we can vie for the same internship.

My stomach rolls.

Yeah, that's definitely it.

"I'm too nervous to eat." I scoop up the carryout container resting on my lap and transfer it to the nightstand. The grilled chicken and kale salad looked amazing when I first opened it, but the mere thought of eating has my gag reflex on high alert. Devin doesn't seem to suffer the same affliction. He just inhaled the world's largest burger, and he's still going strong. "I don't know how you can eat that crap right now."

"I'm hungry." He makes a show of popping a fry in his mouth. "Besides, I plan to work it off before I go to bed tonight."

"Oh, really?" I roll onto my side so I'm facing him and rest my chin in my hand. "How exactly do you plan to work it off?"

He wiggles his brows, amusement dancing in his hazel eyes. "By sleeping with the enemy, of course."

His words take me by surprise. I haven't thought of myself that way in a long time and hearing him say it aloud feels wrong.

"I'm your competition, not your enemy."

"It's about time you figured that out." He grins. "It took you long enough."

I'm about to make a 2PumpChump joke for old times' sake, but I bite it back.

Devin's more than proven our first night together was a

fluke and we're both stressed, even if he won't admit it. I'm not about to kick him while he's down.

Not when there are other, more pleasurable ways we could relieve the tension.

My gaze slides over the length of his hard body.

"What part of the interview process is making you nervous?" he asks, stuffing his trash into the brown paper delivery bag and dropping it on the floor. "Is it the interview, the aptitude test, or the broadcast?"

"All of the above."

We still don't know what the aptitude test entails and despite answering what feels like a million standard interview questions, I know it won't be the same when I'm facing a panel of Sports Stream employees. What if my mind goes blank? Or I forget everything I've practiced? Or worse, what if I just don't click with the interviewers? Devin practically oozes charm. They're going to love him, and I'm not sure I can compete with that kind of natural charisma.

Which is why I've decided to take out my nose ring and wear my hair in a bun. It's about as conservative as you can get when you're rocking a shade of blue called After Midnight.

Should've dyed it a natural color.

No, screw that. I'm not going to change everything about myself to fit some misogynistic notion of what a female sportscaster should look like.

"You have nothing to worry about." Devin scoots down on the bed and rolls onto his side so we're face to face. "You nailed your mock interview. You're ready, Sutton, even if you don't feel it."

"I hope you're right." I toy with a loose thread on my comforter. There's something else that's been bothering me, but I'm not ready to give it voice. Not yet. "I don't want to let Mac down."

"Forget about Mac." He hooks a finger under my chin, forcing me to meet his eyes. "The only person you need to worry about letting down is yourself. Fuck everyone else."

If only it were that easy.

"What about you?" I ask, turning the table on him. "What part of the interview process are you most worried about?"

"I don't know." His lips twist, but I don't push because it's clear he's thinking it over. "Maybe the aptitude test? But I think it's mostly the not knowing that's bugging me."

"Yeah, I'm pretty sure they made it vague as hell just to torture us." I smirk. "Watch, it'll be something completely ridiculous, like memorizing the office coffee order or fetching lunch."

He shudders. "Let's hope not. I'd fail the hell out of that."

"Says the guy who somehow got an entire pan of peanut butter brownies from Daily Grind between morning practice and his eight a.m. class." I curl into him, relaxing as the scent of sandalwood and citrus settles over me. "You never did tell me how you managed it."

He laughs and snakes an arm around my waist, the comforting weight of him pinning me to the mattress. "I see how it is. Trying to unlock all my secret hacks before the interview tomorrow?"

"It was worth a shot." Which reminds me. "Did you talk to Mac about getting accommodations for the broadcast portion of the interview?"

During our mock broadcasts in class, we had the scripts ahead of time, but that probably won't be the case tomorrow. Not if they want to see how we perform under pressure.

Fifteen years of competitive gymnastics should be proof enough.

But not all the interns are athletes.

"No," Devin says, bringing me back to the moment. "I didn't see the point."

"What?" I sit up and he pulls his arm back. "Why not?"

"I don't need accommodations. Or pity." He gives me a meaningful look, which is crap. I've never pitied him because of his dyslexia. "I can do this on my own."

The man has got to be the most stubborn human I've ever met.

"Okay, first of all, no one is pitying you." He opens his mouth to protest, but I swipe a hand through the air, shutting him down. "Accommodations exist for a reason. Using them isn't a reflection of your ability to perform the job or an indicator of future success. They're a tool in your toolbox. No more, no less."

"Easy for you to say." He shoves his fingers through his hair and my thoughts must be written all over my face because he adds, "I'm not ashamed, if that's what you're thinking."

"Good." The word comes out more fiercely than intended and his brows shoot up. "There's no reason for you to be embarrassed."

So what if his brain works differently? That doesn't make it lesser.

"Over the years," he says, choosing his words carefully, "I've dealt with enough snide comments to know that some people don't handle accommodations well. They see it as an unfair advantage or an inconvenience or a combination of the two."

Anger flares red-hot and molten, incinerating every other emotion his words have evoked. "That is complete and utter bullshit, and you know it."

"I do." He nods slowly. "But I don't need those kinds of distractions tomorrow, so I'm going to go in there and do my best, just like everyone else."

"Doing your best means setting yourself up for success, not hoping things go your way."

We stare at one another, deadlocked, neither of us willing to concede.

Did I push too far? Too hard?

It's not my place to tell him what he should and shouldn't do, but I can't stand by and silently watch him roll the dice with his future because he's worried about what other people might think.

"Look, I know you're just trying to help, but I'm good. I know my capabilities and my limits. You need to trust me on this, okay?" He's so sincere, his eyes pleading with me for understanding that when he cups my cheek, his calloused fingers molding to my skin, I cave. "I don't want you worrying about me. You need to stay focused on you tomorrow."

That was our deal, after all.

I nod. "May the best candidate win."

"Thank you. I plan to." A slow smile spreads over his face, and my heart flutters in response. Devin's smile is a thing of beauty and no matter how many times I see it, it still has this effect on me. Probably always will. "Now that we've gotten that out of the way, can I please eat your pussy?"

Heat floods my core, every nerve in my body tingling with anticipation as I match his smile with a wicked grin of my own. "I thought you'd never ask."

39

DJ

Sutton's challenging smile is all the encouragement I need. My cock hardens and in one swift move, I roll her onto her back, pinning her to the bed and caging her small body between my arms. "The next time we do this, remind me to start with dessert."

"It's me, right?" She sweeps her fingertips across my forehead, brushing aside a stray lock of hair. Her touch is featherlight, and a shiver of desire races down my spine. "I'm the dessert?"

"You know it, Shorty."

She's so damn gorgeous, lips parted on a laugh, cobalt hair splashed across the pillow as she stares up at me with bright eyes.

I lower my mouth to hers, and there's nothing soft or gentle about the way I claim her. The kiss is rough and possessive, an animalistic mating of lips and teeth and tongues.

This is what Sutton needs.

What we both need.

A distraction from the internship. From Sports Stream. From reality.

To fuck the stress and anxiety from our lives, if only for a night.

She nips my lower lip and I growl in response, a primal rumble that emanates from deep within my chest.

"Careful, Shorty. Turnabout is fair play."

She bats her lashes, looking far from innocent. "I thought you were into that kind of thing?"

"You know damn well I love it when you use your teeth, but I'd rather not show up for my interview tomorrow with a swollen lip."

"You can say it's a big manly football injury." She smirks. "I'm sure they'd understand."

"Smartass."

"You like it."

"I really do." She rakes her nails down my back and I pull my shirt off, desperate to feel the sharp bite of pain directly on my skin. To feel her marking me as her own, however temporary. "Do that again," I rasp.

Her smile widens, as if she's only just realized she holds all the power. "You forgot to say please."

If Sutton wants me to beg, I'll beg, but only for her.

"Do that again, *please*."

Her nails dig into my shoulders like talons, and as she drags them down my back, pleasure and pain ripple through my body in tandem.

"I'm so fucking hard right now." Desperate to ease the growing tension at the base of my spine, I roll my hips as I pepper kisses along her jaw and throat, working my way down to her collarbone. Her skin is soft and supple, completely at odds with the firm muscles that define every dip and curve of her body. I cup her breast, kneading the tender flesh, and she moans in response, a deep throaty sound that speaks directly to my cock. *Fucking hell.* "Do you have any idea what you do to me?"

I don't give her a chance to reply. I grab her hand and press it to my cock, wrapping her fingers around my shaft so that only the thin fabric of my gym shorts separates us.

Her eyes go wide and I stare, entranced, as she licks her lower lip, making it glisten in the soft glow of the lamp.

"That's all you, Shorty." I thrust into her hand, but it's not enough. I need to be inside her. To feel that slick, wet warmth all around me. "I can't get enough of you. I'm like a goddamn addict, waking up hard, falling asleep hard, thinking about fucking you every waking moment of every single day, and there's nothing I won't do to get my next hit."

"Take off your shorts."

"Did you hear what—"

"Take off. Your shorts."

I don't need to be told a third time.

With lightning speed, I roll off the bed and strip naked.

Sutton does that lip licking thing again and my cock twitches because I'm a hot-blooded guy who likes blowjobs. Though it's one of the few things we haven't tried, I'm not going to force the issue. The sex is incredible and I'm not about to push Sutton into doing anything she's not comfortable doing.

She climbs off the bed and drops to her knees and *holy shit,* is this really happening?

Those big brown eyes settle on mine and the vulnerability in them nearly brings me to my knees.

I cup her face and sweep my thumb across her cheek. "Shorty, you don't have to—"

"I want to make you feel good."

After all these months, she still doesn't get it.

"I always feel good when I'm with you. With or without sex. Just being with you is enough. *You* are enough."

Tears glisten in her eyes, but she blinks them away.

"Thank you." She swallows, her throat bobbing delicately. "I want to do this, Devin. With you."

I nod. "Okay."

Sutton is a smart woman. I won't insult her by questioning her decision. I trust her to know her own mind. Her own desires.

Desires that right now are very much aligned with my own.

I thread my fingers through her hair, snapping the elastic wrapped around her messy bun as she takes my cock in hand, her slim fingers circling my shaft. She grips the base and when she squeezes, applying pressure, a quiet groan bursts from my lips.

"That's it, Shorty."

A smile unfurls on her lips and she seems to gain confidence as her tongue darts out, licking the head of my cock like an ice cream cone.

Pleasure radiates from the point of contact and my balls tighten. Every nerve in my body—hell, every cell—is screaming for more, but I force myself to remain still. To let her set the pace.

To savor this moment and enjoy the ride.

Like the perfectionist she is, my girl gives it her all, alternating between licking and sucking, her tongue swirling over my crown and down my shaft as she works me with her hand. She's relentless. Each sweep of her tongue delivers a fresh wave of pleasure and when she cups my balls and takes me deep, it's all I can do to not fuck her mouth.

"Eyes on me, Shorty." I tug on her hair, forcing her head back. "I want you to know exactly whose cock you're sucking."

Her gaze locks on mine and she makes a humming sound in the back of her throat. It could be agreement. It could be a big "Fuck you." Either way, it feels damn good. The tension at the base of my spine coils tighter, every muscle in my body going taut.

I've imagined this moment countless times, but as usual, the fantasy pales compared to the reality.

"If you keep that up, I'm going to come."

Sutton's lips slide up my shaft and she releases the head of my cock with a loud *pop*.

She smirks, arching one of those perfect brows. "That is the general idea."

She's got you there, dumbass.

It's not my fault. Pleasure has reprogrammed my brain. Brought me back to my basest instincts. I'm like a fucking Neanderthal, barely able to string together a complete sentence.

"I need to come inside you." I scoop her up, embracing my inner caveman, and deposit her on the edge of the bed. "To come with you. Together."

I need to feel her body grip me tight as she shatters into a million pieces.

Sutton laughs as I fish a condom out of the nightstand drawer and hastily put it on. That laugh is my favorite fucking sound in the world and hearing it now is doubly rewarding because it means she's no longer stressing about tomorrow's interview.

"This is going to be hard and fast," I warn, pushing her back on the bed.

She grins and I grab her ankles, positioning them on my shoulders.

From this angle, I've got the perfect view of her pussy. It's pink and wet, her clit swollen.

Ready.

I position myself at her entrance, and with one quick thrust, seat myself to the hilt.

Fuuuck.

Sutton's hot and tight, her pussy sheathing me like a glove.

I pull back, the sight of our joined bodies ripping a possessive growl from my throat, the urge to make her mine rising unbidden.

How the hell am I ever going to give this up?

I'm not. It's that simple.

I press my thumb to her clit as I thrust deep inside her, our flesh slapping together. She cries out, fisting her hands in the comforter as I circle that little bundle of nerves.

"Don't hold back," she pleads. "I can take it."

"I know you can, Shorty." I lean down and kiss her, swallowing another cry as I drive deep, pinning her thighs to her chest. She's so goddamn flexible I'm still in constant awe of her body.

Which is just one of the reasons I'm not going to last long tonight.

From the sounds of it, neither is she.

Thank Christ.

Sweat pools between my shoulder blades as I race toward climax.

Sutton's breath is coming hard and fast, and there's a light sheen of sweat on her forehead as I bear down on her clit, increasing the pressure as my cock slides home, every inch buried inside her tight channel.

"Yes!" She arches her back and her inner walls contract, gripping me tight. "Yes, yes, fuck, yes Devin."

Male pride fills my chest and electricity crackles up my spine as my orgasm barrels through me like a linebacker, obliterating coherent thought, leaving me dazed and weak-kneed as I ride out the aftershocks.

Afterward, as we lie in bed, her head resting on my chest, one leg draped over mine, she sighs. "You're so warm all the time. It's like having my own personal heater."

"Happy to be of service."

Hell, I'd warm her bed every night if she'd let me.

Her eyes drift shut and I pull the comforter tighter around her, the way I always do before leaving. Sutton may be a native Pennsylvanian, but she's always cold, and when I climb out of this bed, I'll be taking my body heat with me.

"Stay the night?"

I freeze. She's never asked me to stay over before. "You sure?"

"It just makes sense." She yawns and scoots closer, sealing every inch of her body to mine. "We have to be up early and we're traveling together."

She says it casually, doesn't even open her eyes, but still, it feels like a big step. Like maybe we're heading for relationship territory.

It's only a big deal if you make it a big deal.

Right. Play it cool.

"Worried I'll oversleep and make you late for your interview?"

Her responding laugh is low and husky, as if she's already on the cusp of sleep.

I've never slept with a woman before—never had the urge to stay over—but I want this. I want to fall asleep with Sutton's head on my chest, her naked body pressed to mine.

I don't want this thing between us to end.

Not tomorrow. Not the day after.

I want more. Have for a while now.

More late-night study sessions. More banter. More everything.

My chest tightens at the realization and I open my mouth to tell her, but then she exhales and her eyelids flutter.

Not tonight.

She's got enough on her mind with the interview tomorrow. We both do.

So even though I want to slice my chest open and let all those messy emotions come pouring out, I'll wait. After all, it's just one day. I've waited this long. I can wait a little longer.

Once the interviews are done, though, all bets are off.

Easy for you to say. Your season is winding down.

Not really. We've got the Big Ten Championship game in Indianapolis Saturday. Then, with any luck, the CFP Semi-Finals and the championship game.

Still, my season will be over by the time spring semester starts and Sutton's will just be ramping up.

It doesn't matter. We'll figure it out. Make it work somehow.

We have a good thing going, and I'm not about to let it slip away.

40

———

SUTTON

"I THINK I'm going to be sick."

Devin turns to me, concern etched in the lines of his face. "Do you want to sit down? Go back to the Jeep?"

We had to park a block from the Sports Stream offices. There's no time to go back to the garage. Thanks to rush hour traffic, we're already cutting it close.

If you're not five minutes early, you're already late.

"No." I close my eyes and suck in a breath, which proves to be a mistake because I get a lungful of exhaust fumes from a passing bus. *Welcome to the Steel City.* "Just give me a minute."

I shouldn't be this nervous. I've competed before thousands of people on a national stage. By comparison, a panel interview with a few stuffed shirts is nothing.

But I was prepared for those competitions. I spent months perfecting my routines. Knew them inside out.

This is no different.

Right. I've done the work. Researched Sports Stream. Practiced interview questions. Triple checked my résumé.

"You can do this." Devin's words are brimming with confidence and when his fingers brush my cheek, I smile.

"Sorry. I don't know what's gotten into me this morning." Truth. Last night was incredible. It was the first time I've given oral, and it was empowering to discover I could unravel the powerful man at my side with a simple flick of my tongue, but even better was drifting off in his arms. Waking to find him curled against my back, the big spoon to my little one. But now everything just feels off. Me. The internship. The fact that I'm going to sabotage both our chances if we don't get moving. "Let's go. We don't want to be late."

The day is gray and overcast, the wind blustering as we approach the Sports Stream offices, which are in a towering metal and glass high rise. According to the sign out front, there are several news and media stations housed in the building, but there's no time to linger and when Devin opens the door for me, I breeze right through, making a beeline for the marble security desk in the center of the lobby.

The guard greets us stoically and we sign in as he assigns us visitor badges.

"Be sure to wear your badge at all times." He gives me a slow once-over. "They'll let you access the elevators, and if you're caught without it, you'll be escorted from the premises."

Heat floods my cheeks.

Yes, I look like a kid playing dress up, but I don't need him to point out that I don't belong. The black pantsuit—which I borrowed from Soraya—isn't me at all. It's ultra-conservative and even Maddie's kitten heels—which she insisted I wear because apparently Docs aren't appropriate footwear for a corporate setting—can't save it.

I clip the badge to my jacket without comment.

The guard barely glances at Devin, whose broad shoulders and trim waist fill his navy suit like it was custom made, though I know he bought it off the rack.

"Which floor for Sports Stream?" he asks, clipping the badge to the lapel of his jacket.

"Thirty-four."

We make our way to the express elevator, and when the doors close, I glimpse my reflection in the gilded surface. I look ridiculous. Wrong. Not at all like myself. But there's no time to dwell on it because the elevator rockets skyward.

My stomach drops and I press my lips flat.

Devin takes my hand, squeezing it gently as we soar upward, the floors ticking by on the overhead screen in rapid succession.

"Can you imagine working here?" he asks, with barely contained enthusiasm.

"No, I really can't." His brow furrows and I hastily add, "I'll bet it's got a great view of the river."

"Which one?"

I shrug. "Maybe all of them, depending on the direction."

The city has three major rivers and they all come together at Point State Park, a fact I only know because my family visited the city for a gymnastics competition when Gabby and I were kids.

The elevator slows as we approach thirty-four and Devin releases my hand just as the overhead bell chimes.

"Thanks. Good luck today."

He doesn't need it. He's amazing and the selection committee is bound to see it.

"You, too."

The doors slide open to reveal a sleek black reception desk with the words *Sports Stream* in bold red script on the wall above. We step into the lobby to find Mac, Kali, and Preston gathered in a tight circle.

Our professor turns to us with a welcoming smile. "Miss Cruz. Mr. Parker. Did you find the place okay?"

Devin grins, turning on the charm as easily as one might turn on the tv. "Couldn't miss it. This is some building."

"Now that we're all here," Preston says, directing a condescending smile our way. "Perhaps we could start the tour?"

Qué cabrón.

The urge to check the time strikes hard and fast and it takes all my self-control to resist. We aren't late. I know we aren't late and I will not let that pendejo get in my head before the interviews have even started.

Kali offers me a weak smile and we follow along like ducklings as Mac leads us from reception and down a long hall that leads to one massive cubicle farm. It's a sea of oatmeal-colored cubes from one end of the floor to the other, each containing a desk, monitor, and a harried looking employee.

Never one to hold back, Devin quips, "That's a lot of cubes."

Mac chuckles. "Not what you were expecting, Mr. Parker?"

"I've always been more of an outdoorsy guy."

The maze of partitions must look like a literal hellscape to him. I can't even see over the top of them, but I can see enough to get the lay of the land and it's like a bad episode of The Office.

"This is where the real magic happens." Mac gestures to the sea of cubes. "Marketing. Finance. Web development. Accounting. Consumer insights. I know it's not as sexy as screenwork, but every one of these departments is critical to ensuring Sports Stream delivers top ratings."

It's a subtle reminder that the intern could be assigned a writer's desk or any number of other positions.

"I'm partial to the studios myself," Preston announces,

completely oblivious as he sizes each of us up. "My father is friends with the CFO, so I got the tour ages ago."

And he wants us to know it. To know he's got the inside track—or thinks he does.

The guy is a creep, but there's no denying he's got the right look for tv. Slick blond hair. Tailored suit. Freaking dimples.

He launches into a story about focus groups, and I sneak a sidelong glance at Kali. She has golden brown skin and her dark hair is pulled back in a sleek bun, much like my own. She's the quietest member of our group, but her dark eyes are sharp and focused. From what I've seen, she only speaks when she has something of value to say, which is a relief since Preston seems determined to fill the room with hot air.

Still, I can't make the mistake of underestimating him.

Either of them, actually.

Devin isn't my only competition, even if it feels that way.

"Shall we move on to the studio, then?" Mac asks.

There's a murmur of assent and we take the elevator to the thirty-sixth floor where we're granted access to the set for The Weekly Roundup, a show that reports on sports highlights, though they rarely include gymnastics.

"Damn," Devin whispers, doing a slow turn to take in the massive set. "This has to be three times the size of the Waverly studio."

"Four." Mac rocks back on his heels, hands in his pockets. "Though, to be fair, the Waverly studio is impressive for a university setting."

"You were featured on The Weekly Roundup not too long ago, weren't you?" Preston asks, directing the question to Devin. "You got shot with a t-shirt cannon, right?"

I instinctively duck my head. But if the question is meant to embarrass Devin, it misses the mark. He just grins and says,

"With any luck, I'll be on again soon when we win the national championship."

"That would be a real boon for Waverly." Mac claps him on the shoulder. "And for Sports Stream, assuming you'd be willing to sit down for an interview."

The wink-nudge is strongly implied, but I can't fault the guy.

This business is all about networking.

We finish up in the studio and as we exit, Mac runs into an acquaintance in the hall.

"Rich! I didn't know you were in town."

"It was a last-minute trip." Rich extends his hand and Mac shakes it vigorously. "Otherwise, I'd have called to collect on that lunch you owe me."

Like Mac, Rich is probably in his forties, but he's far more polished with thick black hair, piercing blue eyes, and a crisp ivory dress shirt that complements his olive skin.

"Interview?" Mac asks, gaze darting to the guy at Rich's side.

"Yeah. I didn't want Jalen facing the vultures alone." Jalen is easily six and a half feet tall, probably around our age, maybe mid-twenties, and he grins at the mention of vultures. I like him immediately. "Jalen, this is my college roommate, Mac."

"Nice to meet you." Jalen extends his hand and they shake before Mac turns to us and makes introductions.

"How'd it go?" Mac asks.

"Smooth, thanks to Rich." Jalen hooks a thumb toward the older man. "This guy should be named sports agent of the year. He got all the questions ahead of time and set clear boundaries for the interview." There's genuine gratitude in his voice when he adds, "Good thing, too. You should've seen some of the shit they tried to slip in there."

"That's the name of the game," Rich says, deflecting the praise. "Never let your guard down."

If only someone had been there to give Brooke the same advice.

"I see you're as jaded as ever," Mac quips, nudging his old friend.

"With good reason."

"I'll take jaded over shady any day." Jalen shrugs. "At least I know Rich has my back."

Brooke could've used someone like that at her side.

"I'm not about to let an overzealous reporter ruin your endorsement opportunities." Rich smooths the front of his shirt. "You focus on your performance and I handle everything else. That's the deal."

"Yeah, well, not everyone takes their responsibilities so seriously." Jalen turns to us, a sheepish smile on his face. "My first agent screwed me over and things got ugly before we parted ways. I was lucky to connect with Rich last year."

"I'm glad things worked out for you." Even if they had to get ugly first. "It sounds like you have a good thing going now."

They're so at ease with one another and it's clear Rich truly cares for his client. Sure, he's paid to look out for Jalen's best interests, but it's obvious he takes pride in his work, protecting his clients from predatory behavior.

This is how it should be.

"On that note," Mac says, checking his smartwatch. "We should get moving. The aptitude test starts in ten minutes."

We say our goodbyes and then he crooks a finger, gesturing for us to follow.

My stomach drops.

Devin was right. Not knowing is the worst. He catches my eye and mouths, "You good?"

I nod, though I'm not sure it's true. "You?"

He shrugs and we trail after our competitors, who are right on the professor's heels.

Mac leads us down the corridor to a glass-walled conference room where four laptops have been set up.

So much for memorizing the coffee order.

"Please take a seat." Mac waits, giving us an opportunity to settle into our temporary workstations. I'm seated across from Devin with Kali on my left and Preston on my right. "You have thirty minutes to complete the test. It's unlikely you'll finish, but answer as many questions as you can in the time allotted. This assessment measures your problem-solving skills, critical thinking, attention to detail, and your ability to learn, process, and apply new information."

Oh, is that all?

My palms begin to sweat and I wipe them on my thighs.

"A bit of advice," Mac adds, stepping toward the door, a sympathetic smile on his face. "Go with your gut and don't overthink the situation."

I glance at Devin and our eyes lock.

If only it were that easy.

41

DJ

"Thank you for your time." I stand and reach across the table to shake hands with each member of the interview panel. It was a surprisingly easy process, like talking with four old friends, and though they didn't mention the results of the aptitude test, I must've passed.

Otherwise, I probably wouldn't be here.

I'm the last candidate to be interviewed, which means I'll be top of mind when they sit down to make their final decision.

At least, I hope that's how it works.

We're in another fishbowl conference room on the thirty-fourth floor with glass windows and no clock. I'm desperate to check the time, but I know better than to whip out my phone, even at this stage of the process. I think I've been in here for at least thirty minutes, but without a clock, it's impossible to be sure.

I timed the other candidate's interviews on my phone—not like I had anything better to do while waiting in reception—but I couldn't exactly time myself.

Kali's interview was only twenty-eight minutes. Preston's

went for thirty-five, but he's a windbag, so who knows if that's actually a good thing. Sutton's interview was thirty-two minutes.

I figure as long as I hit the thirty-minute mark, I'm probably a contender for the internship.

"Good luck tomorrow at the Big Ten Championship," Mitch says, shaking my hand enthusiastically. He's a middle-aged guy with thinning hair, horn-rimmed glasses, and a big personality. "That last game against Michigan was a nail-biter." A conspiratorial grin splits his face and he adds, "I wasn't sure if Waverly was going to pull it off."

"They made us work for it." I grin, though my stomach is tight with nerves. "The rematch should be a good game."

More like a slugfest.

I've been trying not to think about it, but now that Mitch has brought it up, it'll be impossible to shove it back in the box. The team flies out tonight and tomorrow we'll be playing for our conference title and an invitation to the College Football Playoff semi-finals.

Just focus on what's in front of you now.

I have to get through the last portion of this interview process before I can even think about football or bowl games or titles.

"How's the team look?" Dana asks, opening the conference room door. She's the only female member of the interview panel and she asked the hard questions, which I respect.

At least the mock interview paid off.

"Good. Everyone's healthy and with the Michigan game fresh in our minds, we know what to expect. We're ready."

Coach has made sure of it.

I've watched more film in the last week than I've watched in my entire football career. Practices haven't exactly been a breeze either, but it'll all be worth it when we bring home the conference title and secure our spot in the semi-finals.

For now, though, I need to focus on Sports Stream.

On my future.

I rejoin the rest of the candidates in the reception area, but Mac's nowhere to be seen.

"How did it go?" Sutton asks as I take the black leather chair beside her.

"I'd say I nailed it, but I guess time will tell." I roll my shoulders, trying to relieve the tightness that's settled in. "How about you?"

"It was good." She shrugs. "No major mistakes, anyway." Her gaze shifts to Preston, who's messing around on his phone, and she lowers her voice. "From the sounds of it, all the interviews went well."

Damn. Was it too much to hope one of the others had botched the Q and A?

It could all come down to the broadcast.

I have to slay it. With any luck, it'll be something about football or basketball. I'm well versed in a range of sports, but they're the two I'm most knowledgeable about. The two that would be the easiest to improvise, if needed.

Mac appears in the hall, looking rejuvenated.

Probably got his caffeine drip on while the rest of us were slogging through interviews.

"If you'll follow me, we're going to start the broadcast portion of the interview process and then you are all free to return to campus."

We take the elevator back up to the thirty-sixth floor and he leads us to The Weekly Roundup studio. The set is fully lit now, the host's desk aglow with Sports Stream's red and white logo backlit by neon lights. The glossy black floor is polished to such a high sheen, it reflects my image back at me under the harsh glare of the studio lights.

How had I missed that before?

I've watched The Weekly Roundup enough times to memorize the set, but I never noticed the mirror-like quality of the floor.

Mac's voice tears me from my reverie. "Mr. Parker, you'll be up first this time."

Damn. I'd hope to be last again, but it was probably wishful thinking.

"Then Kali, Sutton, and Preston," he continues, reading from his phone. "Filming order was randomly assigned and each of you will read a unique script."

I pay close attention as he explains the process, doing my best to ignore the cameraman and producer that are prepping the stage. The longer Mac's explanation drags on, the more time I have to think about what comes next.

The other candidates will be watching. Probably critiquing my performance and identifying opportunities for improvement. Improvements they can apply to their own broadcasts.

At least they won't be reading the same script.

We're all going in blind on that front.

When Mac finishes, I take the stage, a fine sheen of sweat coating my skin as I settle in behind the desk. The lights are brighter and hotter than those in the Waverly studio, but that's probably just nerves.

I stare at the blank teleprompter. Excellent vision will be an asset today, so at least I have one thing going for me.

The studio is dark beyond the set and I can't see the faces of my classmates—no, my competitors—but it's just as well. I need to put them out of my mind and focus on my performance.

The producer clips a mic to my shirt and we do a sound check and then it's showtime.

My gut twists like a cyclone, and I realize I'm tapping my fingers on the surface of the glossy desk.

Calm the fuck down.

Easier said than done. I have too much riding on this broadcast. On the internship.

I need to get out of my head and on the field.

It's no different from football.

And right now, the only person standing in my way is me.

I square my shoulders and do a quick breathing exercise, inhaling for four and exhaling for six.

I've got this.

"Are you ready, Mr. Parker?"

I nod and the cameraman counts it down.

Three. Two. One.

The teleprompter rolls and I read the intro, striving for energetic, but not douchey.

"Good morning, sports fans. I'm DJ Parker and today I'm filling in for your regular host, Don 'The Grisly' Barringer."

Talk about a trip. The Grisly is an NFL legend and I'm sitting in his chair. My ass is on the same leather cushion he sits on week in and week out. It's a dream come true.

Sure, my broadcast will only be seen by a handful of people, but it doesn't matter. I'm here now, just like I've imagined so many times.

Adrenaline surges through my veins.

I'm actually filming a Sports Stream broadcast.

Unreal.

The next line appears on the teleprompter.

Baseball. It's fucking baseball.

Dammit. The only thing worse than baseball is golf.

It's fine. I know the sport and it's not like I have to offer a running commentary. It's a recap report. Just hitting the highlights of an old Yankees-Braves game.

I read the lines, reciting the matchup history and before I know it, I'm describing the plays even though I can't see them. The producer will add them in the upper right corner of the screen later. Hell, maybe she's doing it as I speak.

"How about that save by Jones at the top of the fifth? Talk about true athleticism. I'm not sure anyone else could've made that play."

I look at the camera and miss the next line.

Fuck.

It scrolls out of sight, and my smile falters. I force it back into place, concentrating on the teleprompter.

No big deal. One line is nothing.

Just read the words on the screen.

"The guy is a beast. If he keeps playing like that, it's going to be a tough series for the Yankees. I don't know who he does it."

How. The word was supposed to be *how*, not *who*. It's a common mistake with dyslexia, my brain mixing up the letters to produce the wrong word.

My pulse accelerates, hammering my temples with a steadily increasing beat.

If I just had more time... But there is no time. No time to make a correction or a joke or to center myself because the words on the teleprompter just keep scrolling.

I drop another line and pick up at the bottom of the screen.

Focus, asshole.

The more frustrated I get, the harder it'll be to concentrate.

But knowing it doesn't make it any easier.

Not when Sutton is watching. And Mac. Kali. Preston.

That asshole is probably enjoying this. I can't see his face, but I can easily picture his smug grin in my mind's eye.

It doesn't matter.

This isn't about him. It's about me. My performance.

I fucked up, but I will not throw in the towel. It's not who I am. I push the fear and anxiety from my mind and focus on the screen, on keeping my energy high.

I give a play-by-play of what must've been an incredible grand slam, and I accidentally say *now* instead of *won*, but it's the only other mistake.

A big one.

When the last line scrolls by and I give the bullshit "Until next time" line, it takes a herculean effort to hold my smile until the cameraman calls "Cut!"

Because despite all the prep work, I just blew my shot at the Sports Stream internship.

42

SUTTON

DEVIN IS KILLING THE BROADCAST. He always has great energy, but seeing him on set? It's a whole other level.

One that will be hard to top.

It doesn't hurt that he looks like a freaking snack.

I don't know shit about baseball, but when he flashes that gorgeous made-for-tv smile, it doesn't matter. The best part? He's enjoying himself, and even though he's following a script, it's easy to imagine him standing on the sideline quoting stats and chatting up athletes.

The man is in his element and it's muy caliente.

If he keeps this up, I just might ride his face later.

Desire stirs low in my belly at the thought of it.

Or maybe that's the nerves.

Kind of hard to tell the difference at the moment.

"At least they didn't give him a football segment," Preston mutters. "That would've been really fucked."

I shoot him a dirty look, but it's Kali who tells him to stuff it.

Like I said, the girl only speaks when she's got something important to say.

I turn my attention back to Devin. He's describing some incredible play at third base and even though I can't see it on the screen behind him, I can easily imagine it.

He's a natural.

Devin pauses and abruptly changes tack.

Did he miss a line?

Anxiety flutters in my chest.

It doesn't matter. It's one line. It'll probably happen to all of us. It's not like Mac gave us a chance to practice and who knows how fast the words are scrolling by on the other side of the teleprompter?

Preston snickers and I shoot him a dark look.

The guy really is a creep.

I get he wants to land this internship—we all do—but he doesn't have to be such a dick about it.

Devin's voice pulls my attention back to the stage. "I don't know who he does it."

What? I take a second to replay the words in my head, to figure out what the line should have been.

My heart sinks.

It's a simple mistake to make, especially when reading from a distance, and that's probably how the selection committee will view it, but mixing up letters—entire words— is a symptom of dyslexia.

I silently curse Devin's refusal to ask for reasonable accommodations.

Processing language differently isn't anything to be ashamed of, but he's so stigmatized by his childhood experiences that he views it as a weakness. One he's determined to keep hidden, even if it costs him this opportunity.

I wring my hands, anxious AF, as he finishes the

broadcast, and when the cameraman calls "Cut!" I heave a sigh of relief.

Devin's smile evaporates and it's clear he's beating himself up over the mistakes. There were only a few in the entire broadcast, and they were barely noticeable. Surely the selection committee will overlook them given his charisma.

Kali and Devin switch places and I smile at him as he takes the spot to my right.

"You did great," I whisper, giving his hand a quick squeeze in the dark.

He presses his lips together and nods, but says nothing.

Give him space.

If our roles were reversed, I'd want time to process before talking.

We stand in silence as Kali's broadcast starts. It's kind of flat, the stage overpowering the quiet girl, and Preston says as much.

Because *of course* he does.

A muscle in Devin's jaw tics. He's probably wondering what kind of shit Preston said about his performance, and my irritation with the platinum-haired douche canoe grows.

When it's finally Preston's turn, he struts onto the set like he owns the place.

Entitled prick.

"I hope he chokes on his mic," I mutter, earning a quiet laugh from Kali.

Preston's performance is fine, but it's clear football isn't his first love. The guy would probably be way more comfortable recapping a regatta or some yuppie sport like polo.

Before I know it, it's my turn.

I take my place behind the massive desk and adjust the height of the chair so I don't look like a Munchkin peering over the shiny black surface.

The producer clips a mic to my jacket and I realize just how ridiculous it was to wish Preston would choke on the damn thing.

Amateur.

"We need a quick soundcheck and then you're good to go," she says, stepping back. "Speak into the mic. It doesn't matter what you say."

"Preston es basura."

"Sí." She gives me a thumbs up and, judging by her knowing grin, she probably has a few Spanish lessons under her belt.

The producer leaves the set and I shift my attention to the cameraman, who's messing with his lens. The lights are hot and sweat pools between my breasts as I wait for him to count it down like he's done with the others.

It's weird being on the set and staring out into the darkness.

I thought I'd be excited, but I just feel...numb.

Because you're exhausted.

The last few weeks have been a whirlwind, and I haven't been getting much sleep.

But no, that's not fair. I slept like the dead last night, Devin's body keeping me warm and toasty all night long, the sound of his soft, steady breath more relaxing than white noise could ever be.

He's out there watching me right now, a shadow in the dark. And even though he's disappointed in his performance, I know he's rooting for me. That's just the kind of person he is. He doesn't need to tear someone else down to build himself up.

The world could use more people like him.

Preston's done his best to prove it today.

The cameraman raises his hand, signaling the start of filming.

Three. Two. One.

I smile as words appear on the teleprompter.

"Good afternoon, Sports Stream fans. I'm Sutton Cruz and this week I'm filling in for your regular host, Jessica Sanders, while she's on vacation."

I read along with the teleprompter, but there's no connection. No excitement. No thrill of victory.

Something's missing.

This is the first step to making my dreams come true. Of realizing the goals I've worked so hard to achieve.

Granted, soccer isn't my first love, but it shouldn't matter.

I should feel *something*.

"Goalkeeper Liza St. Clair is on fire, earning her fifth clean sheet of the season."

The words flow from my lips, but my mind is a million miles away, remembering the day I decided to become a sports commentator. Gabby had just won her first state meet and my family was gathered in the living room watching the Olympics on tv. I'd proclaimed I wanted to be an Olympic gymnast one day and my father had laughed and said that becoming an announcer might be a good backup choice.

That was it.

That was where one dream ended and another began.

It was never really yours to begin with.

I'd just latched onto my father's words, wanting to earn his approval. To make him proud.

Some things never change.

It doesn't matter. It's done. Right now, need to focus on the present.

"The Red Stars better watch out because North Carolina is

coming in hot. Mark my words, this will be one of the best matchups of the season."

I stare into the camera, but it's Brooke's tear-stained face I see, followed by Jalen's, his eyes shining with gratitude.

If only she'd had someone like Rich in her corner, things would have turned out differently.

Maybe. Maybe not.

There are few guarantees in life, but at least she would've had a shot at a better outcome. A chance to reap the rewards of her hard work. That's the whole point of NIL, isn't it? To elevate and reward student athletes who are at the top of their sport, not break them down with false promises and shady backroom deals.

"The Red Stars have won seven of the last eight games between these two teams, but with St. Clair in goal, this one's going to be a toss-up."

There's movement in the studio and I glimpse Devin's stoic face before he melts back into the shadows, his large body disappearing like it was never there at all.

My heart squeezes.

He wants this internship for the right reasons. Not because someone told him it would make a great fallback option, but because he loves his sport and wants to stay connected to it when his college career ends.

I can't be the one to take that away from him.

Not when I have doubts. Doubts about my own goals. My own future.

Fresh text appears on the teleprompter and suddenly it all becomes clear. For the first time today, I know what I have to do.

Fear crawls up my spine, sowing the seeds of doubt and whispering what-ifs in my ear.

But I'm past that now. Past letting fear and doubt and a deep-seated need to earn my parents' approval control me.

I'd rather fail at something I love—at something I believe in—than succeed at something I don't.

I draw a steadying breath, look straight at the camera, and flub the lines.

43

———————

DJ

SUTTON SPOUTS some shit about missed goalies and ends her segment by referring to the Courage as the Courageous. It's an obvious mistake, even to someone like me who doesn't follow women's soccer. Kali winces and that jackass Preston smirks, like she's just handed him the internship on a silver platter.

Hell, maybe she has. He's far from electrifying on camera, but unlike the rest of us, he didn't make any obvious mistakes.

My pulse spikes.

Some mistakes were a little more obvious than others.

Missed goalies? No way Sutton thought that was the line.

She fucking blew it on purpose. She was rolling right along and then, suddenly, the train went off the tracks. No way that was an accident.

Sutton's one of the most focused people I know. She told me once that she had to be. Her exact words were, *"You can't tumble on a four-inch beam or throw a double front"*—whatever the fuck that is—*"unless you're laser focused."*

My palms grow damp and my gut hardens.

She threw those lines. I'm sure of it.

But why?

Her interview went well. She was in the clear, nearly finished with her segment.

Yesterday she was worried about being unprepared and today she throws her shot out the window?

It doesn't make sense.

Unless she did it for you.

No way. We had a deal. Agreed to do our best and let the chips fall where they may.

That was before she watched you crash and burn.

Before dyslexia got the best of me on camera.

The lights go up and my shitty mood descends to a whole new level as Sutton steps off the set and rejoins the group, smiling blithely.

She tries to catch my eye, but I pretend not to notice.

I'm too heated right now and I don't want to get into it here. Not in front of Mac and our classmates.

"Nice work today, everyone." Mac smiles at us and though he sounds sincere, I'm not feeling it. "The selection committee will meet to review your film within the next few weeks and we should have an intern offer prepared by the end of the year." He spreads his hands in supplication. "For now, you're all free to go. Don't forget to turn in your guest badges at the security desk on your way out."

We thank him and then the four of us take the elevator to the building lobby, where we do as instructed and turn in our badges. No one speaks, not even Preston, which is probably a small mercy because the guy is a jackass.

Just the thought of seeing his face on Sports Stream has bile rising in my throat.

The walk back to the parking garage is swift and silent, but the instant we're inside, shielded from howling wind and prying eyes, Sutton places a hand on my biceps, stopping me in my tracks.

"Are you okay?" Her words are laced with concern, and her eyes are wary as they meet mine. "You haven't said a word since your broadcast."

No, I'm not fucking okay. The woman I care about just betrayed me. Broke her word.

"What is there to say?" I loosen my tie and flick open the top button of my shirt. The garage is cold and damp, but I'm sweltering. Suffocating on raw emotion. "You purposely fucked up your broadcast."

Her eyes go round and she opens her mouth—probably to deny it—but I cut her off.

"Don't lie to me, Shorty. I know what I saw."

"What did you see?" she asks, thrusting her chin in the air.

Christ. It's the same look she gave me on move-in day. I deserved it then, but I sure as hell don't deserve it now. I'm not the one who screwed up. Not this time.

"I saw you blow your shot at an incredible opportunity. Screw up your future, and for what? Because you felt bad for me?" I throw up my hands and when she flinches, I lock them behind my head and take a step back. Sutton has such a big personality, it's easy to forget our size difference at times like this, when emotions are running high. But even though I'm pissed, I never want her to fear me. "What did you think? That if you threw your lines, it would improve my chances?"

"Dios mío." She crosses her arms, refusing to back down. "Do you even hear yourself right now? Spoiler alert, Devin. I didn't do it for you. I did it for me."

"So you admit it? You purposely screwed up those lines?"

"Yes."

I'd known it all along, but the admission still hurts like a motherfucker.

"If you'd calm down, we could talk about this rationally." She pulls a face. "Like adults."

"Oh, that's rich coming from you."

She cocks her head and her brows knit together in confusion. "What's that supposed to mean?"

"Come on, Shorty. Pranking the football team isn't what I'd call mature, adult behavior."

She huffs out a breath. "I hardly think that's relevant to this conversation."

"It goes to pattern," I say, pulling some Law & Order bullshit out of my ass. "You saw my fuck up on camera and just like with our term paper, you wanted to play savior. Poor Devin can't read the words, so I'll just improve the odds for him."

"It wasn't like that." She presses her lips flat, as if she's holding something back. "Like I said, this wasn't about you."

"Right. You just sat down in that chair and decided you no longer wanted the internship?" I scoff. "That's bullshit and you know it."

"What I know is that when it comes to your challenges with dyslexia, you've got a blind spot. You always assume the worse. Assume people will judge you or look down on you or pity you, but that's not who I am." She throws up her hands. "It's not who most people are, but you can't see that because you've got a big-ass chip on your shoulder."

"You don't know what you're talking about." My words echo in the cavernous garage, but I could give a shit who hears us. "You have no clue what it's been like for me."

"You're right, I don't." She steps toward me and I take another step back. "But I've seen how hard you work to be the best, Devin. How hard you worked to get this interview and to prepare for it. Despite it all, you refused to ask for accommodations." She pauses, squaring her shoulders. "So which of us is really guilty of self-sabotaging behavior?"

Fuck. That.

I didn't sabotage myself. I wanted that position. Still do. But I wanted to do it on my own.

"Don't you dare try to turn this around on me." I jab a finger in the air. "We agreed we'd both do our best. That we'd keep the internship separate from our arrangement, and accept the outcome, however things played out." I suck in a breath, reaching for calm though my hands are shaking. "I wanted to land the internship on merit, not a hand up. You took that away from me when you decided I couldn't do it on my own, a choice you never would've made if we weren't sleeping together."

Her eyes narrow and if looks could kill, I'd be dead on the pavement. "When have I ever given you the impression I'd toss my ambitions aside for a guy?" She twirls her hand in the air, making a *get on with it* gesture. "Go ahead. I'll wait."

That would be never.

But it's exactly what she did today.

She worked just as hard as I did to get this opportunity, and she pissed it away on some spur-of-the-moment pity jag.

The knowledge burns like hot coals in my gut.

"You are unbelievable," she says, voice cracking.

I roll my shoulders, resisting the urge to go to her. The last time we had this argument, we resolved it with sex and look where that got us.

Nowhere.

All it did was delay the inevitable.

"Look, we clearly aren't going to get anywhere with this conversation." I pull Reid's spare keyring from my pocket and dangle it in the air. "I'll give you a ride back to school, but after that, I need some space to think."

Without a word, Sutton marches past me, making a beeline for the Jeep, hurt and anger etched in the lines of her face.

I don't follow. I need a minute to get my head on straight. To chill the fuck out before I get behind the wheel.

Last night, I was convinced I had everything under control. Convinced I could handle the internship, the playoffs, and a girlfriend. Now I'm not even sure I can handle driving a goddamn car.

In a single hour, I've fucked up my entire life. That's got to be some kind of record.

Nice job, asshole.

I suck in a breath and head for the Jeep. It's going to be a long, awkward drive back to College Park.

44

SUTTON

"Woah." Brooke throws up a hand. "Back the fuck up. Did you just say you've been hooking up with DJ Parker all semester?"

I duck my head and shovel a spoonful of chocolate peanut butter swirl into my mouth. "Yes."

It's Saturday night and Maddie invited Brooke and Soraya over for a girls' night in. We're sprawled out in the living room eating ice cream, as you do when one of your friends gets her heart broken by a sexy football player.

Lucky me.

"I can't believe you've been holding out on us!" Brooke throws a decorative pillow at me, nearly knocking the ice cream carton out of my hands. "How long has this been going on?"

"Since the Sig Chi party." I shovel more ice cream into my mouth, willing myself to stay strong. I will not shed another tear for that pendejo. God knows I shed enough to fill a small lake yesterday, and I have the puffy eyes to prove it. "Not that it matters since we broke things off."

"That's why you're here." Maddie shoots Brooke a

reproachful look. "For solidarity. Not so you can throw shade on their secret relationship."

Technically, it wasn't a relationship, but I don't bother correcting her. It would just give Brooke more ammunition because in her mind, the only thing better than dating DJ Parker would be a no strings fling with DJ Parker.

"Are you sure you're okay to watch the game?" Soraya asks, gesturing to the tv where Waverly and Michigan are duking it out in the Big Ten Championship game.

"It's fine." *Liar*. Okay. It sucks. Every time his smiling face appears on the screen, another tiny piece of my heart is chipped away, but I can't ask them to shut it off, even if I know they would. All of Wildcat Nation is watching, and I won't be the reason my friends miss an epic game.

Soraya frowns and it's clear she doesn't believe me, but she doesn't push the issue. "So, what happened?"

Isn't that the million-dollar question?

"When we started hooking up, it was supposed to be just sex. But then..."

"You caught feelings," Maddie supplies.

I nod. I never meant to fall for Devin. That wasn't the plan, but the more I got to know him, the more I realized I'd misjudged him. Somewhere along the line, between secret hookups and late-night study sessions, he slipped past my defenses.

Blame it on the peanut butter brownies.

They are my weakness.

Maybe I'm one of those people who can't separate physical and emotional relationships, but no, it was more than that. We had a connection. I could tell him things I couldn't tell anyone else and he listened—really listened—without judging or trying to fix my problems.

Devin got me.

With him, I was the best version of myself and it was always enough.

Until it wasn't.

My chest tightens and I absently rub my ribcage to release the tension.

"Anyway, we were both up for an internship at Sports Stream and we agreed we wouldn't let it interfere with our physical relationship." *Dios mío.* We were fools to think that would ever work. "Then yesterday, at the interview, I had a change of heart."

Soraya pulls a face and heat floods my cheeks.

"Not like that." I do, in fact, have some self-respect. "I realized I didn't want the internship, so I purposely screwed up during the final stage of the interview process."

"I fail to see the problem," Brooke says. "So you botched it. Big deal."

"That's what I thought, too, but Devin was pissed." I cringe, remembering the look of devastation on his face when I admitted I'd purposely flubbed the lines. "He thought I screwed up to improve his odds."

Brooke rolls her eyes and props her feet up on the edge of the coffee table. "Men are such fragile creatures."

"So his pride was hurt?" Soraya asks, her expression thoughtful.

"Not in the way you're thinking." How can I explain it without breaking Devin's confidence? He trusted me with his secret, and though we're over, I won't betray his trust. "He's a really smart guy, but he's had some academic challenges over the years and they've stuck with him."

Talk about an understatement.

I meant what I said when I accused him of having a chip on his shoulder.

He's entitled to feel his feelings, but he doesn't have the right to take them out on everyone around him.

"Do you think he got upset because he was projecting his insecurities onto you?"

Yes.

No.

Maybe?

God knows it's an easy trap to fall into. It's what I did when he ghosted me freshman year.

"If he's struggled academically in the past, there might be a part of him that believes he's inadequate," Soraya says, like she's quoting Human Behavior 101. *She is a Psych major.* "It's possible your actions felt like confirmation of his deepest fear, and if he cares about you, that would've made it twice as humiliating. No one wants the people they love to see them as weak or flawed."

I get that. I do, but we're all human.

"I don't know. Part of me understands where he was coming from, but if he'd just given me a chance to explain, maybe he could've seen things from my perspective." I scrape my hair back with my fingers and use the rubber band on my wrist to secure it in a messy bun. "But no, he had to fly off the handle and make a big scene in the parking garage."

"Look, mysterious challenges aside, can we just frame this up differently for a second?" Maddie curls her legs under her body. "You're making it too complicated."

It *is* complicated.

"I don't think—"

Maddie holds up a hand. "You're both athletes. Competitive. Driven. Determined to be the best."

"So?"

"So, how would you feel if Gabby threw a routine or downgraded her tricks so you could win?"

"I'd be furious."

I wouldn't feel like I'd earned it, like all my hard work was for nothing.

She shrugs. "Exactly."

No, not exactly.

"It's not the same thing. I didn't throw the broadcast for Devin. I did it because I realized I was on the wrong career path. Working in sports broadcasting wouldn't have made me happy long term."

"Then you should have withdrawn your name from the candidate list," Brooke says.

It's surprisingly practical advice from our resident influencer.

So why didn't I just withdraw my name?

Because you're too stubborn to do things any way but your own.

Wow. The truth really does hurt sometimes.

I've been toying with the idea of a major change ever since United G screwed Brooke over, but it wasn't until I stepped onto the Sports Stream set that I knew for sure I wanted to go through with it. It all happened so fast. I didn't stop to think how my actions would look from the outside. And, yes, maybe there was a small part of me that thought it might help Devin, but it was a tiny part. The same tiny part that wishes he would've spoken with Mac about accommodations.

That wasn't your call to make.

"Mierda." I cover my face with my hands, shame heating my blood. "I think I screwed up."

Devin's not the pendejo, I am.

Brooke smirks. "Admitting it is the first step."

Yeah, but the first step to what? Devin was furious, and now that I've stopped to consider things from his perspective, I can understand why. Although I never meant to hurt or undermine him, that's exactly what I did.

I hurt the man I love.

Because now that it's over, I can see it for what it was. We didn't have a label or a commitment, but Devin had my heart.

Still does, broken as it is.

So put it back together.

They say time heals all wounds, but screw that. I'm not going to sit around waiting for fate or karma or some other mystical force. I made this mess and I'm going to fix it.

Assuming that's even possible.

It has to be. I refuse to believe otherwise. The prospect is too painful. I don't know how, but I'm going to make this up to Devin, and maybe—just maybe—he'll find it in his heart to forgive me.

"Wait." Maddie's voice shatters my concentration and when I turn to her, her face is screwed up. "If you no longer want to major in communications, what do you want to do?"

I inhale, drawing a slow, steady breath. "I'd like to become a sports agent. I want to help ensure that what happened to Brooke doesn't happen to anyone else."

"For what it's worth, you'll be an amazing agent," Brooke says, tears shimmering in her eyes as she leans over to hug me. Her embrace is warm and familiar, and I hold on until she lets go. "Any athlete would be lucky to have you in their corner."

"Thanks." I force a smile, the warmth of her hug fading fast, and grab my phone. "Let's just hope my parents agree."

Soraya winces. "You're calling them now?"

"Might as well get it over with." I climb to my feet and my gaze slides to the tv. Waverly is up by seven, but it's early in the fourth quarter, so it could go either way. For Devin's sake, I hope the Wildcats can pull off a win. He's already lost one dream this week. I'd hate to see him lose another. "Wish me luck."

I dial my mom and as I head upstairs, Maddie hollers, "There's more ice cream in the freezer if you need it!"

Mamá answers on the second ring. "Sutton? Why are you calling so late? Is everything okay?"

"Everything's fine," I assure her as I flop down on my bed and prop myself up on my elbows. "Is Papá around? There's something I need to talk about with both of you."

"He's right here. I'll put you on speaker."

A second later, his booming voice comes through the line. "Hola, mi corazón de melon."

"Hola, Papá."

"What's going on?" he asks, taking immediate control of the conversation. "What do you need to speak to us about?"

"I had my interview at Sports Stream yesterday."

Not that anyone in my family cared enough to call and ask how it went.

"Was that this week?" Mamá chirps. "Gabby's schedule is so hectic right now. I hardly know what day it is. All this preparation for the National Team training camp is running me ragged."

Of course. Of course, Gabby's schedule trumps mine.

Again.

Frustration bears down on me like a tidal wave and it's all I can do not to scream.

If I don't say something now, I never will, and I'll have no one to blame but myself.

"I know this is a big opportunity for Gabby," I say, fighting to keep my tone neutral. "And I'm really excited for her, but just once, it would be nice if you could put me first."

"I don't know what you mean," she splutters, going on the defensive.

My pulse quickens, but I forge ahead.

"I mean, you promised to come to the Rutgers meet and you canceled. You didn't reschedule. You didn't ask me if it was okay. You just...did it." I roll onto my back, staring up at the ceiling. "You just said yourself that you forgot about my Sports Stream interview. If I hadn't mentioned it, would you have even remembered?"

"Of course." She huffs out a breath. "We love both of our girls equally."

I sit with that for a moment, knowing what I say next could launch this conversation into the stratosphere.

"I know you do, but sometimes it feels like Gabby's gymnastics career comes first and everyone else comes last." I close my eyes and brace for impact. "It's not a great feeling, Mamá."

There's a long pause, and I think she's going to argue, but then she says, "I didn't know you felt that way. How long has this been going on?"

Years.

But I don't say that because this isn't about shaming my parents or rehashing old hurts. It's about trying to move forward with a healthy relationship, something we haven't had for a while now.

"For a long time," I breathe, the words barely a whisper.

Her reply is swift, her tone firm. "You should have said something."

She's right. I never should have let things get this bad, but...

"I didn't know how." And I was afraid that if I did, it would come across as jealousy.

"Lo siento." She sighs, sounding as exhausted as I feel. "We'll try to do better."

Relief washes over me. It's all I can ask of them. "Thank you."

"So," my father says, chiming in again now that the messy emotional stuff is done. "How did your interview go?"

"It was fine, but I've decided not to pursue the internship any further."

"Why not? It's a great opportunity."

My pulse skitters, my fight-or-flight instincts kicking in.

Here goes nothing.

"I'm changing my major." I swallow, pushing the anxiety down. "I want to work as a sports agent."

"Where is this coming from?" my mother demands, voice high and tight. "I thought you wanted to be a sports commentator?"

The old me would've wavered, but I'm not that girl anymore.

Or, at least, I don't want to be.

"That was Papá's dream, not mine. It just took me some time to realize it."

After a lifetime of being judged and critiqued in the gym, I don't want a career in the spotlight. One where my employment is contingent on looking and behaving a certain way. I want to work on the other side of the sport, helping women like Brooke maximize their potential and their earnings. I want to be someone who stands for other women.

"I don't understand," my father says. "Why do you want to work as an agent?"

It's a fair question.

"My friend Brooke recently had a bad experience negotiating an endorsement deal. It made me realize how little support student athletes have when it comes to protecting their interests in the new world of name, image, likeness. I want to help. To make a difference." I smile, though they can't see it. "After all, I was raised by a man who negotiates contracts for a living. Some of that business savvy was bound to rub off on me."

I hope.

He huffs a laugh and I can practically see him shaking his head on the other end of the line. "What about your schooling? Will you graduate on time?"

I bite the inside of my lip, but I can't stall forever. "I may need an extra semester."

Or two.

"I see." He sighs. "Your mother and I won't be able to help with the extra schooling. Not with your sister's training expenses..."

"I get it." I'd expected as much, but hearing it still sucks because my gymnastics scholarship—and my eligibility—expires after four years. "I'll take out loans if I have to."

Which means I really need to get my ass in gear and start studying for finals, because my grades are going to be more important than ever.

45

———

DJ

"Get focused or get off the bench." Vaughn grabs the bar, immediately relieving the strain on my chest and biceps as he slides the barbell into the upright with a clang. "We can't afford any injuries right now."

He's right. I'm distracted. Have been all week. Ever since my fight with Sutton.

If Vaughn wasn't such an attentive spotter, I'd have probably been crushed by three hundred pounds of steel.

"Sorry." I sit up on the bench and use the hem of my t-shirt to wipe the sweat from my brow. "My mind wandered."

"It's been doing that a lot lately." He narrows his eyes. "What's going on with you?"

"Nothing. Just thinking about the Peach Bowl."

It's true enough. With our win over Michigan Saturday night, we claimed the Big Ten Championship and earned a spot in the CFP semi-finals. We'll be facing Clemson on New Year's Eve and there's no doubt it'll be a tough game.

"I'm not talking about football. I'm talking about the fact that you haven't gone sneaking next door since you got back from Pittsburgh."

I freeze, but Vaughn's gaze is unflinching. The big man just stares me down, waiting for a response.

Fucking fuck.

"Noticed that, did you?"

"It was pretty obvious." He snorts. "First Reid. Then Coop. Now you." He flashes me a shit-eating grin. "None of y'all are half as sneaky as you think you are."

I give him the finger. It's all I can manage right now.

I haven't been sleeping well and my brain is fried. Sutton texted a few times, but I haven't responded. It's a shitty thing to do, but with finals and football and the internship in limbo, I'm not sure what to say. Besides, I'm still pissed she threw the broadcast.

Anger churns in my gut and I tamp it down.

Getting mad won't do shit.

The last five days have proved as much, but it's hard to let go when every time I close my eyes, I see her gorgeous smile and hear the words "missed goalies" on her lips.

It's easier to be mad than to admit you're hurting.

Damn right. I was prepared to take things to the next level before she pulled that stunt and now I feel like a damn fool. Like we were in totally different places.

"Want to talk about it?"

Vaughn's face is open, free of judgment, and it's that look that does me in.

The guy is like a vault. Whatever I tell him, it'll stay between us.

I glance around the weight room. It's noisy and chaotic, clanging weights, chatter, and rap music filling the air. No one's paying us a lick of attention.

What the hell?

Maybe getting it off my chest will help. It certainly can't hurt.

"Sutton and I have been hooking up since the first week of the semester. It started off as a no-strings kind of thing. Just a way to blow off steam, you know?" I scrub a hand over my face. "Things were going really well, but then they got complicated."

He nods, and I lay it all at his feet. The internship. Our deal. The botched interview.

Vaughn doesn't interrupt, and when I'm finally done, he speaks.

"Let me get this straight." He holds up his palms and widens his stance. "You're crazy about this girl. You wanted to get serious. And when she screwed up, you didn't even give her a chance to explain?"

"I—"

He frowns, brows pulling low, and I snap my mouth shut.

"When you say it like that, it sounds like a dick move."

"Dude. It was."

Fucking fuck. I've never been in a committed relationship, but it's probably safe to say I have a lot to learn.

"I was too mad to hear her reasons at the time. Like I said, I wanted to get serious and then she turns around and betrays me like that?"

"It sounds like she was trying to help." Vaughn scoffs. "Besides, if she's as strong and independent as you say, do you really think she'd have thrown her future away for some no-strings fun?"

"It was more than that." I know it in my gut. "It started out that way, but..." I throw up my hands. "It was more at the end."

The end.

Christ. It sounds so final.

"The point is, I don't need that kind of help." Hell, I made it clear I didn't want it. "I would never ask her to trade her dreams for mine and I sure as shit don't need her pity. That isn't love."

Vaughn whistles, eyes wide. "Did you just say the L word?"

My pulse skyrockets and the world tilts on its axis, a missing piece of my heart shifting into place.

"Yeah, I did."

Because somehow, over days and weeks and months, this thing between us has become so much more than sex. More than friendship. More than I ever could have hoped for.

The realization cuts like a blade.

Fuck that old saying about how it's better to have loved and lost.

Knowing you had something incredible and lost it? That shit sucks.

"Look, man. I don't know how to say this, so I'm just going to float it out there," Vaughn says, stroking his beard. "Are you really mad at Sutton or are you mad at yourself for internalizing all the nasty shit kids said to you growing up? I know you don't like to talk about it, and I get that, but you let that stuff fester in your head, and it's bound to mess you up."

The fuck?

"Thanks, Dr. Phil, but I'm good." The last thing I need is some B grade armchair psychology. "Not *messed up* at all."

"Says the guy who blew his top without waiting for an explanation from the woman he loves." Vaughn shrugs. "Sounds totally healthy to me."

My stomach drops.

"Word of advice?" He claps me on the shoulder. "If you're focused on the trauma of your past, you're going to miss out on the joys of your present."

That sounds like some bullshit Yogi philosophy, but maybe he's right.

Sutton said I have a blind spot when it comes to my... learning disability.

I hate that fucking label.

I wish I could erase it from my vocabulary, but by the time the world really started to normalize neurodivergence, I'd already been tagged. Picked on. *Bullied.*

Like Vaughn said, it stuck.

So, yeah, maybe I'm a little sensitive. No one is perfect.

Least of all me.

"I'm no expert," Vaughn says, squatting to grab his water bottle off the floor. "But your girl was right about one thing."

I'm starting to think she was right about a lot of things.

I sigh and gesture for him to lay it on me. It's not like my shitty mood can get any worse.

"You shouldn't be too proud to ask for accommodations when you need them. You've got one of the highest GPAs on the team." He twists the top off his Hydro Flask and takes a long drink. "Which, if you think about it, means you should be smart enough to know when you've screwed up."

I stand corrected. My mood can, in fact, get worse.

A dark cloud settles over my thoughts.

Nothing like realizing you've internalized your own stigma.

Maybe if I'd realized it sooner, things would have turned out differently. With Sutton. The internship.

"Thanks, big guy. Wanna rub a little salt in my wounds while you're at it?"

"Not my style." He takes another hit from his water bottle and screws the top back on. "I'd rather know what you're going to do about it."

"What can I do? The interviews are done. I blew it."

"It's only been a few days. If they haven't made an offer, it's not over."

I stiffen, shoulders rigid.

He's right. It may be too late for Sutton and me, but maybe I can still salvage the Sports Stream internship.

"So are you going to sit here and wallow, or are you going to get off your ass and do something about it?"

Option two.

"I'm going to email the professor and disclose that I have dyslexia." It's in my student profile, but that doesn't mean Mac's aware of it. He only teaches part-time, and I never brought it to his attention. There's no guarantee it'll make a difference, but at least I'll know I tried. "If the internship is meant for me, it'll be mine. If it's not, I'll find another opportunity."

But that's a problem for another day. For now, I'm just going to focus on what's in front of me and put everything else in the box.

"That shouldn't be too hard." Vaughn grins maniacally and I give silent thanks he's on my team. I wouldn't want to face him on the line of scrimmage. "After we whoop Clemson, everyone will want a piece of you."

"Here's hoping." I climb to my feet and shove my fingers through my hair, pushing the damp strands off my forehead.

"What are you going to do about Sutton?" he asks. "You can't avoid her forever."

No, I can't, but I'm also not ready to go there.

46

SUTTON

"Ay bendito. This is the smartest thing I've ever done or the stupidest."

"It's genius." Maddie pulls me in for a quick hug. Her cheeks are flushed, but I can't tell if it's from the cold or excitement. "Trust me."

I want to but Wildcat stadium is hella crowded. The pep rally hasn't started yet, but already it's a sea of blue and white, fans decked out from head to toe in Wildcat gear as they take their seats. A massive Waverly banner has been placed at the fifty-yard line and there are enormous blue and white balloon arrangements on either side, creating a makeshift stage.

The pep rally is a send-off for the football team, a chance to show our support ahead of bowl season. The Peach Bowl isn't for a few more weeks, but since most people will head home for the holidays once finals are over, this is our last chance to rally around the team.

From the looks of it, every student, professor, and staff member has turned out, along with half of College Park. It's an incredible show of support, but I'd expect nothing less. Wildcat Nation is notoriously loyal. The fans will make a great showing at the game too, and not just because it's being played in a warmer climate.

An icy breeze whips through the stadium and Brooke tugs on the collar of her coat, pulling it up around her chin. "Why couldn't they do this in the arena?"

"Probably because the stadium's bigger and it's their home turf," Soraya deadpans, eying the azure sky.

Despite the cold, the sun is shining and there isn't a cloud in sight. It's a gorgeous day.

Yeah, a gorgeous day to make a fool of yourself in front of forty thousand people.

There's only one that matters.

Devin.

I miss him so damn much.

Miss hearing him call me Shorty. Miss his playful banter. Miss having his powerful arms wrapped around me as we lie in bed.

My heart squeezes, and I welcome the pain like an old friend.

It's a reminder of what I lost. Of what I'm fighting for today.

We haven't spoken in a week. He's still isn't taking my calls or returning my texts and I'm pretty sure he's avoiding me at the apartment complex, which I know from personal experience takes some effort.

It hurts, but it's no less than I deserve.

Still, I can't let him leave for the holidays without telling him how I feel, without explaining everything. If he chooses not to forgive me, I'll have to live with that, but there's no way I can wait until January to talk to him again.

The crowd roars as the marching band takes the field, Waverly's fight song filling the air as high notes and thumping bass blend in harmony.

I sneak another peek at the crowd and my knees go weak.

Which is ridiculous. I've performed before one hundred thousand screaming Wildcat fans. By comparison, the pep rally crowd is nothing.

Yeah, right.

No one was looking at me during games, not really. They were watching the Wildcat. If I screwed up, or made a fool of myself, it didn't matter. Only Coach Sharpe—and eventually Devin—knew it was me inside that smelly fur suit.

"I don't think I can do this." I grab Maddie's hand, taking her ice-cold fingers in mine. We really should've worn gloves, but that's the least of my problems now. "This was a stupid idea. I didn't think it through. Plan it out."

"Babe, I love you, but the invasion of Normandy took less planning."

I wouldn't doubt it. I've spent the last four days going over every detail. Planning the logistics. Figuring out what to say.

That was the hardest part. There are so many things I want to say to Devin, and maybe, in time, I'll have the chance, but today, every word—every gesture—has to count.

Otherwise, it'll all be for nothing.

My pulse flutters. "What if I screw this up?"

"You're going to do great." Brooke giggles. "Just, you know, make sure your shoes are tied. Wouldn't want you tripping or anything embarrassing like that."

I immediately check my laces.

Maybe I should double knot them.

"Ignore her." Maddie shoots Brooke the side-eye. "She's kidding. You aren't going to fall on your face. You're a D1 gymnast. Strong. Graceful. Confident."

"What she said." Soraya nods to the stands. "We'll be in the crowd cheering you on, no matter what."

I crack a smile. "Even if I chicken out?"

"Girl, you will not chicken out." There's enough authority in her words that I almost believe her. "You've got this."

"Yeah." Brooke grins. "And if this doesn't win him over, we've got a freezer full of ice cream."

"From The Creamery?"

"There's an entire carton of Alumni Swirl," Maddie promises, squeezing my hand.

It's a small comfort, especially when I feel like a human popsicle, but I appreciate the sentiment.

I have no idea how I got so lucky, but I couldn't ask for a better group of women to call my friends. They're loyal and funny and they're always here for me when I need them. Before I came to Waverly, I didn't know it could be like this. Didn't know what I was missing. But now that I know? There's nothing I wouldn't do to protect the bond we've forged.

"You guys are the best. You know that, right?"

"We know," they say in unison, pulling me in for a group hug, our foreheads forming a tight circle.

"Now go get your man."

47

DJ

I've been to a lot of pep rallies over the years, but this one is wild. There must be thirty-thousand people in attendance. The music is loud, the cheerleaders are high on life, and even Coach is in rare form, mic in one hand, clipboard in the other. Despite the cold weather, the old man has the fans on their feet, whipping them into a frenzy with a promise to kick Clemson's ass on New Year's Eve.

"Am I tripping or did Coach just guarantee a win?" Coop asks.

"Think of it as a vote of confidence." Reid grins. "No pressure, princess."

Normally, I'd be the one to crack that joke, but, despite the charged atmosphere, my heart isn't in it today.

"Please." Coop scoffs. "Those southern fuckers—no offense, Parker—won't know what hit them."

"The way Coach is carrying on," Vaughn deadpans. "It might just be his clipboard."

"I know that's right," Smith adds, bouncing on the balls of his feet. "We're gonna own their asses."

We're all lined up on the field, game ready, helmets tucked

under our arms. Coach wants to give the fans one last look at us before bowl season starts, but I'd just as soon head back to the locker room. Finals week wiped me out. Between practice and late-night study sessions, I haven't been getting much sleep. I took my last exam this morning, so at least that's over.

I stare out at the crowd, searching for a familiar face, for that bright cobalt hair.

Wishful thinking, asshole.

Probably. Sutton's never been a fan of football. It's foolish to think she'd brave a twenty-nine-degree windchill, especially after the way things ended between us.

Hell, I don't even know if she's still on campus. For all I know, she's already gone home for the holidays. I haven't seen her around the apartment complex.

She's probably avoiding you.

I can't even blame her. What's done is done.

It's like Vaughn said. It's better to focus on the present.

I emailed Mac a few days ago, and he responded to say he'd be discussing my situation with the Sports Stream selection committee. He didn't make any promises, but he didn't shut me down either, so now it's just a waiting game.

Coach finally passes the mic to the sound of a roaring crowd and one of the cheerleaders directs the crowd's attention to the jumbotron. We turn in unison as a highlight reel fills the screen, and the band kicks off another peppy song.

The first clip is from Homecoming and in it, Coop pulls down a pass that should've been impossible to catch, giving us the lead.

"Hell yeah!" Coop shouts, jostling Reid. "That was our best play of the season."

He's not wrong. I still don't know how he made that catch.

Several more clips roll past, a mix of offense and defense.

There's even a shot of Carter, our new kicker smashing a field goal from the forty-five. Whoever put this together understood the assignment. It's a mashup of all our best plays and the crowd is loving it, stomping and roaring.

When the Wildcat appears on the screen, my gut hardens.

Sutton tumbles down the sideline and then the clip changes and she's holding the t-shirt cannon. I know what's going to happen before I see it, but that doesn't lessen the impact. The cannon goes off, a white blur bursting from the tube and then the camera cuts to me, doubled over in pain.

Just the memory is enough to have my boys crawling up inside my groin.

"That shit never gets old!" Coop slaps me on the back as a bunch of the guys howl with laughter.

"I'm so glad my pain and suffering provide you with endless entertainment."

Reid shakes his head, but the hint of a smile tugs at his lips.

"Fuckers." I shake Coop off just as the Wildcat jogs across the field with a half-dozen cheerleaders, t-shirt cannon in hand.

Oh, hell no.

I don't want that thing anywhere near me.

The not-Sutton Wildcat stops when he sees me, plants his feet, and points the cannon right at my mid-section.

What the fuck?

I debate shoving Coop in front of me, but I'm too slow.

The Wildcat pulls the trigger. Nothing happens.

Thank Christ. I'm not okay being shot in the nuts at pointblank range.

My teammates laugh, like they're all in on the joke as the mascot hands his cannon to one of the cheerleaders. He claps his paws to his cheeks in the universal sign for *Oh, no.*

Oh, no is right. I don't want any part of this skit. It's too fucking painful. A reminder of Sutton and her Wildcat shenanigans.

I must look like I'm ready to bolt because Vaughn leans in close and whispers, "Just go with it."

Like I have any other choice.

We have an audience of thirty-thousand, give or take.

One of the cheerleaders hands the Wildcat a sign, and he holds it up to the crowd before turning to me.

I'm sorry.

The crowd goes nuts as he drops to one knee and tosses the sign aside, clasping his hands together like a beggar.

More like begging for forgiveness.

A couple of guys slap me on the ass and back, hooting and hollering, telling me to forgive the furball.

"Come on, man. Forgive your furry friend," Coop says, shoving me forward.

I look the Wildcat square in the eye. We're the only ones who know the truth. The only ones that know it's not him I need to forgive, but I flash him a smile and nod, playing along for the fans.

The Wildcat leaps to his feet and comes in for a hug, arms outstretched.

Nope.

Too far.

I shake my head and hold out my free hand instead.

He makes a show of being disappointed and my teammates start chanting "Hug it out!"

Oh, for fuck's sake. How is this my life?

The cheerleaders join in, carrying the chant back to the fans and then the entire stadium is shouting "Hug it out!" as the Wildcat raises his arms, encouraging them to get louder.

I look to the stands, to Coach, to my teammates.

This moment takes peer pressure to a whole new level.

I spread my arms wide, helmet dangling from my right hand, and turn to the Wildcat.

He fidgets, like he's the one who should be embarrassed, but makes no move to accept the hug.

The smug bastard covers his eyes and then points to me.

"You want me to cover my eyes?"

He nods.

In for a penny...

I set my helmet on the ground and make a show of covering my eyes.

Long moments pass as I stand there feeling like a jackass, no idea what's going on. The fucker could be mooning me for all I know.

My suspicions are confirmed when riotous laughter fills the stadium.

I drop my hands just in time to see the Wildcat sprint away with my helmet. He's holding it over his head like a goddamn trophy and cutting a line directly for the players' tunnel.

"You've got to be shitting me."

The guys on the team are rolling, but Reid manages to get hold of himself just long enough to suggest I go get my helmet. "You're going to need it for Clemson."

Worst. Pep rally. Ever.

I jog to the players' tunnel, but when I enter, it's not the Wildcat I find holding my helmet.

It's Sutton.

She's hugging the helmet to her chest, her expression guarded.

I take a tentative step forward, anxiety coiled low in my gut. "What are you doing here?"

"You wouldn't take my calls or answer my texts. I didn't know what else to do." She bites her lower lip, looking unsure. "I couldn't let you leave for the semester without apologizing."

That she's doing it on my turf speaks volumes.

"I screwed up and I'm sorry." Her voice wavers and she nods like she's giving herself a silent pep talk. "I never meant to hurt you, Devin. I know my intentions don't matter, but I want you to know that what I did wasn't about you or your shot at landing the Sports Stream internship. It was about me and what I want." She frowns. "Or maybe it was about what I don't want. Both, really."

"I'm going to need you to elaborate, Shorty."

She beams at me and goddamn, I missed that smile.

"After seeing what Brooke went through with United G and Pinnacle, I started thinking that maybe agenting would be a better fit." She gestures to herself with one hand and a self-deprecating laugh spills from her lips. "I mean, I'm not exactly traditional sports commentator material."

"Fuck traditional. You're gorgeous just the way you are."

And fuck anyone who tries to make her feel otherwise.

She dips her chin in acknowledgment, cheeks stained crimson. "The point is, I could make a real impact working with young, female athletes. I could make sure no one else gets burned the way Brooke did."

"I—" I shove my hands through my hair. She wanted that internship as badly as I did, and she worked her ass off to get an interview. "I don't understand. You told me you've wanted to be a broadcaster since you were a kid."

"I thought I did, but that was my father's dream." She lifts a shoulder. "I did a few broadcasts for my middle school news program and when it became clear Gabby was the gymnastics prodigy in the family, he suggested I'd make a good sports commentator. I latched onto the idea because I wanted his approval. I wanted him to be proud of me, and to have something that was my own." She pauses, pressing her lips flat. "I can't spend my life trying to catch my parents' attention."

No, she can't. Nor should she have to, but...

"So, what? You decided in the middle of the interview that you wanted to change your major?"

No way. She's way too practical to do something that brash. She might appear anti-establishment, but Sutton's a rule follower.

"It wasn't quite as spur of the moment as all that." The words carry a hint of her usual snark, and I'll be damned if it doesn't warm my heart. "I'd been thinking about it for a few weeks and then we met Jalen and he shared his experience. Seeing him and Rich interact convinced me there was a better way. NIL has created a whole new world of opportunities for student athletes, and I want to be part of it. I want to make sure the Brooke's of the world get a fair shake."

Fair enough. Noble even. But it still doesn't explain her actions.

"Okay. So you could've easily withdrawn from the interview process or declined the position. You didn't have to throw the broadcast."

"You're right. I wasn't thinking."

Tears shine in her eyes and the sight of them splinters my heart. The urge to go to her, to take her in my arms, strikes hard and fast, but I force myself to remain still.

"When I set foot on that stage, it solidified my decision. I looked in to the camera and I just knew. It wasn't right for me." She shifts her weight from one foot to the other. "I watched your broadcast. I saw the passion and energy you brought to the set, and I didn't feel that."

And there it is.

"So you decided to throw me a bone? Give me a little extra help?"

"It wasn't like that," she says, voice rising an octave. "I'm not used to confiding in other people. Not about the big stuff." She takes a step toward me and then catches herself. "I'm still figuring out how this all works, but I should have realized how my actions would look from the outside. How they would affect you."

I want to believe her. Want to believe her actions had nothing to do with pity and everything to do with choosing her own path.

But how can I be sure?

How can you be sure of anything?

I can't. That's the problem.

A chant floats down the tunnel and it takes me a second to recognize my own name.

"Parker! Parker! Parker!"

Sutton's eyes go round and she tilts her head, listening intently. "Are they calling your name?"

"Sounds like it."

Fuck. I'm not ready. I need more time. Time to figure this out. Time to sort out my thoughts. Just...time.

But the universe is a dick, and time is the one thing in short supply right now.

The Wildcat appears at the mouth of the tunnel, giving an exaggerated wave that I'm pretty sure means *Get your ass in gear.*

"It sounds like you're needed on the field." Sutton smiles, but it's a washed-out imitation of the real thing, lacking her usual warmth and mischief. "You should go."

I should. I really fucking should. I have obligations to my team. To the fans. To myself.

"Yeah." I nod, and it's a struggle to force the words past my lips. "I guess so."

Sutton hands me my helmet and our fingers brush, a final jolt of electricity passing between us. Then I do the hardest thing I've ever done in my life.

I turn and walk away from the woman I love.

48

SUTTON

Devin stalks toward the field, his cleats *tap tap tapping* on the cement. There's no "*Goodbye.*" No "*Let's talk later.*" Not even an "*I'll text you.*"

I watch him go, willing him to turn around, and as he disappears through the tunnel, my heart breaks all over again.

We're done. We're really done.

I knew it might end this way. Tried to prepare for the worst. But can you really prepare to have your heart ripped out?

That's a big fat no.

Tears sting the backs of my eyes, and I blink them away.

I swore I would not cry. Promised myself I would take comfort in the fact that I'd left it all on the field.

At least you didn't tell him you loved him.

It doesn't matter. Even if I had, it wouldn't have changed anything, and it's not like I could actually feel any worse than I feel right now.

Somehow, this has gone from being the best semester of my college career to the worst.

And I have no one to blame but myself.

My phone vibrates in my back pocket and I pull it out to see a new message in the group chat.

Maddie: We got you, babe.

At least I have my girls. With them by my side, I can get through anything.

Brooke: His loss. Obviously.

Soraya adds a Golden Girls group hug GIF and before I can tap out a reply, another message pops up.

Brooke: Just to clarify... I'm Blanche, right?

A laugh-sob bursts from my lips, and I clap a hand over my mouth to smother it. Which is ridiculous because it's not like anyone can hear it over the roar of the crowd. When I've regained control, I type a quick reply.

Me: Thanks. I love you guys.

I press send and when I look up, I'm no longer alone.

Devin stands at the mouth of the tunnel, helmet dangling from his right hand.

My pulse flutters.

It doesn't mean anything.

Right. He probably forgot something or—

He marches right up to me, hazel eyes glowing with determination. "You weren't the only one who screwed up, Shorty. I made mistakes too."

"I thought you were gone." I lean to the side, looking around him. No sign of the Wildcat. "The fans were calling you to the field."

"They can wait." He cups my cheek and though it's freezing outside, his hand is warm and I melt into his touch. "I'm right where I need to be. With you."

Warmth floods my chest and that's all it takes for my shattered heart to piece itself back together.

"When I told you I needed space, it wasn't a blowoff. I needed time to think and to come to terms with some truths about myself I didn't like very much." He exhales and his breath forms a tiny white cloud between us. "You accused me of having a chip on my shoulder and you were right."

"Devin, I—"

He presses his thumb to my lips and a shiver races down my spine.

"Please hear me out. I need to say this, and you need to hear it." I nod and he continues. "When it comes to academic performance, I'm sensitive. Maybe it's because I have dyslexia, maybe it's because I was bullied as a kid, but the why doesn't matter. The truth is, sometimes I see slights and insults where there are none and sometimes, I make assumptions I shouldn't. It's something I need to work through. Something I'm going to work through."

Repairing emotional scars takes time. It won't be quick or easy, but Devin's not a quitter. If he says he's going to do it, he'll do it.

And beat himself up along the way.

"None of us are perfect." I raise my hand to my cheek, covering his. "Give yourself some grace."

God knows he deserves it after everything he's been through.

"I'm sorry for acting like a dick in Pittsburgh. I shut you down when we should have dealt with the issue head on. Together."

"Figured that out, did you?" I look up at him from under my lashes, smirk firmly in place. "Took you long enough."

He shrugs. "Better late than never."

"That's debatable."

"I'm serious, Sutton." That he uses my actual name is proof enough. "I should've given you the benefit of the doubt. That's what it means to trust someone." His eyes lock on mine. "I trust you. You've never treated me differently because of my dyslexia, and I realize now that any perception of pity was my own insecurities talking."

I want to tell him it's okay, that I understand, that I trust him too, but the words get stuck in my throat.

"Forgive me?" He brushes his thumb across my cheek.

"There's nothing to forgive."

We've all got our demons to slay. Naming them is just the first step.

"You're an amazing woman, Sutton Cruz. Have I told you that?"

I cock my head, pretending to think it over. "Not today."

"Well, how about this?" He lowers his forehead to mine and wraps an arm around my waist, pulling me flush to his body. We're separated by pads and clothing and my puffy winter jacket, but it doesn't matter. I'm right where I belong. "I love you, Shorty."

My entire body flushes at his words, heat tingling across my frozen skin from the top of my head all the way down to my toes.

He *loves* me.

Devin loves *me*.

I knew he cared about me, but...

"I love you, too."

The biggest smile I've ever seen breaks across his face as he scoops me up in his arms and crushes his mouth to mine. The kiss is hot and wet, a toe-curling promise of things to come, and when we break apart, I can still taste him on my lips.

"If we're doing this, we're doing it right," he warns. "Dates. Sleepovers. Meeting the parents."

My belly twists. What if his parents don't like me?

"Don't give me that look. I thought you were fearless." He

smirks, and there's a wicked glint in his eyes. "Come on, Shorty. Go all in with me. What do you say?"

There's only one answer I can give. "Yes."

"That's my girl," he roars. "Now let's go make it official."

"Official?"

Before I can protest, he carries me onto the field and as we exit the tunnel, the cheers of Wildcat Nation reach a crescendo, confirming what I already know. This is just the beginning of an incredible journey, one I get to take with the man I love.

EPILOGUE

DJ

"I can't look."

Coop elbows me in the ribs. "Have a little faith, fucknuts. Carter is money."

It's New Year's Eve and the Clemson game has been a knock-down, drag-out slugfest. My ribs are sore as hell, I've got blood dripping in my eye from a nasty cut I got in the third quarter, and my heart is about to beat the fuck out of my chest because it's a tie game and there are only twenty-six seconds left on the clock.

"She's got this. She's a solid ninety-three percent inside the thirty-five," Reid says. "From the forty-five with no wind? She's a solid seventy-nine."

"Of course you know her stats." I roll my eyes, but leave it at that.

No way am I going to remind him that a missed forty-six-yard field goal contributed to our one and only loss of the season. He's right. That was a fluke, and we all made mistakes that day.

Carter's solid. She'll get it done.

Still, my gut hardens as Special Teams takes the field.

We're so close to the championship game I can taste it.

"No need to get jealous." Reid hooks his fingers in the collar of his jersey. "I know your stats, too, Catman."

I raise my hand to flip him the bird, but then I remember we're on national tv.

Catman. Thanks to Coop, it's my new nickname around the house. Like Batman. But with a cat. You know, because I was fucking the Wildcat.

Yeah, make that make sense.

Whatever. I have no shame about my Wildcat exploits. I'm dating the coolest chick on campus, the sex is hot as fuck, and whether we win or lose tonight, I get to ring in the new year with the woman I love.

"Here we go," Vaughn says as our long snapper moves into position.

Adrenaline courses through my veins and it's all I can do to stand still as Carter walks off the steps, preparing to make the kick.

Seconds tick by on the play clock and then the ball is snapped. James, our punter, snatches the ball from the air and places it laces up in the grass. Carter is already moving, one short step followed by two long ones.

Come on, Carter. You've got this.

Her leg powers forward, foot connecting with the ball and sending it arcing into the air. It's a long ass kick and I follow the trajectory, heart racing, as it sails through the air and between the uprights.

Holy shit!

She did it. *We did it!*

We're going to the championship game.

Cheers erupt throughout the stadium, the noise reaching a fever pitch as my teammates and I celebrate on the sideline.

There are still a few seconds on the clock, but that field goal was the nail in the coffin for Clemson. Langley and his boys have been on tonight and our D will shut them down.

Carter joins us on the sideline and before she can even remove her helmet, Reid scoops her up and spins her around. "Game MVP right here!"

"Was there ever any doubt?" she shouts.

The moment is surreal and when the clock runs out and the fans rush the field, I remain on the sideline. There's only one person I need to see, and she knows right where to find me.

Sutton leaps over the railing, landing gracefully before me. When she straightens, I notice she's wearing a Wildcat jersey. It must be new. I've never seen it before.

She follows my gaze and then a mischievous smile curves those gorgeous lips. "You should see the back."

I twirl my finger in the air and she spins, flipping her hair and looking at me over her shoulder. It's the sexiest goddamn thing I've ever seen and when I read the name printed on the back of her jersey, my cock stiffens.

Parker.

"You look good in my jersey."

"Glad you like it." She sashays over and stretches up on her tip-toes, wrapping her arms around my neck. "Some guys like lingerie, but I thought this was more our style."

"Fucking right it is." I pull her in close and there's a little voice in the back of my head that says to keep it PG-13, but screw that. It's New Year's Eve and we're going to the CFP Championship. I kiss my girl hard and deep, a promise of things to come when I get her alone tonight. "I'm going to fuck you boneless while you're wearing my jersey and nothing else."

She smirks. "It's like you read my mind."

A few hours later, we're partying at the hotel with the rest of the team, champagne in hand, waiting for the countdown to midnight. The ballroom is dark, the music is loud, and the dancing is scandalous. Sutton's sitting on my lap and I'm buzzed, which is probably why I'm so enamored with the sight of my name stitched across her back. Most of the other girls changed into slinky party dresses, but Sutton's still wearing her jersey and it's the sexiest damn thing I've ever seen.

She leans forward, nearly spilling her champagne, and grabs my phone off the table. "You have a text."

"Who's it from?" I ask, kissing her neck as she tries to hand me the phone.

"It doesn't say."

"Probably just more well-wishers."

I already talked to my parents, and everyone else I want to celebrate with is right here.

"Don't you want to read it?"

What I want is to take my girl upstairs and make good on my promise.

"Nah." I slip my arms around her waist and begin massaging her thighs. "You can read it though."

"You really don't want to know who it is?" She turns to look at me over her shoulder. "What if it's important?"

"It's not." I get dozens of random texts after every game. Most get deleted without a response. "Trust me."

She turns back to the glowing phone, ass wriggling as I work my way up her thighs.

"If you keep that up, we're going to have a problem."

"Ay Dios mío!" Sutton leaps to her feet and whirls around to face me, cobalt hair swinging around her shoulders.

"Damn, Shorty. It was just a joke."

"Devin, you got it!" She holds up my phone, but I only have eyes for her. "You got the Sports Stream internship!"

My stomach drops. "Are you serious?"

I grab the phone and read the text, pulse thrumming.

UNKNOWN: *Hey, DJ. This is Mac. I got your number off your resume. Hope you don't mind me using it, but I wanted to unofficially welcome you to Sports Stream. The details of the intern position will be emailed to you next week, but it's yours if you want it. The selection committee chose you by unanimous vote. And for what it's worth, you'd have been chosen regardless of the email you sent me. Your interview was impressive and we always expect a few hiccups during the broadcasts. In fact, it's how candidates handle them that are the most telling. Congratulations and Happy New Year!*

"IT LOOKS like we have another reason to celebrate tonight." Sutton wraps her arms around me and squeezes, her smile as wide as I've ever seen it. "I'm so proud of you."

I'm proud of myself. I really thought I'd blown it, but maybe that was my past talking. My parents are going to lose it when I tell them I got the internship, but it can wait until morning. For now, I just want to let it sink in and spend some time with my girl.

"Thanks, but I think you mean two more reasons to celebrate."

She pulls back, brow furrowed. "Did I forget something?"

"Let's not forget you've found your passion and you're ringing in the new year with a new major." It's a big step, but I know she's going to kill it. "Plus, your season starts soon.

I've never been to a gymnastics meet, but you can bet your ass I'm going to be at every single home meet cheering you on."

"Really?"

"You came to all of my games. It's only fair."

She throws her head back and laughs. "I didn't have a choice."

"Well, I do and I'm bringing signs. Glittery ones."

"I can't wait. Speaking of which, do you want to get out of here?"

Hell yeah, I do.

"I thought you'd never ask."

~

SUTTON

"You sure about this?" Devin whispers, glancing around like hotel security might descend on the rooftop pool at any moment. "We might get caught."

"So we'll have to be quick." I peel off my jeans and toss them on a lounger. "That won't be a problem, will it?"

"Not as long as you're wearing that jersey." He pushes me up against the wall, his hard body pinning me to the cool stone. It's chilly, but this is Atlanta, not College Park, and Devin has enough body heat to keep us both warm. "If I had my way, this jersey is the only thing you'd ever wear."

I reach for his belt, making quick work of the buckle. "That would certainly make life interesting."

"It would be just like one of your pornalicious audiobooks," he says, peppering kisses down the column of my neck as I unbutton his jeans.

"What have you been listening to?"

Because that definitely didn't happen in any of the books I own.

"Less talking, more kissing," he orders, attempting to change the subject as I drag his zipper down and free his cock. "We're in a time crunch, remember?"

Oh, I remember. I'll remember to follow up on his most recent audiobook purchases too.

Devin cups my ass with his big, capable hands and desire flares in his eyes, red-hot and molten. "I see I'm not the only one going commando tonight."

I grin. "It's so much faster this way."

He lifts me into the air and I wrap my legs around his waist as he positions himself at my entrance, eyes locked on mine. "I love you."

Warmth floods my body, the tender words wrapping themselves around my heart as I brush my lips across his. "I love you, too."

If someone had told me four months ago that I'd be head-over-heels for DJ Parker by New Year's, I never would have believed them, but now I can't imagine my life without him in it. In just a few short months, he's become as integral to me as gymnastics. As breathing.

And not just because he gives killer orgasms.

"Christ, you're wet." The head of his cock rubs my clit and pleasure ripples through my body.

"I've been waiting all day for this." I roll my hips, desperate to ease the growing ache between my legs. "I need you inside me, Devin."

Right. Freaking. Now.

He kisses me, long and hard, and then, in one fluid motion, he seats himself to the hilt, filling me completely. My body clenches around him and I tip my head back, giving myself over to pleasure as he moves inside me.

I'm on the pill and while we still use condoms most of the time, there are nights like this where I relish the skin-to-skin contact, the feel of Devin's cock sliding into my pussy with no barrier to separate us.

He increases the pace and I lock my ankles behind his back, levering myself upward to change the angle, chasing my own orgasm. In this position, it builds quickly and soon I'm panting, desperate for release.

Devin grips my ass hard, his rough fingers digging into my flesh as his orgasm takes him. He groans and buries his face in my neck and then I'm spiraling over the edge with him, pleasure rocking my body even as fireworks explode at the edges of my vision, brilliant shades of red, white, and purple imprinting on the back of my eyelids.

We ride out the aftershocks together and then he deposits me on the lounger, where I lie boneless, unable to even put on my own pants.

Best. Orgasm. Ever.

I sigh, completely sated. "I think I hallucinated fireworks."

Devin chuckles as he zips up. "If you were hallucinating, then so was I."

"Is that a thing? Shared sexual hallucinations?"

If not, it should be.

"No clue." He squats before me, putting my jeans on. He works the soft material up over my calves before he pulls me to my feet and slides them up over my thighs and hips. "But in this case, I'm pretty sure those were New Year's fireworks."

Right.

I shrug. "Happy New Year then."

"Happy New Year, Shorty." He tucks a strand of hair behind my ear and when he grins, my heart, which is full-to-bursting, melts like a Hershey's bar in a heatwave. "Move in with me next year."

My eyes go wide and something like happiness fills my chest before reality creeps in, bursting the bubble.

"I'm sorry." I shake my head to clear my thoughts. "The champagne and sex must've gone straight to my head because, for a second, I thought you asked me to move in with you."

He chuckles, the deep rumble doing unholy things to my body. "You heard right, Shorty."

Visions of our life together fill my head, images of me falling asleep in his arms every night and waking to his smiling face each day. They're so vivid I could reach out and touch them, claim them, if only I were brave enough.

"You can't be serious." It's ludicrous. My parents will freak. "We've only been dating officially for what, three weeks?"

"Three weeks. Three months. Three years." He shrugs. "I love you, Sutton. Time won't change how I feel, but—"

I press a finger to his lips. "No buts. I love you, Devin, and I want this too. I want days and nights and everything in between."

Just the thought of it has the champagne fizzing in my belly.

His grin widens. "Yeah?"

I nod, a slow smile curving my lips. "Yeah."

Devin wraps his arms around my waist and pulls me in for a kiss. It's soft and gentle, the barest brush of his lips, but it's perfect. We're perfect, if only for this moment. We've found something most people spend a lifetime chasing, and while I don't know what the future holds for us, I plan to hold on tight and enjoy the ride.

Thank you for reading Scoring Sutton! For more of Devin and Sutton's story, visit www.jenniferbonds.com to

download the Bonus Epilogue for a must-read glimpse of their future!

Need more Wildcat shenanigans in your life? Grab Vaughn's story, Protecting Piper!

www.jenniferbonds.com

ALSO BY JENNIFER BONDS

Waverly Wildcats

Holding Harper

Claiming Carter

Catching Quinn

Scoring Sutton

Protecting Piper

The Harts

Miles and Miles of You

Not Today, Cupid

Royally Engaged

A Royal Disaster

Royal Trouble

A Royal Mistake

The Risky Business Series

Once Upon a Dare

Once Upon a Power Play

Seducing the Fireman

ABOUT THE AUTHOR

Jennifer Bonds writes sizzling contemporary romance with sassy heroines, sexy heroes, and a whole lot of mischief. She's a sucker for enemies-to-lovers stories, laugh-out-loud banter, over-the-top grand gestures, and counts herself lucky to spend her days writing swoonworthy romance thanks to the support of amazing readers like you!

Jen lives in Pennsylvania, where her overactive imagination and weakness for reality TV keep life interesting. She's lucky enough to live with her own real-life hero, two adorable (and sometimes crazy) children, and one rambunctious K9. Loves Buffy, Mexican food, a solid Netflix binge, the Winchester brothers, cupcakes, and all things zombie. Sings off-key.

To connect with Jen, visit www.jenniferbonds.com to sign up for her newsletter and be the first to know about new releases, giveaways, and exclusive content! You can also find her on Facebook, Instagram, and TikTok @jbondswrites.

9 781953 794314